I0668380

A HIGHER

VOICE

A HIGHER

VOICE

A Novel

SHERI WREN HAYMORE

A HIGHER VOICE

Copyright © 2013 Sheri Wren Haymore

All rights reserved. No part of this publication may be reproduced, stored in any retrieval system, or transmitted in any form or by any means, mechanical, photocopying, recording, or otherwise, without permission in writing from the publisher, except by a reviewer, who may quote brief passages in a review.

Cover and interior design by Ted Ruybal.

Manufactured in the United States of America.

For more information, please contact:

Wisdom House Books
www.wisdomhousebooks.com

Paperback:
ISBN 13: 978-0-9891821-0-2
ISBN 10: 0-9891821-0-X

LCCN: 2013910221

FIC000000 FICTION / General

1 2 3 4 5 6 7 8 9 10

DEDICATION

To my kind, tenderhearted husband and beautiful, amazing daughter—Always.

CONTENTS

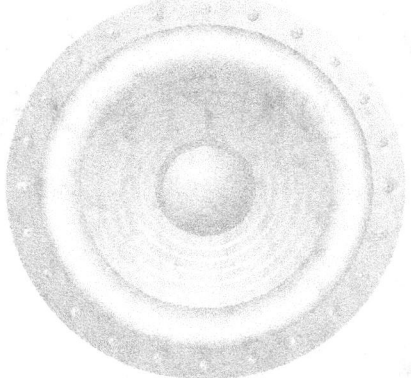

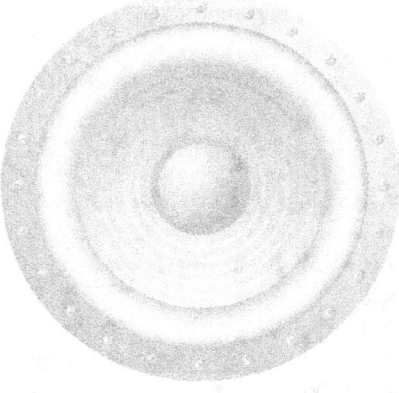

ACKNOWLEDGEMENTS

A good story doesn't tell itself—the storyteller needs a great deal of help. My most wholehearted thanks to—

Melanie, for cheerfully reading through three revisions and steering me toward the perfect title.

Gay, for sitting through the first very rough draft.

Kathy, for insisting that the world needs to hear Britt's story.

Tom, for inadvertently pushing me over the publishing edge.

MAPD Chief Dale Watson, for taking the time to read through a particularly tricky chapter.

The prodigious and gracious singer Melva Houston, for encouragement and stamp of approval on the musical aspects.

The very gifted author Jane Tesh, for excellent, insightful commentary on the story.

Angela Polidoro, editor and saint, for spinning satin out of burlap.

Ted Ruybal, publisher and advisor, for the killer cover design and layout. And more than that, for going beyond all expectations.

And, finally, my eternal gratitude to the One who always does more than I can ask or imagine and who will ever be my soul's Higher Voice.

CHAPTER

ONE

He could have sworn somebody had crammed an electric guitar inside his head. A racket screamed between his ears—half-music and half-insanity—and a riff repeated amongst his tonsils that threatened to drag his gut up to his throat. The racket and nausea had begun to plague him six months ago, and damn if he knew how to pull the plug.

Britt Jordan kicked away the tangle of sweat-soaked sheets, bounded from the bed, and staggered across his dimly lit hotel suite. Bypassing the bar that had been stocked just for his taste, he yanked open the refrigerator door and grabbed a pitcher of ice water. Plunging his hand into it, he splashed a good douse of freezing water onto his face. Twice.

"Aaihh!" he screamed, pounding the wall with his fist. Throwing up, he had learned, did nothing to dispel the nausea that accompanied the racket. Ice water and a good, gut-deep scream, now that helped.

The door of the suite's adjoining room opened, and in stumbled Britt's assistant, tugging on drawstring pajama bottoms, blonde hair tousled. "God, Britt, it's five o'clock."

"And a jolly good morning to you, too, Darrell," answered Britt in his distinct, morning-raspy voice that had made rock and roll history for over two decades.

Darrell glanced at Britt's bed, which hadn't been shared with anyone since the previous summer. "What you need is a woman," he advised.

"What I need is a car. Get me one."

Darrell switched on a light and the two men squinted at each other. "A car? What for?" Darrell asked, looking his boss over suspiciously.

Britt grinned. Tormenting Darrell always started his day off with a bang. He was still holding the pitcher, water dripping from the three-day stubble on his chin and running down his bare chest. "To drive. Where am I, by the way?"

Exasperation crossed Darrell's face. "Britt, you've got a show tonight."

"Right. So if you'll tell me where I am and where I'm supposed to be tonight, I'll just drive myself on in." Britt made a sweeping motion with his free hand, palm down.

"You'll get lost. Go back to bed." Darrell turned to leave.

Britt was fast. In one beat, he had Darrell by the arm, the pitcher poised over his assistant's head. "Where am I?" he demanded, slopping a good measure of frigid water over Darrell.

"Damn it, Britt, stop," croaked Darrell, ducking. "Richmond, Virginia. Your jet is here. Your bodyguard. Me. You know you're not driving off into the sunrise without us."

"Yeah, I am." Britt doused his assistant with some more water. "As soon as you tell me where my show is tonight."

Darrell squirmed in Britt's grasp. He tried to bring his boss to the floor with a kick to the inside of his knee, and when that

2

didn't work, he made a grab for the pitcher. "Why do you need to know?"

"I have a great need to conquer the open road."

"I don't trust you," said Darrell, finally getting a grip on the pitcher. "The name Britt Jordan is not exactly synonymous with 'navigational wizard.' You'll end up in Pennsylvania."

"Instead of where?" Britt asked. Both men had a grip on the pitcher, and Britt gave it a hearty tug, splashing them both in the face. "Tell me or I'll fire you."

"You've already fired me twelve times this tour," said Darrell, wiping water from his eyes, "and given me three raises."

"Really?" Britt asked, astounded. "Then you owe me an answer. Hurry up, boy. The open road beckons."

"I don't think there's much open road in the South."

"Aha! Where did we book in the South?" Britt released Darrell and walked over to the window, still holding the pitcher. He yanked aside the curtain and stared at the pre-dawn city below. "Now I remember. Greensboro, Columbia, Atlanta, then break for Christmas," he recited triumphantly. "North Carolina. If I can just figure out which way is south, I'm bound to hit it eventually."

Darrell shook his head and started from the room. "Go back to bed. You can drive all you want after Atlanta."

Britt turned from the window. "Today," he said. "I'm driving today. Get me a car now."

Sighing in defeat, Darrell padded off into his own room to phone the front desk.

Britt's physical presence didn't overwhelm people. He was not a tall man, and while his compact, athletic build and reckless good looks kept the fans in awe, it didn't give him control over his staff. It was his dogged determination and pure, endless drive that kept them hopping around him.

Catching his reflection in the mirror, Britt slowly raised the pitcher over his head. Britt Jordan was worth a hundred million as far as Uncle Sam knew; only Britt knew the value of his off-shore holdings. He could afford a thousand distractions an hour. But he had not found a single thing his money could buy that would shut up the racket in his head. Without flinching, he dumped the rest of the water over his head in one cold, baptizing shower that streamed from his tangled hair and drenched his boxer shorts.

"Aaihh!" he screamed again, longer and louder than before.

"You're insane, Britt!" shouted Darrell from the adjoining room.

Britt blinked water from his eyes. "Not anymore."

Forty minutes before the concert was scheduled to start, Dena Martin smiled at the polite young man who had ushered Dena and her secretary into a backstage room of the Greensboro Coliseum.

The young man seemed a bit harried, and he spoke quickly, "As I explained, ma'am, Mr. Jordan has cancelled his interviews this evening, and you'll be wasting your time here. If he decides to reschedule for tomorrow, we'll be in touch."

Dena double-checked his name tag, turned her back on him, and settled onto one of the two sofas in the room, the one facing the door to the outside corridor. "Darrell," she said, "you're Britt's assistant, correct?"

"Yes, I am."

"Well, the word is that Britt's not even here," she said. "If that's the case, you have no one to assist at the moment." She smiled broadly at him. "You might as well stay here and chat with us."

Darrell cleared his throat and glanced toward a second door in the room, to Dena's left. Her guess was that it led even deeper into the private backstage rooms. He was undoubtedly eager to escape.

Dena's secretary and friend, Sue Duncan, settled into a corner of the second sofa, her back to the corridor, and let out a resigned sigh.

"So talk to me, Darrell," said Dena, clasping her hands together and leaning forward. "Is it true this is the first sound check that Britt's missed in over twenty years?" When Darrell pursed his lips and frowned, she kept talking, keeping her tone friendly, "It's common knowledge that Britt's punctual to a fault. And the atmosphere around here goes beyond pre-show nerves. More like high alert. I'm guessing that somebody's in trouble. Would that be Britt? Or would that be you, for losing Britt?"

Just then, there was a commotion from down the corridor: a few seconds of muffled screams, as if an outside door had been opened and closed on a hysterical mob, followed by closer shouts, "Britt! Over here, Britt!"

Dena noticed that although Darrell quit talking, he seemed no less harried than before—in fact, he barely turned his head toward the racket.

But he did take a step back when the door to Dena's left opened and an angry-looking man stuck his head into the room, looked around, flung a curse in Darrell's direction, and disappeared again, slamming the door behind him.

"Who was that?" asked Dena.

"Britt's road manager," answered Darrell. "Nothing to be concerned about . . . it happens all the time."

"You're the one who looked concerned," Dena said with a laugh. "Like you thought he was about to throttle you."

Darrell smiled in response. His cell phone tablet jangled just then, and he glanced at the screen and heaved a sigh of relief. "I have to go," he said, looking up at them. "You can wait here until the corridor's clear if you'd like, but really, Britt won't have time for an interview now." With that he left the room in a hurry by way of the corridor.

Dena watched as the door swung shut behind him. "The racket's coming from up the hall," she said to Sue, "but Darrell just took off at a run in the opposite direction. Interesting."

At 7:25 p.m., a Rolls-Royce limousine pulled up to the VIP back entrance of the coliseum, where a throng of security police, media, and fans had been waiting for over an hour. Amidst screams and camera flashes, a man wearing a black leather jacket stepped out of the car and gave a high, straight-armed wave to the crowd. The police closed in around him and moved him inside. "Britt! Over here, Britt!" came from the group of reporters waiting in the corridor.

Just outside a personnel entrance, near the trash dumps, Britt's bodyguard, Len, and a coliseum guard stood their ground. Len took a call on his cell phone. "We should have him in sight any second," he told the guard after disconnecting the call. He sent a quick text and tucked the phone inside his jacket. Within seconds, a state patrol car came into view, driving slowly around the perimeter of the parking lot, avoiding the throngs of people.

When the car came to a stop beside the dumpster, the guard ran up to open the front passenger door, and Len reached inside the car and grabbed the arm of the man who was doubled over in the front seat, hidden from sight. Out stepped Britt Jordan, all business.

"I don't want to hear it," he said as Len hustled him inside the building. "Get me to where I need to be without running into any reporters."

"Britt!" Darrell met him just inside the door. "For once, I'm glad to see you."

"Just get me around that rabble," Britt said, nodding down the hall to where the man in the black jacket stood ringed by frenzied reporters.

"You're the boss," Len said, pushing Britt into a nearby room. "There's a shortcut to your dressing room out that side door."

Britt broke into a run that lasted three steps. He was stopped dead in his tracks by a woman's smile.

"Hello," he said, hopping on one foot to break his stride. He glanced at Darrell and back at the woman.

"Uh, Britt, this is one of your cancelled appointments," said Darrell, flipping his tablet open. "She's with the Deerfield News. I told her she could wait out the crowd in here . . ."

"Dena Martin," interrupted the woman.

"I apologize, Mrs. Martin," began Darrell, "but as I told you, Britt . . ."

Britt held up one hand, still looking at the woman who was sitting on the brown couch in front of him. Darrell hushed. Several seconds passed as Britt stared at Dena. She was beautiful even though she wasn't as young as most of the women who caught his eye. Hazel eyes the shape of dirigibles—and about half as large, by Britt's estimation—were fringed by lush, dark lashes. Thick waves of long auburn hair framed a striking face with high cheekbones and a strong jawline. Sun-kissed skin gave her a healthy glow, and there was an engaging, confident smile on her marvelous, full lips.

Briefly, Britt's thoughts took a tangent as he pondered how many hours it might take a blimp to fly from here to his home in Antigua. When he refocused on those airship eyes, the laugh lines around them began to crinkle in amusement beneath his scrutiny.

She wore a teal green knit dress, belted, with a cowl neckline and sweeping skirt, and she sat with one leg crossed high over the other, her hands clasped at her knee. "So do I get to tell my readers where Britt Jordan has been all this time?" Dena finally asked. Her voice was warm Southern honey, and she didn't appear to be at all shaken by his intense stare.

Britt stuck his hands in his pockets, tilted his head to one side, and squinted at her several seconds longer. "I was lost, if you must know," he answered, "but the whole state of North Carolina doesn't need to know that."

Dena threw her head back and laughed. A woman's laugh, full and melodious, which she made no attempt to stifle.

When the laughter stopped, so did the racket inside Britt's head. He banged his head with the heel of his hand just to make sure. "Do that again," he said to Dena. When she smiled in response, he vaulted over a second sofa that separated them and practically landed in the lap of another woman he hadn't noticed.

"My secretary, Sue," said Dena as Britt settled onto the sofa next to her.

"Sorry about that," Britt said to Sue.

"No problem," replied Sue, holding up a voice recorder. "I'm just the tech guru."

He nodded and leaned forward, his full attention focused on Dena. "Tell me your life history," he said breathlessly, mimicking a novice interviewer.

Dena caught on to his joke. "You're making fun of us small-town reporters," she said.

"Just out of curiosity, how did you manage an interview with me?" asked Britt.

Dena leaned away from him and regarded him coolly through narrowed eyes.

Quickly, afraid he had offended her, Britt added, "My manager keeps so many walls around me, I can't even get an interview with me."

Her face relaxed, and very softly, she answered, "When my husband ran the paper, he not only won awards for his stories, he made a lot of friends. I still pull a few strings occasionally, for the sake of the paper." Smiling, she said, "Now, since you made fun of me, I get to ask a hard question. Where else have you been lost?"

"Oh, that's easy," answered Britt. "The Caribbean. Dozens of times. On purpose. Okay, not on purpose," he said when Dena raised an eyebrow. "But you can't beat the adventure of sitting on a beach with a bottle of tequila, watching the sun set and wondering whether or not the natives are friendly."

"Or speak English?" put in Dena.

"Exactly," said Britt, pleased that she understood.

The door to the room crashed open. "Britt, where the hell have you been?" shouted Britt's road manager, murder on his face. "Get your ass moving."

"It'll happen. Eight o'clock sharp, as always," Britt said smoothly, waving him off. "I'm not that far behind schedule. Get the band's butts into gear, and don't worry about mine."

The man cursed at Britt, barked an order into his headset, and slammed out of the room.

"Pardon my rude manager," said Britt. He grinned and slung his head forward between his knees, sun-bronzed hair touching the floor. He gathered his hair with an elastic band, and when he sat up, he was sporting his trademark jaunty ponytail. "He wants me to go be Britt Jordan for a while."

"And who do you want to be, Britt?" Dena asked.

He stood up and stared hard at her several seconds. "That's a good question," he finally said. He turned to Sue. "When's she going to laugh again?"

"I wish I knew," Sue said. "That's the first time I've heard her laugh like that in two years."

Dena still didn't flinch under his gaze, but she twisted her wedding band, out of habit, Britt suspected. He took her hands in his and pulled her to her feet. He studied her hands, turning them over in his, gently brushing her wedding band with his thumb. Dena's hands were slightly larger than most women's, capable-looking. Natural nails, nude polish. There were calluses on her palms at the base of each finger.

"Do you dance as well as you laugh?" he asked abruptly.

She chuckled in response.

"Please be here when I get back. Please?"

"Sure, Britt," Dena answered easily.

Darrell and Len exchanged puzzled frowns in the corner of the room.

"Well don't just stand there, boys," Britt shouted, "get me moving! We've got a show to do." Edging away from Dena, he clenched his fists and stomped a staccato dance in place, gearing himself up. Without saying good-bye, he turned and ran out the door.

Britt's music was pure rock: three guitars, two keyboards, and a drummer with the quickest hands in the business. He'd written every song he'd ever recorded, and he had a keen ear for turning out radio hits time and again. He had a peculiar way of joining driving rock rhythms, brilliant guitar effects, memorable melodies, and simple, to-the-heart lyrics. Even his worst detractors had to admit that he gave his fans what they wanted. And what they wanted—and paid eighty bucks a seat to see—was Britt. He refused to subject his audience to warm-up bands. He always crashed on stage at eight o'clock sharp and rocked the hall for over two hours, disappearing only once for an outfit change and Gatorade while his band continued to play.

Darrell escorted Dena and Sue to seats behind the sound technicians, and then sat on a folding chair beside the sound board. The coliseum was packed and noisy, electric with expectation. Dena noticed that Darrell glanced at his watch several times as the minutes passed. At five minutes past eight, the band hit the stage, and the coliseum went black. Seconds passed as the mass of human voices quieted, bodies settling into seats. Suddenly, amplified to pulsate through every nerve of every person in attendance, Britt's voice shouted, "My apologies, Greensboro! I'm late, but I'm ready to rock!"

The drummer kicked in with a complicated beat, the guitars blasted in, and then there was Britt, backlit, standing on top of the platform above his band. Dazzling laser lights played in circles around the platform and shot up toward the ceiling. With his arms raised high above his head, Britt appeared larger than life. He laughed a low, growling laugh, the spotlight hit him, and he was in gear. "Baby, I've got you by the heart," he sang, claiming the stage as his own.

For the first hour Britt was in a constant state of motion, working the platform, bounding down to the stage, dancing at the very edge of it so that his fans could touch him, and then returning to the platform. He packed raw energy and a smooth, constrained sensuality into every movement. Dena was soon on her feet along with the rest of the audience, clapping and singing. Sue stood also, armed with earplugs, and appeared to be more interested in watching the technicians and the laser effects than Britt.

At five minutes past nine, Britt picked up a guitar, and five band members left the stage. For the next ten minutes, brilliant guitar music pulsated through the coliseum in deafening waves as Britt and the drummer rolled through an incredible jam session, both musicians grinning. Then the band members returned and took over—no break in the music—and Britt started to disappear through a door inside the platform for his customary outfit change. Just before he turned to leave, he waved in the direction of the technicians and shouted, "Bye, Dena! I'll be back in a minute!" Dena shook her head and laughed along with the rest of the audience.

Just before the show was over, Darrell escorted Dena and Sue back to the waiting room. He explained that Britt wouldn't be joining them for another ten minutes or so.

"Well, good, then you can chat with me some more," said Dena.

"Um, Mrs. Martin, I'm sure you understand that I can't really . . ."

"No hard questions, Darrell," said Dena. "Tell me Britt's bodyguard's name."

"Len."

"You and Len appeared mighty baffled when Britt asked me to wait for him. What was that about?"

"Well, you see, Britt has pretty much kept to himself this tour."

Just then, Britt walked in wearing the unbuttoned, long-sleeved shirt and tight black jeans he had worn on stage, a leather jacket slung over his left shoulder, same three-day stubble of beard, a hungry, demanding look in his eyes.

"Hey, babe, are you ready to rock?" he growled in his classic husky voice.

"Mmm, no, thank you," replied Dena, cocking her head at him. "I believe I'll just stay right here."

Britt slammed a curse in her face and stalked out of the room into the crowded corridor, where applause and screams carried him until he apparently left the building.

"Come on, Dena," said Sue. "Let's get out of here. Britt Jordan's an even bigger creep than I thought."

Dena folded her arms and gave Darrell a cool glance. She wondered what he would have done if she'd left with the man. Britt's assistant held her gaze but made no comment.

Two minutes later, in walked Britt again from the other door, his bodyguard behind him. He was wearing a cashmere jacket, blue T-shirt, jeans, and neon green sneakers. He was freshly showered and shaved, he smelled pleasantly of bay rum, and his expression brightened with unmasked relief when he saw Dena. "Thank you for waiting," he said, his famous voice now a rough whisper.

"Who was that guy?" she asked.

"What guy?"

"The one who looks like you."

"You saw a guy who looks like me?" he asked, glancing at Darrell, who shrugged and nodded his head.

"Sure did."

"But you knew it wasn't me." A smile played around his lips as he looked into her eyes.

"No way," said Dena. "Gray eyes, wrong expression. Who was he?"

Britt studied her for several seconds, the searching look in his green eyes giving way to a relaxed smile. "Can you mambo?" he asked.

"I've been known to," she answered, standing up and taking his outstretched hand. "But my specialty is good old Southern shag."

"Then if you ask me again after we've danced until our shoes are shreds and our toes are bleeding, I just might answer you," Britt said.

Dena chuckled, gave a slight shrug to Sue, and held Britt's hand tightly as they followed Len to the waiting limousine.

─── CHAPTER ───

TWO

B ritt and Dena agreed to forego club-hopping. Too many crowds and cameras. "There's plenty of room in my suite to dance and no one to bump into besides each other," he promised. As soon as they reached his room, Dena excused herself to the powder room, saying that she needed to call her daughter.

Britt summoned Darrell. "Order up a pot of coffee," he told his assistant. "And maybe some, I don't know, cookies."

"Cookies?" Darrell looked his boss over. "Since when do you eat cookies?"

Britt shooed him away just as Len walked into the room. "And play it by the book, Darrell, if she stays past midnight."

Darrell threw an exasperated glance over his shoulder as he left. "I haven't forgotten how to do my job."

"Britt," said Len in a low voice. "What are you doing, man? You're scaring me."

"What's your problem?" asked Britt, knowing exactly what Len's problem was.

"Come on . . . you go six months without a woman and,

out of the blue, pick a married one? Remember your last tangle with some guy's wife? Nearly got your head blown off," Len said. "And mine, too, might I add."

"Maybe I've learned to duck," said Britt. "And don't I pay you to know these things about people before they get to me?"

Len's voice remained low. "I've been a little too occupied looking for you today to waste time looking into a reporter you weren't even supposed to see."

"I'll decide later whether to dock you or give you a raise," said Britt, pushing Len out the door. "Get out of here. You worry too much," he added as Dena emerged, putting her cell phone away.

She walked over to the bar and laid both hands palm-down on the counter-top. "And just what is Len so worried about, Britt?" she asked. "He and Darrell both seem to have their britches in a wad."

He leaned against the counter, opposite her, reached over and lightly touched her wedding band. "That," he said.

"Really."

When she offered no further comment, he asked, "May I pour you a drink?"

"No, thanks. What I would really like is a cup of coffee," she said.

"Coming right up. With cookies."

"Ooh, you sure know how to make a girl happy!"

He pulled out his cell phone. "What did you call that dance, shag? Like beach music?"

"Uh-huh."

He scrolled through the music on his phone. "Not really my forte, I'm afraid. What about Motown? Similar rhythm . . . we can make up the moves as we go along."

"Sure," she answered.

He got the music going, took her hand, and stood still, watching her face. The light in her eyes was confident; the smile on her lips, expectant. He waited until the corners of her eyes began to crinkle with amusement.

"I believe the way this usually works is that somebody moves," she said.

With a grin, he pulled her into his arms, danced an eight-count step, and spun her out before pulling her back in. Her movements were fluid, easy, as if she were an extension of him. Again he watched her eyes, sixteen counts, and laid her back in a dip, her body compliant yet precise, the touch of her hand light on his shoulder. He raised her up into his arms, more slowly than the beat of the music demanded.

"Not really loving this carpet for dancing," she said, "but I think we can make it work."

"What I think," he replied, "is that this is going to be the shortest night of my life."

Several hours later, after they had worked their way through the coffee pot, Motown, Bob Marley, and Big Band Swing, they were chatting at the table in his room. She was telling him about her twelve-year-old daughter, describing their small-town life in charming detail. Britt leaned back in his chair, arms behind his head, and closed his eyes, enjoying the low melody of her voice.

"Oh, my goodness!" he heard her exclaim. "It is four o'clock, and I have put you to sleep."

He sat up quickly. "No, no; I heard every word you said. And it can't be four . . . you've only been here twenty minutes."

She laughed at that and stood up. "I guess I need to wake somebody up downstairs and hitch a ride over to my hotel. Sue will wonder what happened to me."

"You don't have to do that, you know," he said, watching her face carefully.

"Bri-itt." Her voice was low and gentle, and she looked away.

"Darrell left Sue a message," he continued, still studying her face. "And he's reserved a room for you in this hotel." When she met his eyes and he saw the trust return, he added, "Just so you wouldn't have to do that."

"How very thoughtful," she said. "I believe I'll take you up on it." She stuck out her hand, business-like. "Good night, Britt. This has been a fabulous evening."

Instead of taking her hand, he leaned his arms on the table, one fist on top of the other, chin resting on the top fist. He closed his eyes against the dread that was dragging his gut up into his throat. There was something he needed to ask her, and, depending on her answer, that god-awful racket could start up in his head again any minute. He didn't think he could stand it for one more day.

"Britt, are you all right?" she asked.

He drew in a breath. "Dena, would you please sit down for just a minute? There's something I want to ask you." When she hesitated, he added, "My mom taught me to stand when a lady stands, but I don't think I can right now."

He heard her settle back into her chair. She didn't say anything.

Just get it over with, Jordan, he told himself. "Okay, here's the thing, Dena." He kept his eyes closed as he spoke. "You finagled an interview with me, you showed up in a flattering, but, um, full-coverage dress, you . . ."

"I get it," she interrupted. "I haven't shown you any skin, and I haven't flung you across the bed. So you want to know what my deal is." He met her eyes then, and when he did, he saw them soften. "You want to know my motive," she said softly, "because everyone who sees you wants something from you."

He let out a ragged breath, feeling something close to relief. "I need to know," he whispered. *Please be something I haven't heard a thousand times before.*

She reached across the table and put her hand on his arm. "To begin with, Britt, I certainly didn't intend to spend the night with you. Although I will say, it has been a most enjoyable night." She paused. "My motive really had little to do with you, and everything to do with my late husband."

"I'm guessing he died two years ago?" Britt asked. "When Sue said you stopped laughing?"

"Yes. You have been listening."

"Every single word. And I'm still listening."

"Then I'll tell you my story. Do you remember when you started out, how you would play college campuses?"

"Oh, yeah." He smiled at the memory.

"You would get college kids to be your roadies for pennies. Well, my Johnny was one of those kids. I had just met him at that point, so I wasn't part of it."

"Where was this?" asked Britt.

"UNC-Chapel Hill. Johnny was an east Tennessee mountain boy, very smart. Went to Carolina on a scholarship to study journalism."

"Is that where you met?"

"Not exactly. I was at NC State in Raleigh, studying horticulture."

"Ah, gardening, hence the calluses on your hands."

"You're quick! When I did meet Johnny on a blind date, he eventually he talked me into minoring in journalism, and in exchange, he agreed to take dance lessons with me. Came in handy tonight."

"Ah! I'm pretty sure you had rhythm in your soul way before

you took dance lessons."

"Probably. Anyway, Johnny helped set up and pull down your stage that night. Then he spent the rest of the night hunkered down with you over a couple beers."

"Wish I could say I remember him," said Britt.

"Oh, I don't expect you to. The point is, over the years . . ." she squeezed his arm, her hand warm and strong. ". . . well, we didn't print gossip. But an occasional story about you would come over the AP wire, and Johnny would always say, in that Tennessee drawl of his, 'That can't entirely be true. When I met Britt, he was an all-right guy.'"

"So that was your motive? To see if I'm still an 'all-right guy?'"

"Sort of. Mostly it was to do something Johnny would have enjoyed." She laughed that melodious laugh again and stood up. "Well, he wouldn't have enjoyed dancing with you as much as I did."

Britt stood also, then came around the table and wrapped his arms around her. "I have two more questions to ask," he said. She was nearly as tall as he was, and she put her cheek against his. He breathed in her subtle chocolatey-orange perfume. "Is this real?" he asked.

"Do you mean my story?"

"No, I believe your story. I mean tonight, what we had together. Even though it only lasted twenty minutes, it felt real. It felt like something that was meant to last longer than twenty minutes."

She pulled back and looked him in the eye. She didn't answer.

"Because if it was real, then I have one last question. Will you do it again tomorrow? Spend the day with me? Maybe make it last forty minutes?"

"I might make it last a whole hour," she said with a smile. "But I still won't show you any skin."

CHAPTER

THREE

Two mornings later, five o'clock hit Britt hard. He stood at the window of his hotel suite, leaning against the glass, feeling the biting cold against his forearm and bare chest. He had not slept at all.

He and Dena had said their good-byes at midnight. Soon she would be leaving the hotel to drive back to her home in the foothills. She wanted to get back in time to have breakfast with her daughter before school.

After two full days of dancing and laughing, sharing meals and conversation, they were returning to their lives. Dena had a newspaper to run and a daughter to raise. She had family, friends, church. Small-town stuff. A real life. Britt had a show in Columbia, South Carolina tonight. He had a hectic social schedule over the upcoming holidays, a video to shoot, and then he'd be back on the road in January to continue his tour. Life in the big-time. He was engulfed in a frantic machine of his own design.

He and Dena had agreed that their situation was impossible.

Better to say good-bye now, make a clean break, and get on with their lives.

Cold sweat prickled his back, and Britt shivered. Turning, he surveyed his room, glanced at his empty bed. Rubbing his left arm, he looked down at his extraordinary tattoo. It was a singular design that ran from shoulder to elbow, bold colors over a solid black background. The artist had created a tangled mess: his own half-portrait, his ponytail morphed into a fire-breathing sea dragon, which coiled around an imperiled comic heroine. Intentionally shocking. He stuck both arms straight out in front of him. His right arm was covered in full-sleeve ink, delicate as finely-etched scrimshaw. Dena herself had pointed out that his left arm was as incongruous to the right as his life was to hers.

Suddenly, without any idea what he was doing, he took off at a run, banging open the door and letting it slam behind him, sprinting down the hotel hallway bare-chested and barefoot, wearing only sweatpants. Only his band members and Darrell were encamped on this floor, and no one came out to see what the racket was about. His road manager and crew were already in Columbia, setting up for the show. Britt rode the elevator down five floors and sprinted down the hall to Dena's room. He pounded on her door. There was no answer, and his gut wrenched in fear that she had already left. Once again, he pounded.

She opened the door and stood holding it, already dressed for the drive home in jeans and a dark green sweater set. Barefoot. He could smell the freshly bathed, soapy scent of her. She smiled, her eyebrows raised in question.

Britt put his hands at her waist and spoke one word. "Stay."

Lightly, she said, "Well I suppose I could, Britt, but it will be sort of lonesome. You'll be in Columbia."

He smiled briefly at her joke and pressed his forehead

against hers. "I can't go without you," he said simply.

"I can't be your groupie. You know that."

"That's not what I mean." He paused. "I mean I can't go forward without you. I've tried to picture the rest of my life without you." He shrugged. "I can't."

She was silent. He pulled back and studied her. She hadn't put on any makeup yet, but she was still beautiful—her strong features were softer in their natural state, and her skin was clear and smooth.

"What are you thinking?" he asked.

"We've been over this," she said softly. "I can't follow you around."

Quickly, he interjected, "I'm not asking you to."

"I'm afraid Britt Jordan won't fit into Deerfield very well." Her smile was rueful, and she shook her head. "It's just not possible. And the reality is, I still have to live there after you're gone, if it doesn't work out."

"But I have a plan," he said. "You told me Deerfield's airport can accommodate my jet?"

"Yes, several of the industries in town have jets, but . . ."

"Book an entire motel or rooming house or whatever you can find in Deerfield through April, when my tour is over. If there isn't one owned by a manager you can trust, I'll buy a place and hire somebody myself." When Dena's jaw dropped in surprise, he chuckled. "I'm serious. I'll do whatever it takes to be near you. I know you don't want reporters crawling all over town." He cocked his head at her. "I've been doing this for years, Dena. I know how to be incognito. I even have a pseudonym: Daniel Windsor. Would you like to see my passport?"

She shook her head. "Britt," she whispered. "This will never work."

Down the hall, the elevator opened, and he realized that he had come close to compromising her even now, standing in her doorway at dawn without a shirt. He stepped into the room and closed the door, putting his left hand to the small of her back as he did. Quietly, he said, "I know what I'm asking will complicate your life." With a short laugh, he added, "Hell, it's going to make my life insane, jumping from North Carolina to God knows where twice a week until this tour is over." She put one finger to his lips. "But you're worth it," he said. "You're even worth trying to clean up my mouth, if you insist. Please say you'll give us a try."

She didn't answer. She was studying the tattoo on his left arm, frowning.

"You're worth it to me," he repeated. "I know we're good for each other. I know we can make this work." When her only response was silence, he said, "If you can look me in the eye and tell me you don't think what we could have would be worth the complications, I'll leave. Just as we planned."

She closed her eyes and drew in a deep breath. He saw two tears slowly course down her cheeks. When she took a step back, his heart wrenched in his chest. She was looking down, shaking her head slightly. It took him a moment to realize that she was twisting her wedding band, trying to pull it off her finger. When it finally came off, she looked at for a long moment, taking her time, and then wiped the tears from her cheeks and slipped the ring into her jeans pocket. She looked up, and the smile she gave him was warm with acceptance.

When she took him by the hand, he felt as if he had finally begun to breathe again after spending twenty years under water. She stepped so close that he could feel her warmth against his skin, and she slid one incredibly soft bare foot on top of his.

Putting her left hand behind his head, she drew him into a kiss, tender and sweet. Over the years, Britt had been kissed by many lips that had promised him many things, but Dena's were the first to promise him the one thing he needed: completion. He decided to take that kiss for a yes, and he asked no more questions.

"You're kidding, right?" Darrell was standing in front of Britt, tie slightly askew, a dumbfounded expression on his face.

Britt was in a relaxed headstand, one of his morning ablutions, and he stared up at Darrell from his upside-down position.

"Do you really mean to tell me that you're blowing off all your appointments today to fly to Bum-crap, North Carolina, just to see some woman you're not even sleeping with? The one who is married, right?" When he was exasperated, Darrell's blonde hair seemed to spring in all directions of its own accord.

Britt rolled out of the headstand, and onto his feet in one smooth motion. "Yes to all of that," he said. "The married part I intend to make true very soon."

"What?" When Britt didn't answer, Darrell pressed, "What are you talking about?"

"Marriage, my boy. You know, that thing people do. Some people do it several times, but for me, only once." Britt crossed the room and slipped on a purple T-shirt, eyeing his assistant as he did so. The young man looked quite abandoned in his confusion. Picking up his jacket and putting it on, Britt retrieved his cell phone from an inside pocket and unlocked its touchpad code. "Come help me decide on a ring. I've narrowed it down to two designs."

Darrell came closer and made a gesture with his hands, like a signal to settle down a rambunctious puppy. "Okay, okay," he said quickly. "You haven't been yourself in months. I think I get it."

"And just what do you think you get, Darrell?" asked Britt, quirking his mouth to one side to suppress a laugh.

"This extra dose of strangeness started last summer when you and Lori Sink broke up. You finally let yourself meet a woman, and now you think she can fix you." Darrell swiped the phone from Britt's hand and started scrolling through the contacts. "Just let me call one of these women. I can have her here before dinner."

Darrell got quiet, his eyes widening as he looked at the phone. Putting his hands in his pockets, Britt just stood there and watched him.

"What have you done with all of your female contacts?" Darrell finally asked.

"Dumped 'em," came the answer.

Darrell frowned as he continued to scroll. "Well," he said after a while, "you haven't dumped Lori, I see. What does that tell you?"

Britt grabbed the phone and clicked out of the contacts. "All it tells you is that she's better in a sound booth than she was in bed. I might want to collaborate with her on an album again sometime."

"Yeah, right," said Darrell. His expression froze when he looked at Britt.

Britt stared hard at Darrell, following the calculations that crossed the young man's face. Darrell managed to get himself temporarily fired at least once a week, but even after nine years as Britt's assistant, he was never exactly sure how far he could push his boss without finding himself permanently out of a job.

Britt knew it, and he usually got a kick out of watching the young man squirm. Today, however, he was too eager to see

Dena again to bother playing this game.

"You got it partly right," he said. "The thing is, I'm already fixed. Haven't you noticed that I've quit pouring cold water on my head all the time?"

Darrell gave him a look that could only be interpreted to mean, *Tomorrow you'll come up with something even crazier.*

Britt looked away. He had never told Darrell or anyone else about the nausea. The relentless racket in his head. He couldn't explain how Dena's laughter had made both torments go poof. And he wasn't about to tell Darrell that the reason he still had Lori Sink's number was not because he wanted to sing with her again. Britt believed in the adage, "Keep your enemies close." Even though he felt like throwing up every time he saw her name.

He turned the phone off and stowed it in his pocket. "Never mind," he said. "I know which ring I'm going with. It'll take two months to have it made, which is just about how long it will take to get her to say 'yes.'" He started for the door.

Darrell planted himself firmly in Britt's path. "Tell me you're kidding," he said. When Britt faked right and spun around him to the left, Darrell spun too and backhanded him on the arm. "Then tell me why. Why this woman?"

Britt paused, his hand on the door handle. As often happened, an image appeared in his head, along with a jumble of thoughts. He closed his eyes and pictured Dena's smiling mouth, her straight, no-nonsense nose. He drew in the laugh crinkles around her eyes. And then he saw the way her eyes lit up every time he walked into the room. Not in that *Oh-my-God-you're-a-rock-star* way. Her eyes lit up in the, *I've-known-you-a-thousand-years-and-would-like-to-know-you-a-thousand-more* kind of way. Britt had waited a lifetime to see that exact expression on a woman.

"Spill it, Britt. You don't want me to get your manager in on this."

Britt looked Darrell over and saw his feeble threat for what it was: fear. "Just this," he said. "She doesn't need me." And then he rumpled Darrell's hair and left.

Late that same evening, Dena was saying goodnight to Britt after driving him from her house to the small inn where he'd be staying. The day had been pleasant, and Britt had certainly done his part to remain incognito. No entourage. His jet was registered under a holding company, and he'd even kept his face hidden while riding in her car.

He had brought a gift of luxurious organic Caribbean chocolates for her daughter, Bonnie, and he had been funny and engaging with the child while keeping his distance. He had even joked that if he'd had a kid at sixteen, and his kid had had a kid at sixteen, he could be Bonnie's grandfather. Just the right touch—she seemed neither overwhelmed by him nor in danger of developing a crush on him.

Now, standing in the foyer of the inn, he put his left hand at the small of Dena's back and drew her close. So far she had kissed him exactly three times: *Good-bye* at midnight two nights ago, *Yes* at dawn yesterday morning, and *Hello* today. She wondered what this kiss was going to say.

But he didn't kiss her. He looked intently into her eyes for a long moment. And then he spoke three words, "Marry me, Dena."

She choked and sputtered over a surprised laugh. "Oh, my word; I was not expecting that!"

"Yes, you were," he said. "Well, maybe not today, but eventually.

You have to admit that it's crossed your mind." When she looked away without answering, he touched her cheek, and she lifted her chin and met his eyes. "You're just a little afraid to marry me, aren't you?"

"Britt, I, we barely, I mean . . ." She stopped. There was enough truth in his statement that she really couldn't argue.

He chuckled. "Hell, I'd be afraid to marry me. But I have something to tell you . . . Are you listening?"

When she smiled her assent, he kissed her. It was a kiss that started out sweet and warm, and built in intensity until she tasted his passion, decadent and complex as Caribbean chocolate. When she tasted something else, a shiver shot through her, and she drew back and stared at him.

He scrutinized her face in return, waiting for her reaction.

She realized she was holding her breath and let it out carefully, keeping it under control. What his kiss had told her was this: Britt Jordan didn't pour himself out on the stage night after night because it was an act. He did it because it was his essential nature. He would pour his very heart out of his chest and lay it at her feet if that was what she wanted. He would climb to the heavens and bring down the moon if it were humanly possible.

She breathed in and breathed out. "You're all in or all out, aren't you, Britt?" she asked.

"Yeap." He smiled, his dimples inviting her to smile back. "You get me."

She thought about that. Britt Jordan's public persona was raucous and irreverent, not really her type of guy. But this Britt, the one smiling at her now, was playful yet intense, and yes . . . she did get him. She wasn't sure why, she just did. She returned his smile. "Then I can honestly say I'm not afraid. There's just a whole lot to consider, my daughter above all else."

"Exactly as I expected," he said.

She brushed her lips across his. "Tell me more," she whispered.

"Okay."

There was humor in his voice, and she pulled back to see his eyes.

"Here's more," he said. "Be careful where you are when you answer 'yes,' because I might start some bodice ripping then and there."

Bursting into laughter, Dena backed away and pointed a finger at him. "Mood-killer," she accused.

He put his hands in pockets. "You're the one who told Bonnie you'd be back in twenty minutes."

At that moment, it hit the center of her brain: He had her best interests at heart. She smoothed her hair, even though he hadn't mussed it, blew him a kiss, and left him standing in the foyer, still smiling at her.

———CHAPTER———

FOUR

The furthest thing from Britt Jordan's mind was his Grammy nomination for Best Rock Performance. Having blown off the red carpet and slipped in through a back entrance, he stood shirtless before the mirror in his dressing room, the muffled sounds of the awards show drifting past his closed door. Cool green eyes stared back at him, giving no clue to the wheels that were turning in his brain. Tilting his head, he checked out his hasty shave job. A three-day stubble was part of his brand, and minutes before, the room had been filled with people whom he paid well to make sure he looked the part. He had kicked them all out and gotten rid of the beard. Jutting his chin, he checked it once more. Just last week, a reporter, thrashing about for words to describe his sculpted jawline, had compared the angle of his jaw to Jimi Hendrix's Gibson Flying-V guitar. Absurd hyperbole. The image of the billowing forward staysail on his ship in Antigua floated through his thoughts. A better comparison, if he were to write it.

Britt knew everyone was wondering what he was up to,

since he'd announced that he was using a recording for back up tonight instead of his normal band. What he'd hinted to no one was that he was planning a miracle. And he had been known to work miracles, especially in a sound booth. With a bit of technical wizardry, he had mixed tonight's recording so that his own recorded voice would override his live voice on certain notes. He had no choice.

The truth was plain and simple. He was losing his voice.

His pitch and range had been plummeting this entire tour. Twenty years of abusing his voice had finally caught up with him. The damage to his vocal chords was irreversible, and even surgery wouldn't bring back the top notes. He had managed to hide it from the audiences so far by screaming out his lyrics through swollen vocal chords, further escalating the damage. Not even his band members guessed at the pain he'd been suffering after each show. Britt's career was crashing, and he knew it. The recording would ensure that it didn't crash tonight and that his failing voice wouldn't interfere with his plan.

A knock at the door interrupted his thoughts.

"Yes!" he called and turned, smiling. His smile froze as the door opened and in stepped a young woman. Achingly beautiful. Very young. And a big part of his life just last year when the tabloids had labeled her "Britt's handful of TNT."

"Lori," was all he said. He stared straight into her eyes as she crossed the room, coming to a stop right in front of him. The dress she was wearing, he knew without looking, left little to the imagination. He folded his arms across his chest and tried to send his imagination on a vacation.

"Britt, you look fantastic." Her voice enveloped him. He felt her place a hand on his bare chest, and he closed his eyes, standing his ground. Sweat began to form on his neck.

"I've been thinking about last year, about us," she murmured. She was standing so close that her blonde hair brushed his arm. She continued, "I've been hoping that it could be that way again."

Britt felt her other hand slip behind his neck, and he opened one eye. A low noise growled in his throat, causing her to step back.

At that moment, the door opened again and in walked another woman. Beautiful. Not so young. "Dena," he said with relief. The door shut, cutting off the backstage racket. No one spoke.

Britt uncrossed his arms and grabbed a towel to mop the sweat that was pouring down his chest. Turning his back on both women, he stuck his hand in a pitcher of ice water and splashed his face. He swallowed a scream and waited for the nausea to pass. It had hit him the moment Lori's hand touched his skin.

When he turned around, both women were staring at him, Dena with no expression whatsoever on her face, Lori with an expression Britt preferred not to interpret. "Dena Martin, Lori Sink," he said, picking up a shirt and slipping it on. "Lori is singing with Adams this year. She just came by to wish me luck, I think. That was all you had to say, wasn't it, Lori?"

Lori looked from Dena to Britt. "Of course. Good luck." She turned, giving Dena a hard stare as she left.

Britt didn't watch her go because his eyes were on Dena. His plan balanced on a pin in his mind, waiting for her next move.

Just as Lori brushed past her, Dena cut her eyes sideways and said sweetly, "Come back and visit any time now. Oh, I'm sorry, dear, I forgot your name."

"Lori Sink." Lori gave Britt a drop-dead look over her shoulder before stepping out the door and shutting it behind her.

Britt's eyes took in Dena's emerald green dress, fitted through the bodice in a way that sculpted her curves yet allowed room for imagination. He called his imagination back from vacation and smiled at the way her auburn hair shone in its classy twist. When his eyes met hers, the laugh lines she could never hide crinkled upward.

His voice twisted with laughter. "'I'm sorry, dear, I forgot your name?'" he sputtered. "You knocked her out of the room with that one."

"I thought you'd get a kick out of that." Then she laughed, pure, hearty notes that seemed to dispel Lori's perfume from the room. She crossed the room and picked up his tuxedo vest, holding it out to him.

At her touch, as light as it was, a feeling swept through Britt that was far from nausea. "Marry me," he said.

"Britt, I swear, you have a one-track mind."

"You've had nearly two months to decide."

"I've barely known you for two months." She handed him his tie.

"Ample time," Britt insisted, his eyes on hers as his fingers arranged the tie. "Why won't you say yes?"

She adjusted his tie, not meeting his eyes. "After today, it's going to be pretty hard to keep you a secret from the neighbors, that's for sure. But I'm still trying to wrap my brain around how two hearts as incongruous as ours can form a successful marriage."

Britt looked away. He knew exactly what she meant. Her heart was like the cabin of his ship in Antigua, everything in order. His heart was more like a shipwreck, with flotsam and jetsam everywhere. It made him sick to think about it.

Still, he had a plan, and he would persevere in his attempts to convince her. With his hand cupped as if testing a rope, he measured the space between them. "There," he said. "Right there is the cord that runs between our hearts. It can't be broken; it can only be ripped out, causing much pain and a very loud shout."

Dena shook her head at his poetry and moved to pick up his tuxedo jacket. She held it for him, then turned him around and looked him over. The sparkle returned to her eyes. He was as dressed up as he ever got, with jeans and yellow sneakers under the tux. No socks. "Marry me, Dena," Britt said, pulling her close. "You keep soldiers marching between us all the time. Some of them have guns pointed right at me." He waited for her smile. "Fire those soldiers and marry me. It's right. It's inevitable. And you know it."

She kissed him, her lips warm and sweet. "I'll pray about it," she said. "That's all I can promise."

Just then an usher knocked on the door and called, "It's time, Mr. Jordan, if you want the lady seated before your segment."

Britt watched as Dena left the room, then turned to the mirror. "She said 'yes' this time," he told the mirror. "Don't argue with me. She didn't say 'no.'"

Minutes later, the Grammy audience waited expectantly for Britt to come crashing on stage. The set went dark, and the crowd watched for bright lights and shocking special effects to blast from the three video screens that dominated the set. Instead, though the stage was still dark, Britt's voice could suddenly be heard singing an eerie melody with no lead-in.

Instinctively, Dena looked to her right, where she saw Britt in silhouette, striding down the runway toward where she was seated. The cameras began to pick up his face, still in shadow, and throw it bigger than life onto the screens. Dena never looked at the screens but continued to watch Britt's silhouette. He appeared relaxed, singing into his headset, his left hand still in his pocket.

Never had Britt Jordan crooned such a song. It was mellow yet catchy, like something from the forties, and the audience settled back uneasily, not sure what to expect.

Britt sang the first verse and the chorus while the entire arena was still in darkness:

Someday I'll meet her:
The shadows will fall away.
Even the trees will step back
To light the path.
She'll be the one.
She'll be the one.
One time in a row.

Love for me has been a dark thing:
Never right, never light.
A hot pursuit,
Talking in my sleep:
Who knows how to make it work
Just one time in a row.

During the second verse, the runway was gradually illuminated. As the shadows fell away from Britt's face, the cameras pulled back, losing the detail of the sweat that was pouring down his forehead. Dena could tell that Britt was staring straight at her as he continued to approach her. Her eyes still on Britt, she failed to notice a camera that was easing toward her from the left. Britt was singing:

Today I saw you;
The wind brushed your hair.
And I reached to touch your face,
Caress your lips.
Are you the one?
Are you the one?
One time in a row?

The runway was fully illuminated. The chorus again. The bridge:

Never could make it work;
Never could get it right.
Never, not ever, Baby.

Suddenly he stopped singing; his voice continued on the tape, barely audible at times:

Tomorrow I will hold you.
Don't know if I can do it—
Hold tight to this feeling—
Hold you for good.
Please be the one.
Please be the one.
One time in a row.

As the audience strained to hear the recording, Britt's voice came through the speakers again, this time speaking the words in that oddly clear yet husky voice of his. A break in the song. Now a second voice, deep and omniscient, came over the sound system: "Dena, will you take Britt as your husband?"

Dena's mouth flew open, and she started to slide down in her seat. Glimpsing her face magnified on one of the screens, she lifted her chin and stared back at Britt.

"Dena, say yes," Britt whispered, stopping directly in front of her. The last verse began playing again. "Say yes," he repeated, leaning toward her, his right hand extended.

Dena could not possibly know the time pressure Britt was under, but she could hear the urgency in his voice, and she stood up. Nearly deafened by the screams and whistles from the shocked crowd yelling its approval of Britt's latest coup, she allowed the two men seated closest to her to steady her up the single step onto the runway. When she took Britt's extended hand and looked into his eyes, he mouthed the one word he had spoken to her minutes before in the dressing room: *Inevitable.*

She took a deep breath and said, "Yes."

"Do you, Britt, take Dena to be your wife?" resounded over the system.

"Yes." Britt's hand came out of his pocket and opened. In it he held a magnificent diamond and emerald wedding band. Dena kept her eyes fixed on Britt's face as he slipped it on her finger.

The deep voice continued, "Then by the power vested in me by the state of California, I pronounce you married. Britt Jordan, you may kiss your wife."

Britt's lips touched Dena's just as the last note of the song played and the control booth cut to a commercial. The audience roared with laughter and cheers, everyone rising to their feet, applauding.

Britt kept his arm around his wife as they made their way back up the runway. He could feel her body shaking against his side, and he could tell that she was struggling to hold it together from the way she bit her lip. Ignoring his peers' hands, which were extended in congratulations, he moved her as quickly as possible through the crowd and into the backstage area.

Cell phone cameras clicked all around them, and Dena buried her face into the folds of Britt's jacket. Walking backward, he pulled her down the corridor to his dressing room and shut the door quickly. She was visibly shaking.

"I have never heard of anything so outrageous in my entire life!" she cried. "On what planet did you think this was a good idea?"

Britt held his shaking wife close, not sure whether she might faint on him. With his right hand, he lifted her face so that he could meet her eyes. She was frowning, lips pursed, hazel eyes glaring at him in outrage. Good—she was okay.

"On this planet," he said. "At this moment some thirty million people know for certain that I love you outrageously."

She buried her face in his jacket again, still shaking.

He held her close, not sure what else to do. "Dena, my wife, the love of my life, it's not official until we sign the papers," he said. "If you don't want to, you don't have to."

"Papers! Britt, have you lost your mind? We haven't applied for any paperwork. I am not your wife."

A tall, elderly man stepped into the room. "Actually, Dena, you are," Britt said. "Meet my friend, Judge Roberts. He's bringing the license bureau to us, so to speak."

Dena raised her head from his jacket and looked at the judge skeptically. "It doesn't sound legal to me," she said.

"Mrs. Jordan, I assure you, this is unusual but not at all illegal. The papers will be properly filed. You are legally married."

"Do you mean all the words it takes to marry two people are 'Will you, will you, kiss her?'" Dena demanded. Britt began to relax. He leaned his head back, eyes closed.

"Yes, technically, it is," answered Judge Roberts.

"Please say yes," Britt whispered.

The shaking subsided to a tremble, stopped. "Technically, Britt, I already have," she said. When he opened his eyes, she flashed him a broad smile.

Britt missed the rest of the Grammy show, and he didn't win the award. He jumped around the hotel suite shouting, however, like a kid who had won his first blue ribbon. When Dena came out of the suite's dressing room, she took one look at his face and burst into laughter.

"What?" he asked, finally standing still.

"You look like a ten-year-old," she said.

"I've never been married before. How am I supposed to look?"

"Come closer and I'll show you."

He obeyed.

"I didn't say 'yes' to your proposal," she said firmly. "You took a big chance tonight."

"You did say 'yes.' I heard you."

"I said I would pray about it."

"Same difference. Anyway," he added with triumph in his voice, "there must have been a yes in there somewhere. Here you are, an unprecedented territory of skin bountifully in view."

She chuckled. "You shocked me into a desperate cry for help more than a prayer, but you're right." She put her arms around him, her hands firm against his bare back. "Here I am."

"You've fired those soldiers, haven't you?" he asked.

She smiled at her husband. When she looked into his eyes, she didn't see the raw, conceited rock star most people assumed he was. She saw what they missed: kindness. "Yeap," she said. "I've fired them for good."

Britt pulled her close and stood motionless, his face buried in her hair. Dena felt him take several deep breaths, but otherwise, he stayed motionless. He was still for so very long that Dena finally whispered into his ear, "I hope you're not always this boring, Britt."

He leaned back, flashed a wicked dimpled grin, and slid his hands down her body with unabashed intimacy. "I was writing my own marriage manual in my head," he said. "Chapter One: To begin the best marriage in the world, the couple must not sleep for the first twenty-four hours."

"Goodness, Britt, are you planning an expedition?"

"Haha," he growled, one of the most famous laughs in the world. "Lewis and Clark only wished they had such territory to explore."

Outside on the sidewalk, Phillip Jordan stood leaning against a car, staring up at Britt's hotel suite. "Pretty slick, there, Bro, marrying that Southern honey in front of the whole damn country." He drank deeply from an old fashioned glass and wiped his mouth with the back of his hand. "Yeah, pretty slick. Get your name in the papers and a good-looking piece all at the same time."

The doorman, who had been watching the man with concern for ten minutes, stepped out onto the sidewalk. "Come inside, Mr. Jordan. This is no place to spend your wedding night," he said.

Gray eyes defiant, Phillip drained his glass and hurled it crashing against the hotel wall. "You got that right," he said and walked away, slinging his black leather jacket over his shoulder as he went.

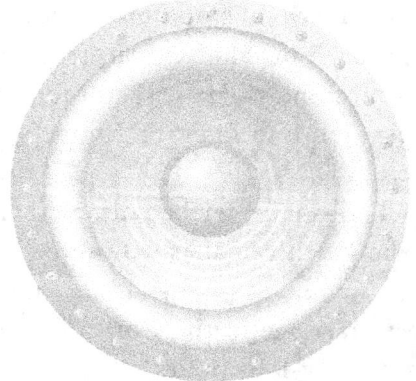

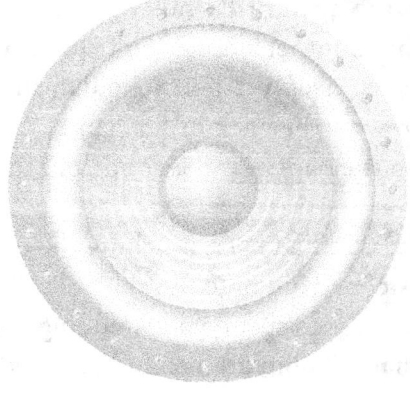

———CHAPTER———

FIVE

Unannounced, the Jordans flew into Dena's hometown just three days after their wedding. Noel and Arlene Carter, Dena's parents, met them at the airport. While Arlene boarded the Gulfstream jet for a tour and a chat with her daughter, Noel drew Britt aside on the tarmac, out of earshot.

He wasted no time in getting to the point. "When I asked you last month why you were in such an all-fired hurry to marry my daughter," he said, "you didn't give me a straight answer."

Britt looked him in the eye and made no reply. Noel hadn't really asked a question.

Noel gave an aggravated grunt. "You know, Britt, a little heads-up would have been nice before you married my daughter in front of half the world."

"I respect your opinion, sir, but Dena is a grown woman."

Noel looked Britt over. "Yes, and you're a grown man with quite a reputation. Does it shock you that I'd be concerned?" When Britt didn't answer, he added in a low voice, "In this family, we take marriage seriously."

Britt kept his face passive and let several seconds pass, even as he continued to look Noel in the eye. "Noel, I'm going to let you in on a secret, just between you and me. Here's how seriously I take my marriage: I didn't ask Dena to sign a pre-nup, but I signed one." Britt let that statement sink in before continuing, "I may never tell Dena about it, but I'm telling you. The one I signed says that if I do anything to screw up my marriage, anything, Dena gets everything I own. Everything I've worked for my entire life will be hers."

Noel's face worked, trying to comprehend what his new son-in-law was saying. "That's the most extreme thing I've ever heard. And downright strange, I might add."

"Exactly what my lawyer said, right before he keeled over in a dead faint. That's just the way I roll." Britt stuck out his hand for a shake, which Noel accepted. "If my wife ever hints to you that she's unhappy with me, feel free to tell her."

Dena's voice called across the tarmac from the jet's portal, "Daddy, would you drive Britt home to wait for Bonnie, please? I'm going to run by my office and the grocery store."

Dena's errands took a few hours. When she finally arrived home, Britt and his new step-daughter, Bonnie, were waiting at the kitchen door. Britt watched as Dena walked around his silver car in the garage, looking it over. He had told her about his rare 1970 Monteverdi 375S, but she had never actually seen it. The car had begun its journey from California on a car hauler the day of the Grammys. "James Bond wishes he had this," she commented.

When she stepped into the kitchen, he kissed her right in front of her daughter. "What took so long?" he asked.

"Let's see," she began. "Shoulder-to-shoulder reporters in my office, well-wishers at the grocery store, and more reporters camped out on the lawn."

He hung his head. "Sorry. The police have evicted the reporters from the lawn twice already. They've promised to enforce a curfew for this whole block after eight tonight . . . hopefully that will help."

Bonnie broke in with impatience. "You're not going to believe what Britt did!" she laughed, strands of sandy blonde hair waving around her face as she bounced on her toes.

"I'm afraid to ask," said Dena as Bonnie took her by the hand and led her through the kitchen and dining room and into the living room. There, smack in the middle of the room, crowding out every other piece of furniture, sat Britt's Steinway. A concert grand. Nowhere to sit anymore besides the piano bench.

"What . . . how?" Dena sputtered.

Bonnie squeezed past a desk to get around the piano and sat on the bench, cracking up with laughter.

"Darrell thought I might need some company," explained Britt seriously.

Dena turned on her heel and walked back into the kitchen. When Britt followed her, he found her leaning over the sink, shoulders shaking.

"Your mama doesn't take surprises well, does she?" he said to Bonnie, who now stood at his side.

Laughter exploded from Dena, echoing in the sink. "Britt, I swear, give me a little warning next time." She straightened up and looked at him, wiping her eyes. "How on earth did you get it here so fast? Isn't that the same piano I saw in your living room in California this morning?"

"Darrell can work wonders . . ." he began.

"I know, but . . ."

"They've invented these wonderful things called airplanes . . ."

"I know, but . . ."

"Actually, it's done with mirrors," he finished.

At this, Dena and Bonnie both burst out laughing, Bonnie's staccato, girlish laughter punctuating her mother's rich notes.

"You don't mind then?" Britt asked.

Dena looked him in the eye. "It's a little late for you to be asking. Why don't you and Bonnie go see if you can arrange the room so that we can walk through it while I start supper?"

The two of them went off to do as they were told.

"I didn't know you played the piano," Bonnie said to him as they surveyed the crowded room.

"I thought all my fans knew that," he replied. He slid himself prone on top of the piano and ran through a scale from his upside-down position, grinning at her. Bonnie blushed beneath his teasing gaze but held her ground, not intimidated. Britt smiled, pleased, and hopped down. "Yes, I've played since I was ten," he said. "I went to college to study music. Big dreams of concert halls. I, uh, sort of got side-tracked. Never did finish, which I now regret. I did get to do the concert scene, though," he said, nudging her with his elbow.

"You're funny," she said. Hands on her hips, she surveyed the room. "You know, if we move any furniture, everything else will have to move too."

He looked around, taking in "everything else." Dena's eclectic taste was evident everywhere he looked. There was a Navajo bowl on an intricately carved table. Above an African drum hung a delicately designed Amish quilt; beside the quilt hung a mandolin, which had belonged to Bonnie's father. Britt had been teaching himself to play the mandolin during his visits.

Britt's eyes took all this in, stopping at a huge, bold abstract painting that dominated one wall. Another painting, a seascape in the same style, hung above it, near the ceiling. On the far side of the piano, in an alcove that was bathed in the last glow of sunset, a bright carnival scene stood on an easel amidst a scattering of unframed canvases.

"We can't move your art," he said. "That would be a sacrilege."

"Therefore, we can't move any furniture," she said.

"Exactly." He spread his arms and turned in a slow circle. "The room is perfect as it is."

Bonnie giggled. "Come see what I'm working on."

She squeezed past the piano while Britt hopped on it and swung across to the other side. He followed her into the alcove and looked over her shoulder. Besides the easel and canvases, there was a wooden table loaded down with paint jars of various sizes, tubes, brushes, and palettes. The table top was covered in layers of multi-colored paint, and the brown tile floor was splattered with paint too. Although he detested ordinary domestic clutter, Britt loved this. Honest work of any description intrigued him.

Bonnie bent to pick up two small canvases and held them up on either side of the carnival scene. Each was an unfinished study of a small child, very detailed, yet bright and colorful. "The abstract party scene will be set in the middle, with the children on each side, as if we've focused in on them while there is music and movement going on all around them," she explained.

Britt looked at his step-daughter with respect in his eyes. "I'm impressed," he said. "You hadn't even started these children when I was here last. You're really good. Great, even." He chuckled, gesturing at the haphazard array of canvases in the alcove. "Prolific."

Her head bobbed eagerly. Bonnie was a substantial child, not heavyset, but rounder than Dena and with a fuller face. Above her outrageous smattering of freckles, her startling blue eyes implored him. "Tell Mama I'm good. She's determined to send me away to art school."

"I know you're good," Dena called from the kitchen. Britt and Bonnie shrugged sheepishly—neither of them had realized she was listening. "That's why I want you to go to a good school."

"What do you think, Britt?" Bonnie persisted. "Don't you think I'm doing fine on my own?"

Britt cleared his throat. He hadn't expected to be called upon for fatherly advice quite so soon. "Tell me why you don't want to go to art school."

"I just don't want to leave home," she said. "Besides, I'm not sure I can work anyplace else."

Britt nodded in understanding. "I can tell you two things. First, I am an artist too, and I know that it takes more than raw talent to be the best. It takes a lot of skill. You'd be surprised by what you can learn from new teachers." Bonnie looked skeptical. "Second, while this may always be your favorite place to work, you'll find that your art can spill out anywhere." She laughed at his pun. "I much prefer to work in my home studio in L.A., but I can work anywhere. I wrote my most popular song while sitting in a boat."

Bonnie frowned in disappointment. "So you agree with Mama?"

"I didn't say that. Tell me why you don't want to leave home."

She shrugged. "I just don't. Anyway, Mama needs me. She's not exactly Goddess of the Sparkly House, you know," she added conspiratorially.

"She's not?" Britt asked in mock astonishment.

Bonnie giggled. "Not even close. She cooks pretty good, but she hates housework. If you send me away, the dust bunnies will eat you alive in a month."

"Then we must do something. Today. Before this gets out of hand." Britt crossed over the top of his Steinway once more while Bonnie squeezed around it, her eyes bright with anticipation. Britt marched into the kitchen and slammed his hand on the counter beside the stove where Dena stood. "I am the man of the house," he announced. "You must do as I say."

She calmly dumped dried basil leaves into her hand from a jar and crushed them into the marinara sauce that was simmering on the stove. "Is that a fact?" she asked.

"Yes. I have a plan."

"Oh, no. No plans. Please don't inflict one of your plans on my daughter."

"When will you admit that our wedding was a pure stroke of genius?" he demanded.

"Never."

Bonnie giggled. "I liked it. It's all my friends talk about."

"Mine too, no doubt," said Britt. "But never mind that. This is an even better plan than that one. It's . . ."

Dena raised a hand to stop him.

"It's from Chapter Two of my marriage manual," Britt whispered.

She smiled and let him continue.

"I will hire a tutor for Bonnie," he declared.

"A tutor?" Dena tasted her sauce with the handle of the spoon, raising both eyebrows at him.

"Yes, a tutor. I can afford the best art teacher in the country. Someone qualified to teach advanced studies in other subjects as well as art. It's settled." He slammed his hand on the counter once more. "Bonnie stays here."

Bonnie bounced around the room as only a twelve-year-old can, looking hopefully at her mother.

"Okay," said Dena with a shrug.

"That's it?" exclaimed Britt. "That's all there is to being the head of a household? Ha! I can do this!" he shouted, raising his fists in the air.

Dena winked at Bonnie and held her arms wide for a hug. "I never wanted you to leave home," she murmured, rocking her child in her arms. "I just want you to have the best instruction possible."

Bonnie pulled away from the embrace and looked her mother square in the eye. "Does this mean Britt's going to live here with us?" she asked.

Dena glanced at Britt and bit her lip. She didn't answer Bonnie, so Britt made no comment.

After supper, while Bonnie was doing homework, Dena pulled Britt into the den and shut the door. "Britt, I want to ask you something," she began.

"Ask away. I have the answer right here," he said, tapping his head.

"This is serious. Your home is in Antigua, right?"

"Yeap. Antigua and California."

She spread her arms, palms up. "You've told me you plan to live here with me, and you've moved your two most important possessions here, but I still have trouble believing it. Think about it, Britt. This is Deerfield, North Carolina. You're *you*. You can't possibly be satisfied living here."

Britt smiled. "Chapter Three: Working out the transcontinental marriage. Part One: I will never, ever go to Antigua without you. I promise. Between having my studio in L.A. and being on the road a good portion of the year, I don't get to spend much time there, anyway. In fact, I haven't been since late last May." He stopped. Sweat broke out beneath his collar and he swallowed hard against the nausea that rose whenever a particular morning last June was called to mind. "I've been too busy working to get back there, although I miss my home dreadfully," he finished softly.

"Tell me about it," she said.

"I'll do better than that; I'll show you." He fetched a photo album from a box of personal belongings that had been flown in with the Steinway.

She settled beside him on the sofa and turned the pages of the album, chuckling. "There's nothing in here but pictures of boats."

Britt pretended to be offended. "These aren't just boats, Dena. Never. This one is called a cutter. She actually qualifies as a ship."

"Excuse me."

"You're excused. I had her custom-made—you can tell in this picture. She's made of mahogany and teak."

Dena looked closely at the pictures. "This must be her name on the back, Shirl?"

"On the stern. Yes, Shirl. After Mom."

"Okay. Is that your house?"

"Yes, that's home," he said.

"Pretty impressive."

"Yes, it is. Thank you for noticing. I look forward to showing it to you."

She smiled, studying the house, and turned more pages. "Check out those fish!"

"Pretty, huh? I took these pictures snorkeling."

"Hey, look at this," she said, pointing to a photo. "Now that's a fish!"

"Trophy sailfish. You can see the deck of my cruiser, Jane."

"Who's Jane?"

"The boat there."

"Ah, I don't have to call it a ship, huh? Did you keep it?"

"The boat?"

"No, the fish," she said.

"Of course not," he said. "Do I look like a barbarian?"

"Pirate, maybe."

"Okay, here we're in California." Britt pointed at a picture.

"I miss the Caribbean," she said.

"Yeah, me too. Anyway, that's my other sailboat, Jessie."

"All these women!" Dena teased.

"She's a sloop. I just keep her around to play with when I get tired of working. Ever heard me sing 'Sea-green Mistress'?"

"Who hasn't?"

"Well, I wrote it while sitting right there."

"On this picture?"

"You're confusing me," said Britt.

Dena flipped back to the pictures of Britt's home in Antigua. "This is what I asked about."

Britt took the book from her and laid it aside, wrapping both arms around her. "We can make this work, Dena. Me in a small town; you in Antigua. Wherever we are, we'll be happy. When I finish this tour, we'll go to Antigua together, just the two of us, for our honeymoon. And you can decide for yourself how much time you want us to spend there."

Just as he was about to seal his promise with a kiss, the door burst open and Bonnie rushed into the den to announce, "It's snowing, y'all."

"Then we must go for a walk," suggested Britt. "Our first family outing. Maybe the reporters have obeyed the curfew."

The three of them walked the quiet, small-town streets hand-in-hand, listening to the soft pat-pat of snow on the winter grass. A police cruiser followed from a distance, watching for reporters. Deerfield lay in the northwestern foothills of the state, just close enough to the mountains to receive smatterings of snow that frequently fell on the nearby Blue Ridge. Tomorrow morning, the mountains would probably be white with six inches of snow when they looked out their window, yet there would likely be only an inch in their yard. And tomorrow Britt would return to his tour and the hectic schedule he had kept since December, flying in and out of Deerfield between shows. Only now he would be staying with Dena instead of in the small inn where she had successfully kept him hidden.

"I'm already spoiled. I won't want to leave tomorrow," Britt commented as they returned home, stomping snow off their shoes on the garage floor. He reached over and lovingly patted the hood of his Monteverdi, then jumped and drew his hand back. The hood of the car was warm.

"Stop," he said to Dena, who was just about to step inside. He opened the car door, and cigarette smoke filtered out. Although the car hadn't been moved, someone had been in it just minutes before, idling the engine and smoking.

"Both of you wait here." Britt opened the door, and entered the house alone. The smell of fresh paint instantly stung his nose. "Call the police on your cell phone," Britt called back to them in a low voice. "I'm going to take a quick look. I won't be long."

Dena nodded and drew a protective arm around Bonnie, pulling her close as she made the call.

More puzzled than afraid, Britt walked into the living room.

There, scrawled across Bonnie's huge framed abstract were the words, "Dena is Britt Jordan's whore." On the wall itself was painted, "Britt wanted a blonde, not a bitch."

"Don't move!" he yelled back to Dena and ran toward the bedroom. An open window awaited him there. Footprints in the snow tracked across the yard, leading to the street. They could have belonged to a woman or an average-sized man; it was difficult to tell in the light snow.

By the time Dena finished her call to the police, Britt was beside her. "We've been vandalized," he said. "And it's obviously a lunatic who's mad at you for marrying me." He put his arms around them both. "Bonnie doesn't need to see what they wrote, and I would prefer that you didn't, either, Dena. Please take Bonnie to your parents for the night. I'll wait for the police."

When Dena started to protest, he added, "Let me take this hurt for you, Dena. You just take care of Bonnie. And I want you two to come with me tomorrow. I'll arrange to have a security system installed and the walls repainted while we're gone. Please." Dena's eyes searched his, and when he saw her relent, he said to her daughter, "And Bonnie, they ruined your abstract. I'm so sorry. It will have to be destroyed."

Tears slid down Bonnie's face as she nodded, trying to be brave. Just that night, he had told her that moving her painting would be a sacrilege. Now his first act as her step-father would be to destroy it.

Britt stood in the garage and watched them leave, arms folded. After they were gone, he inspected his car, which didn't appear to be damaged. Back in Los Angeles, Britt's home was secure and well protected, and he was accustomed to leaving his key in the car. Today his key was in his pocket, and the key he had given Dena was inside a locked cabinet in her kitchen. He checked the lock. It didn't appear to have been tampered with, and when he opened the cabinet, the key was precisely where he had placed it. Even so, he would have the security company install a coded lock-box for both keys.

The insanity of his life had invaded Dena's sooner than he had anticipated.

CHAPTER

SIX

Britt's jet touched down in St. Louis mid-afternoon. His body-guard, Len, was there to meet him, and he pushed the steps up to the plane himself. As often happened, a small crowd of fans was there to welcome Britt, lined up behind barricades between the jet and a limousine that was waiting fifty yards away.

Britt sighed when he saw them: middle-aged women, young businessmen, college students, a couple of kids—his music had a broad appeal. These people were his bread and butter, and he knew that they'd taken off work or skipped school to see him. It just wasn't a good time, not after the vandalism the night before.

Britt squeezed Dena's hand and stepped through the portal first, giving the crowd a wave and a grin. In two bounds, he was down the steps. Len grabbed his arm, but Britt shrugged him off, whispered briefly into his ear, and ran unescorted toward the crowd.

As Britt greeted the line of fans, giving handshakes and hugs while an airport guard tagged disinterestedly behind him, Len ushered Bonnie and Dena down the stairs, moving them past the crowd. Len's frown grew deeper by the second. A woman was clinging to Britt's lapels, screaming.

"I don't like this situation," Len muttered. When the airport guard attempted to pull the woman loose, he only managed to knock down another fan with the barricade. Len let go of the two women, and rushed over to Britt, moving him away.

Britt wheeled around. "When I tell you to guard my wife," he growled, "that's what I mean for you to do."

Len opened his mouth to protest, then swallowed and said, "Yes, sir."

Moving smoothly, Britt quickly had his arms around Dena and Bonnie, and he pulled them to the limousine. Len got in behind them and slammed the door.

Until the car left the airport, the only sound was Britt and Len breathing heavily.

"It's okay, Bonnie," Dena said. "Britt's not mad at you. Don't cry."

Britt looked over to see Bonnie staring at him, her eyes narrow, lips trembling. He leaned forward and put his hand over hers.

"It's all right now, Bonnie," he said soothingly. "That was my fault. I just got a little scared. Everything is okay now."

She bounced her fist on top of his hand, a conciliatory gesture. "What are you scared of?" she asked.

Britt glanced at Len who stared out the window, arms folded. "Well, I've been shot at twice," he said. "Len here saved my life both times."

Bonnie drew in a breath. "Shot at? By who?"

"Once by a crazy fan," said Britt, leaning back. "The other time, I, uh, I guess I sort of deserved it." He put his arm around Dena, who patted his leg. "I just don't want anything to happen to you or your mom. From now on, I want you to hold your mom's hand and don't let go anytime we're in public. Stay close to Len whenever he's around. He'll protect you. Understood?"

Bonnie nodded solemnly.

Len frowned, shook his head almost imperceptibly, and continued to stare out the window.

Britt Jordan had performed for millions over the years, and he gave every single person who came to see him the best show he knew how to give. The fans continued to pack every concert because they knew they'd get their money's worth: a full show of high-energy Britt, with a voice and stage presence no one could imitate. Britt's music was rooted in classic rock, but he pushed the boundaries of tonality and rhythm to create a twenty-first century rock archetype that was all his own. Even a mellow tune would keep the audience on its feet and spellbound.

When Britt performed that night, Dena and Bonnie were there, standing just off-stage. Bonnie was absolutely beside herself, jumping all over the place, playing air drums. After the first set, Britt disappeared while his band continued to play, as was his habit. Dena knew he had gone to strip off his sweaty clothes and put on a fresh outfit, and she grabbed the opportunity to give her ringing ears a break for a few minutes. She took her daughter by the hand and started back stage.

Suddenly Bonnie was tugging on her arm. "Mama, who is that man and why is he staring at me like that?" she asked in a whisper.

Dena looked up, jumped, and instinctively put her arm around her daughter. "Uh, Bonnie, this must be Britt's brother, Phillip. Mr. Jordan, my daughter, Bonnie."

The man walked toward them, a beer can in his hand, a swagger in his walk. Dressed exactly like Britt, he looked amazingly like his famous brother. Although he was younger than Britt, a little taller, a little slimmer, anyone who had never seen Britt up-close would assume that it was him. Britt had told her that he had just begun using Phillip to keep reporters out of his face last fall, and so far the media hadn't caught on.

But while Britt's face usually exuded humor and boyish curiosity, Phillip's was drawn into a hard sneer. He had not deceived Dena the night she'd met Britt, and it was all Dena could do not to shove her daughter behind her. "So we meet again," he said to Dena, looking her over. "One of these days, I'll fool you, and you may just be glad that I did."

Dena frowned and tried to side-step him. He blocked her path.

"And this is my new niece," murmured Phillip. "Yes. Very nice." His hand touched Bonnie's hair; Dena tightened her grip and pointed down the hallway.

"Phillip," she said, "We were heading for Britt's dressing room." A lie, she was looking for a soda.

"Then you're lost." He pointed back the way she had come. "Britt changes in the room under the platform, and I think you knew that." His eyes narrowed at her, hard with challenge.

Her own mouth tightened, and Dena firmly guided her daughter in that direction. "I'll see you girls again, I trust. Soon." Phillip's laughter followed them as they escaped.

Dena was trembling when she found an empty room and pulled Bonnie inside, quickly closing the door.

"Mama, do I have to call him Uncle Phillip?" asked Bonnie.

A few names she would like to call him ran through Dena's mind. "No, honey."

"Good. He's not like Britt up-close, is he?"

"I know what you mean," sighed Dena.

When Dena and Bonnie returned, Britt was back on stage,

working it hard. The audience was rocking, loving him. But something was wrong. Britt was ad-libbing a lot, getting around the higher notes, and he appeared to be concentrating intently. Britt Jordan had always made his job appear easy, great fun. He could bounce from one end of the stage to the other all night without missing a note. With forty-five minutes left in this show, Dena could tell he was struggling to keep the momentum going. She looked over at Roger, his road manager, who was frowning and rubbing the back of his neck. The drummer never took his eyes off Britt, his face intent, his style less relaxed than before. One of the guitarists glanced at Roger with a worried expression, and then stepped up to a mic and gave Britt some harmony support.

The concert ended one song short. Britt didn't finish with the song he had done at the Grammys, as was the plan. When Dena saw the haggard look on his face as he left the stage, she grabbed Bonnie's hand. "Pay attention," she commanded.

With one quick motion, Britt had his arm around his wife, and then Len had them both in his grasp, pushing them quickly down a hallway toward the waiting limousine. They were pulling away while the crowd was still screaming for an encore. Dena kept her arm around her husband. He was doubled over in the seat, his face hidden in his arms, breathing heavily. The sight subdued even Bonnie, and Dena, just four days into her marriage with the singer, couldn't imagine what was going on with him.

Back in their hotel suite, Britt headed straight for the shower without a word. When he came out of the shower, he could hear Bonnie jumping around in the next room, loudly singing one of his songs. He lay on top of the covers in bed and stared at the ceiling.

In a minute Dena slipped into the room and shut the door. "What's wrong?" she asked as she sat on the bed beside him.

He didn't answer. He didn't know how to tell his wife his career was crashing to pieces around him. Britt had not thought his voice would hold that last hour . . . He had needed to visualize every single note and hang his voice on each one. It had taken every ounce of strength he possessed just to keep going, and his body had nearly faltered in the process. His hectic schedule and the demands he made of himself on stage were finally catching up with him. He was exhausted, worn down by the pain of pushing his damaged voice. After a long silence, he pointed at his throat.

"Britt, take some time off," she said, her voice insistent. "Give your throat a rest."

Britt shook his head. Rest would ease the hoarseness, but it would not restore the notes he had lost. Not even the shots of cortisone his doctor had inflicted on his vocal cords could do that. Nothing could. In a rough whisper, he said, "This tour is draining the life out of me. I just want to finish it."

"Why not quit?" she asked.

Bonnie's voice, singing one of Britt's songs, floated in from the suite's living room. He nodded toward the door. "That's the main reason: the people who come to hear me sing. There are still about a quarter million people who have paid good money to see me complete this tour, and they deserve a good show. And there's the small matter of the contracts I have to honor. Not to mention a whole herd of people on the payroll, counting on me." He paused as she rubbed his throat gently. "You've seen how it used to be for me. I would put everything I had into my concerts, and the crowd would multiply it back. I'd have more energy when it was over than when it started."

She leaned down and kissed him gently. "Like when you danced with me for hours when we first met?"

"Exactly. Now I pump myself up, and it's like a slow leak through the whole show. I am completely drained by the time it's over."

"I can't believe this has happened so quickly, and I haven't even known about it," said Dena. After a pause, she asked, "Britt, have you ever thought about changing your show?"

He growled low in disgust.

Her words were measured. "Do you know the most mesmerized I've ever been by you? You were just sitting in my kitchen, your back to me, playing a twelve-string. Waves of music, this, this," she seemed to be searching for the right words, "pure unearthly racket poured out of you. I've never seen or heard anything like it. Just do that the last hour. Just sit on a stool and play guitar."

Britt blew out a noisy, deliberately rude breath. "I think Ben Harper holds the market on that show. The day you see me turn into a white Ben Harper will be the day I quit forever."

There was a long silence.

"There's something you're not telling me, Britt," she finally said. "I don't think your voice is the only thing that's bothering you. I know you've only had a wife for four days, but that's why people get married. To have someone who will help them with the hard stuff."

He closed his eyes. The fear of losing his career was such hard stuff—it was nearly breaking him. He didn't possess the words to explain it to her. Instead of trying, he said, "Hit me with something besides the Ben Harper image, please."

After a pause she asked, "Do you know the story of Paul from the Bible?"

"Nope," Britt whispered, his eyes still closed. Britt had no use for religion, but Dena's faith seemed to make her happy. He would tolerate her story insofar as she remained happy. Besides, her voice was sweet medicine to him right now.

"Well, this man, Paul, had a lot on his mind too. Let's see. He was beaten six or seven times, stoned, shipwrecked twice, thrown into prison."

Shipwrecked. That was a pretty good description of how Britt felt, but all he said was, "I haven't been stoned since college."

She chuckled at his pun and continued, "Even after all that, Paul believed that anyone could achieve peace of mind by keeping their mind fixed on things that are true, honorable, and excellent, even lovely."

A minor crash came from the living room. "I think you'd better see about your daughter," he whispered.

"I think you're right." Dena stayed with Bonnie until two o'clock, when she finally calmed down enough to go to sleep in her own room.

As soon as Britt felt his wife slip into bed beside him, he wrapped his arms around her.

"Why aren't you asleep?" she asked.

"I was lying here, thinking of something lovely."

"I believe you missed the point," said Dena.

"Not necessarily."

"I thought you were exhausted."

"I am, but I'm not dead," he retorted.

"Oh," was her only reply.

Two weeks passed. Six more concerts. Britt continued driving himself hard. The seventh concert was in Phoenix, and his doctor met him there the morning of the show. Britt flew out of Phoenix two hours later, too dejected to even send Dena a text that he was returning home. The doctor had shot him with more cortisone, and then advised him to keep his mouth shut for at least a week. Britt had canceled a handful of concerts over the years due to weather, and once because his entire band hand landed themselves in jail, but never once had he been the reason for the cancelation.

Late that afternoon, Britt rode up Dena's driveway in the one limousine the local airport had at its disposal. Dena was washing the Monteverdi, energetically but haphazardly, Britt noticed. He marveled at how she could put so much effort into such a sloppy job.

She scratched her head as he approached. When he stepped out of the car, she gave him a quick hug, getting him slightly damp. "You can't sing tonight," she said, pulling back to take a look at him.

He shook his head.

"Have you quit?"

He shook his head again, more emphatically.

"Your doctor's making you rest?"

He nodded.

"Good. It's about time," she declared.

He didn't smile.

"How many shows will you be missing?" she asked.

He held up two fingers, then three, shrugged.

"And you're not allowed to speak at all, I see," said Dena. She finished hosing off the car and started into the house. "Maybe you should get in out of this cool air."

He stopped her, got two dry towels from a shelf in the garage, and started drying the car. He tossed one to her, still was not smiling.

"I'm sorry, Britt," she said. "I'm not being too sympathetic, am I?"

He pointed to his nose. *You got it.*

"Look, it's like this: I'm a bit distracted, and you aren't going to be too happy, either. We weren't expecting you home until tomorrow, and I told Bonnie she could have a few friends over. We, uh, we have a houseful of twelve-year-old girls."

He leaned across the car hood, spread eagle. Defeat.

Dena laughed at this, her laughter bringing back the warmth between them. "I'm so sorry," she said. "You aren't going to leave me now, are you?"

He made a show of considering, then spread his arms open wide, shaking his head. She gave him a genuine hug then, wet but welcoming.

Once inside, Britt stood in the kitchen and watched her knead pizza dough, feeling very lost. Bonnie appeared, followed by a troop of giggling, ogling girls. Britt hugged Bonnie and solemnly shook hands with all the others.

Dena herded them out of the kitchen. "Look, girls, Britt is here to rest his voice, and he doesn't need you to help him. Y'all go play a game or something."

After the others had disappeared giggling down the hall, Bonnie returned, a big grin on her freckled face. She spread her arms wide. "Welcome home," she said.

Britt smiled and wandered into the living room. Two gigglers appeared out of nowhere. He rubbed his hands over his face, walked into the den, and shut the door. Maybe some TV for a while. No such luck—two more gigglers came in and picked a random book off a shelf, knocking things around as they stared at Britt. When he saw Bonnie pass by the now-open door, he snapped his fingers to get her attention, and then crooked his finger at her. As soon as she was close, he pointed toward the kitchen and mouthed, *Go get your mother.*

Dena laughed as soon as she entered the den. "Uh-oh, stormy weather on your face. Hang in there, dear. I have a plan of my own." She went out, closing the door. Britt heard her say, "Stay out of the den, girls. I mean it."

In a few minutes, Dena reappeared. "Get your jacket and follow me." She hustled him out the back door before sticking her head back inside. "Bonnie, watch that pizza," she called. "Grandma will be here in a few minutes to look after you."

A picnic basket and a quilt were stashed behind the seats of the Monteverdi. Britt got into the driver's seat, and Dena directed him. As they drove out of town, she pointed out landmarks and told him colorful local stories.

"This is rich," she said. "I get to do all the talking. Let's see, where do I start? I was a beautiful little baby. Best baby ever. I . . ." He reached over and put his hand over her mouth. "Britt, where's your sense of humor?" she asked.

He jerked his thumb toward the car window. *Gone.*

They headed toward the nearby mountains, and soon they were in Virginia, at an entrance to the Blue Ridge Parkway. She indicated for him to drive around the single barricade, explaining, "Nobody's going to come after us. That's there to keep the tourists out, because the parkway facilities are closed. The locals use it year-round."

The late afternoon sun was bleeding orange into the distant haze when Dena motioned for him to pull over onto a grassy knoll. The March evening was settling over the hills with a damp chill. They pulled on jackets before spreading the quilt on the grass. From here, they could glimpse the foothills to the southeast as the lights started to blink on. To the west, the Blue Ridge plateau stretched lazily toward the last glow of sunset.

They ate in the chilly dusk, a simple meal of baked chicken, potato salad, and fruit. As the night settled, they lay on their backs, watching the stars come out.

A little later they were wrapped in the blanket, having shucked their clothing. Britt had momentarily forgotten his voice woes, as his focus was entirely on the extraordinary beauty of holding his wife in his arms.

Suddenly she pushed away from him and—still within the confines of the blanket—rolled onto her belly, laughing harder than he'd ever heard her laugh. He looked up to see the beam of a flashlight playing along the side of his car, moving in their direction. The light moved over their quilt, stopping in the grass at Britt's head, just in front of a pair of brown boots. As Britt's eyes moved higher up, so did the light, showing him green trousers, a gray shirt with a National Park Service emblem, and finally a man's seriously grave face beneath a Stetson hat. If Britt had a voice, he still would have been speechless.

The quilt continued to shake with his wife's now silent laughter. When Britt glanced her way, he saw that her head was buried in her forearms, her face hidden by her hair. He reached one hand out of the quilt and tapped her shoulder insistently. This sent her into noisier peals of laughter. She wasn't going to be any help for a while.

The park ranger coughed. "Excuse me. Would you folks care to tell me what you're doing here?"

Britt opened his mouth, but no sound came out.

"Okay. Sir, do you mind?" The ranger pointed toward the picnic basket. Britt reached over and opened it. After the ranger had looked inside only to see empty water bottles instead of the wine bottles he no doubt expected, he looked back at Britt, who looked at Dena, who finally looked up. Britt made a quick motion with his hand: *Cut it out.* This sent Dena into another bout of helpless laughter.

Britt heard the ranger heave an exasperated sigh. "I hate to break up the party," the man said, "but you folks are going to have to come with me."

Britt nudged his wife with his elbow in exasperation. She lifted her head, brushed the hair away from her face, and looked the ranger in the eye. "I am so sorry, sir. I know we must look absolutely crazy." When she glanced at Britt, she sputtered and had to compose herself again.

The ranger shifted his feet.

"Let me explain. I'm Dena Jordan. Believe it or not, I own the newspaper down in Deerfield. This man is my husband, Britt Jordan. He has lost his voice from singing too loudly."

By the glow of the flashlight, Britt saw recognition dawn on the ranger, who asked, "Um, don't you people have a home?"

"Yes, sir. But it's full of twelve-year-old girls at the moment. I mean, they're bouncing off every wall. And my poor silent husband here needed cheering up in a bad way."

Britt buried his face in his arms, pulled the quilt over his head, and awaited his fate. He heard the ranger sigh again before turning and walking away. He heard the flashlight click off, and then the man said, "I didn't see a thing," as he got in his car.

Britt came out from under the blanket and put both hands around Dena's neck. She laughed, warm and low, and pried his fingers loose. "Welcome to the South, Britt," she said, as his arms slipped around her and he buried his face in her hair, his shoulders now shaking with laughter. "Glad you got your sense of humor back."

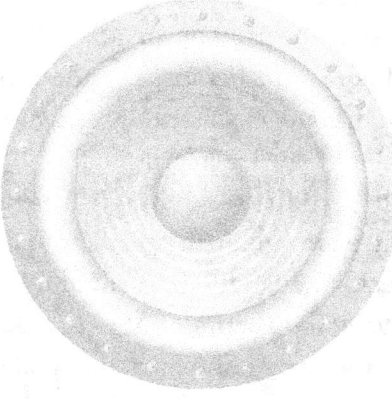

CHAPTER

SEVEN

When Britt went back to work the following week, he had eight concerts left in his tour. Dena stayed home and paced the floor the night of the first concert until her telephone finally rang at midnight.

"One down, seven to go," Britt spoke in a voice that was hoarse and shaky with fatigue. "I'll see you tomorrow." He hung up without saying another word.

When he arrived home the next day, morose and distracted, Dena was waiting for him. "Come with me," she said, taking him by the hand. "Bonnie is at a softball game at school. We have an hour or so."

Britt wasn't sure he was up to whatever he imagined she had in mind, but he followed her anyway. To his surprise, she had a hot bath waiting for him. She left him alone to soak in her large tub with classical music playing in the background. Very soothing. After a while, she reappeared. "Would you like a shampoo?" she asked. He nodded. Slowly and luxuriously, she washed his hair, massaging his scalp with her hands. He wished it would never end.

71

Too soon, she pulled him from the tub. "I'm sorry, but we're on a time crunch here," she explained. Britt knew he wasn't up to what she had in mind now. Again she surprised him.

Pointing to a quilt on the floor of the bedroom, she had him lie face down. She covered his body with warm oil and began to massage him with her strong hands, slowly, rhythmically, expertly.

Britt wondered where she had learned to do this, but he didn't ask. He was grateful that she didn't expect him to say or do anything. A long half-hour passed in silence. "I like having a wife," he whispered.

The back door slammed—Bonnie was home. Dena stood up. "I need to go," she said, covering him with a sheet. "Don't move until you're ready."

When Britt emerged after a long nap, his still-damp hair pulled into its familiar ponytail, he felt rested, nearly himself again. After a peaceful dinner, he and Dena settled onto the sofa in the den, at opposite ends, facing each other. Britt placed her feet in his lap and rubbed them gently. Dena's feet mystified Britt—they were softer than her hands, as soft as a baby's skin.

She smiled at him. "I'm glad you're feeling better," she said.

"Actually, I feel shipwrecked and beaten," said Britt. "What else did that guy in the Bible have to say?"

After a hesitation, she replied, "Well, Paul said to be kind and tenderhearted to each other and forgive each other."

"Was this before or after he was shipwrecked?" asked Britt.

"After."

Britt squeezed her feet. "And you managed to be that way without even being shipwrecked. Ha!" Abruptly, he changed the subject. "Did Darrell send my box of Tuesday night stuff?"

"Excuse me?"

"He should have sent it. There would be a ball cap, my

sweater, a golf club . . ."

"Oh, yes," Dena replied. "I didn't know what to do with it, so I put it in the garage."

"In the garage! Poor babies." Britt went off to retrieve them.

When he came back in a few minutes, he had the cap on backwards, the sweater around his shoulders, and his arms were loaded down with a huge bag of chips, a long neck beer, a can of soda, a harmonica, and the golf club. "Tradition," he explained. "Darrell and I had a date every Tuesday night before I met you." He handed her the harmonica. "You be Darrell."

He plopped down on the sofa, offered her the soda, and turned the television to a sports channel. The sweater smelled faintly of cigarette smoke.

"Does Darrell smoke?" she asked.

"Only on Tuesday nights." The show was a post-race NASCAR wrap-up. "What's the matter with this TV?" he asked. "It's broken. There's no Andretti."

"I wouldn't say that too loudly in this part of the country, if I were you," she advised. "The woods are full of stock car racers."

"No kidding!" He looked out the window. "What are they doing there?"

She chuckled. "They're not *literally* in the woods anymore," she said. "Some of them used to be in the woods, though, running moonshine."

"Do they do that these days?"

"What, run liquor? I should think not. If they wanted any, they could afford to have it driven in to them."

Britt stared at her. "Do you mean people still make liquor around here?"

She laughed. "I suppose it could be obtained for a small fee."

He stored this information away. "I'm buying a new TV

tomorrow," he said, taking a swallow of beer and setting the bottle down with a grimace.

"Change channels," she advised.

Eventually, he settled on a baseball game.

"What's the golf club for?" she asked.

"To murder the umpire." In fact, it looked battered and twisted enough to be a murder weapon. "From my last time out on the golf course," was his only explanation.

He chose a team arbitrarily for the night, as was his habit. The game was going badly for them.

"Aiiaah!" he screamed, waving the golf club at the screen. "Are you blind?" He threw a sofa pillow at the TV. This continued until he was out of pillows.

"Darrell always retrieves my pillows for me," he stated. He pointed at the pillows with the golf club.

She looked at the pillows, and then back at him. "Yeah, right," she said.

"It was worth a try," he said. "Wait a minute. Look at that. All right! Good show." He stood up and lifted his arms in a classic wave. "Come on, Dena. You're supposed to do this too. Blow your harmonica, while you're at it."

Dena sat still and looked up at him. She crossed her ankles.

"You're not as much fun as Darrell," he observed.

She raised one eyebrow. "Is that a fact?"

He took one swallow of beer and grimaced.

"You would not make a very successful drunk," she pointed out.

"Believe me, I've given it a good try in my day."

Bonnie, hearing Britt's racket, came out to join them. Dena handed her the harmonica. Bonnie, of course, did a more satisfactory job of playing Darrell's part. There was lots of shouting and harmonica tooting and, of course, pillows sailing from one end of the den to the other.

"See?" Britt said to Dena. "Bonnie is a fun date."

"Uh-huh."

Later, when Bonnie was safely asleep, Dena turned off the TV and threw Britt's cap and sweater across the room. She did this with a vengeance. His shirt and jeans followed.

"I take it back," he said. "You're way more fun than Darrell."

"I already knew that," she told him, pulling him down onto the sofa with her.

"Dena, do something for me," said Britt.

"I am," she murmured against his neck.

"Come with me tomorrow. I can't do this alone. I can't get on that stage again if you're not with me."

She sighed and sat up, rubbing his cheek with her hand. It pained her to watch him perform now that she understood how hard he was struggling, and he knew it.

"A tenderhearted wife would do it," he said.

"What chapter is this in your book?" she asked, settling down beside him again.

"The chapter on being your shipwrecked husband's only life preserver," he whispered just before he kissed her.

———CHAPTER———

EIGHT

I t was with some trepidation that Dena left behind her business and her child to fly into Chicago with Britt the next day. Trying to run a newspaper via email was going to be a headache. To ease Bonnie's burden at home, Dena hired her neighbor, a seventeen-year-old girl named Rhiannon, to do housework and keep an eye on Bonnie while she painted after school. Bonnie would be spending the nights with her grandparents.

Dena stayed by Britt's side through the sound check, his pre-show nap ritual, a handful of scheduled interviews, and the thirty minutes before he went on stage, when the pre-show jitters hit him. She held his hand and danced with him in his dressing room to keep his mind off the ordeal that faced him. Then, at a minute to eight, Britt screamed and stomped his feet and left the room at a run . . . without her.

Dena joined Britt's road manager in a balcony seat. From there she could watch the audience rock. Entire sections of people were on their feet from the moment Britt went on stage, dancing, singing the lyrics, laughing at the jokes he cracked between songs. Britt made his concerts fun, and before long, the entire audience was on its feet. It was always this way—his fans expected it, and not one person in the audience seemed to notice what Dena knew to be true. Britt was shaking with fatigue after half an hour.

Dena turned to see Roger frowning, leaning forward as if to move closer to his star, sweat beading on his forehead. "What's your plan?" she mouthed to him.

"I don't have one," he mouthed back, and abruptly got up and left.

A few minutes later, Dena could see him standing beside the stage, seemingly heedless of the huge amplifier next to his head, his lips moving as he spoke into a headset. Dena stayed in the balcony until it was nearly time for Britt's break, and then made her way downstairs, past the security guards and into the belly of the coliseum. Len was there, pacing at the bottom of the ramp that led to the stage, his eyes on Britt.

Just as she started up the ramp, Len glanced at her, shook his head, and jerked his hand toward her. She stopped. Len moved toward the stage, out of her vision. She heard the band shift into "Don't Miss Out," twelve minutes early. Desperate as she was to see her husband, she stood still at the exact spot Len had stopped her.

The moment Britt sang the last note, the stage went black. There was a collective gasp from eighteen thousand people, and then the band swung through a rampage of guitar riffs into its planned interim music as if the darkened stage were nothing out of the ordinary.

With a strangled cry, Dena started to run toward Britt. A hand on her arm stopped her, and she turned to find her face inches from Phillip's face. By the dim light from the hallway behind them, she could see his features hardened into a contemptuous glare. Stunned, she struggled to pull free. Phillip put his mouth close to her ear and said in a gloating voice, "He's done for. They'll haul his ass down here, closer to an ambulance." He held her in a tight grip until a cortege of security police appeared at the top of the ramp, flashlights in hand. As she watched, the circle of police opened to let three people pass—Roger, Len, and Britt. Britt hung limp in the two men's grasp, soaked in sweat, his legs dragging the floor.

"Britt!" she cried. He did not open his eyes, but the fingers of his right hand circled into the universal sign for "Okay." She turned to follow him, and Phillip caught her eye. He held up both hands, fingers extended in the sign for "Rock and Roll," an unholy look in his eye that sent a shock through Dena. She brushed past him and followed Britt, shaking.

They were moved quickly into a small room. As soon as the door closed, Britt shrugged off Roger and Len and sank to the floor on his own, breathing hard, hugging his knees, head down. Sweat continued to pour off his body.

Roger put a hand on his shoulder. "That's it, Britt, I'm pulling the plug."

Flinging Roger's hand away, Britt gasped raggedly, "I'm okay; I'm okay. Just give me a minute." A tall sport drink was placed in his hand, and he gulped it noisily, waving away two paramedics who banged through the door with a gurney. Britt leaned forward again, arms over his head. For several seconds, he remained motionless while the power of the rock and roll machine he had created pulsated on above them.

Suddenly his head came up, and he frowned at a subtle falter in the drummer's rhythm. At that moment, Roger cursed loudly into his headset. Two seconds later, a male voice blared through the sound system, singing one of Britt's songs too loudly, the voice not quite Britt's. Britt screamed, "Phillip, you . . ." His curses were drowned by Roger's yell into the headset, "Kill the mic; get that fool off the stage!"

"No!" shouted Britt, as he staggered to one knee. "That'll make it worse! The whole damn country will think that's me being dragged off." His right hand sliced through the air as he shouted commands in quick succession, repeated by Roger's shouts into the headset. "Pick up the pace; pick it up; pick it up. Drop his mic. Keep the lights moving and off him." Britt's voice became an angry, heart-stopping growl. "I want him off-balance stage center when I murder him!"

Britt lurched to his feet, took one step, and dropped back to one knee, retching. A paramedic grabbed his arm. Britt came up, shoved him backward into the gurney and shouted, "Get away from me! Save that buggy for my brother after I'm done with him!" This time Britt made it as far as the doorway before another wave of nausea hit him, and he slammed the doorframe with his fist, bent forward, cursing.

At that moment, Dena stepped to his side, her hand firm between his shoulder blades, and she whispered into his ear. He turned, locked eyes with her, and straightened up. Seconds passed as the awful parody of Britt's voice continued to sing on above them. In a very quiet voice, looking steadily into Dena's eyes, he said, "Ben Harper it is, then."

In one smooth motion, Britt stripped off his sweat-soaked shirt and flung it across the room. With another, he yanked the band from his ponytail and swung his head, spraying droplets. Dena didn't flinch. His hair hung in wet strands, nearly hiding his eyes, and his tattoos glistened. Head lifted, jaw clenched, he spoke two words to Roger before walking out of the room:

"Drum solo."

Within seconds of Roger's order, all sound came to a sudden stop except for a confounding, complex cacophony of drumming. Len pushed past Dena, who shouted to Roger, "Get him a guitar!"

Britt walked up the ramp alone, picking up speed as he went. The guitar tech rushed forward with a guitar, and he grabbed it effortlessly, never breaking stride as he lifted the guitar high above his head.

"He's coming up the ramp, hit him with the lights in five, four, three, two . . ." muttered Roger into the headset.

Dena stopped still at the bottom of the ramp, captivated by her husband's silhouetted figure against the blinding white light. Her right hand raised involuntarily, the palm out toward him, until Britt moved from her view.

Screams thundered through the coliseum as Britt strode onto the stage. Even shirtless, hair down, swinging a guitar over his head instead of blasting onto the stage with raucous vocals, there was no mistaking the *real* Britt Jordan.

Taking control of a mic, Britt shouted, "Say hello to my brother Phillip," and without giving the audience time to respond, he pulled an ear-splitting shriek from the guitar and yelled, "And good-bye!"

The crowd roared with laughter. The lights only on Britt now, few people noticed the obscene gesture Phillip aimed at his brother or how Len had to haul him off the stage.

Britt gave a quick hand signal to the drummer, who segued easily from his solo into a heavy four-count beat. With a few strokes on his guitar, he showed the rhythm guy what he wanted, and then growled into the mic, "Are you ready to make rock and roll history?"

While the crowd screamed its approval, Britt dove into a complicated guitar solo that the bass guy soon underpinned and the lead punctuated with clear, high notes. This lasted three minutes, and then Britt motioned for the drum and rhythm to push harder into the four-count. He got the crowd to move into a high hand clap on each down-beat, which one of the keyboard guys continued to lead while Britt's fingers flew to pull another wave of notes from the guitar.

Stepping back to the mic, Britt sang a simple, melodic chain of, "Oh-oh-oh-oh, oh-oh-oh-oh, oh-oh-oh-oh, ooohh!" At his nod, the other keyboard guy urged the crowd to repeat the melody until soon the whole stadium was clapping in rhythm and singing this new tune. At that, Britt rocketed into a heart-stopping guitar riot that wove its way through the song now rocking the coliseum and then screamed above it in a sound so pure it was lyrical.

As if a collective sigh passed through Britt's band, the men relaxed into the music for the first time in weeks. They were the best in the business, and Britt paid them well to back him up. If he suddenly started pulling tunes out of his backside in front of a live audience, it was all the same to them—at least the job was fun again.

The incredible music went on and on. Just when the audience started to become subdued, as if attempting to absorb this unprecedented glimpse into Britt's brilliant mind, he would step up to the mic again and get them singing. At one point, he had one side of the room going on the chorus of one of his hit songs while the other side was rapping out a brand-new line that somehow fit. Each time the crowd would think he was winding to a close, he'd rock into yet another phenomenal, fresh guitar creation that kept the crowd on its feet.

Dena had moved and was standing beside the stage. Although Britt never glanced her way, her heart told her that he knew exactly where she was. She stood still, head high, fighting tears; she did not want him to look up and see her crying. After a while, Len joined her and caught her eye. He gave her a slight nod and a small smile, his first sign of acceptance.

Dena missed the inevitable signal that Britt gave his band, but she heard the shift from his guitar to the lead guy's instrument, and she looked up to see her husband jump from the darkened edge of the stage to land right next to her, holding a mic. He yelled into it, "Good night, Chicago! Thank you for an incredible evening!"

And with that, he turned his back on his career and walked down the ramp, holding Dena's hand.

Once out of sight of the crowd, Britt collapsed against a wall, still on his feet. Dena held him in her strong arms, his scent of sweat and bay rum covering her. When she felt his breathing slow, she spoke into his ear, "What do you want me to do?"

He looked at her, his face etched with exhaustion, eyes intense, and whispered, "What did you call me back in that room? Say it again."

"A gentleman," she said carefully. "I reminded you that above all else, you are a gentleman."

He laughed shortly. "Nobody's ever called me that before."

"It's the truth," she said. "And you knew what I meant. But Britt, I never said for you to pull a Ben Harper. I never said walk away."

He looked up at the ceiling, his head against the wall. "Given the circumstances, I thought that was the only thing left for a gentleman to do."

Clearing his throat, Len broke in. "We need to get moving,"

he said, hustling them out to the waiting limousine.

As soon as the car door closed, Britt spoke one word to the driver: "Airport." He leaned back against the seat, eyes closed. Dena stared hard at him, puzzled, and he answered her unspoken question. "I need to be somewhere tonight besides a hotel room. Home." Just speaking those words seemed to require all his strength.

"Home?" asked Dena. "Do you mean Deerfield?"

Something close to gratitude softened his face, and he nodded his assent and murmured, his voice thick with fatigue, "I know I promised you a honeymoon in Antigua once this tour was over, but I'm crashing. I may need to sleep the next two weeks."

Sleep, he did, all the way to the airport, rousing himself when they arrived for only long enough to make a phone call to his publicist. "You are to make one statement," he told her brusquely. "'Britt Jordan has retired due to throat issues.' Say absolutely nothing else. I won't make any comments or take any interviews." He hung up in the middle of her protests. And he slept hard during the flight back to North Carolina.

Dena didn't sleep at all on the plane, overwhelmed by all that had occurred in the space of one evening. As she studied her sleeping husband's face, she wondered what Britt would be like once it hit him that he had performed his last concert. She thought about where Phillip might turn up next, and decided against telling Britt that his brother had frightened her tonight. Mostly she contemplated the appropriate action a tenderhearted wife should take.

———CHAPTER———

NINE

Early the next morning, after about three hours of sleep in her own home, Dena stood beside the bed and looked down at her sleeping husband. She touched his forehead and then his cheek, gathering courage. With resolve, she yanked the covers back and commanded in her best drill sergeant tone, "Geedup-geedup! Whadoyouthinkthisisboy, a rest home? Rollout!"

Britt opened one eye and shut it quickly. "What time is it?"

"Oh, seven-hundred, boy—you're sleeping your life away." She dropped his running shoes on his stomach. "Put these on and be ready to roll in two minutes."

In less than two minutes, Britt walked into the kitchen, wearing nothing but his shoes and a grin. "I was a very success-ful G.I.," he explained. "Always did exactly as I was told." Dena stifled a laugh as he produced a pair of shorts from behind his back. "Where are we running off to, by the way?" he asked.

"Oh, just around a few blocks." Dena looked out the window. "I don't see any reporters camped out on the lawn yet, but your announcement's just now hitting the streets. I'd say they'll be here soon. Let me show you the back way out of here. It might come in handy later."

She led him down through the yard and under a thick hemlock grove. Her lawn was terraced above her back-door neighbors' lawn by a rock wall. They climbed down the wall into the adjoining yard, where they were met by a massive Rottweiler. It stuck its huge nose against Britt's belly and growled low. Britt froze.

"Shame on you, Brandy," Dena said, taking the dog's jaws in her hand. "Can't you tell he's with me?"

The dog backed off, eyeing Britt as he edged his way past. They crossed the yard, Britt walking backward to keep an eye on Brandy, until they reached a chain link fence.

"I hate to tell you this, but there's no way out of this yard except over the fence," said Dena. "My neighbor is extremely paranoid. Sleeps with a loaded gun beside the bed."

"Whatever it takes to get out of this yard," said Britt, then added brightly, "You're my hero."

She laughed as she hauled herself over the fence. "Brandy may wind up being your hero before it's over. She keeps our backs pretty well covered. I don't know about the front. Once people figure out that you've settled in here for good, we may need a brick wall around the place."

Finally reaching the street, they began to run, Dena setting the pace. As they left her neighborhood, the wide, tree-shaded lawns gave way to turn-of-the-century Main Street yards. Each was split in two by a straight sidewalk leading to a boxwood-lined house, a pair of trees standing at symmetrical attention on each side of the sidewalk. Between the houses, they could glimpse the distant Blue Ridge, the misty slopes glowing in the early morning light.

Britt was becoming winded, as his body had not yet recovered from his ordeal the previous night. Dena kept a watchful eye on him—the purpose of this run was to pull him from his post-adrenaline crash, not break him. Soon she heard him whistling a catchy tune through his teeth, and she relaxed. Getting him up and moving had been a good idea.

They started to see people emerging from their houses, all of whom waved. "Southerners are . . . a friendly lot," observed Britt between gasps.

Dena slowed to a walk when they returned to her neighborhood. He grabbed her arm. "No, no," he said in a falsetto voice, "please don't feed me to the dog."

"Come on, wimp," Dena said with a chuckle. "Better the dog than the reporters."

They reached the fence. In one leap, the dog was on top of the doghouse, eye level with Britt. She licked her chops. "I wish you wouldn't do that," said Britt, staring her down. The dog wagged her tail once.

"I believe Brandy likes your voice," Dena declared. "If you come this way by yourself, just sing to her."

"Singing lunch," muttered Britt. "I don't know what worries me more, the dog or the lunatic with the gun."

"You should worry more about the lunatic's teenage daughter," said Dena.

"Oh, boy," said Britt. "Now I really feel safe. The father will shoot me, the dog will chew me up, and the daughter will spit me out. I can't wait."

Before she left for work, Dena cornered Britt with a concerned look on her face. She was wearing an intimidating gray business suit and heels, and Britt said "Yes, ma'am" when she said she wanted to talk.

"I really don't feel good about leaving you here alone after what you went through last night," she began. "Are you sure you're all right?"

Britt rubbed his chest and considered how to answer her. As far as the world knew, he had quit at the top of his game. That was not a bad impression to have left. He was a survivor, and mentally and physically, he would recover. Right now he was more afraid of being consumed with hatred toward his brother rather than regret over his career.

He spoke carefully. "We didn't make any vows in front of the judge when we got married, but I made some promises to you on our wedding night. Do you remember?"

"Well at one point I remember you promised you would never drop me off the bed," she said lightly.

"Did I?" he asked.

She shook her head with a smile.

"Do you think I ever will?"

"No, Britt—I trust you."

He put his arms around her, business suit and all, and looked deeply into her eyes. "I promised you I would always be your Britt, the man you married. I knew you felt there was a lot about me you didn't know, and I promised I was not going to turn into a stranger on you. I'm not going back on that promise any more than I would drop you on the floor. Whatever it takes, I will deal with this. My voice is shot, my career has crashed, and my brother is an asshole, but I have you. I'll be okay."

Her lovely smile reflected the confidence and trust she had in him, and she touched one finger to his lips.

"I'll even keep trying to work on my mouth for you while I'm at it," he said. She kissed him lovingly in response. When she left for work, her hair was rumpled and her suit was a little less crisp, but she was still smiling.

After she left, Britt stared out the windows of Bonnie's alcove at the reporters who were already setting up camp on the lawn. He sure wanted to be in Antigua right now. With a sigh, he went into Dena's den, where he couldn't see the reporters, and started making some calls.

First he woke up his manager, Don McQueen, and fired him, just because he didn't feel like arguing with him about his decision to retire. Then he called his secretary, Phyllis, to fill her in on what had happened. She was sympathetic and supportive between yawns. Next he woke up one of his lawyers, who nearly had a heart attack when he heard that Britt was not finishing the tour. They argued about the financial and legal repercussions of the situation until Britt hung up on him. He did not call his agent. After thinking for a few minutes and making some on-the-spot calculations in his head, he called his comptroller and gave him detailed instructions concerning severance pay for his band, Roger, and the crew. When the comptroller, who had not yet had his morning coffee, started to nag Britt about his excessiveness, Britt told him to just do it or figure out his own severance pay. Then he hung up.

Britt leaned back and closed his eyes. He guessed he had pretty much done a day's work in about twenty minutes. He thought about calling his mother, who would be reading the morning paper back in Sheboygan, Wisconsin. His mother was no fool. She knew Britt and she knew Phillip, and she would probably piece together the entire story just from the few words his publicist had released to the news media. He decided to put off the call until later.

His eyes opened, and he almost expected to see a reporter

peering at him through the den windows. Dena's backyard was closed in by a wooden fence on one side and an impenetrable hedge on the other, but Britt guessed it would only be a matter of time before the news hounds gave up on waiting for him in the front yard and squeezed their way into the back. Feeling like a mouse stuck in its hole with the cat just outside, Britt stood up with sudden resolve. He got a steak out of the freezer, thawed it in the microwave, and went out the back door, carrying the steak, warm and dripping.

"Brandy," he called softly before reaching the hemlocks. "Here, girl, come to Daddy. There's a girl." Britt backed his way across the neighbor's yard holding the steak high, then dropped it in front of the dog and clambered over the fence.

He spoke to the dog through the fence. "Good, huh? The best thing about this lunch is that it doesn't scream when you bite it."

Dena returned home from work that afternoon in a distracted mood, her head hurting from lack of sleep, aggravated by the reporters she had nearly driven over to get to her garage. Dena's paper had printed no more news about Britt's retirement than any other, but her telephone had rung off the hook all day. Everyone from the gossip sheets to the AP were looking to her for details. All she wanted was a bite to eat, a couple aspirin, and a few minutes alone with Bonnie.

She stepped into her kitchen to find Rhiannon, the teenage neighbor she had hired to keep an eye on Bonnie, dreamily ironing Britt's undershorts.

Dena let the door slam behind her. Rhiannon jumped. "If you're going to iron Britt's undershorts, then you'll have to iron mine and

Bonnie's too," Dena stated flatly. "That's just all there is to it."

The girl flipped her blonde hair over her shoulder and gave Dena a hard stare.

"You're done for the day, Rhiannon," said Dena. "I'll call you again when I need you."

When the girl continued staring, Dena turned and headed toward her room, high heels clicking on the hardwood floor. In a few seconds she came back. "Rhiannon, where's Bonnie?" she asked.

The girl was folding Britt's undershorts carefully, and she didn't look up. "When I went to pick her up after school, she said some teacher had asked her to stay and make posters. She said somebody would bring her home."

Dena sighed, closed her eyes, and covered her face with one hand. She didn't know whether to be angry at Rhiannon or the school, but 'somebody' bringing her child home was not going to cut it. Not with the whole town swarming with reporters. She heard the kitchen door slam shut and realized that the girl had left. It was just as well—she was in no mood to deal with an impudent, star-struck teenager anyway.

She had just received confirmation from Bonnie via text that she was already on her way home when the door slammed again. Britt was home. She looked up from her cell phone to see him cradling Johnny Martin's mandolin under one arm.

"What have you been into today, Britt?" she asked.

"Some real work," he answered, mischief back in his eyes. "You're going to be so proud."

"Am I now?" she responded, downing two aspirins.

"Did you know that there's a recording studio right here in town?" Britt appeared quite pleased for having made this discovery.

"Yes, I know that. The local bluegrass groups use it."

"I made a recording today," he announced. "Me and the Elk

Gap boys. Aren't you proud?"

She sputtered into laughter, like cranking an engine. Once she got started, the laughter flowed from her, long and full, and she leaned on the counter for support.

Britt watched her for a full minute. "I didn't know my gainful employment would cause you so much amusement." He tapped her on the shoulder with something. "Here. I have my very own recording of the day's work. Listen to it with shame, woman, for doubting my abilities." She had nearly collected herself, but that sent her into another round of laughter. "That would be me on the mandolin. I'd like to think your late husband would be proud," he said and started from the room.

"Wait, Britt." She wiped her eyes. "I have to know one thing. What did they pay you?"

"Money, money, money—that's all you ever think about. I'll have you to know I received a very nice commission for my work."

"Well what was it?"

"Here, if you must know." He reached behind him and produced a quart jar of clear liquid, holding it up to the light for her inspection.

"I don't believe this," she said.

"Believe it," said Britt with conviction. "I am very proud. I'm told it is the finest in the country."

She unscrewed the lid, touched a drop to her tongue, and coughed. Pure moonshine. "No doubt in my mind." She handed it back to him. "Put it out in the garage. Bonnie has never seen contraband brought into this house."

"In the garage!" He held the jar protectively away from her. "You have a strange way of showing your gratitude for your man's hard day of work. My fingers will never be the same." He held out his left hand. She took it in both of hers and inspected it, smiling. Britt's hands were nicely shaped and well kept, but a bit broad for a mandolin player. "Besides," he continued, "this is medicine. Cough medicine."

"So I've heard. One whiff and your cough will get up and run to the next county." Dena rubbed her head. "As a matter of fact, I think that may be what happened to my headache."

"See? Now aren't you proud of this fine commission?" Britt stood on tiptoe and pushed the jar to the back of a top shelf. "I want to save this. I've got some friends who will get a kick out of it. And you never know when you may feel a cough coming on," he added with a fake hack.

Dena shook her head at his silliness and opened the refrigerator door. "What would you like for supper?" she asked.

"Supper? Forget supper! We can be in Antigua by nine o'clock." When she shot him a hard look, he declared humbly, "I'm all better now, Dena."

She looked him over. Even standing still, he was fairly twitching with adrenaline. "You just think you're better, honey," she said sweetly. "I don't believe a person can get over what you went through in a single day. You may crash and burn a couple more times yet." When he put on his finest imploring face, she added, "I'll tell you what, you do your best to rest for another week, and then we'll see."

Britt stood behind the open refrigerator door and banged his head against it several times while she pulled out supper ingredients. Finally he said, "I think I need some cough medicine."

After Britt showered that night, he walked into the bedroom still dripping water, wearing his boxers. He stood before Dena and with great drama reached inside his undershorts and pulled out a piece of pink paper. "Who's Rhiannon?" he demanded, grinning.

93

Dena snatched the paper from his hand, glanced at the girl's declaration of love in curly letters, and crumpled it. "She's fired is who she is," she said.

"Oo-*kay*," he said, amused, and turned on his heel and walked back into the bathroom.

The next morning, Friday, the Jordans were awakened by reporters pounding the front door, shouting for a statement from Britt. The police were called to evict them from the lawn, and two policemen escorted Dena to her car. The minute she left for work, reporters shouting to her from the street, Britt slipped out through the back again on foot. He followed the same procedure as the day before, dangling a steak to distract the dog. Just as he reached the chain link fence on the other side of the neighbor's yard, he heard a voice say, "I don't think Daddy would like you to do that."

He turned to see a buxom young girl sitting on the screened-in back porch. "Which, feed the dog or climb the fence?" he asked.

"Either one." She opened the screen door and stood on the step, one hand on her hip.

"Why aren't you in school?"

"I'm sick." She made a face, giggled nervously. Perhaps she had meant to say something else. Running her hand through her hair, she invited, "Why don't you come in through the house?" She tipped her head coyly and twisted a blonde strand.

Britt looked her over; she was every bit of seventeen. "I know your daddy wouldn't like that," he said and scrambled over the fence. He walked away without looking back.

He took the same route as yesterday, stopping as before to watch a construction crew frame a new house. Today they were setting roof trusses. Britt stood, hands in his pockets, watching their progress.

A voice called down to him, "Son, are you looking for a job?"

Britt looked around.

"Yeah, you." A hefty man, who looked to be about sixty, swung down off a beam and approached him. "I seen you hanging around here yesterday morning. You need a job?"

Britt kicked a rock. He did need a job, so he couldn't answer in the negative.

"You have done carpentry work before, haven't you, son?"

"Well, yes, but . . ."

"I figured." The man nodded. "Healthy fella like you. What's your name?"

"Jordan."

"Jordan what?"

Britt blinked. "Jordan Martin."

"Well, do you want the job or don't you?"

Britt looked up at the trusses and back at the man, suppressing a laugh. "Ah, what the heck."

"Well you get on up there, boy. Johnson there will show you what to do."

Britt took off his T-shirt and hung it on a tree limb. "By the way, Mr . . ."

"Just call me Big Jim."

"Okay, Big Jim. What do you pay an apprentice these days?"

"A what?"

"A new boy."

Big Jim looked him over. "How about eight-fifty?"

"Wow." Britt swung up by way of the corner braces and

balanced himself beside Johnson on the top plate. He was told that his job was to catch the end of the truss as the crane swung it toward them and hold it in place while Johnson braced it. Britt had, in fact, done some carpentry work in high school. Like riding a bicycle, the balance came back, and he followed Johnson's instructions on catching and placing the end of the truss. They had their end set within seconds of the men on the other end. Johnson straightened up. Britt looked him in the eye. "How did you ever manage this without me?" he asked.

Johnson spat a stream of tobacco juice and motioned for Britt to move two feet down to the next mark. By way of an answer, he flipped the hammer around and handed it to Britt. "Here, wise guy, let's see if you can drive a nail."

None of the men seemed to recognize him. Somewhere below, country music was playing on the radio, most of the notes trapped between the din of the hammers and the growl of the crane. Evidently, he was anonymous to country music fans.

Britt enjoyed the work for a while. The feel of the hammer in his hand, the pure sharp notes of metal biting into wood, the hot sweat scalding his back all returned him to a time in Wisconsin when he'd been nothing more than a talented kid with big dreams. For three-fifty an hour, he had worked his tail off, saving money for college. Owning his own car had been out of the question; his father was already working two jobs to pay for the best piano teacher in town, music camp in the summer, and stacks and stacks of sheet music. And Phillip? Phillip was a good kid then, following Britt everywhere, even to the construction sites, sweeping and picking up the sites for free just to be near his big brother.

A truck pulled up. Britt looked down and saw a younger version of Big Jim step out and stare up at him before motioning for his father. A brief conversation ensued, and then both men looked at him.

Big Jim motioned for Britt to come down. Britt handed the hammer to Johnson. "That's the way it goes," he said.

Johnson eyed him warily. "What'd you do, pull time?"

Britt grimaced and swung down. Perhaps a ponytail and tattoos were not an asset in a small town.

Big Jim was standing with his hands in his back pockets. "Your name Britt Jordan?" he asked.

"Yes, sir."

"My boy here says we ain't got enough insurance to cover you."

Britt looked at the boy. He was probably forty. "Your boy may have a point there."

"Dang shame. You was catching on real good."

"Thank you, sir." Britt retrieved his shirt and, holding it away from his sweaty body, started up the street at a run. He was late for an appointment anyway.

Sometime after midnight that night, Britt still hadn't fallen asleep. His shoulders ached from the unaccustomed work. More than that, his brain was revving, urging him to get back into tour mode. He told his brain to shut up. He managed to get both arms around Dena without waking her up. After lying that way for several minutes, enjoying the smell and warmth of her skin, he became restless. One foot flexed, then the other, and then both moved from side to side. "I'm bored," he said aloud.

Dena jumped. "What?"

"Oh good, you're awake." He hauled her over on top of him where she lay facedown, arms beside her. She began to breathe deeply again. "You're no fun anymore," he told her.

She jumped again, rolled away from him, and put the pillow over her head. "Go away, Britt," she said.

Britt bounced out of bed. "Go away, Britt? Go away! Do you realize there are one million women right now who would not tell me to go away?" He waited for a response. None came. "One million, Dena."

She mumbled something about him finding one, and he was afraid to ask her to repeat it.

He started down the hall.

"Britt!"

He jogged back to her side. "You had a change of heart."

"Put some clothes on. Bonnie might wake up."

He rummaged through a drawer, put on sweatpants, and headed down the hall. After pacing the house several times, he sat down and began to play his piano. That diversion lasted only until he heard a door slam down the hall.

He marched back into the bedroom. "I'll have you to know," he said to his wife, "I was told this morning that I would make a dang good carpenter."

Dena moaned and opened one eye. "Yes, I heard all about that," she said. "Big Jim Tate can't afford to have you playing around on his roof, you know."

"I wasn't playing," said Britt, offended. "He paid me a whole eight-fifty an hour. Maybe he should consider getting more insurance. I'm going to be available next week if you don't hurry up and take me on my honeymoon."

"Let me ask you something," she said. "Where did you go after Jim fired you?"

He didn't answer.

"There were Britt Jordan sightings all over town yesterday," said Dena. "But you disappeared today. Care to explain?"

"No." In the dim light of the room, he saw her smile and close her eyes. He smiled too, and then left the room.

CHAPTER

TEN

Saturday morning, Dena went to work again, trying to catch up. Britt and Bonnie joined her for lunch downtown, and afterwards they walked her the three blocks back to her office. People smiled and waved, recognizing him. The reporters had given up and moved on, at least for the day. Britt decided that small town life wasn't so bad.

One woman approached him on the street, a concerned look on her face. She said in a low voice, "I was so sorry to hear about your throat. Are you taking any antibiotics?"

Britt lowered his voice also, making it classically hoarse. "Madam, I've had the best doctors in the country climb in and out of my throat on ladders. They say nothing can be done."

As they approached Dena's office building, Bonnie was still giggling and Dena had a smile on her face. Through the smoky glass, Britt could see a pudgy man standing beside Sue's desk in the outer office. His mood shifted at once—apparently his agent had shown up for a confrontation.

"You haven't called me, Britt," Bob Johnson said as soon

they walked in from the street.

"May we use your office, Dena?" asked Britt.

"Of course."

Britt led the man into the office and closed the door behind them. "I haven't called you because there's nothing left to say, Bob."

Bob Johnson turned to face Britt, the singer whose career he had nurtured for twenty-two years. Both men stayed standing. "Nothing to say," Bob repeated. "A man drops out of sight, just like that," he snapped his fingers, "at the height of his career, and you say there's nothing to say?"

Britt looked him in the eye but did not respond.

"When were you going to call me, Britt? Next week? Next month?"

Britt didn't answer.

"Tell me your plans, Britt."

"I don't have any plans."

"Britt Jordan with no plans." Bob ran his hand through his graying hair. "That is a statement that frightens the life out of me."

Silence.

"I want you to tell me what's going on with you," demanded Bob.

"I have lost my voice."

"Damn, half the singers your age have lost their voices. You don't see them walking away. Their fans don't notice or don't care."

"I care."

"Then go to a voice coach," said Bob.

"I can never regain what I've lost," replied Britt. "It's gone."

"Don't hand me that crap," Bob said, turning away and pacing the office.

"Give me a little credit for knowing what I can or can't do."

"With some work, you can have a new voice. You know that," Bob said, still pacing.

Britt stood his ground. "If I can't sing my songs with my voice, what's the point?"

Bob stopped pacing and put one hand on Britt's shoulder. "The point is that a man like you can't just walk away from it. You can't turn your back on a career you've worked so hard to attain." He added quietly, "Or on a relationship that has lasted two decades. I signed you on the day you got out of the Army. God, you were a talented kid. Got your first label within a month. Do you remember that?" Britt didn't smile. Bob continued, "I know you better than anyone else in the business. I know what it has cost you to get where you are today. And I know what you stand to lose by quitting."

"I won't be losing a thing that's worth keeping," Britt said, his chin up.

Bob leaned against Dena's desk and ran his fingers through his hair again. "You look me in the eye, right now, and tell me that you haven't enjoyed the hell out of every minute of it: the fame, the money," he ended in a sharp whisper, "the women."

Britt looked him in the eye. "I've had it up to here with the fame. Do you know that it costs me a steak every time I want to walk out of my own house?"

Bob's eyebrows went up, puzzled.

A brief smile tugged at Britt's mouth. "And I have more money now than my wife will ever figure out how to spend."

"And the rest of it, Britt?"

"The rest of what? The big parties, people mooning in the mirrors over their own reflections? How about all the bashes that I don't even remember because I was too drunk? And all my great flings?" He took a dried flower from an arrangement on Dena's desk and crumpled it to dust in his hand. "It amounts to this. You blow it away, and when the dust settles, there's not a damn thing left." He demonstrated.

"Well, aren't we poetic?" said Bob sarcastically. "Half the men in the country would kill to have had even one of your flings, as you call them. And here you are talking about dust settling." When Britt didn't respond, he continued, "It's more like gold dust, in your case. The name Britt Jordan turns to greenbacks when you say it, and you know it as well as I do."

Britt's eyes narrowed, and Bob stepped back and stopped talking for a few seconds.

"Look, Britt," he said more quietly, "you have a career. That is *real*. You have talent. You have accomplished tangible things in this industry. You've made a difference to your fans, to the next generation of musicians, to the music. Don't give it up, for your own sake, if nothing else." Bob's voice shook with emotion and he grabbed Britt's shoulders with both hands now. "A man like you will shrivel and fall headlong into hell without work. I've seen it happen, and I can't let it happen to you. Just think about it. There's too much at stake here—your own sanity, maybe even your life. Think about it."

"I have thought about it," said Britt in an even voice, "and there's nothing left to say."

Bob dropped his arms and sighed deeply, and then he turned and walked out the door.

Britt placed both hands on Dena's desk and leaned all his weight against it, his eyes closed, his breath ragged. He stayed like that for several seconds until a shudder passed through him, and then he straightened up, stretched, and left the office.

He looked around for Dena, but she and Bonnie were nowhere to be seen. Sue was at her desk—she'd come in today to work some overtime and help Dena catch up. After staring at her for several seconds, Britt passed one hand over his face and walked over to her desk. "Sue, will you do me a favor?" he asked in a low voice.

Sue looked up but didn't smile. "What do you need?" she asked impatiently.

Britt didn't flinch. "Dinner tonight," he said. "I'd like to treat you and your husband to dinner at the Green Leaf Inn. All I need is for you to drive Dena and Bonnie there so that it'll be a surprise. I'll meet you there."

Sue's face reddened and she sputtered, "The Green Leaf Inn!"

Britt laughed heartily. "You thought I was up to something . . . admit it," he cackled, pointing his finger in her face. "You heard I was at the Green Leaf yesterday afternoon, and you assumed I was having a little tête-à-tête."

Sue opened and closed her mouth twice before getting out, "I don't know what to say."

"Just say you'll do it," he said. "Then you can see for yourself what I've been up to."

Sue stammered, "But, but . . ."

Britt bent down, his eyes level with hers, and said in the same rough, teasing voice that had captivated millions, "Come on, Sue. You know you want to like me."

Sue laughed a little, her face going even redder. "I never met anybody quite like you," she admitted. "And you're right. I did think you were up to something. I just wasn't sure whether to tell Dena yet or let you hang yourself."

He laughed again, pleased with her honesty. "This is a small town. I expect Dena knows every move I've made the past two days. So you'll do it?"

"Well, see, the Green Leaf Inn—I mean, are you sure they're even serving tonight?"

This time Britt doubled over with laughter. "Why wouldn't they be?" he asked.

"Well, uh, it's like this," Sue stammered. "I don't think Carlene

Jenkins usually serves anyone besides the guests who are staying there. And most people in town wouldn't eat there even if she did. Carlene is, shall we say, discreet. She has been known to let certain executives meet their ladies there."

Britt kissed noisily in her direction. "I know Carlene is, as you say, discreet. Dena made me stay with her for two months, from Christmas until the Grammys."

Sue's eyes widened, and if her face could have gotten any redder, it would have.

Britt crossed two fingers and whispered mysteriously, "Carlene and I are this tight." He straightened up. "Be there at six, okay?" Then he turned on his heel and walked out without waiting for her reply.

Carlene Jenkins met her four guests at the door that night with her new waiter by her side. He looked remarkably like Britt Jordan in a tuxedo. Dena hooted with laughter as she followed the waiter to the dining room where the only table was set for four.

Carlene lit candles as her guests were seated. She was one of those women of indeterminate age: dyed black hair, robust bosom, open face. She was the kind of woman that men want to be close to, if only to flirt, the kind who seems to understand men, yet who is rarely understood by other women. Before she returned to the kitchen, she gave her new waiter a cozy smack on the lips.

The waiter composed his face into a prim, snooty pucker and stood at attention beside the table, a towel draped over his arm. "My name is Pierre," he lisped. "I believe I know the ladies. And you, sir?" he asked Sue's husband, extending his hand.

"I'm Charlie. Charlie Duncan," returned Sue's husband pleasantly.

"Yes. Nice to meet you, sir," said Pierre. "I'll be your waiter and your chef tonight." Dena started to sputter. Pierre looked at her. "Madame, really."

Bonnie whispered dramatically, waving her hand around the empty dining room, "Mama, don't. You'll embarrass us in front of all these people."

Dena leaned her head in her hand and tried to hold back her laughter. Pierre disappeared into the kitchen, reappearing soon with salads, which he set down with a flourish. Dena touched her finger to the dressing and tasted it. She said in a choked voice, "This is not the dressing I ordered."

Pierre answered in his most offended voice, "We only serve one dressing here."

Dena excused herself and went outside, where she could be heard laughing. Pierre asked, "Has she always been this way?" Three heads nodded in unison. He followed her outside, sat on the steps beside her, and wrapped both arms around her.

"What brought this on?" Dena asked after her laughter subsided.

"I didn't want to be useless in my retirement," he said. "Carlene is teaching me to cook."

"You've gone to a lot of trouble just for me," she said.

"Of course. Of all the million women I claimed would take me in, no one actually did besides you." He kissed her cheek. "You're keeping me afloat, Dena. I would have sunk to the bottom and drowned by now if it weren't for you. This is my way of hanging on."

She closed her eyes and leaned into him with a sigh. After a minute, he stood up and said, "I'm going to lose my tip if I don't get back to work." He held his hand out to help her up. She shook her head and rested her cheek on her knees, arms circling her legs, and stayed on the step as he went inside. Pierre was serving the second course by the time she joined them.

It was an interesting meal. Stuffed artichokes followed the salad. Next came chilled gazpacho, then London broil, rice pilaf, marinated asparagus, and a fruit slaw.

"I'm quite impressed," Dena told him.

"You ought to be. Of course, every time I cook for you, this is what you'll get, since it's all I can do."

"Get Carlene to give you more lessons," Dena advised.

When it came time to serve dessert, Pierre walked in holding an apple pie and set it down in the middle of the table. Pulling up a chair, he joined his customers, removing his tie. "Carlene made this," he said. He nudged Sue. "My tête-à-tête was too short yesterday for pie lessons."

Sue blushed and cleared her throat. "Britt, I am so sorry . . ."

He held up his hand. "Think nothing of it. You're going to think I'm up to worse before this has blown over. I can hear the rumor mill now, buzzing like a hornet's nest, because I haven't fed it one drop of anything since Chicago. Just do me one favor . . ."

Sue nodded sheepishly.

"Don't believe anything you read about me in the tabloids. Ever."

The adults talked until late. Britt discovered that Charlie had always wanted to learn to sail and volunteered to teach him soon. The Duncans left around midnight, taking Bonnie with them.

Britt looked at Dena. "I'm waiting for my tip," he said.

She kissed him there in the dining room, long and warm. Eventually he pulled her into the guest room that Carlene had waiting for them. Sometime between midnight and dawn he murmured with a contented sigh, "I've been in the wrong business all my life. I should have been a waiter."

ELEVEN

On Sunday morning, Dena insisted on picking up Bonnie and returning home early to dress for church. Britt was playing the piano when his wife walked into the living room looking innocently radiant in a softly draped dress, a Bible tucked under her arm.

"Where are you heading?" Britt asked.

"To church, Britt. It's Sunday."

"You're going off and leaving me alone again?"

She shrugged. "Come with us."

Britt considered this. It seemed like a social, Southern thing to do. "I believe I will," he said. "What should I wear?"

"A tie would be nice," said Dena. Then she added with a smirk, "And pants."

He grinned wickedly over his shoulder at her as he headed down the hall. In a few minutes, he returned wearing a linen jacket with the sleeves rolled up, a yellow T-shirt, a green tie, khakis, and green sneakers.

"Cool," pronounced Bonnie.

When they arrived, Dena led him to the balcony. No one else joined them. Apparently, Dena had reserved it, thinking that he would prefer the privacy. Britt sighed—what he preferred in potentially boring situations like this one was to have people to watch.

When the service began, Britt looked around for the acolytes. Seeing none, he closed his eyes and reminisced about having served in church as a boy. He remembered the smell of the candles as he lit them, the swish of the robes as he walked. He had burned his fingers once. The pain had made his eyes smart, but he'd hidden it from the other boys. They already called him a sissy since he played the piano and was smaller than they were. When he reached middle school, he started lifting weights and bloodying noses, and they stopped calling him that. Britt looked at his hands and stretched his fingers. It was a wonder he hadn't broken his fingers with all the punches he'd delivered. He smiled to himself, thinking of another time when he'd waved to his brother behind his back in church, making Phillip giggle. He and Phillip had both been spanked for that. That made him think of the terrible fights he'd had with his mother when he turned fourteen and announced he was too old to attend church. He hadn't set foot inside one since, with the exception of his father's funeral and one of Phillip's weddings. Britt frowned, trying to remember which of Phillip's four wives that had been.

Music began to play, drawing Britt out of his reverie. He stood up when Dena did, hands in his pockets. The piano needed tuning, he noticed. They were singing something about "higher ground." Britt could remember Van Morrison singing about higher ground, and he decided he liked Van's version better.

During the second verse, Britt began rocking up on his toes, making a gesture with his right hand, palm up. "What are you doing?" Dena whispered.

"Trying to lift them to higher ground. They're flat."

Dena looked shocked. "All of them?"

"Well, it can hardly be helped with that piano."

"Am I flat?" she asked.

Britt eyed her chest. Not even her modest dress could completely hide her figure. "Not hardly."

"Bri-itt."

The song over, they sat back down. Britt studied the three stained-glass windows behind the choir for a while, and then tilted his head back and studied the one behind him. After that he turned his attention to the rafters, imagining how much scaffolding it must have taken to set them in place. Finally he sighed and began to drum on his knees with a pencil. Dena covered his hand with hers.

A woman stood up and began singing a solo. "Is she flat?" asked Dena in an undertone.

Britt squinted. "Maybe I need glasses. I can't tell from here."

"Britt, you're a case," whispered Dena.

Britt wasn't sure what a case was, but he had the feeling that he might not be far from a spanking. Church could be a painful place.

Sue's husband Charlie was in the choir, and when the choir began to sing, Britt could hear the man's bass voice clearly, on pitch. He closed his eyes and followed Charlie's voice in his mind, picturing the notes.

Britt's natural range fell between tenor and baritone, perfect for a rock singer, with a raspy growl that sounded like no one else. Screaming for twenty years, however, had destroyed the upper notes of his range. But the bottom notes . . . Britt listened carefully to Charlie. He had never pushed his voice to sing lower. *What if I could pick up four or five bass notes?* he wondered.

Develop a low baritone voice. He'd still have a two-octave range. New music. New style.

Britt leaned back after the choir finished, hands behind his head, eyes closed. He pictured what he knew the inside of his throat looked like, the vocal chords rough and swollen, the muscle walls thickened. His mind went over and over the damage, willing it to disappear.

In deep concentration, Britt propped his feet up on the back of the empty seat in front of him. Scraps of melodies dropped into his brain, but he wasn't sure what to do with them. What could he do with a baritone voice? What kind of music would he write? Who would buy it? Perhaps he could sell this new music on his name alone, without concert tours. Maybe acoustic instruments only. The thought excited him.

He knew of a voice coach in New York who had a reputation for working wonders, teaching an operatic style that saved even the most ravaged voices. He'd have Darrell call the guy on Monday. Britt wiggled his feet in anticipation.

Suddenly, he became aware that somebody was staring at him. In horror, he realized where he was and what he had done. He opened his eyes and spread his feet wide, like a fan. There, framed between his green shoes, the faces of the entire choir were gaping at him. Charlie appeared relaxed, arms folded across his chest. He grinned at Britt.

Britt closed the fan, his feet blocking out their faces. He looked at Bonnie, who was staring at his shoes. He guessed that he had managed to embarrass her.

He dreaded seeing Dena's face, but he turned his head toward her nonetheless. She wasn't looking at him. He shifted slightly. She would not look at him. Britt brought his feet down and leaned forward, forcing her to meet his eyes. When she did, there was no expression whatsoever in her hazel eyes.

I wish she wouldn't do that, he thought. It scares the willies out of me. He sat still for the rest of the service, hands folded in his lap. As soon as the pastor finished speaking and the congregation stood to sing, Dena slipped off the seat, and settled down on the floor. Britt followed her. Bonnie, not knowing what else to do, followed suit. The three of them sat for a moment, their backs leaning against the seats behind them, their legs under the seats in front. The seats behind them began to shake, and Britt realized that Dena was laughing silently, the tears rolling down her face. He looked at Bonnie, and saw that she was bent over too, her shoulders shaking. He decided that it was in his best interest to stay quiet for now.

Finally Dena spoke. "Britt, I swear. Is there no chance that you might settle into a routine for just a few more days without getting into trouble?"

"Probably not," he said humbly.

"We can't go on a honeymoon in a week," she declared.

His heart stopped.

"I'll be insane by then," she continued. "Call your pilot; we're leaving tomorrow."

Britt sighed with relief and rubbed his chest. It hurt when his heart started up again. He drew in a breath. "Dena, do me a favor. Please don't take that dress to Antigua."

Dena folded her arms and looked at him. "Ha! Now I know how to punish you. You're taking me out dancing tomorrow night, and I'm wearing this dress."

Britt blinked. He didn't have an answer for that.

The music had ended, and the service was over. Dena didn't seem disposed to leave, so the three of them continued sitting on the floor. Finally she said, "Britt, please do me a favor. When we get back, I want you to pursue an occupation. I don't care what it is—write songs for somebody else, go to work for Jim Tate, for all I care—just do something with yourself. You seem to be desperate for work."

"I'll become Carlene's new chef," he said, deciding to keep his idea to write new music for his new voice secret until he actually *had* a new voice.

The sound of footsteps filtered up to them, and a few moments later Charlie appeared. He didn't seem surprised to see them sitting on the floor, he just sat sideways in front of them, looking into Britt's eyes with concern. "Are you all right?" he asked.

"Sure," answered Britt. "Never better." He lowered his voice to a whisper. "I get to go on my honeymoon tomorrow."

Charlie smiled. "Just so you know, you've probably started a trend around here. I can see it now: a whole row of teenagers, sneakers waving. Assorted colors. It'll keep the preacher on his toes. I never saw him in such a frenzy, trying to get your attention."

Britt covered his face with one hand. Charlie held his own out for a handshake. "Just make sure you come back to see it, Britt—I mean it."

Taking Charlie's hand in his own, Britt used it for a boost. Once on his feet, he looked his new friend in the eye, but didn't answer him. Some things, like gratitude, aren't generally voiced between men. He helped Dena to her feet.

"Let's go home," she said. "We've got a lot to do."

Britt looked at her dress. Personally, he didn't have much to do besides make three phone calls: one to Darrell about the voice coach, one to his pilot, and one to his staff in Antigua. That and make sure this dress didn't find its way into Dena's suitcase.

That night, Dena finally heard back from Rhiannon, whom she had been trying to reach all weekend. She got right to the point. "Rhiannon, I need you to bring Bonnie's key over." When the teenager didn't answer, Dena said, "I don't think I need to spell out why I'm firing you."

There was a long pause. Finally the girl responded, "I'm not even at home. I've been on a hunting trip with my father."

Dena had no idea what kind of game people hunted in April. "When will you be back?"

"Um, I'm not sure. Tomorrow night, I think."

Shoot. Dena had wanted that key in hand before she left. She drummed her fingers on the desk, deep in thought. The day she caught Rhiannon ironing Britt's undershorts, she had been so irked that it hadn't even occurred to her to ask how the girl had gotten in the house. Later, Bonnie had explained that Rhiannon had asked for the key so that she could 'catch up on the ironing.' As if Britt's undershorts had been in dire need of tending to.

Well, Dena decided, it really didn't matter about the key—the security code was automatically re-set every Monday at ten, and she and Britt would get a text with the new code. "All right, Rhiannon, I'll get it from you later. Don't you have school tomorrow?"

"Bitch!" The line was disconnected.

Dena was still holding the phone, staring at it, when Britt walked in.

"Problem?" he asked.

Dena sighed. Britt had put up with star-struck females for years; he didn't need to worry about the one in his backyard. She skirted the issue. "Child care problem. Until we hire an art tutor for Bonnie, I don't want her in anyone's care after school besides family. Understood?"

Britt appeared perplexed, but he answered, "Absolutely. Totally. Count me in." He put his arms around her. "What you're saying is that if your parents didn't live in town, we wouldn't be leaving for our honeymoon tomorrow."

"Exactly."

"When your father gets over resenting me for marrying you, I'll thank him."

------CHAPTER------

TWELVE

t was lunchtime the next day when Dena stepped out of Britt's car in front of his home in Antigua. The colors of the place were instantly welcoming. The sun was bright and hot, and the sky was an unreal blue that turned almost violet where it met the sea at the horizon. Then there was the sea itself, that indescribably rich, cerulean blue-green that sparkled through the darker green foliage of the lush trees surrounding the house. Everywhere, there was a profusion of flowers—they even cascaded in bright pink bouquets from the house's second-story balconies. And the whole place smelled like an intoxicating mixture of salt spray, sweet amaretto, and earthy-green Eden. There was a constant, pleasing breeze, steady as an old lover, promising endless pleasures to sailing buffs.

Dena stood still, eyes closed, and breathed deeply before turning to face Britt's house. It was large but not palatial. The outside walls were formed of fine stucco with a foundation made of rocks that had been hauled in from the cliffs of the eastern coast. Each balcony was framed by intricately detailed wrought-iron work, and the front door and surrounding window casings were made of mahogany.

Walking slowly, Dena ascended the outside steps, her hand gliding along the iron railing, and allowed Britt to open the door for her. Crossing the tiled foyer, she stood stock-still at the entrance to the living room and dropped the travel bag she was carrying.

Dena stayed completely silent as she took in every detail of the spacious room in quiet wonder. Straight ahead was the front of the house, which faced the harbor with seven sliding glass doors that had been opened to the sea breeze. Above them were seven tasteful, bold nautical paintings similar to Bonnie's in style. To Dena's left was a long wall painted a color that was a cross between melon and coral, with pure white trim. Because the room was two stories high, the effect of the bright color was doubly dramatic.

There were three separate upholstered groupings of furniture, all done in a rich green leaf and floral pattern, the flowers reflecting the bright wall and contrasting with the sky and sea framed by the glass. Every table in the room was warm mahogany. The effect was startling, yet surprisingly tranquil. In the far left corner a baby grand piano stood next to the windows. Dena's attention was drawn to the wall opposite the coral wall. "A rock fireplace in Antigua?" she asked aloud.

"Every home needs a fireplace," Britt said with a shrug. Not even Dena laughed at that statement, the effect was too impressive.

A large motherly woman stepped into the room from the kitchen to the right. "Mr. Britt," she said warmly, regally. "Mrs. Jordan. You're finally home." She shook both their hands at once, and then embraced them both in her great, fleshy arms.

"I'm Ruby," said the woman in her calypso accent, taking Dena's hands in hers. "I take care of Mr. Britt when he's at home.

You, too, now." She smiled at Dena benevolently, her warm brown hands caressing hers like a benediction. "You'll want to see the kitchen."

Ruby led Dena into the gleaming, commercially equipped kitchen. Dena walked around the room, hands behind her back, examining everything in wonder. The floor and countertops were covered in warm brown tile, the equipment and utensils were stainless steel, the walls were sparkling white, and the cabinets were mahogany. Dena opened a cabinet door just to feel the weight swinging on the hinges.

From the kitchen, Dena walked into the dining room, which also had a wall of glass doors. Here again was mahogany—a long, richly grained dining table and matching sideboard. The twelve chairs were upholstered in a green leaf pattern that matched the living room chairs, with no floral design. This room alone was carpeted, in white. Decidedly formal.

Through French doors to her right, Dena entered a peaceful sun room with a circular sofa in soft green and yellow and a table for two. From here Dena could see the view from another angle, and it was stunning.

Britt's house faced south on a high hill overlooking a slender finger of water that formed a sheltered bay. The hill plunged to the sea so steeply that Dena could see a wide expanse of brilliant Caribbean water across the treetops. The lush green hill seemed to be almost ablaze with flamboyants, their bright red flowers shouting their presence among the Antiguan palms and tamarinds. Caressing everything was a profusion of red bougainvillea, and the grounds were edged with plumbago, the blue and white spikes perfect exclamation points to the whole scene.

Britt's home had a series of wide decks that descended the hill toward a white beach, ending in a long dock, which stretched into the bay. A cruiser was stationed at the end of the dock, and several sailing yachts were anchored in the harbor, the only evidence of neighbors whose homes were hidden by the trees.

"This room is my favorite," Dena told Ruby, who smiled with approval.

"Come upstairs, and I'll show you my favorite," said Britt, strolling in from the living room, his wife's travel bag in one hand. Ruby's smile faded as Britt pulled Dena into the foyer and up the stairs.

Dena only caught a quick glimpse of the balcony that looked out over the living room from above the foyer before Britt pulled her into the master bedroom. It was a large and masculine room, with windows overlooking the harbor and a state-of-the-art entertainment system installed against one wall. Britt strode into the room like a captain taking possession of a ship and dropped Dena's bag on the floor. Unaware of what she was doing, Dena picked up the bag and took a step backward, her eyes fixed on Britt's bed, where he had brought so many other lovers, shaking her head ever so slightly.

Turning back from the window, Britt caught her expression, and keen pain flickered across his face. Crossing the room quickly, he put a strong hand on her back and steered her out of the room. "Come on, Dena," he said in a quiet, sympathetic voice, "this is a big house. We'll find another room."

They finally settled on a guest suite facing the sea, decorated in the same green and yellow as the sun room. Dena breathed a sigh of relief and dropped her bag for the third time on the floor. The room surprised her with its odd yet charming details: a large arrangement of fresh flowers, a bowl of fruit, and a plate of freshly baked sweets. Their luggage was already in the dressing room, having been brought in by Britt's handyman, Bogey, while Dena was touring the kitchen. Evidently Ruby had had a hunch that Dena would choose this room.

After Dena unpacked, carefully keeping one bag hidden from Britt's eyes, she joined him on the outside balcony, where the wind quickly whipped her hair into disarray. Britt's hands gripped the balcony rail tightly as he looked out into the bay. "Which one is she?" Dena asked. He pointed to a single-mast cutter, as sleek and trim as a sixty-foot ship can be. "Will we sail today?" she asked.

He shook his head. "I have a peculiar love affair with my ship," he said. "I need some time alone with her. Maybe tomorrow afternoon."

After a lunch of Ruby's lobster salad, sliced fruit, and warm coconut bread, Dena went outside to explore. She tested every one of the decks, plopping down into a dozen different chairs, as Britt looked on in amusement. When she reached the lowest deck, she took off running down the long dock, leaving Britt behind. He stood with one foot propped on a deck rail, watching her with pleasure. The wind tore her scarf from her hair, and she stood with her back to him, hair streaming, her long, gauzy skirt billowing in the wind. When she motioned for him to join her, he strode down the dock, hands in his pockets. "Are you in love with Jane too?" she asked, indicating his cruiser at the end of the dock.

He looked at Jane, all gleaming white fiberglass: a nice forty-foot Hatteras, made in North Carolina. She did not inspire passion in his sailor's heart. "Would you like to go for a spin?" he asked. When Dena nodded happily, he helped her aboard and led her up the steps to the flybridge. As they headed for open sea, Dena settled back and watched the shoreline, the sailboats, the frothing waves, and the scudding clouds.

Britt was as relaxed and happy as she had ever seen him. He let his hair down, and the wind lifted and tangled it. Even though he kept his hair trimmed to his collar bone, just long enough to pull to the crown of his head in a ponytail, it was thick and wavy, and it tangled easily.

She reached over and pulled a strand between her thumb and forefinger, feeling its texture. "I'll bet your hair streaks golden pretty quickly in this sunshine," she observed.

He grinned in response. "I'll be a different man by Friday."

They spent the afternoon riding around, and then headed back to the house. At sunset, Dena found him on the balcony once again, hungrily watching the sea turn to bronze. "Hey, you," she said, "you're supposed to take me dancing tonight."

He kissed her. "Forget dancing," he whispered. "Let's honey-moon awhile."

"Nuh-uh. I'd like to go dancing tonight."

"Will you be wearing whatever it is you've been hiding in that bag?" he asked.

"Most definitely," she assured him.

"It is a dancing dress, right?"

"Right."

He appeared relieved. "You'll love the band tonight," he said. "They've managed to achieve a curious blend of Beach Boys, David Sanborn, and Hugo Montenegro all at the same time."

"You're kidding," she said. "No steel drums? No Reggae?"

"This isn't Jamaica, mon," he replied.

She waited until he was completely dressed and calling for her to hurry up before emerging from the dressing room, her hair up, wearing her church dress, shoes in hand. She dashed past him before he could stop her and ran down the stairs.

"Dena!" he shouted down to her. "Can't you punish me in some other way? You can't dance in that dress."

Dena ran out the door and jumped into the car. "You deserve this!" she laughed as he walked out the back door.

"Nobody deserves this," he grumbled, getting in the driver's side.

When they arrived at the restaurant, Dena walked in, her head high. Britt followed, hands in his pockets, resigned to his punishment. They were seated at Britt's favorite table, and he ordered dinner for them both.

After a few minutes, Dena began to fiddle with the back of her dress.

"Is there a problem?" Britt asked.

"My back itches," she said.

"Do you need any help?"

"No . . . Yes, actually. Can you go get me a piece of bread? I'm starving."

He frowned slightly and raised his hand to summon the waiter.

"Please," she said with uncharacteristic insistence. "I'm really hungry."

A perturbed look crossed his face. He passed one hand over his face and got up and did as he had been bidden.

When he turned back to his table, she saw him do a double take to make sure he had the right one. She flashed her most charming smile at him when his mouth dropped open. She had kicked her church dress under the table and was now wearing a hot pink dress with a shocking décolletage.

"How did you do that?" he asked so loudly that all the heads in the restaurant turned in his direction.

She laughed and shook her head.

He crossed the room and sat down in front of her, placing the forgotten bread on the seat beside him, staring at her as if he were seeing her for the first time. "Dance with me, Dena," he said hoarsely.

"There's no music, Britt," she answered.

"Surely there must be somewhere."

She laughed at him once again. "There's something I want to give you." She dug into her handbag. "I've saved this for tonight." She held out her hand, fist closed. He reached out, his palm open. Into it she dropped a gold-inlaid titanium wedding band. He stared at it without moving.

"You don't like it," she said, reaching to take it back.

He closed his hand. "I apologize for my slow reaction. You've shocked me twice tonight. It just struck me that never in my life had I expected to wear a wedding band."

"Read the inscription," she said.

He held it up, squinting in the dim light, and read aloud, "B—I'd do it again—D." He looked at her. "You'd do what again?"

"Britt, this is a serious moment."

"I am serious. I'd hate to miss it if you did something again." He slipped the ring on and winked at her.

Their salads arrived, and she picked up her fork. He pushed his plate aside.

"Look, the band's about to play," he said. "Come dance with me. I want to get a better look at that dress."

She chuckled and started to lift a forkful of salad toward her mouth.

"Britt!" a voice screamed, and a woman's fanny landed on the table, right where Britt's plate had been.

Dena paused, fork in midair.

"Kathleen," Britt said formally, "my wife, Dena Jordan."

"Hello." Kathleen's voice suggested complete indifference. She slipped off the table and tugged at Britt's arm. "Everybody's been looking for you. We all heard about the tour. Come dance with me. I've been bored out of my mind with you away."

Levelly, he said, "I'm having dinner with my *wife*."

"Come, come, come," Kathleen insisted. "She's eating. Everyone wants to see you."

Britt hesitated, shooting Dena a look as the persistent woman continued to pull at him.

"I am indeed eating," said Dena, putting the bite of salad into her mouth.

Britt let Kathleen pull him to his feet and across the room, glancing over his shoulder at Dena. The band started up as soon as they reached the dance floor. Dena took another bite of her salad and watched as her husband danced a few polite steps with Kathleen before bowing elegantly and starting back to the table. He was immediately grabbed by another woman. By the time a third woman had snagged his arm, Dena could tell by the set of his jaw that he was about to cease being polite. Perhaps she had better rescue him before things got ugly.

Dena pushed her plate aside and dabbed at her lips with a napkin. Before she could stand up, Britt's seat had been occupied by a man who stared at her without introducing himself. "Hello," she said, extending her hand, "I'm Dena Jordan."

The man chuckled as he shook her hand. "Everybody knows that. We just don't know why."

Dena raised one eyebrow.

"I'll bet I can guess why," said a voice by her side.

She looked up into steel-gray eyes. They weren't looking into hers, however, because they were focused on her décolletage. "Would you care to dance?" this man asked.

"Thank you, but no," she replied.

He shrugged and walked away.

The first man grinned at her. He still hadn't introduced himself. "My bet's on that one," he said, nodding toward the fourth woman who had her husband in a dance grip.

"Your bet?"

"The first gal he'll slip out on you with. We're all taking bets."

Dena looked him in the eye. "This conversation is over," she said firmly and stood up.

Just then a woman plunked down on the edge of the seat, practically in the man's lap. "Hello, the first Mrs. Jordan," she said. "The women are all curious about what kind of pre-nup he made you sign."

Dena raised both eyebrows. She spread her hands on the table and leaned forward, a curt reply on the tip of her tongue. The woman's eyes dropped from Dena's face to her hands on the table and her eyes widened. Dena looked down at her hands. They looked quite capable—in fact, they seemed strong enough to strangle somebody. What the woman was staring at, however, was her exquisite diamond and emerald wedding band. Dena decided no words were necessary.

"Excuse me," she said. She walked slowly across the room toward the music: pop tenor, light jazz, dark Latin. Bizarre. Britt was already making his way toward her, impatiently shrugging off any hands that reached for him. His eyes caught hers and the music seemed to flow between them, an ocean wave cresting. When he reached her side, he looked into her eyes for a full eight counts before he moved. She was ready, swinging easily through a dip, then spinning away from him, the full skirt of her dress flowing around her.

The entire room held its breath. They had seen Britt Jordan dance many times, but they had never seen him dance with his wife. And they had never seen him dance when he was ready to blast them all out of the room. Dena could read the anger in his eyes—somehow he understood that these people had collectively chosen to insult his wife.

Dancing with Britt while he was in this mood was a transcendent experience for Dena. It was like being in motion and static at the same time: an unhurried river that appears to stop as it meets the sea. Or molten metal caught at the precise moment it meets the mold. It was hearing one voice sing harmony and melody at once. Their dance was unhurried yet complicated, flowing precision, restrained passion. When the music stopped, the dancers stopped. No one else in the room moved.

Then Britt did something Dena realized was deliberate. He set his face into a hard glare that had even more impact than the more openly angry look he'd sported earlier in the evening. Just like turning a faucet, he turned on the Britt Jordan whose phenomenal strength of will had made him an international success. This was the man who could throw fans into a swoon with a single glance, send musicians scattering with the wave of an arm. This was the man who had brought down the house in Chicago even as his career crashed around him. He did this to show her that he could turn that man on in an instant, with enough power to destroy the room.

It was his way of telling her that he would stand between her and a tsunami wave, and she would be safe.

They drove home with the top down and the music loud. The Australian band The Temper Trap was singing "Sweet Disposition," all driving bass and soaring male vocals. Britt let his hair down, and the wind quickly tangled it. Dena studied her husband as he drove. His psyche was complicated: creative, abstract, quirky right-brain; analytical, detailed, obsessive left-brain. He was at once restless and disciplined, passionate and controlled. Right now he was angry, and his expression was steely, but she was confident that he was capable of flinging aside his mood in an instant.

When they reached the house, Britt's handyman, Bogey, opened her car door. She got out, walked toward the house, and waited on the bottom step until Britt caught up with her. From this vantage point, she leaned down, her right hand weaving through his hair, her left forefinger touching his right cheek, and kissed him with lips that trembled.

He pulled back. "Have I frightened you?" he asked.

"I've never felt safer," she answered.

Walking backwards so that he could face her, he led her up the steps to the landing at the door. She kissed him again, insistently. She was asking, with the authority of a wife, that he drop his mood on the doorstep.

Slowly, taking his time, he removed the pins from her hair, letting them fall. Her hair tumbled to her shoulders, and she stroked her left forefinger against his cheek once again.

Then he spoke. "Would you really, Dena?"

"Would I what?"

"Marry me again."

"Absolutely," she replied.

Just above her finger on his right cheek, she caught a glimpse of a dimple. He looked into her eyes, connecting with her, and then his eyes went a little unfocused. No telling what that brain of his was concocting.

"What chapter are you on in that marriage manual you're writing?" she asked.

He let her see both his dimples and slid his hands down her back to rest below her hips. "My favorite chapter yet," he said. "This is the chapter where the groom has a spectacular revelation. He realizes that some nights are far too short for a man's body to say all it needs to say to his perfect mate."

She laughed, warm and low. "And you wondered why my lips were trembling."

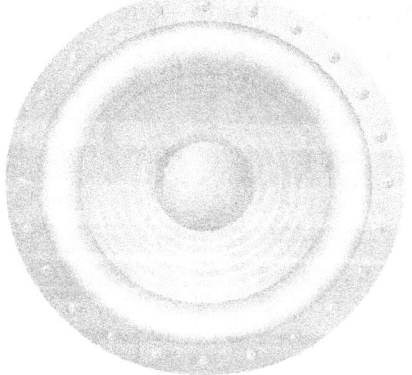

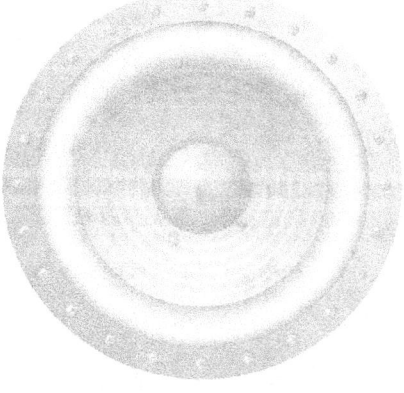

——CHAPTER——

THIRTEEN

Britt spent the next morning puttering around on board his sailboat. He didn't sail her, but he carefully checked over the entire rigging system. He ran his hands over every inch of the ship, every cleat and pulley, every fitting. He raised and lowered all the sails, including the racing sails, which he refolded and meticulously put away. He fired both engines, cut them off, and then re-fired them one at a time, listening intently. He checked every line, cable, light, bilge pump, the hot and cold water, the radio, the horn, and the fire extinguishers. He scrubbed the head, even though it was already gleaming. In his way, he was making love to his ship.

He joined Dena for lunch in the sun room, the bright sunlight painting the Caribbean in vivid colors once more. "Will we sail this afternoon?" asked Dena.

"No," he replied.

"Gracious, Britt, how long does it take to reintroduce yourself to your boat?"

He grimaced. "Ship, Dena." He pulled binoculars from a

drawer. "Look at the clouds."

She looked. They were scudding along as they had done the day before.

"Now look at that sailboat on the horizon," he said, pointing.

She focused, and then gave a small shriek. "It's about to fall over in the water!"

He chuckled. "It's pitched leeward at a thrilling angle. Too much thrill, I'm afraid, for someone who's never sailed. You might not come with me again."

"Okay, whatever you say," she said. "So what will we do?"

"We'll do the tourist thing," he declared.

"What's that?"

"Walk on the beach holding our shoes."

She laughed.

"Take pictures of each other with the sea in the background, one at a time, still holding our shoes," he continued.

"What else?"

"Let's see. We'll go to Nelson's Harbor and stare at the yachts, wishing they were ours."

"That's what tourists do?" asked Dena.

"Yes." He was on a roll, gesturing with his right hand. "Then we'll watch the other tourists walk around holding their shoes. We'll vote on which ones look the tackiest."

"Tacky is a Southern word," she pointed out.

"Don't insult me like that. Oh, I nearly forgot. We must keep our cameras around our necks at all times. That's a rule."

She chuckled. "You're really into this thing, aren't you?"

"Yes, and when our camera batteries die, we'll have to stop taking pictures because we forgot to recharge them. The rest of our vacation will be a blank in our scrapbook." Britt smacked his hands together and stood up, ready to go. "We'll end the day making love on the beach."

"Goodness, is that what tourists do?" she asked.

"I think so."

They took their time doing everything on their list except for making love on the beach. Dinner was chicken grilled in the open air by a local vendor, eaten while strolling the docks. They returned home late to discover that their home had been invaded by about forty of Britt's friends.

"What on earth!" exclaimed Dena.

"I'm sorry," he said. "I should have warned you. Everybody just comes on over whenever I'm home. I assumed that they'd give us a break since we're on our honeymoon."

He took her hand as she stepped out of the car, his eyes appraising her with approval. She was dressed in a flattering slip dress, appropriate for the tropics, her hair down and shining. "Come dance one dance with me," he said. "Then we'll split."

She followed him without protest to the front of the house, where the decks overflowed with people. Music was playing from hidden speakers, and the guests seemed to have already helped themselves to Britt's well-stocked bar. Applause and shouts announced his arrival.

Without acknowledging his guests, Britt pulled Dena close, letting his fingers tangle in her hair. Their eyes locked. When he spun her away from him, she looked exquisite, her shapely body a tantalizing sight. It was his way of introducing his wife to them. It was his way of shutting them up.

When the dance was over, the hosts slipped into the house and disappeared. They met in the basement ten minutes later, Dena with a travel bag and Britt with two coolers in hand. Their plan was to leave on Britt's ship without being seen. In order to accomplish their goal, they snuck through the trees down to the beach. They managed not to stumble over anything until they reached the clearing, where they stumbled over lovers in the sand.

"Tourists, no doubt," said Britt loudly, stepping over them.

"I don't think so. They don't seem to have a camera," she said, equally loud.

"They were holding their shoes," he said.

"They were not," she argued.

"I distinctly saw shoes."

They stepped onto the dock and strode past a few guests without speaking. With their coolers and bag, they pushed off in the dinghy and motored over to Shirl. Britt hauled their things aboard before helping Dena in, and then moored the dinghy and climbed aboard. He wasted no time before firing up the engines, hoisting the anchor, and steering clear of the surrounding yachts.

A cheer went up from the shore. They looked up to see their uninvited guests lining the dock and beach.

"What happened to the tourists?" She asked.

"Trampled, no doubt."

They headed for open sea, turned north, and then followed the western coast until they reached an undeveloped cove. Once they had anchored the boat, Britt suggested they sleep on deck, one of his favorite things to do. For this purpose, he had designed the L-shaped seat in the cockpit to fold down into a double berth. He placed two deck cushions on it, and they spent the night in each other's arms, listening to the splash and trickle of the water, the sail lines singing in the breeze, and the moans of the ship itself. It was peaceful, but not necessarily restful. Pink and yellow clouds were gliding overhead when they sat up as one.

Dena stood up and stretched. "I need to exercise," she said, twisting back and forth. "Come swim with me."

"I have a better idea for morning exercise," said Britt, patting the cushion with a sly grin.

"Nuh-uh, my back aches from lying in one position all night." She slipped into the water off the stern, nude, and disappeared.

"Dena. Dena! DENA!" he shouted, standing at the rail to look for her in a panic.

"What?" came her voice from beyond the bow of the ship.

"Stay close by where I can watch you."

"You pervert."

"I'm serious. I'm afraid I'll lose you." Britt moved a cushion and lay down in the bow of the ship. He watched her swim until his eyes became too heavy to focus.

"Come up here with me," he said. "I'm too sleepy to watch you, honest."

"I'll be fine," she called up at him. "Throw me some flippers and a snorkel, and I'll look at the fish while you nap."

"Okay. Here." He threw a life preserver down to her along with the snorkel gear and checked that the line was secured. "Keep that close by. And scream if a shark bites you."

"I will."

The sun had climbed midway in the sky when Dena eased out of the water, crossed the deck, and lay down on top of her husband's dreaming form. He woke up with a start.

"Aaiish! Woman, get your cold, wet body off me."

"No way."

"Why not?" he demanded.

"You'll see."

"I was dreaming about you," he said, "but it didn't have to do with anything cold and wet."

"Quit talking and show me what you were dreaming," she murmured.

He obliged, fascinated as always with the intensity of their intimacy. Dena's passion was fearless and trusting; her humor and imagination complemented his exactly. The eloquence of her love obliterated every other woman from his memory. She was his perfect wife.

When Dena left her husband's arms, the sun was high overhead. Britt lay with one foot propped on the gunwale, his arm resting on his forehead. She raised her arms and stretched luxuriously. Immediately she dropped to the deck.

"Britt!" she exclaimed. "There are two boats parked over there."

"Ships. Anchored. I know, they've been there for an hour."

"You scamp. Why didn't you tell me?"

"You had other things on your mind." He shut one eye and squinted up at her. "Relax. I haven't seen anyone on deck with binoculars. Smile and wave and see if anyone waves back."

She hurried below, grumbling, "I oughta smack you." He could hear her rummaging around in the cabin, and in a few seconds, a pair of shorts landed on deck. "Put those on," she ordered.

He smiled to himself as he obeyed. Dena. Every inch of his body still tingled where her flesh had touched his just moments before. He longed to tell her that she touched places in his heart where no woman had ever been, but he studiously refrained from mentioning his past lovers to her. They had no place in his life with Dena.

This passing thought of former lovers brought a shudder through his body, followed by a wave of nausea. Britt sat up and looked over the rail at the rich waters of the Caribbean. He wished he knew if this sickness was going to haunt him for the rest of his life. He wished that throwing up would help. It took a while, but the nausea finally passed. With a shaky sigh, he lay back down.

Dena came up on deck then, dressed and carrying a plate of sandwiches. "You sorry thing," she fussed in her Southern tone. "You haven't moved a muscle since I left."

He smiled a wistful smile without commenting.

After lunch, Britt said it was time for them to sail.

"Finally," said Dena. "Am I to be your crew?"

"I don't see anyone else. "Think you can handle the mainsail halyard there?"

She looked up at the mast. "Hmm."

Britt laughed. "Dena, can you even tie a knot?"

"Sure, Britt," she said.

"Show me."

She tied a granny knot.

"That knot stinks," he announced.

"I apologize," she said with no humility.

"No need for an apology. Just watch," he said and tied a neat bowline. "Now you try." She did. "That's not a knot, Dena, that's a calamity." He tied one again. "Your turn," he said. "Interesting. Again." She tried a third time. "Nuh-uh," he said. A fourth time. "Better." On the fifth knot, he said, "There it is—a wonderful knot. Absolutely the finest knot ever tied."

"Thank you," she said with a proud smile. Her face fell when he said, "Now do it again. This time make it even better."

Britt convened a class in sailing and pointed out every part of the rigging, making her practice her job as first mate over and over again. Actually the ship was beautifully engineered for pleasure sailing without a crew, but he led her to believe that it was of the utmost importance for her to learn it all perfectly. He even gave her a quiz. When she confused some of the terms, he announced that they'd be starting the course over again.

"Britt, I'm getting bored," she complained. "Surely all these terms aren't necessary to keep us afloat." She caught a glimpse of the answer in his eyes and pounded her fist against the teak deck. He winced. "You rascal," she said. "Here you had me thinking that we'd sink or something if I didn't get everything right. Who cares what a tack cringle is? Get this boat moving, Skipper."

"Okay, okay," he said, unperturbed, and he soon had them underway. When the boat picked up some speed, she shrieked and laughed as salt spray hit her face, hanging onto the gunwale for dear life. Closing his eyes, he imagined it was the first time for him also, feeling the wind, the break of the waves, the impatient surge of the ship in every pore of his body.

After a while, once she had recovered from her terror of being flung into the sea, Dena let go of the railing, first with one hand, then the other. He motioned for her to come and stand in front of him, which she did gingerly, bare toes gripping the deck. She grasped the wheel in both her strong hands. In a minute he let go, nearly throwing her off balance. "Maybe you should do this," she said, and he took the wheel from her.

Everywhere around them there were other yachts, preparing for the races in May. They made it a point to wave at each one. The shoreline was also dotted with colorful windsurfers and day-sailers. Eventually Dena sat down in the cockpit and watched them through binoculars. Britt sat and leaned back too, one hand behind his head, his bare feet on the wheel, his eye on the sails, adjusting the main sheet winch from time to time. He looked the part of a sailor, and his face had an expression of pure bliss as he squinted at the sails, his hair tangled by the wind.

Midway through the afternoon, they turned south, tacking into the wind with Dena manning the jib-sheets under his direction, enthusiastically if not expertly. Britt had just noticed a group of college students aboard a passing yacht and was in the process of giving them berth when he heard a woman screaming his name. Accustomed to attention from his fans, he half-turned toward the other yacht to give her a wave. His open hand turned into a fist, which he slammed against the wall of the cockpit. One of the girls had her bikini top off, waving it at him, and not even the wind could erase the obscene invitation she was screaming at him.

The yacht was barely out of earshot when Britt began to lower the sails, a cold sweat dripping down his back.

Dena joined him in the cockpit and put her arms around him. "You have a hard time being Britt Jordan sometimes, don't you?" she asked.

"Yes, I do," he said emphatically.

Britt thought about this as they motored home. Sometimes he wished he could change identities with someone, just leave Britt Jordan behind. He'd like to make a fresh start, if such a thing were possible.

It struck him how bizarre it could be, being himself. On the first night of his honeymoon, he had danced with women he'd taken to bed before, right in front of his wife. His friends probably thought it was quite normal. He was, after all, Britt Jordan. Well, Britt didn't think it was normal—he thought it was disgusting. But what could he do about it? Even if he sat with his legs crossed for the rest of his life and never danced again, people would still see him as the famous Britt Jordan and react accordingly.

He looked at Dena, who smiled at him. To him, she represented all that was good, clean, and fresh. All the things he had never been.

"Penny for your thoughts," said Dena.

He shook his head and killed the engine. They were at the

entrance of their own bay. "Tell you what," he said. "I don't want to go home in this mood. Let's anchor here and eat supper. You can tell me a few of your corny jokes, and I'll be all right again."

They stayed on the quiet sea, watching the lights blink on along the shoreline. Yachts glided by, running lights lingering on the waves. "Britt, look at that," she said suddenly, pointing toward his house, high on the hillside.

"I've already noticed," he said. Silhouettes could be seen moving around in the light streaming from the glass front. His friends were back. "I'm sorry, Dena."

"Are we going home?" she asked.

"Yes, we're going home," he said, starting the engines for emphasis. "It's my house."

"Don't do anything rash," she implored.

"Me? Rash? I'm never rash."

She kissed him on the cheek. "I think I see a plan cooking in your brain. It scares me."

"I'm a performer, remember?" he said. "The crowd will love me—they always do."

By the time Britt had moored his ship, the beach was alive with people waiting to greet them. The two of them stood on deck and waved to their guests. "Does this remind you of anything?" asked Dena.

"Maybe it's still last night, and we just imagined today," he suggested.

"Maybe they've waited for us all day. All lined up on the beach."

"If so, those two tourists ought to be sufficiently trampled by now," he said as he reached for the dinghy line with the gaff.

They were both laughing when they reached the dock. There were plenty of hands ready to pull them from the dinghy.

"Nice day, Britt?" somebody called.

"How's the honeymoon going, Jordan?"

"Mighty fine tan. Didn't you spend any time in the stateroom?"

The rum was flowing freely, and the laughter rang across the water.

Britt flashed a good-natured smile, grasped Dena's arm with one hand and motioned toward the house with the other. "Follow me, folks. I've got a surprise for you."

When they reached the living room, Britt and Dena immediately went over to his piano. The forty-odd people gathered around, as polarized as if Britt were a magnet.

He played through a few bars of a melody and said, "This is a song I wrote for my wife. I had intended to sing it for her alone, by candlelight. With no one else around. You know, like on a honeymoon."

Somebody lit a candle and set it on the piano. There was laughter all around. Britt played a few more bars. This was the sort of song that came to him easily. In fact, this would be the first time he had ever sung or played it, though he had whistled it to himself while he puttered on Shirl. It was an easy song in a key with only one note that he couldn't reach with his damaged voice.

He continued pointedly. "Since the prospects of spending our honeymoon alone are looking slim, I shall play it for all of you. Then you can go home and talk about me. Just don't talk about my wife."

His guests laughed, loving it. No one else could have thrown them out with such aplomb.

He began to sing. The tune was catchy, familiar in that way simple songs often are:

Mmmhmm.
Well it happened to me, baby,
Uh-huh.
In the early morning sunshine.
Mmmhmm.
I felt my ship was sinking.
Oh, yeah.
I was searching for a lifeline.
Uh-huh.
Then I looked up and saw your smile
And I knew I could hang on for a while.
I felt it,
I knew it,
I waited for you, girl . . .

Sometimes you never know when
Uh-huh.
The waves are gonna drown ya.
Mmmhmm.
With a crash you'll hit rough water,
Oh, yeah.
The ocean will surround ya.
Uh-huh.
Then I looked up and saw your smile
And I knew I could hang on for a while.
I felt it.
I knew it.
I waited for you, girl . . .

You gave me back my life,
You gave me back my dreams;
I want to thank you, girl,
You're heaven and earth to me.

Mmmhmm.
Just want to thank you, girl.
Uh-huh.
For giving me your laughter.
Oh, yeah.
For throwing me a lifeline.
Mmmhmm.
You're all that I was after.
Uh-huh.
I looked up and saw your smile;
You know I'll be here more than a while.

Just want to thank you, girl,
Uh-huh.
Just want to thank you, girl,
Oh, yeah.

"Thanks, Mrs. Jordan," he finished.

There was laughter and applause, and all eyes turned toward Dena.

"Maybe you should think about doing this for a living," she said.

"What, and miss my calling as Carlene's chef?"

This exchange meant nothing to the guests, and they took it as their cue to leave, good-byes following them out the door.

Alone again, husband and wife looked at each other. "Thank

you, Britt," she said.

"For what, throwing them out?"

"For the song. It means a lot to me." She paused. "You didn't have to throw them out on my account."

"Come here." He reached for her. She stood in front him, leaning slightly against the piano while he remained seated, his hands on her waist. "I'm trying to make a home for us." He looked away. "I hadn't realized how difficult that would turn out to be," he added, mostly to himself.

He drifted into his private thoughts, and she kissed him and left him to go upstairs. After a long shower, she found him on their balcony, running his hands along the rail as if caressing it, looking out to sea. She stood beside him, not touching him.

Eventually, she spoke. "I never told you how proud of you I am," she said. "It took courage for you to give it your all right up until the end, and then walk away. Most people would have been satisfied with half an effort and half a voice." His lips pulled tight, and he shook his head briefly. She kissed him goodnight on the cheek, leaving him on the balcony.

Britt's thoughts were darker than she could have guessed. He wasn't thinking about losing his career. He was thinking about his house, about how this could never be their home when they had to sleep in the guest room or on a boat. The memories contained in the master bedroom had turned sour for Britt. In fact, the whole house had taken on a sour note, and it nearly wrenched his heart in two. He had always loved this place.

He had thought his home was a puzzle and Dena the final piece to be set in. Now he realized she was not the missing piece. She was from another picture entirely.

Standing in the doorway with the insistent wind behind him, Britt watched his wife sleep in the moonlight. He left the room without touching her and walked slowly down the hall, his hand sliding along the wainscot molding. When he reached his own bedroom, he stopped for several seconds but did not step inside. He did stand for many minutes at the upstairs balcony, running his hands along the white railing, looking down at his living room in the dim light. He went down the steps, letting his fingers run along the rail, and entered the living room, walking slowly, touching everything he had viewed from above. Standing before the rock fireplace, he placed both hands on the mantel, leaning forward, forehead resting on one arm. Several minutes passed before he moved again. He made a circuit through every room downstairs, taking his time, picking up bric-à-brac as he went and setting them back down. Finally he went outside on the upper deck and stood still, inhaling the sea breeze.

When Dena searched for him early the next morning, she finally found him in a chair on the dock, facing the sea, his feet on the railing. Deciding to look for something to eat before joining him, she opened the freezer door and stood staring at its contents. Something drew her attention, and she reached inside and pulled out a small plastic bag.

"Must be the spices Ruby uses to make that lobster salad so interesting," she said aloud and opened it, sniffing its contents. She closed it quickly and walked down the series of decks to the dock.

She approached Britt slowly. He glanced up, and then looked back out to sea. She asked carefully, "Why do you have a bag of marijuana in your freezer?"

"I don't," he said.

She held it out.

Again he glanced up and looked away. "Must be Phillip's."

"Phillip?"

He didn't move.

"What does Phillip have to do with it?"

He shrugged and shifted slightly. "He uses the place sometimes when I'm not here."

"You mean, you just let him take over your house and do whatever he wants?" she asked incredulously.

He shrugged, still looking out to sea.

"Not in my house, Britt," she said flatly and dumped the contents of the bag into the sea.

He winced as if she had slapped him.

"You disagree with me?"

He shook his head and looked up at her. His eyes were weary and scared and imploring.

"Do you feel all right?" She crossed the few feet that separated them and put her hand to his forehead.

He put one arm around her, his hand at her waist. "It's just that . . ." He stopped and looked at the water for a long time, his face working, biting his lip. "Let's go home, Dena," he said finally.

"Home?" In his eyes, she caught a glimpse of the jagged rip in his heart. Without saying another word, she turned and climbed slowly back up the steps to the house.

Ruby was standing in the living room, looking through the glass at Britt. She turned her steady gaze on Dena when she entered.

"I can't explain it, Ruby," Dena said in a quiet voice, "but I have a terrible feeling that I'll never see you again." She turned and looked at Britt, who hadn't moved. "Something has come over him. I don't exactly know what it is."

"Do not think this is a bad thing, Mrs. Jordan. It is a good thing."

Dena looked at Ruby, puzzled.

"There's another plane to life, yes?"

Ah, a spiritual plane. "My Britt has a very complicated mind; you know that, Ruby. His thoughts take him to deep places where I can't follow. He can flip a million-dollar song out of his brain, like he did last night, as easily as another man might flip pancakes, and yet . . ." Dena broke eye contact with Ruby, returning her gaze to her husband. "And yet, he can't comprehend the existence of God."

"Hear me well, Mrs. Jordan. Mr. Britt has spent many years being the man other people wanted him to be. But there's another man deep inside him, the man he was always meant to be. It will take much unraveling to get to the real man, but be patient. Have faith."

The two women embraced for a long moment before Dena went upstairs to pack. When Britt finally came inside, she had already informed the pilot and prepared their bags.

He went to the piano and played a few notes, gave Ruby a long hug, and walked straight out the door. He had said goodbye to everything else the night before. The salt smell of the sea he carried to North Carolina on his skin.

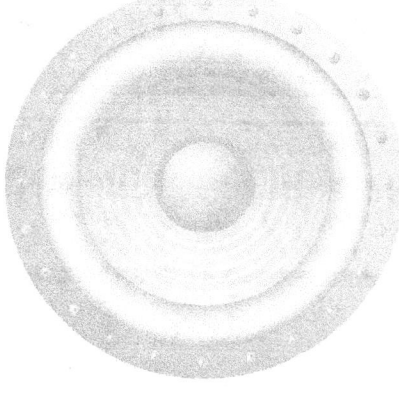

———CHAPTER———

FOURTEEN

B ritt spoke very little on the flight back to Deerfield—instead he fiddled idly with the Twitter feed on his cell phone and stared out the window. Dena held his hand and said few words herself.

When they arrived home, she unlocked the kitchen door and keyed in the security code. Walking into the garage behind her, Britt reached over and patted the hood of his Monteverdi, jumping back when he realized that it was warm. It was a reenactment of the night their home had been vandalized.

"Dena, stop!" he shouted.

She did not stop. Instead, she shot an irked look at him over her shoulder and charged into her kitchen, determined, evidently, to see for herself whether the vandal had struck again.

With the same voice he'd used to bring an entire coliseum to its knees, Britt roared, "Stop!" But the command had no effect whatsoever on his wife. If anything, it propelled her forward more swiftly.

Dena had momentum in her favor, but Britt had agility,

honed by years on the stage, and he maneuvered in front of her, grabbing her by the arms, his body now traveling backward. He glimpsed one quick flash of anger in her eyes, and in the next instant there was a bright flash, a deafening *BOOM*, and he felt himself being launched off his feet by a blast from behind. He was slammed into Dena's forward-moving body. With a horrifying, sliding thud, he landed on the floor on top of her, her body splayed awkwardly beneath him.

"Dena!" he gasped, scrambling to move.

Her breath was coming in quick gasps, no exhalations. Her mouth moved, trying to form one word: "Bo..*gasp*..Bo..*gasp*."

"Bonnie's okay," he whispered quickly. "She's at school. We've got to get out of here. Can you move?" He got to his knees and began to lift her.

She clung to him, uncomprehending, sobbing her daughter's name.

"Bonnie's okay; she's okay." Then, more forcefully, "We have to get out of here. Can you move your legs? I'm going to lift you."

She nodded her understanding, and he gently lifted her to her feet and guided her onto their front lawn, where she stood clinging to him, shaking and sobbing. A neighbor ran toward them, his cell phone pressed to his ear.

Time and events passed of which Britt would later have little recollection. A fire truck arrived first, and then a police car. More fire trucks, more neighbors. Ambulances. Dena refused to let the paramedics check her over, waving away their every attempt to have her sit down. She leaned into her husband, whose arms were wrapped tightly around her.

Britt felt no pain. His entire being tunneled to one pin-point of concentration: He could feel his wife's heart beating against his chest. Her breathing would slow down as she relaxed into him for a few seconds. And then it would quicken, the trembling would start again, and she would cry raggedly as another wave of panic hit her. He rode this crest with her time and again, his every cell focused on carrying her safely through it.

She didn't lift her head until her father, Noel, arrived. She caught the angry glare Noel shot at Britt, and quickly whispered through her tears, "Daddy, Britt saved my life," burying her face even deeper into Britt's embrace. Noel stood close enough to place his hand on his daughter's head, close enough to growl into Britt's ear, "My daughter didn't have an enemy in the world until she married you."

Dena's church friends showed up, touched her shoulders, spoke into her ear. A bomb squad arrived. A canine unit. Noel left Dena's side to speak urgently with the police chief, and then a detective approached the couple. "Mr. Jordan," he said. "It would help us if you could answer a few questions."

Britt reflexively nodded, still focused on his wife.

"Who else has a key to your car?"

"My brother, my assistant, Lori Sink."

"Where is your brother?"

"In hell, for all I care."

"What's your assistant's name?"

"Darrell Olmstead."

"Would he do this?"

"No."

"Where is he now?"

"He was in California when I talked to him on Sunday."

"What's your relationship to Lori Sink?"

"We dated."

"Do you know where she is?"

"New York, according to Twitter. Her number's in my cell

phone." And Britt unlocked his phone and handed it over without looking at the detective.

"Does your brother want you dead?"

"Probably, but not my wife."

"Does your assistant hate you?"

"Some days."

"Is Lori Sink capable of doing this?"

A beat. "I doubt it."

It wasn't until Sue Duncan arrived and spoke to Dena that she stirred in Britt's arms. "What time is it?" she asked.

"Two-thirty."

"Oh! Bonnie! I have to . . ."

"No, no," said Sue. "Your mother and Bonnie were picked up a while ago and taken to a safe place. Your father arranged it with the police."

Dena began pushing away from Britt. "I—I have to go, I have to see if she's okay. Oh, Britt," she whispered, her voice choked and thin, her words running together. "If we hadn't come home early, if we hadn't come home from Antigua when we did, that would have been Bonnie and Mama. They would have come here after school."

Her features were contorted, the hurt and fear in her eyes so raw that all Britt could feel was his heart twisting in his chest. Her eyes held his a moment longer, and then she started backing away, out of his reach.

A thought slipped into his brain, the first coherent thought that endless afternoon: *My home in Antigua. If that's the price I have to pay to keep this pain out of my wife's eyes, so be it.* He couldn't have said with whom he made this transaction. A God he didn't exactly believe in? The universe? Didn't matter—to his mind, it was a done deal.

"Dena!" he called after her, his voice hitched and rough,

"We can be in California before dark. I'll take you anywhere in the world . . ."

She was shaking her head and moving away. Sue's arms were around her and other people were reaching for her too. Then her father was face-to-face with him, blocking her from his view. Noel's voice was flat and matter-of-fact. "Oh, no, you won't. This may be a small town, but these investigators are good, and I trust them." Noel spat those last words in Britt's face. "Don't you even think about taking my daughter out of this state."

Britt, the man who had held thousands in the palm of his hand, nodded once and stepped back. When his eyes found Dena once more, she was farther away, approaching Sue's car. Two paramedics were standing in front of her, and she was shaking her head, emphatically telling them, "No."

Another detective was firing questions at him. "Who else has a key to your home?"

"No one, not since the new system was installed after the vandalism."

"Are you sure? What about pest control service?"

"No."

"Furnace maintenance?"

"No."

"Cleaning service?"

"No, there's no one." Britt put his fingertips to his forehead and tried to think. Dena had fired somebody? Something about child care? He had no clue what that had been about. Only four keys had been issued—he was certain of it. And all four were in the hands of family.

Just then, a squabbling, barking racket erupted from the backyard. The canine unit had met up with the neighbor's Rottweiler at the top of the rock wall separating the two yards. Britt saw Dena turn toward the noise before reaching to open the door of Sue's car.

Before he knew it, the first detective was at his side, giving him something. "Here's your cell phone." Britt stared, no memory of having handed it over. "Your brother's number is no longer in service. There's another Jordan in here: Marcus. Any relation?"

"My nephew, why?"

"Would he know how to contact your brother?"

The words seemed to be coming from far away. Britt stared at the cell phone in his hand, and a second coherent thought slipped into his brain. *I handed private numbers that the President can't even get to a total stranger.*

When Britt looked up, Sue's car was turning the corner, and Dena was no longer within sight. The phone dropped from his hand.

He grabbed his hair, stood still, his breathing hard and rough. Suddenly, he bent over double. A loud, feral groan exploded from him, along with a yellow stream of vomit. Guitars were blasting, heavy metal in his head, and he staggered backwards from the sheer weight of the racket, that infernal racket . . .

"Britt, stay with me; stay with me, Britt." He became aware of a reassuring hand on his shoulder, a low, firm voice in his ear. The screaming guitars faded. He opened his eyes. Water was pouring off his face, droplets hitting the grass. No way to tell sweat from tears from spit. He steadied himself, hands on his knees, gasping for air.

"Where did you go, Britt?" the voice asked. "You left us there for a minute."

Britt drew in a couple of ragged breaths, spat, and then wiped his face on his sleeve. "No place you ever want to be, Duncan," he answered. Then, "Charlie, I need you to help me."

"Of course, Britt. I'll go with you to the hospital."

Still bent over, Britt squinted through salt-filled eyes and looked up into Charlie Duncan's concerned face. "What?"

"Britt, don't you even realize that you're hurt?" Charlie asked quietly.

"We've been trying to help him for the past hour, Charlie!" came a new voice. Britt noticed for the first time that two sets of shoes were directly in front of him, and he looked up to see two paramedics, the younger one gesturing excitedly. "Mrs. Jordan insisted she was fine, and Mr. Jordan never even acknowledged us."

Britt's gaze moved farther upward, behind the paramedics, to find Noel's face. There was a softening in Noel's eyes, a relenting in the tight line of his mouth. The man nodded, stepped back, and then turned and left the scene.

"Damn, I thought he was just being stoic for the cameras," said the detective at his side.

Britt looked beyond the gathered crowd to see that news crews from two nearby cities had already been set up. Uniformed officers were keeping them back as far as the sidewalk. He blew out a breath. "Charlie, I've got to get out of here; there's something I need to do. Please help me."

"Okay, I will, after they . . ."

"You don't understand." Britt forced his body into a standing position through a ripping groan. "We have to go now, while there's still daylight. Where's your car?" Britt retrieved his phone and started off toward the street, already dialing.

Charlie got in front of him, hands up. "Whoah-wo-wo-whoah!"

Britt changed course, striding purposefully toward his own car, which was now part of a crime scene. Once again, Charlie was in front of him, waving his arms like a referee. "Okay, okay, we'll do this your way. But first . . ."

Britt held up his hand, and Charlie hushed. After a terse, one-sided conversation, Britt clicked off the phone and put it in his pocket. "But first what?" he asked.

In a quiet, steady voice, Charlie said, "Here's how this is going to go down."

Britt raised one eyebrow. In a different mood, he would have been amused—not many men stood up to him.

"You can't go anywhere bleeding like that. And you've probably got stuff shaken up inside that you don't even know about." Charlie's arms were crossed now, and it was clear that he wasn't budging. "You're going to let these boys clean and patch you up a little, I'm going to give you the spare shirt I keep in my car, and then we'll go do whatever it is you're so hot to do in the daylight. But when it gets dark, I'm carrying you to the hospital." He paused. "Got it?"

Britt closed his eyes, grimaced, and nodded. Pretty soon the paramedics had him seated and were cutting his bloody shirt off. He barely glanced at it when they threw it aside.

The younger guy whistled when he saw Britt's back. "Whew, that's gotta hurt." He reminded Britt of a Spaniel puppy.

The older guy said, "Sir, you really need to get this wound properly cleaned and stitched up. We can't really . . ."

"Just patch it up," Britt snapped. The older guy reminded him of his drill sergeant in the Army, whose bulldog face he'd never forgotten. "You've got four minutes."

Britt pulled out his cell phone again. He figured he should at least send his nephew Marcus a heads-up, so quickly he typed: *Police looking 4 your dad. Throw him under the bus. Take care. B.*

Right about then, one of the detectives ambled over to check in with him. "Oh good, they've given your cell phone back. We might need to call you if something else comes up." The man's voice cracked, making a joke, "We've got your number."

Britt glanced from the man to the phone in his hand. *Yeah, and you've got Bono's number now too, you just don't realize it,* he thought.

"Hey," said the Spaniel. "You got anybody famous in that phone?"

Britt's frown turned into a wince, and he grunted with pain. Whatever they were doing hurt like heck. Maybe it would be in his best interest to play along.

"Who would you like to talk to?" he asked smoothly.

"Skynyrd," cracked the Spaniel.

Good grief, a comedian. That great band had crashed a decade or so before Spaniel was even born. "Can't help you there, son," said Britt.

"Taylor Swift," the guy quickly shot back.

Britt closed his eyes and swallowed hard. Strikingly pretty, scorchingly young. "Can't help you there, either." With a half-hearted leer, he shook the phone and said, "Beyonce?"

"Naw, dude, pick somebody that ain't already married," said the Spaniel.

Annoyed, ready to be done with the game, Britt flipped to the J's in his contact list and started to say something about calling her husband, when the Spaniel, looking over his shoulder, said, "Wait. Jag. You got Mick Jagger in that phone?"

Britt looked down at the phone in his hand and coughed out a short laugh, the first one that day. Any really private numbers were well hidden behind codes only Britt understood, so if he had Jagger's number, it sure wouldn't be listed under "Jag."

"What would happen if you called him?" asked the eager Spaniel.

"If I called Mick Jagger, you mean?" responded Britt. "Well, it would be a really short conversation considering that the man despises me."

"Send him a text and see what happens," the guy said.

Britt shook his head. "You've got a minute and a half," he

pointed out to the paramedics.

He flipped through incoming texts. From Darrell, simply: *???? Call me.* From Marcus: *Done. No prob. Hope u r ok.* From Dena, nothing. Britt leaned his head on his folded hands, elbows on his knees. He rocked forward slightly, picturing her pained face, trying to hold it together.

"Hurts, huh?" said the Spaniel.

Abruptly, Britt started to stand. "You're done," he told the paramedics. "I have to go."

Bulldog spoke for the first time. "Four minutes isn't up, and we're not quite done. Keep your seat."

Britt looked up to see the police chief approaching, and this time he did stand, Bulldog still taping the dressing. He shook the police chief's outstretched hand and nodded toward Charlie's waiting car, then started walking.

"For the record," said the chief, "you should be in the hospital."

"Duly noted," said Britt. "Tell me what you've got."

"Not as much as I'd like," admitted the chief. "The one thing tying the vandalism to the bombing is your car, which makes it seem like it was the same perpetrator as last time. But motive? They went from offensive graffiti aimed at Dena to trying to kill you both? Doesn't make sense."

Britt didn't speak as he retrieved the shirt from Charlie's car and began easing it on, grunting with the effort.

The chief continued, "Your security company says someone used a key at your kitchen door and entered the alarm code, no miss-keys. Six a.m. this morning. I haven't seen the video feed myself yet, but your people say it doesn't show much. Whoever did this knew where the cameras are. And they didn't key in the lock-box that holds your car keys."

Still not speaking, Britt began rolling up the sleeves of Charlie's button-down shirt.

"So we've got somebody who already has the key to your car and the code to your house." The chief paused. "Are you listening, Mr. Jordan?" When Britt nodded, the chief continued somewhat impatiently, "So far, your assistant and the Sink woman seem to check out; they appear to be in California and New York, just as you said they'd be." When Britt didn't respond, he said with emphasis, "This brings it back to you. This was personal. Somebody had a key to your car and took the time after setting up that bomb to sit in it with the motor running. Who do you know who would do that?"

"No clue."

The chief folded his arms, getting nowhere. "So I'll just say it, Mr. Jordan. You've either forgotten something mighty important or you're hiding something."

Britt's felt his face go hot with anger. He fisted his hands and crammed them into his pockets, a quick motion. And he stared very hard at the chief.

The chief stared back, cracked his knuckles, and waited for Britt to speak.

Britt finally spoke. "For the life of me, I cannot imagine what I possibly could have said that would make you think I'm hiding something."

"Stand in my shoes and think about it, Mr. Jordan. It has to be one or the other."

At that moment, the car door behind Britt slammed. He heard Charlie's voice, "Denny, what are you doing? Back off."

The chief's eyes shifted to Charlie, then back to Britt. He stood his ground.

Britt's brain was getting into gear again, in fits and starts, like a stalled engine coughing back to life. With it came his trusted intuition, which rarely failed him. He scrutinized the chief for a long moment through squinted eyes. The man was good-looking, about forty, no wedding band. He'd bet a platinum album that the chief had a thing for Dena. And still was willing to defend Dena, even against her famous husband. Britt could hardly fault the guy for that.

The chief's jaw clenched, and he cracked his knuckles again, waiting for Britt to speak.

Britt took his hands out of his pockets and smacked them together, done with the conversation. "Look, I get it. I'm the outsider here. But I'm not the bad guy. Chase another angle. And by the way, the security code reset Monday after we left. Figure that one out."

Just before he got into the car, Britt added, "And Chief, don't waste your time trying to find my brother. When he comes at me for throwing him off my stage last week, it'll be a sucker punch. Not this."

The police chief watched Charlie's car pull away, shook himself a little, and looked over at the nearest detective. The man joined him on the sidewalk.

"I've got just one question," said the chief. "What kind of man lets a former girlfriend keep a key to a half-million dollar car?"

"Maybe a man with entirely too much money," said the detective.

"Or maybe one with entirely too many secrets," the chief said. "Wasn't he arrested for cocaine possession a few years back?"

"Yeah, seems like I remember it. Not quite sure what happened after the arrest, though."

"Look into it for me, would you?"

---CHAPTER---

FIFTEEN

Within seconds of pulling away from the curb, Britt folded over double in the passenger seat, forearms on his knees, face buried in his hands. Charlie glanced at him with concern. Was Britt hiding from the cameras or was he sick?

In a tight voice, Britt whispered, "Please get me to the airport."

Even as he put on his turn signal to comply with the request, Charlie kept glancing at the other man. Charlie noticed that Britt's shoulders were shaking, and soon he became so still that Charlie wasn't sure he was still breathing. After a couple of minutes, Britt breathed out a long sigh, sat up, and wiped his cheeks with the heel of his hand. "Here, Britt," said Charlie, "I snagged us a couple sodas."

Britt grunted a hiccup of a laugh, popped the top, and took a long drink. "Thank you kindly," he said, his voice rough. He stared at the drink in his hand a long moment. "Do you realize how sick this is, Charlie? Never in a million years did I dream I would bring something like this on Dena. But to bring it on her child?" His voice cracked. "It's unthinkable." Britt stopped for a moment, trying to compose himself. "This animal knew where the cameras were. What if they . . ." He paused, as if unable to say the words aloud. "What if they knew we were supposed to be away for the week? What if . . ." After a long silence, he asked, "Charlie, do you have any words of wisdom for a drowning man?"

They were on the highway now, minutes away from the local airport. Charlie wasn't sure what he could possibly say to comfort him. He had only met Britt five nights ago, right after the singer had shocked the rock and roll world by announcing his retirement. Britt had appeared to be in good spirits in spite of it all. Clearly he was in love with his wife, yet they had returned from their belated honeymoon after only three days. Something must have gone terribly wrong in Antigua, and everything had gone appallingly wrong when they got home. Charlie sensed that there were battles waging inside this man that were too fierce to be won with a few short words.

Britt's voice exploded in the small space, "Good God, Duncan, how do you make a living as a salesman?"

Charlie laughed in spite of the awful circumstances. That certainly sounded more like Britt Jordan. "Maybe it would help if you could tell me where you're headed," he suggested.

"We. Where *we're* headed," said Britt, his voice stronger. "We're headed to find my wife a new home, of course."

"Oh. Well, then," said Charlie, "I suppose that the wise thing for you to do would be to focus on what you think Dena would want in a home." Charlie's mouth twisted. He hoped this venture wouldn't require a passport, since he didn't exactly keep one in his pocket.

"Finally!" came from Britt. He adjusted the seat as far back as it would go, making room for thought. When he started to lean back, he winced, and leaned forward instead. His words came quickly, with animation. "Security is our first priority." With that, he pulled out his phone, dialed, carried on a quick, one-sided conversation, and clicked off. "Done. Now let's think this through. Dena would be happy-ish anywhere. Australia. Italy. Kind of like she's happy-ish with my big-ass piano in her living room. But I don't want any more ish-es for her. I want her to thrive." He emphasized the word.

Britt's face puckered in thought. "What's north of here, Charlie?"

"Virginia."

"We can rule that out; her father has made his thoughts clear on that subject." He was becoming more animated. "West?"

"Mountains."

"Summer, yes; winter, no. I'll buy her a mountain house in June if she wants. East?"

"Couple of small cities."

"Ish," said Britt. "South?"

"The next county south is mostly woods and fields," said Charlie. He glanced at Britt as the singer shuddered visibly. Charlie wondered whether a couple swallows of soda had done this to him. Britt had certainly thrown off his foul mood in a hurry.

"Dena wouldn't be happy if I were completely miserable," stated Britt. "So nix on the woods and such. Let's see. I've seen a big lake somewhere from the air; I think south of here."

"You've probably seen Lake Norman. It's huge."

"There you go." Britt declared. He pulled out his phone, dialed, said, "Lake Norman," and clicked off.

They were pulling off the highway now, about a minute from the airport. Britt began popping his fists together rhythmically. "Breathing room. Nice big living room for my piano, assuming it survived the blast. That darn thing has been a—what do you

161

call it?" Britt snapped his fingers a few times. "You're no help, Duncan. Oh, yeah, a metaphor." His words were coming faster. "A metaphor for how I plopped my insane life in the middle of hers. But not a palatial house—we wouldn't want to lose each other. Space for Bonnie to paint. Not too far from Dena's parents." He popped his fists together one last time. "There. I guess that covers it."

They had arrived at the airport, and Charlie started to park the car. Britt motioned with one hand for him to drive toward the gate, and with the other hand, he waved at a young man who hoofed it out of the little office to unlock it. Cautiously, Charlie drove on through, glancing toward the jet hangars where everyone in town knew Britt housed his Gulfstream. When Britt gestured with his hand, he drove instead toward a four-passenger single engine Cessna that was sitting out on the tarmac, two men standing in front of it. Pre-flight check, evidently.

"Just leave your keys; they'll take care of it," instructed Britt.

Charlie got out, nodding at Todd, the airport manager. He didn't know the other man, the one holding a clipboard. He started toward the plane and heard Britt curse under his breath. The man with the clipboard gave Britt a sharp look, and then went back to his clipboard.

Charlie looked the small plane over skeptically. When Britt caught him eyeing it, he approached the man holding the clipboard, his hands out, palms up. "Eddie, what the . . ."

"Short notice," said Eddie.

"There you have it," said Britt to Charlie. "Short notice. Thus we ride in a grasshopper, which beats a paper airplane by not much." He turned to Eddie. "Tell Charlie you can fly a . . ."

"Yes," said Eddie. "Now be quiet."

Britt gave Charlie a sheepish shrug, started up the steps

to enter the plane. Immediately he grabbed the rail with both hands and groaned, his head buried against his arm. This time Eddie watched him and didn't look away for a long moment.

Charlie approached Britt and spoke in a quiet voice. "Come on, man. What are you doing? This can wait."

"Charlie," said Britt, in an equally quiet voice, "I bruised a kidney once when an amplifier collapsed under me. I felt as bad then as I do now, and I finished the concert." Britt's face was nearly hidden by his hair. "I'm going to finish this. Trust me; I have no intention of making my Dena a widow again." With that, Britt pulled himself into the seat next to the pilot's.

Charlie shot a questioning glance at Eddie, who looked up from his clipboard once more, giving Charlie an appraising stare. "What do you weigh, about two-ten?" asked Eddie.

"Two-fifteen."

"Center of the bench-seat," said the ever-concise Eddie.

The south-bound flight was uneventful and reasonably quiet, considering the drone of the engine. From time to time, Britt would speak a few words to Eddie that Charlie couldn't quite hear, and then the pilot would speak a few words into his headset. Charlie surmised that he was relaying information to someone on the ground.

Charlie wasn't surprised when Eddie conducted a north-south, lengthwise flyover of the lake. Sure, get the lay of the land, he thought. It made perfect sense to him when Britt spoke over the engine noise, "No, it's too populated down there. It would be too difficult to keep it secure. Come around toward the north again."

What floored Charlie and left him completely speechless was when Britt turned to him and said, "Okay, here's what I want you to do, Charlie. See that house there? Too big. Dena wouldn't want a lot of excess room. Now see that house? Too open. Think sharp-shooter. What we're looking for is a place with a lot of tree cover, preferably on its own peninsula, but without too large of a footprint. Got it?"

When Charlie's jaw dropped and he just stared at the singer, Britt's mouth twisted with impatience. "What's your problem, Duncan?"

"Um." Charlie coughed, getting his voice in gear. "Most people would set the plane down and go find a real estate agent."

Britt turned his head away from Charlie, looking out the window. Even so, Charlie caught what he said next, "I'm not most people."

Eddie followed the eastern shoreline as he flew north. Discovering that this shoreline involved countless miles of many-fingered peninsulas, the men narrowed their search area to a manageable swath of land and traversed it twice. Britt and Charlie commented back and forth on potential houses while Britt noted navigational positions on his cell phone. As the light began to wane, Britt said, "I think we're in agreement on these three. Let's fly over once more, Eddie, so that I can make sure I've got the coordinates nailed down." A few minutes later, that mission accomplished, Britt said with finality, "Okay, I'll shoot these numbers to Darrell. He should have the owners' names and hopefully phone numbers by morning." After a quick glance at Charlie's face, he blew out an exasperated breath. "Now what's your problem, Duncan?"

Charlie decided not to ponder an answer this time. "Most of these are summer homes, for starters. Getting in touch with the owners may not be easy."

"Nobody said anything about easy, Charlie. What else you got?"

"Okay, I'll just say it. Money. Money doesn't always talk. Some of these people . . ." he hesitated, plunged ahead, ". . . a lot of these people don't need money. If they don't want to sell, it won't matter how much money you throw at them."

Britt snorted a quiet laugh. "Charlie, how do you think I got where I am?"

Having learned not to contemplate an answer too long around Britt, Charlie blurted, "Like everybody else in the country, I've seen the pirated videos of your last concert, Britt. It was brilliant, and it pretty much devastated every critic you ever had."

Britt's mouth pulled into a hard line, and he said, with brutal candor, "What's truly devastating is that I'm ruthless. I've slit a lot of throats and left good men to bleed out, Charlie. Professionally speaking, of course." Britt looked Charlie in the eye. "And when that doesn't work, there's always good, old-fashioned salesmanship, which is why you're here." With a smile, man-to-man, more a crinkling of his eyes than a flash of his dimples, Britt finished, "It took a little of both to make a bride out of Dena."

Up until this point in the flight, Britt had appeared to be reasonably comfortable as long as he stayed perfectly still. Charlie had noticed him wince a few times when he changed positions. Now in the fading light, Charlie could see sweat beading on the man's temples.

Charlie heard Britt mutter to Eddie, "Where is he?" and he heard Eddie mutter back, "Stuck in traffic out of Charlotte." He heard Britt grunt and saw his face go very pale.

"Eddie?" Charlie said sharply.

"Way ahead of you," said Eddie, already banking the plane.

Eddie set the plane down at the Lake Norman airport. To Charlie's relief, an Iredell County ambulance was waiting for them there. Turning toward Charlie, Eddie instructed, "Ride with him. Len is still twenty minutes out."

Having no clue what that meant, Charlie did as he was asked. Nineteen minutes later, he was standing in the emergency room waiting area, stretching his back, which ached after four hours in the cramped plane. In walked a big guy, taller and more muscular than Charlie, who scanned the room quickly, drew a bead on Charlie, and started toward him.

Charlie had played tight end in high school some twenty years ago, and he made this guy for a former fullback by the way he moved, covering a lot of ground in no apparent hurry and with even less effort. The guy walked straight up to Charlie, his right hand extended, palm down. "Duncan," stated the guy. Not really a question. His steel-gray eyes were fixed in a habitual no-nonsense expression.

"Len, I assume?" said Charlie, extending his hand. Instead of a handshake, the guy dropped a car key in his hand.

"Your ride is a white Pontiac—the plate number's on the key fob. Hotel reservation info is in the passenger seat." Len ignored the question in Charlie's eyes, glancing instead at his cell phone when it buzzed. In a sharp whisper, Len said, "Dammit, Britt."

Len had barely paused for this exchange. As he continued moving toward the reception desk, he stated, apparently to Charlie, who had not moved, "Britt won't let them touch him if I'm not there." Len showed something to the receptionist, who buzzed him through immediately. Still in motion, now headed toward the door leading into the bowels of the hospital, Len turned halfway to Charlie and said, "One of Britt's many quirks." Just before disappearing behind the closing door, Len turned directly toward Charlie, walking backwards, "Try to get a good night's sleep. Britt rolls out early when he goes off on one of these tangents."

The doors closed, leaving Charlie standing in the middle of the room, a key in his hand, completely baffled.

At a quarter to five the next morning, Charlie was awakened by an insistent knocking at his hotel room door. He jumped out of bed and thrashed around, finding his slacks and pulling them on. He felt the same annoyance he had felt as he fell asleep the previous night. Somehow he had gone from accommodating a friend to feeling like one of Britt's employees, scrambling to do what the singer wanted. Charlie wasn't much of a scrambler.

Standing at his door was a young man wearing a polo shirt with the insignia of the hotel on the pocket, holding out Charlie's button-down shirt. Freshly laundered after having been worn by Britt the day before. When he dug in his pocket for a tip, the young man hastily said, "No, sir. Everything's been taken care of."

Charlie closed the door and flipped a light switch. Attached to the hanger was a handwritten note, apparently in Britt's own hand: *Thanks, Charlie. It means a lot. If you have time to see this through with me, I'm out of here at 5:30 a.m. P.S. You're on your own for underwear.*

He had to laugh. Okay, being Britt's friend might not be much easier than being an employee, but Charlie had to admit, it was pretty interesting. Sure, he'd see it through with Britt. He was a little curious about just how ruthless Britt was going to have to be to get his wife a home.

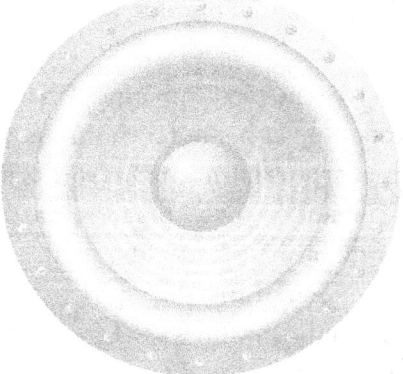

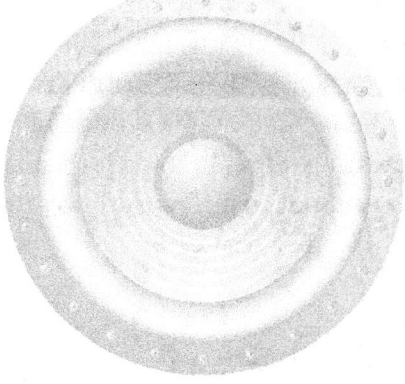

———CHAPTER———

SIXTEEN

Britt was pretty ruthless, as it
turned out. And not at all the
kind of guy Charlie had expected. The negotiations on Britt's
preferred home took all morning, and in the end, Britt did slit a
throat. His own. And he seemed pretty happy to do it.

The day began when Charlie pulled the car through the
patient pickup portico of the hospital, and Britt bounced
through the doors as if he had just checked out of a fancy hotel.
"A good morning to you!" shouted Britt as he eased himself
into the front passenger seat a bit more carefully than usual.
In response to Charlie's raised eyebrows, Britt explained, "All
stitched up, shot full of antibiotics, good drugs I no longer
need." He flipped a prescription bottle into the backseat which
Len caught in his large paw.

"Ibuprofen," said Len, slipping the bottle into his pocket.
"We'll see."

"Don't just sit there, Charlie," said Britt, "we've got a boat
to catch!"

"I've got a coffeepot to catch first," stated Charlie as he

pulled away from the hospital.

In fact, by six a.m., they were all in a boat, Britt at the wheel, headed to view the three properties from the water which he had chosen from the air. The first home he rejected because he wasn't satisfied that the trees offered enough cover when viewed from the water. He bypassed the second because Darrell had not yet located the owner. At the third, he slowed the boat, and they viewed the home from every water angle. It dominated its own peninsula, facing west toward the main body of lake, with a shallow cove toward the south. Around the north of the peninsula ran a deep cove. Only one other home shared the point, set far back into the cove.

"What do you think, Len?" asked Britt.

"Impressive cover. The seawall can be secured. If the owner of the other house will let us come behind his property with a fence and share a private gate, it might work."

"Might won't cut it," said Britt.

Len considered for a full minute before finally saying, "Australia would be better, but I can make this happen."

By noon, it was a done deal.

It was mid-afternoon when the men and their wives met up at an intersection several miles off the highway, close to the lake. Sue was driving Dena's car, and Charlie was behind the wheel of the rented Pontiac. At Dena's request, Britt and Sue traded places.

Britt eased his aching body into the driver's seat of Dena's car. There was an awkward silence, which Dena interrupted with a short laugh. "I just realized I never asked what meds they have you on . . . Can you even drive?"

"Yeah, I'm good," he answered. He kept the vehicle in park while Charlie drove away. Taking his time, he studied his wife.

Dena was dressed in jeans, worn leather boots, and a soft long-sleeved T-shirt: comfort clothing. Her hands were lightly fisted, tugging the sleeves down to cover her knuckles. Her hair was swept back in a loose ponytail. She wore no makeup, and she didn't meet his eyes.

Britt put the car in gear and laid his right hand palm-up on the console that separated them. She laid her left hand palm-down in his open hand, her hand still fisted around the fabric of her shirt sleeve.

Before easing the car back onto the road, Britt looked once more at his wife's face. Her marvelous lips were neither smiling nor pulled tight with tension. They were slightly puckered, a sure sign that she had something to say.

She said, "Daddy went by the house and picked up a few things. You have some clean clothes in that duffel in the back. He said your habit of keeping your piano closed probably saved it. The case is scarred, but the sound shouldn't be affected."

Her honey-soft voice spoke this in a serious tone, but this was only part of what she wanted to say. He waited for her to get to what was really on her mind as he drove.

She said, "You haven't told me much about what you did yesterday or this morning. I'm guessing you've found us a place to stay on the lake."

He almost smiled at the way she put it, "you've found us a place to stay." He continued to wait.

She said, "Bonnie and I have talked. She knows things are going to change, but she really wants to finish out this school year in Deerfield. I'm going to . . ." She paused. "We're going to

171

make that happen for her."

He nodded but didn't say anything, still waiting her out.

She said, "Britt . . ." Her voice was a choked whisper. She un-fisted her left hand, the fabric of her sleeve still between their palms. "Britt, whatever Daddy said to you, you know it was in the heat of the moment. You know . . ." Her tears began to flow now.

Britt bit his lip and concentrated on every nuance of her voice, even as he managed to keep the car on the road.

She continued, "You know I will live anywhere in the world you want to make a home for us. You know I will be happy as long as Bonnie is safe."

He almost smiled again. Someday he would tell her about wanting more than happy-ish for her. Right now he just listened; she was nearly there.

She entwined the fingers of her left hand with his. He glanced down at her wedding band, which was now peeking out beyond her sleeve, and squeezed her hand. With her already soggy right sleeve, she wiped tears from her face.

"This is what I wanted you to see, Britt," she said. "I'm a mess. I can't stop crying . . . I haven't slept. I keep getting hit by these panic things. But in here . . ." She let go of his hand and made a fist again, rapped it twice between her breasts. She drew a breath as if to speak, but instead, her left hand made a gesture, deliberately measuring the distance from his chest to hers. He recognized what she meant immediately—it was the gesture he had made during his proposal the night of the Grammys. The gesture marked the cord that bound her heart to his, the cord that couldn't be severed.

She laid her strong hand back in his open palm and squeezed as she entwined her fingers with his once more. "On the inside,

I'm not shaken." Even spoken through tears, her voice was the most beautiful thing he had ever heard. "I'm shaking on the outside, but inside, Britt, I'm not shaken." After a pause, she said, "Aren't you going to say anything?"

He couldn't. The pure poetry of her words had left him speechless.

After many twists and turns on narrow roads, the two cars finally came to a stop behind a modern two-story house on a private point on the lake. Britt bounced out of the car, stopped and leaned on the hood a few seconds. "I forgot that I need to move slowly now," he explained through clenched teeth.

Dena came around the car and stood behind him, gently lifting his T-shirt away from his body. She drew in a sharp breath when she saw his bruised and battered back. "Britt, I . . ." Her tears began to flow again, and she wiped her cheeks with the hem of his shirt. "You saved my life, and I wasn't even there for you last night."

He held out his hand, and she took it. "We were both where we needed to be last night," was all he said. "Now let's look at our house."

Together they walked up the steps onto the side deck. A white-haired gentleman, vaguely familiar, with the courtly manner of a movie star from another generation, opened the door and invited them inside. "What do you think?" Britt asked as soon as Dena stepped through the door.

She looked at the owner and said politely, "Your home is very nice."

The man laughed. "It's not mine anymore. It's yours."

Eyebrows raised, Dena looked at Britt, who bounced on his toes, mischief in his eyes. "Uh, Britt, let's take a walk outside," she said firmly.

He grinned at her and led her straight through the spacious living room to the front deck of the house, overlooking the lake. Neither spoke for a minute as they walked down the long hill toward the dock.

"What have you done?" she asked finally.

"I've found a home for us," he answered.

She opened her mouth to speak and then closed it. After a long pause, she said, "I sort of assumed you were renting a place for us. You know, until we could decide together where we should live." When he didn't speak, she said, "Okay, so instead of finding us a place to stay, you found a home. Tell me what a home is to you."

Britt spoke with measured words. "A place that is ours alone, with our own memories, where we can make a fresh start." Taking her hand, he continued, "A place where my wife can thrive. A place that is safe, where you and Bonnie don't have to be afraid."

She studied his face as he spoke. "Tell me what makes this place safe."

Britt pointed as he spoke. "We've looked at this property from every angle. You can't see the house at all from the road, it barely shows up from overhead, and it's adequately hidden from the water. We don't have the best view of the lake, but that's a plus when safety is the priority."

Dena nodded, her eyes following where Britt was pointing. She waved at Len who had been there since noon and was already going over the property with a security team.

Britt pointed toward the driveway. "See where the driveway

forks?" he asked. "We can put a security gate there to serve both our home and the neighbor's home." He pointed to the south side of the property. "Our line runs along that fence, cuts across east, there, to where the gate will be. Our neighbor has given us permission to connect the dots by continuing our fence on along the other side of his house, down his far line, which will enclose us on three sides. I've been told that the property behind us can be purchased, giving us a buffer of forest."

"What about the lake?" asked Dena.

"I've always felt safe facing water as long as my back is covered," he answered. "But as far as security goes, we will have sensors put along the seawall when we have the security system installed."

"Good grief, Britt, we'll hear bells every time a cat walks through the yard." Dena put her arms around him gently. "Tell me what your plan is," she said. "This house is over an hour away from my work and Bonnie's school."

Britt met her eyes. "Dena, you know my heart. You know that I would never try to control you. I only want to get you away from lunatics and bombs." A soft breeze ruffled around them from the lake just then, teasing strands of hair from her ponytail to cover her eyes. Gently he pushed her hair aside. "When school starts back in the fall, Bonnie will be spending half-days with her new art tutor. And as for your job," his eyes searched hers, "I know that you're harassed every day by reporters looking for me." She relented a little. "Perhaps you can rearrange your schedule so that you can do part of your work from home and not have to go to your office every single day. Our biggest concern is going to be keeping reporters and lunatics from following you home. Len has a plan worked out for protecting you on the road."

She stepped back and looked at him intently. His face was

tanned to a Caribbean bronze from sailing his ship just two days ago. Smile lines defined his sea-green eyes and his lips were full and perfect. When he wanted to, Britt could translate his good looks into a reckless attraction that could charm women into giving in to him without fail. There was nothing rash in his expression at the moment, however. He had thought this through, in his own way, and it was obvious that he meant the best for her, even if his methods were a bit peculiar.

"I'll move into this house if you will truthfully answer one question," said Dena, her soft voice belying the steel-hard strength of will she had just bent for him.

"Anything," he answered.

"How much did it take to persuade this gentleman to sell his house to you? I didn't see a for sale sign."

Amusement twitched the corner of his mouth. He didn't offer a reply.

"What did you do?" she continued. "Just knock on the man's door and present him with a small fee for his house?"

"Actually, I started out with a large fee, but he insisted his house wasn't for sale."

When he didn't add anything to his story, she prodded, "So what did you do? It must have taken a tidy sum to persuade him to sell his home."

"No, actually, it took a bit more persuading than money to get him to turn it loose."

"More persuading?"

His mouth worked. "I—uh—I traded him my house in Antigua."

"You did what?" Her voice rang across the water and sent a pair of ducks into quacking flight.

"Don't be mad, Dena," he said, a boyish grin on his face.

Dena stared at him, hands on her hips. Money meant nothing

to Britt. He had told her once that the money came in faster than he could spend it or hide it from Uncle Sam. But to give away his home just one day after leaving it, like whacking off a gangrenous limb! Such a sacrifice was beyond her comprehension. It must have torn a huge chunk out of his heart, and yet he stood looking at her with his heart in his eyes, apparently intact.

"I . . . I don't know what to say," she said.

"Say you still love me and you'll try to make a home with me here," he said.

"Of course." Taking his hands in her strong grasp, she lifted them toward her face and shook them for emphasis. "Pay attention, Britt. Just listen to me. This will be our home, I promise you that. But you can't expect to settle in here and be happy like a normal person."

There was playful shock on his face and exaggerated offense in his voice as he said, "I can't?"

"No. You're not normal. I don't think you even realize how peculiar you are. And you're still bouncing from your career hitting the stage just last week."

He choked back a laugh at the intensity of her lecture.

She continued to shake his hands, trying to get her message through to him. "You've spent half your life on a stage or in a jet or at a party. Always in the spotlight. You can't play Mr. Britt Homebody, and you can't sit here waiting to scare the boogeymen away. Please, please tell me you're going to find some venture to occupy yourself."

"I am deeply offended," he said with exaggerated primness. "What did I do to merit being called an insane bouncing oddball?"

She rewarded him with a smile. "Whom I admire with all my heart. You get harder to understand and easier to admire each day. I don't know how to thank you for making such a sacrifice to get a home for us."

He leaned forward and whispered in her ear, "I'll think of something."

Just then the Duncans stepped out onto the deck of the house. Charlie yelled down to them, "Hey, Jordan, you owe me dinner. I told you it would take longer than five minutes to talk her into it."

"I had her charmed in the first thirty seconds. We've just been discussing where you're going to buy our supper," Britt yelled back.

They started up the hill toward their new home, holding hands. "I have to ask one more question," Dena said. "What will you do with your boats?"

"I suppose I'll sell Jane. But a mistress like Shirl . . . Well, it would be sacrilege to put a price on her. I may have to put her in dry dock for now, though," he said as mournfully as if he had mentioned calling the mortician. He snapped his fingers, and his voice picked up speed. "That reminds me, I got a nice little sloop in this deal." He pointed to a twenty-two foot sailboat at the end of their dock. "I'm still waiting for her to tell me her name. And I also have my eye on a vintage Chris Craft power boat, all mahogany. She just needs a little fixing up, and she'll be better than new."

Dena smiled as they joined their friends on the deck. Some things could always be counted on with Britt. Boats being one of them.

CHAPTER

SEVENTEEN

Sitting alone in the sauna of her penthouse apartment, Lori Sink closed her eyes and let the steam melt her body. Britt had given her this apartment the previous year, and he had never asked for it back. She knew he still had the key, and she expected him to return very soon. Licking her lips, she touched her body where Britt's hands had left their imprint two hours ago—the small of her back, her face, her hands. Innocent places, but his heat had seared her flesh. And she had pressed her body with hard insistence against the body that she knew so well, sliding her hands along the contours of his solid back. Without words, she had told him that she wanted him back.

At two o'clock this morning, Britt had tracked her down in a Manhattan club. With intensity in his half-closed eyes and a set to his jaw that had thrilled her, he'd pulled her away from her companion and the music, leading her into a quiet corner of the room. There he'd danced with her and asked her questions about the recent details of her life. With intimate brashness, he'd taken her face in his hand and studied her eyes as she talked.

He'd left after ten minutes, but not before a photographer had spotted them and taken a picture.

Lori knew her body had made an imprint on his, so firmly had she held him. She slipped out of the towel and ran her hands down her body, where she could still feel his heat. She knew he must be thinking of her at this very minute. Desire melded her thoughts to his.

She wondered when the photograph would hit the streets. The world, and particularly his wife, needed to know that Britt Jordan would soon be hers again.

At the exact same time, four a.m., Dena woke with a start in the Deerfield hotel suite she and Britt were sharing with Bonnie. Another panic attack had hit her. She slid one foot behind her on the bed, just to touch her husband's leg and know he was near. Britt's side of the bed was empty.

She rolled over and pulled his pillow tight against her chest, her breath coming in quick, shallow gasps. When she buried her face into the pillow to cry, she encountered a slip of paper. For several minutes, not caring what the note might say, she wept sad, weary, and angry tears all at once. What mattered at that moment was that her husband wasn't there for her.

Suddenly, she sat up, drawing in long breaths to calm herself. Grabbing her cell phone from the nightstand, she used its flashlight to read the note. "Trust me," was all it said. Drawing her knees into her chest, she wondered: *How long has it been since Britt has slept? A week?*

Just then, Bonnie tiptoed into the room, sliding into bed next to her.

"I'm sorry," said Dena. "I didn't mean to wake you up."

"I've been awake all night, waiting for Britt to come back," said her child. "Where did he go?"

"I don't know; I wasn't even aware . . ." began Dena. "What time did he leave?"

"Five minutes after you turned out your light at eleven," Bonnie replied.

Dena shook her head. She must have crashed as soon as her head hit the pillow. Drawing her child close, she whispered, "It's all right; we're okay. Let's try to get some sleep."

In the dark, Bonnie snuggled into her mother's embrace and whispered, "Mama, why do grownups say 'it's okay' when it's not?"

"Um," began Dena, "partly because we so much want every-thing to be okay for our children. And partly," she continued, settling onto Britt's pillow, "because we know it *will* be. We're going to be better than okay soon, Bonnie, I promise you."

Mother and daughter did eventually fall asleep. In fact, the dawn's soft glow was filtering in around the curtains when Dena opened her eyes again. Instinctively she turned her head to discover her husband sitting on the floor beside the bed, back against the wall. His eyes were staring straight into hers. Although there wasn't enough light in the room yet for her to read his expression, she detected a shift in the lines of his face from steel to marshmallow.

Carefully, trying not to wake Bonnie, Dena disentangled herself from her daughter's arms and slipped from the bed, taking Britt's pillow with her. Positioning it against the wall, behind their backs, she arranged her body on the floor, easing into her husband's ready embrace.

"Where were you, Britt?" she whispered, her face against his neck. "I needed you last night."

"I'm sorry," was all he answered. He bent his head forward, and she felt a shudder run through his body. "Trust me, Dena," he whispered, a hitch in his voice. "Please trust me."

She could feel the pulse in his neck racing against her cheek. Placing one hand against his chest, she could feel his heart pounding. She whispered, "Britt, you need to sleep. Please, sleep."

She felt him draw in one deep breath before slowly letting it out. His body slumped against hers, and his heart rate slowed against her hand. Apparently he had fallen asleep. Even Dena was startled at this. Leaning into him, she closed her eyes.

When she opened them again, the room was brighter and Bonnie was stirring in the bed. Stretching, Bonnie stood up, looked over to see Dena and Britt huddled against the wall. Bonnie's mouth twisted, her eyes rolled heavenward, and she stomped toward the bathroom, shaking her head.

Dena closed her eyes. In a couple of minutes, she heard Bonnie open the refrigerator door in the kitchenette, clattering around as she fixed herself some breakfast. She listened as her daughter moved into the other bedroom, where she crunched on her cereal.

A few minutes later, Bonnie went back into the bathroom, the sounds of the child energetically brushing her teeth bouncing throughout the suite. Then Bonnie's imperious voice hit her ears, "Am I going to school or not?" When Dena opened her eyes and looked wearily at her daughter without answering, the girl shook her head and stomped back into the bathroom.

She returned an instant later, still holding her toothbrush. She stood there until Dena said, "Bonnie, it's Saturday."

"I told you last night, they're giving a makeup test in Probability this morning. It's because practically the whole class flunked it on Thursday, including me, since the police got me out of school before I could finish. Britt said he'd go over it with me."

Bonnie disappeared into the bath again, and Dena softly bounced her head against the wall, a reverse version of the way Britt had banged his head against her refrigerator door just over a week ago.

"Probability," came Britt's sleepy, raspy voice. "I'm on it."

As Dena continued to hit the wall with her head, Britt asked quite seriously, "Dena, do you want me to go over to the house and get that jar of cough medicine for you?"

When Bonnie returned to the room to find the two of them leaning into each other, laughing helplessly, she put her hands on her hips and said, "Somebody needs to be the adult around here!"

At this, Dena collapsed sideways onto the floor, laughing. Britt drew in a deep breath, cracked his neck, and slid into a standing position, shoulders pressed against the wall. "I guess that just leaves you and me, Bonnie," he said.

Trapped in the space between his wife's prone body and the bed, Britt chose the bed, stepping up onto it. He bounced once, ricocheted against the ceiling with his hands, and dropped cat-like onto the floor on the other side, bits of ceiling plaster raining down on him.

"Britt, you broke the crappy ceiling," Bonnie stated matter-of-factly.

Laughter-strangled, Dena asked, "What was the probability of that happening?"

While Bonnie was at school, Dena snoozed as Britt slouched in an over-sized upholstered chair, glancing through his Twitter feed. At around noon, his courier service knocked at the suite's door and presented him with a fat packet.

"What is it?" Dena asked drowsily.

"It's from my secretary," he answered, tapping the packet against his hand, deciding whether or not to open it. "Phyllis is old-school. As if being slammed in social media weren't enough, she continues to think I need to beat myself up with print media as well."

With a sigh, he slit open the envelope and flipped through the contents quickly. "The world will collapse at any moment unless I get back on the stage," he announced and threw the clippings into the trash. With a puckered brow, he studied a separate envelope for a moment. Posted on the outside was a note in his secretary's handwriting:

> *Britt, this will make you sick, and I advise you to trash it without opening. You'll hear about it soon enough. Suffice it to say your brother needs his butt kicked and his head examined. –Phyllis*

Britt sat back in the oversized chair. Glancing at Dena, he pressed his lips together and opened the second envelope. Inside was a clipping from a tell-all tabloid, one everybody would soon see at the grocery counter. The caption read, "Now we know, Britt . . . Does your wife?" There was a clear photo of Phillip in a sensual embrace with a young man. With a soft curse, Britt spun around in the chair, propping his feet up on the back, letting his head hang off the seat.

"I don't know whether to laugh or cry," he said to Dena, making a paper airplane out of the clipping and sending it her way. "If it weren't for this being so dang hurtful to you and Bonnie, I'd call him and shake him down for not coming up with some better form of revenge." Under his breath, he muttered, "Well, I would if he hadn't changed his cell number. I'm really, really sorry about this, Dena."

Dena glanced at the clipping, balled it up and tossed it toward the trash can without comment.

"You know this is just a start, don't you?" asked Britt. "He won't stop until he's satisfied that, in his mind at least, I'm ruined. God, I should have murdered him when I had the chance."

Dena stood up. "Bonnie should be finished with Probability by now. I promised we'd show her our new home today. We'll have a talk about handling slander on the drive." She glanced sideways at his upside-down position. "I'm buying one of these big chairs for the lake house—I kind of like you like this."

She danced just beyond his grasp as he slithered out of the chair onto his back on the floor.

"Ouch! I keep forgetting," he said, his face a pained grimace.

Later that afternoon, they were finally allowed full access to Dena's house. She had steeled herself to see her dining room completely blasted, but a clean-up crew was dismantling what remained of the room when the Jordans arrived. She'd thought she was prepared to see the damage to her living room, and had even told Britt on the way over that all the upholstered furniture in the room would surely need replacing.

It was worse than she'd imagined. Tables were toppled, lamps smashed. All the interesting and beautiful things she had collected over the years were now scattered across the floor, covered in rubble from the dining room. She was struck afresh with the horror of what could have happened, and her tears began to flow once again. The enormity of the job of cataloging all the damaged pieces for insurance, let alone trying to figure out what could be salvaged, hit her hard.

With resolve, she stepped through the mess and opened the door to the den. The same acrid stench that filled the rest of the house met her there. She stood still in the doorway and looked around. For the first time, it struck her how much this room reminded her of Johnny Martin. The den had been his haven.

Britt stood behind her, and she leaned into him. "I need to give all this up, don't I?" she stated.

He held her tightly. "No, you don't," he answered.

"But I need to," she said. "If we're going to have our own home, a fresh start, I need to." After a pause, she said through her tears, "It's so hard, Britt. I'm not as strong as you are."

"That's not true . . . you're stronger. You've been keeping me afloat all this time," Britt said. He pulled her away from the den. "You don't have to decide now. Let's just do what we came to do and get out of here."

Together they made their way around Britt's Steinway to Bonnie's alcove. The piano had shielded the paintings from the blast. Altogether there were eight beautiful works of art to be transported to their new home.

Just then, a small moving van pulled up. Bonnie's paintings would leave the house first, today. Moving from this home into the new one without leaving a trail for the bomber or reporters would be a logistical nightmare. Len had arranged a total of four moving vans, each following a strategic protocol to ensure they weren't followed. Now, Dena realized, the final destination for two of them would be a storage warehouse or donation center.

Sunday morning, Dena returned to the house armed with boxes, determined to sort through photographs, books, and mementos belonging to Bonnie's father to be stored until Bonnie had her own home. As she tackled the job, she seemed tense to Britt, wound up, almost angry.

When she cranked up the volume on the stereo—gospel music since she was missing church—Britt decided that the best thing for him to do was get out of her way. He remembered that Carlene Jenkins could concoct a Bloody Mary mean enough to make a man forget his own name. With a nod to the uniformed officer guarding the house, he set off across town on foot to pay Carlene a good-bye visit.

Britt floated back into Dena's house a few hours later, a silly grin on his face, to find his wife sitting on a clean blanket in the living room floor, cradling Johnny's mandolin. She handed it up to Britt, explaining, "Your habit of putting this away in the closet with your guitars saved it. It's yours now."

Carefully, he laid the mandolin on top of his Steinway and settled down on the blanket behind Dena, knees bent on either side of her, forming a chair of sorts. She leaned back against him with a sigh.

"You've been to see Carlene, haven't you?" she asked.

"Yeap."

"God bless that woman, she may have saved our marriage today. I was a little cranky this morning, wasn't I?"

"Yeap."

"I've wrung out every tear I could possibly cry. Now I'm just ready to move. You've got your wife back."

"Of course," said Britt. "Exactly as I expected."

Bonnie came down the hall just then, shirts draped over one arm. "What is the deal with you people sitting in the floor? Are we even going to have a couch in the new house?"

When Dena patted the blanket, Bonnie plopped down behind Britt, back-to-back, and leaned into him. He winced, grunted softly, but didn't ask her to move. When she finally quit wiggling against him, he announced in a contented voice, "I have everything I will ever need right here on this blanket."

"I don't," said Bonnie bluntly. "I've washed these shirts twice and they still stink. I need some new stuff."

"I'll tell you what," said Dena. "We're moving Wednesday. If you'll spend that night with your grandparents, we'll have a girlie shopping day in Charlotte on Saturday. On Britt's card. Deal?"

"Cool," said Bonnie and Britt simultaneously.

The photograph of Britt and Lori dancing hit the stands on Monday. Dena didn't ask Britt about it, and he didn't bring it up.

On Wednesday, she woke up in her usual good humor. The last of the four strategically orchestrated moving vans was expected at seven. "I'll tell you what," she said to Britt, stretching and smiling. "If you don't mind going over to the house to wait for the movers, I believe I'll go for one last run and meet you there in a half an hour."

"Sure," he smiled.

Dena walked for a couple of blocks before breaking into a run. She noticed the spring flowers growing in newly green yards and neighbors who waved at her, but she didn't notice the car that had been tracking her for six blocks. She turned a corner. The car turned too, and then sped away. Two blocks later, just as she stepped off the sidewalk into an alley, the car pulled out in front of her. She slammed to a stop against it, her hands on the hood to break her fall.

A man jumped out and grabbed her arm before she could regain her balance. She gave a quick scream before glimpsing his face.

"Phillip!" she cried.

He kept a grip on her arm, his face smug.

"What are you doing here?" she asked, her voice cold, her breathing hard.

"My dear sister-in-law, I would expect a friendlier welcome from you, Southern girl that you are."

"Let go of my arm," she demanded, twisting to get away from him.

He didn't release her. His eyes were cold gray, cruel. So unlike Britt's.

"What do you want, Phillip?"

"I have a message for my favorite brother," he said, his voice low and husky.

She attempted to jerk her arm away, his grasp painful. "I told you to let go of me!"

He still didn't budge.

She looked him in the eye. "You are a loathsome man."

He laughed in her face.

"What do you hope to gain by ruining Britt's reputation?" she demanded.

A car horn honked just then, and a man's voice yelled, "Dena, are you all right?"

She relaxed against Phillip and turned to the man with a smile. "Yes, thank you. Everything's fine." All she needed now was for the town to think Britt Jordan was hurting her on the street.

Phillip murmured into her ear, "I'll gain nothing but the pleasure of watching him fall. You tell him that. Tell him I hate him that much."

He released her and got back into the car and drove away, leaving her to fight her tears alone on the street corner. Retracing her steps, she ran to Sue's house and vented her tears of frustration in her friend's kitchen before going home to face Britt.

As soon as he saw Dena arrive in Sue's car instead of on foot, Britt knew something was wrong, and he met her halfway across the lawn. Dena waved good-bye to Sue and stood still, looking into her husband's eyes.

"What's wrong?" he asked, gently touching her face. She continued to look at him, her eyes sweet with concern, the morning light touching her cheeks with a vibrant glow. When she didn't answer, he checked her over as a parent might a small child and quickly found the ugly red mark on her arm where Phillip's hand had bound her. "Who did this?"

"Britt, I want you to sit down," she said. She tried to steer him toward the front stoop, and when he resisted, she looked him in the eyes and said, "I'm not hurt, but I am terrified of what you might do. I need your promise that you won't fly off in a rage and kill somebody. Will you do that?"

He relented and sat down beside her on the steps. He gently covered the red mark with his hand. When she spoke, she grasped his leg in an iron grip. "Phillip did this," she said.

The rage boiled with such black heat inside his head that he was temporarily blinded. Then he felt her hand on his face, cool and sweet, and heard her voice demand that he look at her.

"He didn't mean to hurt me," Dena said in quick words. "He wanted to control me. He knew he was being cruel, but I'm sure he didn't mean to hurt me."

"What did he want?" Britt asked through clenched teeth.

She was quiet a moment before she spoke. "You were right. He wants to destroy you. And the only reason he gave me is that he hates you."

Britt looked at her arm. "He did this to you just to tell me that?" he demanded. "Hell, I already knew that!" He released a long sigh, and Dena let go of his leg. After a moment, he asked, "Did anyone see him with you?"

"Yes, I'm afraid so." Then she added lightly, "But I don't believe the local newspaper will be reporting the story."

"Oh, Dena, what have I gotten you into?" he asked softly.

"Shh, it will be okay," she answered, patting his knee. "My biggest worry was that this might push you over the edge."

"I'm already over the edge," he responded. "The only thing holding me is that cord that runs between our hearts. If you ever drop me, I swear I'll keep falling for the rest of my life." He leaned against the porch rail. "You know, unless I actually do murder Phillip, there's not a lot I can do to stop him."

"Can you explain something to me?" asked Dena. "I can't for the life of me understand why Phillip hates you so much."

Britt looked away, rubbing his face with one hand.

Dena prodded, "You've told me that he idolized you when he was a kid and that you deserted him when you went to college." When he didn't pick up the story, she continued gently, "You said you wasted two years—"

"I said I spent two years wasted," Britt broke in. "Drugs terrify me to this day." He looked away, not wanting to continue.

"When you flunked out, your dad pretty much forced you into the Army," she said, still digging for the truth. "And after your discharge, you didn't speak to him or go home at all until he died. So Phillip was neglected for about six years, and he still hates you for that." She made a helpless gesture with her hands. "That was a long time ago. I don't get it."

Britt rubbed his hands together, looking down at them. "My father's funeral nearly tore me apart. He had done the toughest thing he could do to save me, and I knew it. I knew I should have thanked him instead of punishing him, but I was young and stupid. And then it was too late." He glanced up at her face, and saw concern where he'd been expecting condemnation. "And Phillip. There he was, a younger version of myself, but more messed up at seventeen than I'd been at nineteen. Only he didn't have a dad to pick him up by the scruff of the neck and turn him around. And I had been away for too long to have the right to do that for him, you know?"

She nodded kindly, searching his face, trying to understand.

"Guilt and the Army put an edge on me that drove me to fame. Lots of people have talent," he said, "but I have something inside me—I don't know, more arrogance, more guts, more discipline—that got me where I wanted to be. Unfortunately, Phillip was the one person who knew that edge was fueled by guilt, and he knew just how to put his finger on it to get what he wanted from me most of the time."

Britt stopped talking. Dena waited.

"I wish those movers would get here so I wouldn't have to keep talking about this," Britt said suddenly with a short laugh.

She leaned toward him, nudging him. "I think talking about it is doing you good. Keep going."

Britt drummed his hands on his legs, deciding. "Okay, but you're still not going to understand. You see, one problem was that Phillip looked like a younger me, and he taught himself to sing sort of like me. But he couldn't see that a face and a voice didn't give him talent. He never understood that the reason he couldn't be me was that he *wasn't* me. Does that make sense?"

She hugged her knees and shook her head slightly, smiling.

Britt tried to gather the right words. "Phillip blamed having my face and my voice for his general lack of success in life, and specifically for his lack of success in music. It was always my fault, not his. The same damn piano sat in Mom's living room that I had always played, but he never bothered to learn to play it. The day I first picked up a guitar, I played it for eight hours straight, and I practiced eight hours a day for years until I knew I could play a riff that would bring Clapton to his knees. I gave Phillip a guitar, and he learned about three chords. He just thought, I guess, that all he had to do was show up in a recording studio and be his charming self and sing a couple of songs and somebody was going to make him a star. He has never understood that I have dynamite inside me while he has, at best, a firecracker. And he's too lazy to take that firecracker and make his own blast." Britt slammed his fists together and made an explosive noise with his mouth for emphasis. "He could have made a fine blast out of his life, but he still wouldn't have been me, and so he hasn't bothered to do it." The movers pulled past the driveway just then, and he stood up with relief.

"And that's why he hates you enough to destroy you?" asked Dena incredulously.

"No. That started last year when I bought his ass out of jail." He started across the lawn toward the moving van, finished with the conversation.

"His butt was in jail?" Dena repeated, prodding him, trotting to stay by his side.

"Well, his whole miserable body was on its way there for failing to pay child support," said Britt, striding across the lawn, waving his arm to direct the driver to back on in the driveway.

"What could I do, let my own nephew starve with his fool father in jail? I arranged to put Phillip on my payroll so I could draft the payments myself. It worked out pretty well for me, considering that Phillip has lived hard enough to age himself so that he now looks exactly like me." Britt put his lips together and let out a piercing whistle that stopped the van just before it hit the house. "Or maybe I'm getting younger, which do you think it is?"

Dena chuckled and shook her head. "I'll bet you've been very generous in your payments to Phillip's ex-wife, and that your nephew knows it's really you taking care of him. And he hates his father and loves you."

"Damn, you're smart." Britt looked twice at Dena's face. "I mean, darn. Sorry, I keep forgetting to work on that."

She gave him a squeeze. "We're starting a new life today," she said. "I hope a lot of things get easier for both of us."

Britt nodded in agreement. He sure hoped so, too.

At noon, Charlie drove by Dena's house to see if the movers were still there. Only Britt's Monteverdi sat in the driveway. Puzzled, Charlie pulled in and got out of his car. Piano music, too powerful to be contained within the confines of the house, met his ears and stopped him in his tracks on the sidewalk.

The music was a rampage of sound—brilliant, flawless, and driving. It spoke of dangerous rage, passionate remorse, and deep heartache. And it told Charlie more about Britt's heart than he wanted to know.

Charlie entered the house without knocking and watched Britt play, in complete awe of the man. It was the loneliest sight Charlie had ever seen—nothing in the room besides the Steinway, the bench, and Britt. The music, driven by a talent beyond description, beyond anything Charlie had ever imagined he would stand this close to, filled the room with notes that were almost visible. Crashing toward an ecstasy of fulfillment, the music poured from Britt's broken heart with a power so strong that Charlie had only to put out his hand to feel its force. This was, he realized, Britt's way of healing himself.

Abruptly, Britt stopped playing and turned to look at Charlie. The two men stared at each other without speaking. Britt was the one whose expression changed; amusement pulled at the corners of his mouth.

"You didn't know I could play, did you?"

Charlie shook his head. "Not like that."

There was silence for several moments. Britt spoke again. "Is there something I can do for you?"

Charlie answered, "I came over here thinking there might be something I could do for you. Help with the moving." He shrugged. "Or listen if you wanted to talk about your brother." He scratched his head. "Now I don't see how I could have thought there'd ever be anything I could do for you."

"Huh! You've already helped me plenty, my friend," said Britt. "I couldn't have risked tracking Lori Sink down that night without you coming along to vouch for me. Dena hasn't asked me about that picture of me and Lori, so I suspect she thinks the tabloids pulled out an old photograph." Britt's husky voice continued very quietly, "My wife has always trusted me, but a man like me, with a reputation like mine—it wouldn't take much to lose that trust." Britt folded his arms and stared hard at Charlie. Uncomfortable, Charlie almost took a step backward. Then Britt smiled and said, "So you see, I still owe you."

Charlie laughed a short chuckle, still so awe-struck he barely knew how to talk to Britt. "Let's call it even. I had never ridden in a private jet or a grasshopper until I met you."

A horn blasted in the driveway. "Good," said Britt. "The piano movers are here. I can finally get my baby here loaded up and go help Dena move in." As he started outside, he said over his shoulder to Charlie, "I'll take a rain check on that help. The way things have been going lately, I might need you again."

Charlie put his hands in his pockets and watched Britt leave. It occurred to him that Britt's statement was his way of keeping their friendship in balance. Britt Jordan, who had been everywhere and knew everybody, who had turned the rock and roll world upside down for twenty years and had enough influence to take over the Grammys, was struggling to be friends with a simple tool salesman.

CHAPTER

EIGHTEEN

The first night in their new home, Dena presented Britt with a letter bearing the insignia of the state of California. Britt read:

Dear Mr. Jordan and Mrs. Martin:

It has come to my attention that due to the unusual circumstances of your wedding ceremony, your marriage is not binding. The State of California cannot honor your marriage license. Should you wish to refile . . .

Britt looked up, frowning. "Where did this come from?"

"Daddy gave it to me when I dropped Bonnie off," she answered. "Evidently it was forwarded to their house."

"I'll call in the morning and straighten this out, Dena. There must be some mistake." Britt started toward the stairs that led up to their bedroom.

"Where do you think you're going?" she demanded.

"To bed."

"Oh, no. You can't sleep with me until you get this settled."

His frown went deeper. "This is ridiculous. We're not any less married because of this letter."

"According to the letter, we never were married. Do you know what this makes me?" She didn't wait for a response. "I'll make up the bed in the guest room for you."

"No, I'll sleep on my boat." He went out the door without saying goodnight and spent a hard night on the double berth, arms folded.

The next morning, he walked back into the house and up the steps, arms still folded. He leaned against the door frame and watched as Dena bent across the dresser in the guest room, putting on earrings. She was wearing a suit jacket and slip.

"We have to talk," he said.

"I should say so."

"If it turns out that we really aren't married, we can take care of this today at your local courthouse."

"Nuh-uh. I want a real wedding this time. Southern-style," she said.

He turned on his heel and walked out, then came back, arms still folded. "Okay. How long will that take?"

"Two weeks."

"Two weeks!"

"Yes." Her voice was calm and firm.

"You can't be serious," Britt sputtered. "Two weeks? This is just not going to work at all."

She sat down on the edge of the bed and began to pull on a pair of stockings very slowly. She didn't say anything.

"Dena, we can't sleep apart for two weeks," he argued. "We've already spent a rather dry week in that hotel room with Bonnie, remember?"

She raised one eyebrow, still pulling her stockings on, taking her time.

"Dena, we are married. You are my wife. How can you possibly think that things have changed between us because of that letter?"

She raised one leg and smoothed her hand down her calf. "What I think is that you shouldn't be standing there watching me dress."

She stood up and slipped her skirt on. He stayed rooted to the spot, arms still folded.

"Dena." He kept his voice very low, very stubborn.

She picked up the letter from the dresser and brushed past him in the doorway. When she was two steps away from him, she tore the letter in two over her head. "Gotcha!" she said and took off running across the balcony from the guest room toward the master bedroom.

He caught up with her halfway there and wrestled her to the floor. "What brought this on?" he demanded.

She lay on her back on the floor and laughed heartily, her laughter filling every crevice of the house with warmth. "You should have seen your face when I said you'd have to wait two weeks," she sputtered.

He leaned his head on his left hand, elbow on the floor, and watched her laugh. The moment would remain fixed in his mind as the first memory in their new home. When the laughter subsided, he asked again, "Why did you do this?"

"Oh, I thought you might need an anecdote for that book on marriage you've got going in your head. The chapter on the consequences of making big decisions without consulting your wife."

"You scared me half to death," he whispered. "I thought I had lost you."

She touched his wedding band and laced her fingers with his. "Never. I wanted you to understand that I meant what is inscribed on your ring. I would marry you again. No matter what has happened or will happen. We are meant to be together."

He started to kiss her, and stopped, his mouth poised above hers. With a challenge in his voice, he said, "You punished me terribly, making me sleep in the boat on our first night here."

Wicked mirth danced in her eyes. "But there might have been a 'no' between us last night, we were both so tired. I wanted there to be no doubt in this house's mind that the people who live here love each other with a resounding 'yes.'"

"Or resounding shock," he rejoined as his hand discovered she was wearing nothing underneath the jacket. "You keep shocking me, Dena. I intend to find that inch today."

"What inch?"

"Somewhere on your body there is an inch that I have not yet tamed. I will find it if it takes all day."

"And you plan on taming this inch?" she asked, amusement in her voice.

"No, just finding it. I'll feel safer knowing where it is." He kissed her, then sat up and slowly, deliberately removed her stockings. "I believe I'll start with these soft feet," he murmured, caressing her foot in his hands.

The toes wiggled at him in anticipation and she held out her hand. "Help me up first. I still have a surprise for you."

He pulled her to her feet and they stood close, looking into each other's eyes, all the chaos and pain of the last week dissolving. Then she took him by the hand and led him to their bedroom. Pushing the door open with her foot, she made a sweeping gesture with her free hand. "Here we are, Britt," she said softly. "A fresh start. Our own memories."

He looked around the room with surprise. She had purchased a new bedroom suite, solid cherry, and had it delivered without his knowledge while he waited for the piano movers the day before.

"Does this meet with your approval?" she asked.

"Oh, yes," he responded in a deep voice. Then he was speechless for a very long time as he kissed every inch of her skin, beginning with her toes and lingering over the bend of her knee, the small of her back. He saved for last a certain spot on the back of her neck. As he had known would happen, merely brushing this inch of skin with his lips elicited a moan from her. He whispered, "I think I've found it." He kissed the spot more deeply, describing his love to her with practiced hands until he tasted sweat on her neck and felt her body yield to his touch with abandonment. "I don't believe this can be tamed," he told her.

That afternoon, Dena drove back to Deerfield to work a couple of hours and pick up her daughter after school. She had not been gone ten minutes when Britt's secretary called, frantic.

"This letter just came up from the mail room!" Phyllis cried, nearly hysterical. "It's addressed to your home in Deerfield, but your post office must have forwarded it to us like they do your fan mail. What's going on down there?"

"Just calm down and read it to me," Britt said.

"I can't . . . it's too horrible. I'm going to email it to you right now," she said, her voice shaking.

The note came through on his cell phone, handwritten. It read,

> Britt,
>
> *You're moving. I don't like that. This means I have to find you and it will take longer for you to be mine. I had planned to kill her alone. Now I will wait until you are together, when I can splatter her brains across your face. Throw that slut away and come back to me.*

"Britt! Britt!" Phyllis's voice screamed to him from the phone in his hand, but Britt didn't respond. He stared at the words, rage and fear shaking within him. His throat closed so tightly he thought it was impossible for words to escape, and yet he heard himself say to her in a terrible, trembling voice, "I'm calling Len. Good-bye."

His heart nearly propelled him out the door after his wife. He wanted to grab her and run to the far corners of the earth—Australia, Russia, anywhere away from this lunatic. But something made him stand still. There was nowhere he could take Dena where she would be safe. Everywhere he went, he was recognized. This house, with the security system he had installed, was as safe for now as anywhere.

Dena would want to know about this note. But she would never agree to be a prisoner in her home. She would insist on continuing her life, going to work, always looking over her shoulder in fear. Britt was repulsed at the thought of shattering the sweet peace that surrounded her. Not yet. Not until it was absolutely necessary.

Within minutes, Len was walking through the front door. He had already read the note on his cell phone and argued with Britt that he must call Dena's cell and have her return home.

"She won't come back until she has her child with her," Britt repeated as Len came to a halt in the exact center of the room. "You'll have to catch up with her."

Len's frown grew deeper as Britt continued to talk, not wasting words.

"That guard you have acting as an intern in her office isn't enough. I want you by her side every minute. And that 'teacher's aide' inside Bonnie's school isn't enough either. Shoot the note to the police chief and ask him to double the guards he has outside the school."

Len's voice was low and even. "Britt, tell Dena to come home now and have an officer pull Bonnie out of school. This is crazy."

"Three weeks, Len. Just make it happen for three weeks, until school's out. If I can't convince Dena then to stay home with Bonnie for the summer, I'll show her the note. But until then, I don't want this image, these awful words, in her brain." Britt turned from Len to stare out at the lake beyond the trees, his left arm braced against the window frame.

Len began tapping a quick rhythm with his fingers against his leg, a sure sign that he was ready to make a move. "Okay," he said, "but you're going to have to do two things. Number one, you have to leave her."

Britt glanced up at the balcony, where the warmth of his wife's laughter still lingered. He didn't respond or even look at Len.

"The threats started when you married her. If you want to save her, you're going to have to end it."

Britt half-turned from the window and stared at Len, considering, rejecting, considering again. He closed his eyes, pictured the sweet delight on his wife's face the moment he whispered to her that he had found her inch. Britt instinctively understood something deeper than Len's professional observation: It was Britt's job to protect his wife's heart, not break it.

"Not an option," growled Britt. He turned his back on Len, facing the window. "Not within these walls. But out there," he jerked a quick nod toward the outside world, "I can make it happen."

"Then number two," said Len, "this note tells me that this person doesn't know where you are. Come up with a plan for Dena to make only one trip to Deerfield a week."

"Done," said Britt, still looking out the window.

Now that a plan was in motion, so was Len, headed for the

door. "That photo of you and Lori Sink," he said over his shoulder, "You've already started it."

"Inadvertently, but yes," answered Britt. "How did you know it was a current photo?"

Len had reached the door, pulling it open. "You pay me to know things, boss," he said, and then he broke into a run.

Dena would be furious with him for putting a bodyguard at her side without her consent. But perhaps she could be convinced to chalk it up to Britt's eccentricity. Perhaps she would only be furious, not afraid.

With eyes half-closed in anger, Britt read the note once more. *I will wait until you are together . . . throw that slut away.* Taking a deep breath, he dialed Dena's cell phone.

"Hello, beautiful," he said in a steady, husky voice when she answered.

"Hey," she said with a chuckle. "Whatcha want?"

"You're going to be so proud of me," he said. "I'm going back to work."

"You—well, good. Great! Can we talk about this tonight? Traffic's pretty heavy."

"But this is important." He made his voice light, argumentative. "I'm going to be gone three days a week."

"Okay." She sounded agreeable, unconcerned.

"I'll be gone in the middle of every week for a while."

"Okay."

"Well, aren't you going to say you'll miss me?" He was trying hard to push her into thinking he had become even more peculiar.

He heard her grunt with impatience. "Of course I'll miss you. Look, can we talk about this later? I'm trying to drive."

"That's what I want to talk to you about," he said. "Why

don't you plan to stay those nights at your parents' house so you won't have to drive? I would be worried about you being on the road every day."

"Well, okay. Whatever." He heard her horn honk. "It might be easier while Bonnie's still in school anyway."

"And would you consider staying home Mondays and Fridays with me? Please?" he whined.

"Bri-itt." She drawled his name in exasperation. "I don't know. I'm so far behind now I can't turn around. Maybe later."

"Please?"

"We'll see. Just let me get caught up. I've gotta go. I'm turning onto the interstate right now."

"Wait. Let me tell you what I've done." He could almost hear her thinking, *What now?* "With much persuading, I've gotten Len to agree to look after you in my absence."

"What!" Dena didn't say anything else for a few seconds. He could picture her pulling off the road. "Britt, what is it with you? I've only been gone twenty minutes. Do you just sit around while I'm not there and think up ways to torment me?"

"Yes," he answered in an offended voice.

"This is just not going to work." She sounded mad. "I can't deal with a bodyguard. I'm already tripping over that so-called intern you stuck in my office, and Bonnie is well guarded. The police are doing a good job keeping an eye out for potential bombers. And on top of that, nobody knows where we live. I'm good . . . *really*."

"It's just for a while," he implored. "Just long enough to make sure nobody follows you home and finds us here. Okay?"

"No, it's not okay," she responded. "But I doubt I can do much about it. Once you get on these kicks, you're like a bulldog. But I am not putting up with this for long. Do you understand?"

"Yes, ma'am," he answered and hung up. Okay, good. So far she was mad but not suspicious of his motives. Not afraid.

Britt looked around their living room. Dena had worked so hard yesterday to turn it into a home. Even though the room was not yet fully furnished, lamps were on tables, books were on shelves. The largest wall in the high-ceilinged room was devoted to eight of Bonnie's paintings, some hung high on the wall to be viewed from the upstairs balcony. Dena's loving, tasteful touch was everywhere. Closing his eyes, he could still hear her laughing at him this morning, still feel her body pressed with heat against his.

The one thing he desired most—to run to her and stand beside her and protect her—was the one thing that could get her killed. *Now I will wait until you are together, when I can splatter her brains across your face.*

He felt a wash of raw anxiety flow over him. He shook that off and stormed into the kitchen with determination. From the wine rack he grabbed a bottle of stout red wine, and he opened and slammed drawers until he found an opener. Uncorking the bottle, he carried it out to the deck and sat down in a chaise. Deliberately, without the benefit of a glass, he turned the bottle up and forced the wine, rich and fiery, down his throat. Unless he got himself drunk right then and there, he knew that his heart would carry him to his wife's side.

He had not had a bite to eat all day. By the time Dena returned that evening, he was still passed out on the deck.

That same afternoon, Rhiannon walked through the Jordan's empty house in Deerfield. The key Bonnie had given her no longer worked in the lock, but the security system had not been replaced and the police had finally left. It wasn't that difficult to break in through the basement door.

For the life of her, she couldn't imagine why Britt Jordan had married Dena Martin. But one thing was certain; there was no way it would last.

Anybody who knew anything about Britt Jordan knew he was a stickler for punctuality, and he liked everything ship-shape. There was no way he could stand Dena's haphazard housekeeping for long. Rhiannon's father had taught her how a real man, a military man, liked his things. She understood precision. She understood what a real man wanted in a woman.

On the same day that Dena had made such a fuss over ironing Britt's undershorts, Rhiannon had searched the house and found Britt's cell phone in his desk drawer. Carefully, she had lifted the phone and turned it over in her hand. Of course it was code-locked. She had thought about taking the SIM card and having it cloned, but a man like Britt Jordan would undoubtedly have codes behind codes and possibly an alarm.

That day, when Rhiannon had put Britt's phone back in the drawer where it belonged, she had seen something else in the drawer, an item much more useful than Britt's locked cell phone.

Today, she stood in the empty room and wished Britt hadn't moved away.

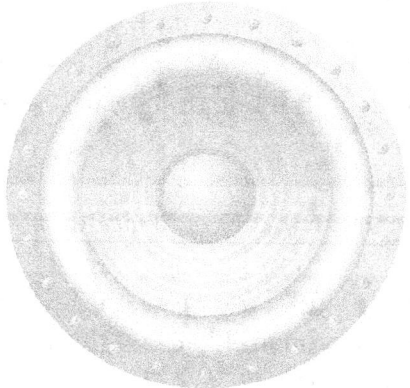

———CHAPTER———

NINETEEN

Gregory Marcello sat behind a desk in his studio and studied Britt Jordan's doctor's report. He had seen cases like this before—rock singers who had abused their voices until their throats were irreparably damaged. Never did these fools bother to come to him when they were first starting out, when he could really help them. Instead they came to him after their voices and careers were destroyed expecting Gregory to snap his fingers and give them their voices back. Rarely did he find one of these aging, has-been rock singers who had the discipline to sacrifice his own voice to the regimen of scales and exercises that would give him a new voice.

Gregory did not expect Britt Jordan to be any different from the rest of the pack. Judging from the man's music and reputation, this Jordan fellow would probably be the worst one yet. He certainly had the most to lose of any who had come to Gregory. The voice coach stood up and looked out the windows of his studio at the Manhattan skyline, running his hands through his thinning hair. He had contempt for the whole lot of rock singers who had come to him. They were all a waste of his time. And this one in particular was wasting his time now, making him wait.

The door opened, and in strode Britt Jordan. Gregory recognized him at once from his signature ponytail and tattoos, and watched as he crossed the room. He appeared very relaxed, and yet there was an intensity about him that Gregory could not quite define.

"I apologize, Mr. Marcello, for making you wait," Britt said in a very distinct, husky voice. "The airport was a madhouse this morning."

Gregory acknowledged the apology with a slight nod, and then made Britt wait while he studied him.

Where was this man's breaking point? How far would Gregory have to push him before he gave up and got out of Gregory's hair, allowing him to concentrate on his real students, the ones with talent, the ones with a future? Oh, Gregory Marcello was paid quite well to babysit these rock singers, but the sooner he could get rid of them, the better.

This one rocked up on his toes, hands in his pockets, and commented, "You have quite a view here, Mr. Marcello." Then he looked Gregory in the eye, and Gregory detected a shift within the man. Britt Jordan was through with introductions.

"Mr. Jordan, exactly what do you expect me to do for you?"

Britt took one hand out of his pocket, still looking Gregory in the eye. "I have destroyed my own voice," he said matter-of-factly, rubbing his throat. He leaned against the piano and crossed one foot in front of the other. "There's nothing to be done about it. What I need is to start over, from the bottom, and develop a new voice within the range I have left."

Gregory blinked. Britt did not. "And what do you propose to do with this new voice?" asked Gregory.

Britt did not answer.

Gregory rubbed his hands together and looked at them. His fingers were fine and tapered, unused to labor. "Do you expect to return to giving stage performances? Do you plan to transpose your songs into your new range? What are your plans, Mr. Jordan?"

Britt looked at him levelly. His words were very distinct. "My plans for my voice are none of your affair. Whether I sing to myself in the shower or join an opera company, your job is to teach me to sing again."

Gregory's face twitched slightly. "What was your range before?" he asked.

Britt hit two A's on the piano. "Two octaves, easily."

Big deal. Gregory could sing three octaves, easily. "And what range do you expect to attain?"

Britt hit two D's on the piano.

"You want to lower your range?"

Britt's answer was to look him in the eye again.

"Why?"

"I know it is attainable. I don't know how to do it by myself, at least not in the way it needs to be done." Britt rubbed his throat again. "My voice has had time to rest. Now is a good time to put it to work."

"You're living in North Carolina now, I understand?"

"Yes."

"We can meet once a week . . ."

"Twice a week," said Britt flatly.

"What's your rush, Mr. Jordan, if you're going to be singing in the shower?"

Britt looked away for the first time. He had to keep himself away from Dena long enough for the lunatic to think they were separated. And he wanted to see real progress on his voice before he told her he was working under a coach. With authority he said, "Tuesdays and Thursdays, Mr. Marcello."

Once again, Gregory's face twitched. He did not like to be told what to do. "When I'm done with you, Mr. Jordan," he said crisply, "you will either have a new voice or you will wish you never had a voice."

"Precisely what I expected," said Britt.

Gregory looked Britt over once again. This man's breaking point could be more difficult to find than he had imagined, but he would find it. He definitely would find it.

Britt managed to return from New York the same day without Dena realizing he had been gone. When she and Bonnie walked into the house that afternoon, Bonnie immediately ran into her room downstairs and slammed the door, and Dena started up the steps without speaking.

He stood at the bottom of the steps and inquired of her back, "Are you still not talking to me?"

She gave him an irritated glance over her shoulder and continued up the steps.

"Are you mad because I got drunk yesterday or because of Len?" he asked.

"Both," she said, still climbing the steps.

"What happened to being kind and tenderhearted and all that forgiving stuff?" he called when she reached the top of the stairs.

This stopped her, and she turned around slowly.

"I would forgive you if you got drunk," he insisted softly.

There were tears in her eyes as she descended the stairs. Putting her arms around him, she buried her face against his neck.

"Britt, I love you with all my heart, but you're just so darned hard to . . ." She stopped. He wondered if she meant he was hard to love or hard to understand. More emphatically, she said, "I hate having a bodyguard in my way all day. I just hate it. And there's no reason for it."

He tried gently to get her to look at him, but she kept her face buried stubbornly, hidden by his hair.

"All this is too difficult for Bonnie," she continued. "Bonnie knows you haven't done anything wrong, but this makes three weeks in a row that she's had to deal with the kids at school making remarks about the tabloid stories." Before he could speak, the rest of her pent-up feelings poured out. "And having Len drive us home just made her afraid. We had told her there would be a car following to keep reporters away. Len's presence reminded her that the bomber could be following also." Dena raised her head and looked him in the eye. "I want you to put a stop to this bodyguard nonsense, Britt; I mean it."

"I have a better idea," he said. "We can be in Australia tomorrow. By the time we've explored the entire continent, the tabloids will have moved on to something else and the police will have caught the lunatic."

She groaned in disgust. "I don't want to run away. All I want is for our lives to make sense again, and you can start by firing Len."

He held her tightly. "Not yet. Soon, I promise. But not yet."

Pushing him away, she frowned at him. "Is there something you're not telling me?"

He froze. He would rather cut off his tongue than lie to her. Taking a deep breath, he gave her a boyish grin. "Of course not. I'm a bouncing insane oddball, remember?" He touched the frown lines on her forehead. "Do you still love me?"

She relented enough for him to kiss her.

"I'll go talk to Bonnie," he said. "As long as she still trusts me, maybe she'll understand that this is just a precaution." He went to Bonnie's door and knocked. Just before she opened it for him to step inside, he caught a glimpse of Dena's face as she started up the steps. Her expression was not angry . . . it was worried.

Tuesday evening, Britt stood alone in his apartment in New York, looking out over the city toward the river beyond. His first lesson with Gregory Marcello had not gone well. Nothing he'd ever done before could have prepared him for the intense set of exercises the man had put him through. Before it was over, Britt was angry with himself, his voice, and his coach.

Thoroughly disgusted when he left, Britt had the driver carry him up and down the streets of the city, letting the noise and the surge of human power surround him and pulsate through his veins. He had poured himself a drink in the limousine and another once he had reached the apartment.

Britt glanced in the direction of another building, just two blocks away, where Lori Sink was no doubt spending the evening in the apartment he had given her. With a sigh, he turned from the window and surveyed the living room. It was very masculine, decorated in black and hues of butterscotch, the lighting dramatic. Actually, the place belonged to Jordan Enterprises and was used occasionally by members of his staff, but it was definitely considered Britt's. The Steinway was kept tuned and ready for him, and the bar was always stocked to his taste. If he made a phone call on the morning of his arrival, there would be food in the refrigerator and fresh flowers on the tables by noon. And no matter who else used the apartment, no one else ever, ever used Britt's bedroom.

Dena did not know of the existence of this apartment.

Britt looked back out at the city and felt its power echo in each beat of his heart. It was here that he had put together the most profitable deals of his career. It was here that he had performed to some of the largest, most spellbound crowds. And in this city, he had romanced a few of the most exciting women in the world.

In New York, he was absolutely, irrefutably, wickedly, Britt Jordan.

Night had enclosed the city while he stood at the window. Britt sipped his drink, watching the lights of the city, and thought about all the things that were available to him. One phone call, and he could have box seats at the theater. Another, and he could have the best table at any of several world-class restaurants in town. He could call a press conference and there would be reporters scrambling over each other to get to him. He had only to snap his fingers, and a private masseuse would be there within an hour.

Britt turned and looked at the leather-bound address book on his ebony desk. Nearly a year had passed since he'd been in this apartment. Even so, the book held names and numbers of people he could call and get almost anything he wished. In particular, there were women listed in the book who would drop what they were doing and be ready for him to pick them up in an hour.

Britt turned through the book and dialed a number. After a quick conversation, he notified his driver to be out front. He looked around the room. There were no pictures of Dena on the desk. There was no Bible on the bookshelf. Nothing in this room reminded him of the life he had made for himself since he married Dena. Without hesitancy, he slipped off his wedding band and laid it on the desk. Then he left the apartment. He would not be back until four a.m.

By the time Britt returned home Thursday evening, the Page Six headline gossip in the New York Post applauded Britt Jordan's return to the city. The singer had been spotted all over Manhattan the night before, popping in and out of clubs, dancing, drinking. Although the column did not claim a lead on which woman Britt might have taken home at dawn, the consensus was that Britt Jordan, after less than three months of marriage, had finally come to his senses.

The next week, the tabloids carried a photograph of Britt and Lori Sink walking a city sidewalk, holding hands. He looked intense and masculine, three-day stubble defining his clenched jaw, very much Britt Jordan. Her eyes were cat-like, her face turned slightly toward his, quite sophisticated in a low-cut dress. It was a very recent photograph, but Dena did not mention it. Neither did Britt.

Three weeks went by. On the night before Bonnie's last day of school, Britt kept the same schedule as he had the previous two Wednesday nights. At eleven o'clock, he left his apartment and headed for a glitzy Manhattan night spot. Before the driver dropped him at the front entrance, Britt sent a quick text. He stepped out of the vehicle dressed in tight black jeans, a summer-weight black jacket slung over his right shoulder. The left sleeve of his purple T-shirt was slit from hem to shoulder seam, making the shocking sea dragon tattoo impossible to miss. This was a calculated move; after Phillip's last foray into the print media, Britt's publicist had issued a statement disclaiming any photo in which Britt's tattoos were not clearly visible.

He bypassed the onlookers on the sidewalk and strode straight to the front door, which was gladly opened for him. Immediately every cell in his body was assaulted by the pounding music, pulsing lights, and sheer sexual energy emanating from the place. Within two minutes, he had made his way to the bar and had a drink in his hand, which he knocked back at once.

Flashing a wicked grin at the people who were pressed closest to him, he placed both hands on the top of the bar and launched himself onto it, standing high above the crowd. Getting his photo bounced around on the Internet didn't require the paparazzi; these days, all it took was an anxious guy with a cell phone device. Britt scanned the room until a familiar beautiful face returned his smile, and he tilted his right hand in her direction—a request for her to wait for him where she stood. After calculating the trajectory from the tallest cell phone addict to his target, he sprang off the bar and cut straight through the crowd, deliberately brushing against the tall guy with the cell.

"Oh, sorry, man," he shouted into the guy's ear. "Crazy crowd tonight."

Banking on the guy following him, Britt continued a swift course until he reached the woman on whom he'd set his sights. Gathering her up in his arms, his face set in a smoldering glare, he danced with the woman for just long enough to make sure the guy got an unmistakable shot. Usually several people snapped photos, but Britt left nothing to chance.

Twelve minutes after entering the front door, Britt hit the back door, where his driver was waiting. He repeated a variation of this performance countless times throughout the night, until exhaustion drove him home.

The party crowd was thrilled to have Britt Jordan back. The online gossip sites lit up quickly with the juiciest dirt in town.

For Britt, it was a waltz through pure hell.

The very next day, there was an interesting photo of Britt in the tabloids. It was very innocent, actually: Britt talking with Darrell, his arm across his assistant's shoulders. Ordinarily, the photograph would have been rejected by the tabloids. However, with the public clamoring for more dirt on Britt, the gossip sheets were able to make something quite disgusting out of this pose.

Dena pulled up the photo on the web and magnified it on the screen. Aggravated, she left her office in such a hurry that she nearly gave Len the slip. Since it was the last day of school, she'd had Len pick up Bonnie early. She intended to be at home when Britt returned in the afternoon.

"Again, Mr. Jordan." Gregory Marcello's voice was flat, with a hint of impatience. There was no sympathy in it whatsoever.

Britt closed his eyes and tried to give the man what he wanted. Again and again. It was grueling.

"Your voice has the capability. Do you have the will to attain it? Then show me."

Britt's voice would not cooperate. His head was splitting. His shoulders were beginning to hurt from the tension. And his mind was on Dena.

His wife did not know he'd been visiting New York for the past three weeks. She thought he'd been staying in his studio in California. He had gambled a dangerous game, staking his reputation that the monster would read every online gossip column, hedging his bets that Dena wouldn't. Yet despite the online chatter, he had no certainty that his message had gotten through to Dena's would-be killer.

Now, after six lessons with Marcello, he had nothing concrete to show for his time. He dreaded confronting Dena with his deception.

"You are not concentrating, Mr. Jordan." Gregory saw a flash of anger in his student's eyes. Ah, he had at last reached the man's limit.

Britt brought his hands up behind his head and twisted back and forth a few times, then put his hands in his pockets. "You are absolutely right, Mr. Marcello. May we start at the beginning, please?"

Gregory's face twitched. "Of course. As you wish. Take your hands out of your pockets and remember your breathing."

"Yes, sir."

Three hours after leaving Gregory Marcello's studio, Britt stepped off a leased Leer jet onto the tarmac of the Lake Norman airport. In an effort to remain incognito, he had instructed Eddie to house his recognizable Gulfstream at the Charlotte airport. Instead, he'd been flying the small, nondescript Leer. An equally nondescript car and driver were waiting for him, and Britt ran across the airstrip toward it, his hair hidden under a ball cap. Just in the few seconds he was outside, he could tell it was hot. Miserably hot. This was not California heat. This Southern air was heavy, sticky. And it didn't do his headache any good.

Britt kept his eyes shut and his head down until the car pulled up to his house some twenty minutes later. There was Dena in the yard, working like a farmer, her gloves and hat lying forgotten under a tree. She was wearing very short shorts and a button-up blouse, sleeves rolled up. She was trying to move the unwieldy soil with a shovel, arms straining as she pushed on the blade with her foot. There was no reason for her to be doing that, none whatsoever.

He stepped out of the car. The heat hit his pounding head immediately.

"Dena," he called across the yard, "why in the hell don't you hire a gardener?"

——CHAPTER——

TWENTY

Dena dropped the shovel when she heard Britt yell across the yard, and she turned and faced him, hands on her hips. Sweat was running down her arms, smearing patches of dirt stuck to her skin. "What's it to you?" she called back.

"You are a rich woman. You don't have to grub in the dirt."

"I happen to enjoy it. I find it a most pleasant, relaxing occupation," she responded, her hands still on her hips. "Why don't you get your sorry butt over here and see for yourself?"

She saw him wince. He knew he was in trouble when she reverted to Southern slang.

Still, he proceeded. "I don't enjoy grubbing in dirt."

"How do you know? You've never tried it."

Britt rubbed his forehead. "Are we having an argument?"

"I'm sure the neighbors will think so."

"Dena, I apologize. Really." He pulled at his collar. "How can you stand this darned heat? And where is Len?"

She looked at him but did not answer.

"I'll tell you what," he said. "Give me a few minutes to change clothes and take a couple of aspirins, and then I'll give grubbing a try." He started for the door.

"Wait!" commanded Dena.

He stopped without turning around.

"Turn around. I want to get a good look at you," she said.

He did as he was told with military precision.

She pushed her sunglasses on top of her head and looked him over. He hadn't slept; she could tell from the weary lines around his eyes. And he had that twitchy adrenaline thing going on again.

"Hold out your hand," she commanded.

"Which one?"

"Either. Please." When he stuck out both arms, she saw that his hands were shaking. "Britt," she said, "have you eaten anything today?"

He opened his mouth, and then closed it. Looked up to the right. He had no idea.

"I made pimento cheese; it's in the fridge in a white bowl. Fix yourself a sandwich," she told him.

She watched as he clicked his heels, turned, and marched up the steps. After three months of marriage to the man, she was just getting a handle on his odd body rhythms. It occurred to her that in some very basic ways, Darrell had probably been a better wife to Britt than she was.

Dena put the shovel aside and stripped off her gardening shirt, under which she was wearing a bathing suit top. After rinsing her face and arms with the hose, she set to work weeding a long-untended flower garden.

She looked up to see her husband standing on the steps of the house, shirtless, lighting a cigarette as he watched her. That was a first. He kept a pack in the drawer with his undershorts, but she had never actually seen him light one. When he started toward her, she asked, "Did you eat something?"

"That cheese stuff you made didn't look edible," he stated.

Apparently he was serious. Another first. Any previous commentary on her Southern cooking had always been accompanied by a wink.

As he walked closer, he said, "I had a chunk of unadulterated cheese and a pear; thank you for asking."

He came to a halt directly across the flower bed from her, and she squinted up at him, looking into the sun. Perhaps it was because his face was in shadow, but he had a rocker's hard, road-weary look to him today. He was studying her through narrowed eyes above his cigarette, closely assessing her, it seemed. *Well*, she thought, *if you want to know my mood, Mr. Jordan, just stick around.*

He squatted opposite her, the flower bed between them, just as a breeze began to stir from the lake. "Is there something on your mind?" he asked.

"You've been in the tabloids again," she said, slamming a weed against the ground to shake the dirt off its roots.

"Yes, I know that."

"The photo of the week is of you and Darrell," she said, pulling up another weed.

"Yes, I know," he said.

"When was it taken?" she asked.

"Last week."

She looked him in the eye. "I want to get something straight between us. You do not have to explain to me where you go or why. But you led me to believe you have been in California. That photograph was not taken in California. There were eastern deciduous trees in the background."

Britt nodded his head slightly, not taking his eyes from her face.

"If you don't want me to know where you're going, that's okay. I assume you have your reasons. But don't let me believe you're somewhere you're not, Britt. You deceived me, and I don't appreciate it."

His answer was to take another drag of his cigarette. He had yet to pull the first weed.

Dena returned to her furious attack on the weeds and asked, "Do you not agree?"

"Well, the thing is, I deceived you deliberately."

She stopped and looked at him, perplexed.

"This is difficult for me to explain," said Britt.

"Well, try. I'm all ears," she said, pulling at the weeds again.

"Okay. I was in New York," he said.

"All three trips?"

"Yes."

"Business or pleasure?" she asked.

"Dena," he reproached her.

"Excuse me," she said sweetly. "Do you wish to reveal your business in New York?"

"I'm trying to." He took a deep breath and said quickly, "I'm seeing a voice coach."

"Good," said Dena.

Britt leaned forward and pulled at a few weeds. There was silence between them as Dena continued her battle with the tenacious plants. Finally, she said, "I really don't see the mystery, Britt. I mean, I think it's terrific that you're working on your voice, but I don't understand why you'd deceive me."

"It's hard to explain," admitted Britt. "This was something I had to do for myself, and I wanted to tackle it with everything in me. I thought that by today, after six lessons, I could say to you, 'Dena, I have a new voice,' or 'Dena, my voice is totally shot.' As it is, I don't know any more than I did three weeks ago, and I am pretty annoyed with myself."

"In other words," she said as she reached behind her for a trowel and waged a heavy ground attack on a stubborn root, "you've held this secret hope in your heart that you might someday sing again, yet you deliberately withheld it from me."

"That pretty well says it."

She looked across the flower bed at him. He took one last drag, having smoked the cigarette down to the filter, and stubbed it out. When he held his hand out in front of her, it was no longer shaking.

"It's complicated to explain," he said. "I don't want my voice back. I want a new voice, and I want to write new music. A whole different style. I didn't want to talk about it until I was certain it was going to happen. Now I still don't know."

"Britt, honey, you go about things the hard way," she said. "You've gone to a lot of trouble to hide this from me, when all you had to do was tell me. I could have hoped right along with you. Two hopes can make a big difference."

"You're so wise," he said.

"You're so sorry," she rejoined. "Look at your pile of weeds and look at mine."

"I'm not into weeds," he grumbled.

"Tough. This is your punishment." She pointed at his side of the flower bed. "You missed one there." She moved farther down the row and paused to wipe sweat from her forehead. "But think about it," she continued. "If you haven't resigned yourself to your voice being shot, then there's still hope."

Britt smiled and made an effort to increase his pile of weeds.

A butterfly flew between them, and she watched it land on a yellow dandelion. "Why did you need Darrell in New York?" she asked.

"I didn't."

There was a long silence. Finally, she blurted, "I declare, sometimes you are so hard to talk to."

"I don't mean to be," he said humbly.

"Well, are you going to tell me why he was there, or is it none of my business?"

"I don't mind telling you . . . it's just a bit personal." He reached for her trowel and made a stab at the dandelion, sending the butterfly fluttering away. "This yellow flower's pretty," he said. "Why don't you just plant the whole flower bed in them and forget about it?"

She threw a chunk of dirt at him.

He looked her in the eye. "Darrell came to New York to turn in his resignation."

"I'm so sorry. What happened?"

"Nothing. That's the problem. The boy doesn't think I want him anymore."

"Well, give him something to do." She pointed at the dandelion. "How does he feel about weeds?"

Britt chuckled. "You could hire a busload of gardeners for what I pay Darrell."

"What's he good at?" she asked.

"Handling me."

She glanced up at him. "The tabloids would just love to get hold of that statement!"

"You know what I mean. He's kept me going in the right direction for nine years. Made sure I didn't get lost." Leaning across the flower bed, Britt puckered his lips at Dena. "Fortunately, he wasn't doing his job the night I met you."

She pointed at the weeds again. "You can't do two things at once, can you?"

Britt sat back and delicately picked at a tiny plant. "And he nagged me all the time, like a good wife should," he said slyly.

Dena pursed her lips. "Is that the real reason he's quitting? Because I've taken his place as your wife?"

Britt burst into laughter. "I'm going to tell him you said that; he'll think it's hilarious." More seriously, he added. "Darrell needs to be needed. I've asked him to stay on for awhile and give me time to get myself organized. If my plan works, and I get a new start on my career, I want him to be my new producer."

"Darrell knows music?" she asked.

"Sure. He plays a mean bass guitar. And he's hung around me for long enough to know all the ropes. He knows what needs to be done and how to get it done. He'd be quite good at it, with me to help him."

She looked into his eyes. "You really love him, don't you?"

"Uh, well, yeah. He's like a brother. Beats the heck out of the one I've got." Britt stabbed at the ground with his trowel.

Exasperated, she pointed at the ground between them. "Look, I keep having to do half your side and all of mine. If you can't do any better, head on into the house."

He promptly stood up, brushed off the back of his shorts, and marched toward the house without another word.

"You come back here!" she shouted after him.

He turned, chuckling. "I enjoyed that," he said.

"Do you really hate this?" she asked.

"Yes, I do. I hate it," he answered. "Why don't you at least get a high school kid to help you with the heavy work?"

She sighed. "That high school kid thing didn't work out too well in Deerfield."

"Oh, was that who you fired? That high school girl?" he asked.

"Yeah."

He thought about that for a few seconds. "That kid didn't have her own key to our house, did she?" he asked.

"Of course not." Dena decided not to bother him with the detail that Bonnie had loaned Rhiannon her key the day of the undershorts incident. After the house was bombed, getting the key back from the girl had pretty much become a moot subject.

She stood up. "Speaking of heavy work, see that camellia right there? It needs to be over here."

He walked over to the camellia and inspected it. "You mean this bush here? It looks fine where it is."

"No, it doesn't," she argued. "It needs to be moved."

"And I suppose you want me to move it for you?"

"Yeah, while you're in the mood."

He pronounced each word slowly. "But . . . I'm . . . not . . . in . . . the . . . mood."

"Sure you are." She handed him the shovel. "You can tell me about your voice lessons while you dig."

"I don't want to. It's depressing." He examined the shovel very carefully, as if he could get out of the job if he found a defect.

She folded her arms, containing her impatience. "Then tell me what you did between lessons."

"I practiced." Studiously, he put the point of the shovel to the soil.

Dena grunted with exasperation. "Day and night? I know you, Britt Jordan. You did not sit in some hotel and hold hands with yourself."

Britt put his weight into making the first slice with the shovel. "You're right; I didn't sit in a hotel. I have my own apartment in New York."

Her mouth dropped in astonishment. "You've never told me that!"

He rubbed his left arm, smearing dirt over his tattoo.

"Britt, are you going to dig this hole or aren't you?"

With a grimace, he made another slice with the shovel.

"Why haven't you told me about your apartment?" she asked.

In a quiet voice, he answered, "It's one of many things I try to forget."

She watched him for a moment as he continued to dig. "Make the hole a little deeper," she said. "I'm going to bring the hose around and start filling it with water when you're done."

When she returned, he was standing still, frowning at her. "Aren't you going to ask me what I did at night?"

"What did you do at night, Britt?"

"You won't believe me if I tell you."

Only the whoosh of the water filling the hole could be heard until Dena turned the hose full-blast on Britt's stomach. His yell could be heard halfway across the lake.

"What was that for?" he demanded.

"For being so darned hard to talk to," she said.

"Well, I don't think you're showing enough concern over how I spent my nights," he answered.

"How did you spend your nights?" she asked again.

"Put that hose down, and I'll tell you." He shouldered the shovel like a rifle and marched over to the camellia. "Is this the bush you want moved?"

"It's a camellia."

"Whatever." He jabbed the shovel into the ground next to the shrub. "I amused myself," he stated. And then he looked up at her, his eyes dead serious.

Suddenly Dena had an uneasy feeling in the pit of her stomach that his deception had involved more than a voice coach. She watched him make a couple of cuts with the shovel. His jaw was clenched, and she didn't think it was from the manual labor.

Finally he spoke, his head down as if he were concentrating on digging. "I know a guy who runs a small recording studio, and I called him my first night in New York. His equipment is a little dated, but his rates are reasonable, so a lot of groups who are starting out use him. He let me come in as a pick-up player, like studios did back in the sixties and seventies."

"You mean Britt Jordan played for some unknown band? That must have been a hoot!"

"Yeah. The poor guys kept waiting for me to tell them what to do, and I was just there to play guitar." He dug once more with the shovel. "Is this deep enough?"

"Not quite," she answered. "You need to get the whole root ball."

"Heaven forbid we leave that behind," he said. "Anyway, it was while I was playing that I ran into Lori Sink, if you've been wondering about that photo of us walking along a sidewalk."

She was shocked, and she stared hard at him. "I thought that was an old photograph."

"No, it was taken that first night I was in New York. Word gets around among musicians, who's where doing what, and she showed up when she heard I was playing."

"Did she stay?"

His face reddened a little. "No. After an argument you really don't want to know about, I did walk her out and hail a taxi, which was when that photo was snapped." He glanced at her face and added quickly, "Hey, you're the one who called me a gentleman. I was trying to act like one."

"You weren't wearing your wedding band in that picture."

Softly, he said, "I hate that apartment. It reminds me of things about myself I wish I could forget. I haven't been there since . . ." He stopped and bit his lip. ". . . since last June. The

230

only reason I used it this time was because I needed the piano to practice my voice lessons. And it nearly froze my soul to be there. There was nothing of you in the whole place." He looked into her eyes. "I left my ring so the apartment would be warmer when I got back."

She looked away and made no response.

He lifted the camellia onto the burlap Dena had laid at the edge of the hole. Together, they dragged it across the yard. Carefully, words spoken distinctly, he said, "That's what I did on Tuesday nights. I showed up at the studio and played guitar."

Now Dena was the one who quit working. "I'm getting a sick feeling," she said, "that I don't want to hear what you did on Wednesday nights."

Britt bent over and picked up the camellia, set it in the hole. When he straightened up, he looked her squarely in the eyes. "Please stay with me while I try to explain. I went club-hopping."

"Okay," she said slowly.

He took a deep breath, and it seemed like he was having a tough time saying the words. "I was trying to . . . trying to make the lunatic think that I had left you."

She caught on quickly. "So what you're saying is that if I typed your name into a search engine, I'd see pictures of you partying all over Manhattan without your wedding ring."

"Exactly," he said. "It was intentional."

She took a step back, clicked her tongue before speaking. "Let me see if I've got this straight. You made this decision involving your public character, and now the whole world thinks I can't keep my man. And it never even occurred to you to run it by me before you did it."

He rubbed his chest and frowned. Switching gears, he asked, with a hint of panic in his voice, "Where's Len?"

"Don't change the subject," she stated flatly. "I'm not through talking about this."

Picking up the shovel, he began moving dirt into the hole around the camellia. The sick look on his face matched the sick feeling she had in the pit of her stomach.

"Here's what I think," she began, trying not to sound angry. She simply wanted to give him the facts as she saw them. "What we have here is an accountability issue. Look, I know that you are who you are, and you need the freedom to go off and be creative without your wife looking over your shoulder. I get that." She put her hands on her hips. "But you have messed with my repu-tation for three weeks without telling me. And you should have explained that photo of you and Lori Sink the day it came out."

He dropped the shovel and closed the distance between them. His words were clipped, his voice low and serious. "I was not entirely unaccountable," he said. "The night after our home was bombed, I tracked Lori Sink down, just to settle in my own mind that she didn't do it."

Dena's mouth dropped open.

"When you saw the photo of me dancing with her, what you didn't see was Charlie hanging close-by. I took Charlie with me, so that there'd be no misunderstanding my intentions. And over the past few weeks, I sent Charlie a text every night that I was in New York so that someone besides Len knew what I was doing."

She stared at him incredulously, turned away from him to face the lake, trying to absorb his words. Just then, Len came into view, walking along the seawall, tracking a fishing boat as it motored out of the deep cove. A second boat seemed to be tracking it also, a boat she had seen come and go every day.

Suddenly, the pins began to drop into place, and she turned back toward her husband to see the truth etched in the weary lines of his face. Quietly she asked, "You've had some sort of communication from the bomber, haven't you?"

"Yes." He paused before adding, "The day after we moved in. I didn't want you to know, Dena. I didn't want you to be afraid."

"What . . . what did the lunatic say?"

"I'd rather not tell you," he answered, his voice still very low. "Please, Dena, if you trust me, just let me do what I can to keep you safe." There was another long pause before he added, "And now that Bonnie is out of school, there's something else I need to ask you to do."

She turned from him again, looking out at the lake, the familiar boat on the water, Len. Thinking about the slight catch of panic in his voice just now, when he'd thought Len had gone missing, she glanced at the beautiful home that he had sacrificed so much to attain for them. It was all starting to make sense to her now, and it was obvious what he was going to ask next.

And she had a choice. She could insist on going to work, making her husband sick with worry. She could stay home, which she knew he was going to ask her to do, and be resentful. Or she could simply lean into the gift of safety he was offering her.

Dena looked Britt over once more. In some everyday ways, being married to him was a bit like raising a ten-year-old. But when she stepped back and looked at the big picture, he had an extraordinary gift for marriage. An extraordinary gift.

Suddenly she kicked off her shoes. "I know what you're going to ask," she said, "but I need to process all this before I answer. In the meantime . . ." She glanced once more at his tired face, the sweat that had started dripping off his chin. "You asked how we Southerners stand this heat. Take your shoes off, and I'll show you."

As he toed off his shoes, she started running across the yard, past Len, down the long dock toward the lake, where two armed men in a boat looked on from a distance. With a skip in her stride, she planted her feet on the end of the dock and dove smartly into the water.

When her husband stepped off the end of the dock and plunged feet-first into the water a minute later, she was ready for him, hanging from a brace underneath the dock by her arms. She gave him time to surface and draw a breath, and then she grabbed him around the waist with her legs and dragged him under the dock with her.

The light beneath the dock was green and the air was cool, slightly fishy. In this light, he looked more like a tired, relieved husband than a hardened rocker. She spoke, her lips against his ear, "Welcome home, honey. You know, we Southern gals keep a few tricks handy to cool down hot-blooded boys like you."

CHAPTER

TWENTY-ONE

"Yes, I am very pleased with the way this project turned out." The voice coming from the television was polished and professional, a young woman's voice. Dena did not look up from tying her shoelaces to see the face that belonged to the voice. Instead she glanced out toward the lake sparkling beyond the trees. She and Bonnie were going sailing with Britt this morning, and the day promised to be sunny.

"Hey, I'm ready," Bonnie's voice called from the bottom of the steps. "What's taking y'all so long?"

"We're coming," Dena called back. "Make sure to put on plenty of sunscreen."

Dena brushed her hair, pulled it back in a ponytail, and searched her walk-in closet for a hat. She heard the interviewer ask the young woman about her role in the television movie that would be shown that night, but all Dena was interested in hearing right then was the weather broadcast. Hat in hand, she walked back into the bedroom and grabbed the remote to flip the channel. At that moment, she heard the interviewer say,

"And now I understand that there's something new you've been working on. Don't look so mysterious, Lori. Tell us about it."

Dena looked at the TV screen for the first time to see Lori Sink's face, bigger than life, her lips upturned in a catty, secretive smile. The young woman's tousled blonde hair gave her the look of someone who had just tumbled out of bed.

"I've found that I enjoy acting so much," Lori was saying, "that when I was offered a role that would give me the opportunity to combine my singing and acting skills, I jumped at the chance. Of course, we haven't started production yet on this new movie. We're having a little trouble convincing the one guy who is perfect for the role to be the leading man."

"And who might that be?" asked the interviewer.

"Why, Britt Jordan, of course."

The interviewer's face revealed both surprise and amusement. "What makes you think Britt would be interested?"

"Oh, he's interested, all right," said Lori, running her tongue along her lips, her eyes half-closed.

Just then, Britt walked into the room from the outside deck. "Oh hell, what now?" he said, reaching for the TV remote. Dena held it away from him.

Lori continued, "Britt came all the way to New York just to see me last month. A guy with as much energy as Britt—wow! He's gotta have something to plug all that energy into . . . my movie." Her voice matched her smile, secretive, seductive. "Maybe something else."

"Like what?" asked the interviewer.

"Anything but marriage," she answered slyly. "Britt can't even say the word monogamy."

With a touch of his finger, Britt killed the television. He looked at Dena, rubbing his chest, waiting for her response.

She asked pleasantly, "Was a single word of that true?"

"The part about monogamy was the biggest lie ever told," he answered.

"That's what I figured," she said. "Come on, skipper; let's go sailing."

There had been no additional communication from the lunatic or suspicious activity. Yet, even though this early June day was sunny, the breeze exhilarating, the boat quick, and the crew amiable, Britt could not let down his guard. He eyed every approaching boat with suspicion. When one man waved as if in recognition, Britt brought the sloop about, using the mainsail to hide Dena and Bonnie.

"We're going to have to sail at night or wear disguises," he grumbled.

"A disguise?" asked Bonnie in delight. "Even me?"

"Especially you," said Britt with a wink.

They claimed a little island for themselves, spread out their blankets and lunched and drowsed the noon hour away in the shade. The hum of passing motorboats and the chatter of leaves shivering in the breeze over their heads lulled Britt into an uncommon laziness. Lying facedown on the blanket, he finally murmured, "Anybody ready for more sailing?"

"I think my freckled child has had enough sun for one day," said Dena, sitting up and yawning. "Let's sail again in the morning."

"What will we do this afternoon?" asked Britt lazily.

"Work on my studio," broke in Bonnie. She sat up quickly and began packing the picnic basket.

"What?" Britt rose up on one elbow.

"I sketched it out last night," said Bonnie. "There's enough space in that storage room behind the garage for me to work. If you'll help me move that old work table that's in there and throw away some of the junk, and if Mama will move her rakes and things . . ."

"Whoa," said Britt, sitting up. "I thought you were going to use the bay window in your bedroom as a painting area."

"There's not enough room, and besides, I keep splattering the window," she retorted.

"But that storage room is too dark, honey," said Dena.

"Not if Britt knocks out the wall and puts in a sliding door," said Bonnie. Her blue eyes searched Britt's hopefully.

He jumped to his feet. "You would trust me with such a major remodeling project?" he shouted.

"Yeah," Bonnie said with a giggle.

"Why are you still sitting there? Get in the boat, and fire up the engine!" He splashed out into the water, getting his shorts wet, and heaved himself on board. Dena and Bonnie paused to roll up their shorts, and then followed carefully, Dena holding the blankets and Bonnie carrying the basket over her head.

When they returned home, Dena went inside to make lemonade, and Britt ran next door to borrow a sledge hammer from their neighbor. He was on his way back, the heavy hammer slung over one shoulder, chuckling as he watched Bonnie fling stuff out of the storage room, when his cell phone chirped. It was an email from his secretary, Phyllis, which read:

Britt, You all need to come back to California. I'm really worried. P.

With a sigh of defeat, Britt opened the attachment. As before, Phyllis had scanned a handwritten note that had arrived with the fan mail.

Britt, I'm at my limit. You've been partying with other women. I don't like that. You're supposed to be with a blonde. I want you back. Why won't you tell me where you live? The sooner I see you with her, the sooner I can kill her and take her place. You will never regret it.

Britt stood still for a long time, fear prickling the back of his neck. It wasn't over.

Who could it be? Britt read over the note again. *I want you back . . . You will never regret it.* He knew any number of women, so that didn't help narrow it down any. But only one of the women he knew also had a key to his car. Lori Sink. She definitely wanted him back, and she was blonde. But the night that Britt had tracked Lori down, she hadn't appeared to be hiding some monstrous secret, certainly not one as big as bombing his house.

Of course, this kook could be a stranger, someone with a vivid imagination, someone with no other access to Britt beyond his fan mail. But the more he thought about it, the less likely that seemed. Whoever the lunatic was, she had known the exact day he and Dena had moved in together and the exact day they'd moved out of the old house.

At least, she didn't know where they lived now. Not yet, anyway.

Britt sent the email along to Len. His bodyguard would shoot it to the Deerfield police chief, along with the suggestion that Lori Sink should be questioned again.

That evening, Britt and Dena sat on the deck watching the lightning bugs twinkle like effervescent stars in the trees. A warm, comforting breeze stirred from the lake, bringing the cheerful song of tree frogs chirping. Twice Britt got up and walked the perimeter of the property.

When he returned to the deck the second time, Dena caught his hand before he could sit down. "Why are you so jumpy?" she asked.

"*I'm jumpin' all over for the woman I love,*" he sang, dancing in place in front of her.

"Silly," she chided him affectionately. "Something's on your mind. What is it?"

He swallowed. So far, she'd been safe here, in this house. There was no real reason to tell her about today's note from the lunatic.

She looked closely at his face. "Has something else happened that you're not telling me about?"

"Not knowing who this monster is makes me nuts, that's all," he said smoothly. "I guess I'll just be a bit kooky until they're behind bars."

She stood up, gave him a pat on the behind, and started inside.

"Where are you going?" he asked.

"To kiss Bonnie goodnight. I'll be back."

"Kiss her for me too. Wait a minute, Dena." He pulled her back. "I think we need a dog."

"A dog!" In the soft light coming from inside the house, he could see her smile crook sideways, as if she were thinking, *Now what?* "What brought this on?"

"A guard dog," he stated.

Dena sighed. "First a bodyguard, then a boat in the water, now a guard dog. Listen, I don't want some guard dog that's going to turn on Bonnie or me. Do you understand?"

"You knew how to handle that dog in your backyard," he said.

"Well, go buy Brandy then." She turned abruptly and went inside.

Ten minutes later when she stepped back on the deck, he said, "I'll go tomorrow."

"Go where?"

"To buy that dog from your neighbor." His voice rose with the impatience of a ten-year-old kid.

She stood over him, gesturing for emphasis. "Britt, I was kidding about Brandy."

"I'm buying that dog." He clicked a note of finality inside his cheek.

She gave his ponytail a yank. "You're driving me nuts," she said. "Take your boat out for a few minutes; maybe that will calm you down."

"Can't do it," he said, shaking his head. "I don't love that boat. She won't tell me her name, and besides, her lights don't work. I got a warning ticket the other night." He pulled Dena into his lap with a mischievous laugh. "I guess you'll have to be my entertainment tonight."

She let his hair down and ran both hands through it, her fingers sending a delicious tingle across his scalp. "Too bad for the boat," she said.

Sometime after midnight, Britt slipped out of bed. He stood and watched his wife sleep, her face peaceful in the moonlight. In his mind, his life with her was one continuous song, a simple melody with a complicated harmony. The song flowed between them daily, the most beautiful thing he had ever heard, and yet there were times when he realized his part was out of tune.

Discordant.

He did not know why.

Britt studied his dreaming wife. Everything about her life exuded harmony and purpose. Britt's greatest fear was the discontent that gnawed at his heart at times, like now, trying to take the harmony away from him, trying to pull his life out of tune. How well he knew his own restless spirit.

He was fighting with everything he had not to shatter the life he had made with her. Yet the secrets and memories that stabbed at his heart overwhelmed him still. The truth was, he needed her peace more than she needed him.

And he didn't know what to do about that.

Dena would try to explain her peace by quoting something from the Bible, that much he knew. But the shipwreck of his heart couldn't be fixed by Dena's God. Such a thing was impossible for a man like him. Impossible. He would have to take his own life in hand and put it back in tune.

Dena awoke at three a.m. to the sound of Britt's piano filling the house with indescribably complicated music.

On Monday morning, Dena tried to slip out early without waking her family. She had a publisher's meeting in Charlotte and wanted to get on the road before the traffic got too heavy. Len had gone ahead earlier to check the place out and would be meeting her there. She wasn't even aware that Britt was awake until he came bounding down the steps, grabbed her keys from her hand, and ran out the door.

"I'll drive your car around for you," he called over his shoulder. "Just wait there."

She waited about a minute. When she didn't hear the car start, she headed for the garage. What she saw would change her heart forever.

Britt was sliding out from under the car just as she turned the corner. He stood up, reached inside the car, and tentatively turned the key in the ignition. When the car roared to life, he jumped back as if shocked. She knew in an instant. He'd been worried that her car might be wired with explosives. The image of Britt turning the key that way would never leave her memory. She wiped away the tears that sprang to her eyes as he got into the car.

Britt caught her watching him in the rear-view mirror as he started to back out. He took his time turning the car around, his face unreadable. She watched him closely until he finally stepped out of the driver's seat.

The look in his eyes nearly took her breath away. There was that dogged determination that sometimes made her nuts, only now it was directed toward her with the keen force of pure kindness. They held each other close, and then Dena got into her car and drove through the gate. Neither of them had spoken a word.

When Dena returned home late that evening, she found a new addition to the family. Apparently, Britt had managed to talk her former neighbor into selling his dog.

"Poor Brandy," she said when the Rottweiler met her in the garage. "What have they done to you? Are you lost?" The dog, of course, looked quite dejected at being uprooted from her home.

"Come on, let's see if we can find you some supper," Dena said to the dog. "I hate to tell you this, but it's my fault you're here." She led the dog around to the deck where Britt was grilling two fine bass amid splashes of lemon juice and garlic butter. He and Bonnie must have found time to do some fishing in addition to adopting a dog.

"Britt, this is pathetic," Dena began as she stepped onto the deck, the dog at her heels. "You have torn this poor dog from her home and set her down in the middle of nowhere. See how sad she is?"

"She likes it here," said Britt, eyeing the dog warily. "This is a major improvement over being cooped up with your fruitcake ex-neighbor, believe me."

"Speaking of neighbors, have you asked our new neighbor whether he minds having a dog in his yard?" Dena sat down, and the dog put her head on her knee.

"He shouldn't complain," said Britt. "He's getting a free guard dog."

Dena laughed. "Guard dog? Look at her. She doesn't even know where she is, let alone what she's supposed to be guarding."

"Think not? Watch this." Britt walked over to where Bonnie sat and reached out his hand as if to touch her. The dog lifted its head and growled a warning.

Dena laughed again. "Have you always had this much trouble getting along with dogs?"

"No, just this one. As long as she does her job, she can growl at me all she likes."

"You're going to think differently when she leaves her dentures in our neighbor's backside," said Dena.

Britt chuckled as he sprinkled parsley on the fish. "I'm telling you, the dog is better off with us."

"You could be right," she admitted. "Her former owner was a pretty strange fellow."

"Strange doesn't begin to cover him. The man has an arsenal in his house. I mean, automatic weapons, the kind used in the military. He kept trying to hand them to me to sight down the barrels. When I tried to explain that having been on the wrong end of a gun puts a whole new perspective to things, he called me a wuss." Britt pointed at his chest, exaggerated indignation on his face. "Can you believe it? Me! I'd like to see him stand in front of a few thousand people and shake his buns."

Dena sputtered into laughter, causing the dog to lift its head from her knee and look searchingly into her eyes. She asked with a cackle, "Did you try to save face by telling him you'd been in the Army?"

"Exactly," said Britt. "Big mistake. He wanted to hear all about it. I hated to disappoint him, but all I did was load ammunition—or sometimes unload it when it failed to discharge, which got a little hairy." Britt shook his right hand and kissed it, as if he was happy to have all his fingers intact. "He still thought I was a wuss. Had to tell me all about blowing up stuff in the desert in Iraq. I thought I would never get away from him. Finally I just had to take my dog in hand and leave." Britt popped a piece of fish in his mouth and gave Bonnie a thumbs up. "Actually, Bonnie took the dog in hand, but that's beside the point."

"How did you get the dog home?" asked Dena.

"My new truck," said Britt with pride. "Didn't you see it parked beside the garage?"

"You bought a truck to haul one dog fifty miles?" she asked in disbelief.

"Of course not. I bought it for you to haul bushes and such in." He looked at Dena wisely. "You need a truck if you're going to live in the country."

"Britt Jordan driving a truck!" Dena leaned forward to laugh. The dog licked the side of her face.

Britt transferred the fish to a platter. "When you're through laughing at me, come inside for supper." He sidestepped the dog and walked into the house, followed by Bonnie, who gave the dog a pat as she passed.

Dena was left to collect herself. "Well, Brandy," she told the dog, "your new master is a different kind of nut from your old one. Try to be nice to him, okay? He's the good guy, I promise." The dog gave one small wag of her tail. "Maybe it will help if he brings your supper." She started for the door. "Just keep in mind that he's not the supper."

—— CHAPTER ——
TWENTY-TWO

B ritt stood in Gregory Marcello's studio, surveying the city through the window. The day was fair and breezy, and he could spot sailboats on the river in the distance. He rocked up on his toes. It felt good knowing that Dena was thinking of him right at this moment, hoping his lesson would go well. *If only Marcello would get here*, he thought.

Britt turned quickly from the window. People rarely kept him waiting. Seating himself at the piano, he began to play an impromptu musical dialogue that incorporated lines from show tunes and lines from operas. Broadway meets the Metropolitan Opera House.

Gregory Marcello himself despised being late. He pushed his way off the elevator rudely, hurrying toward his studio. He wasn't particularly anxious for his next lesson to begin, but he always made a point of being punctual.

As soon as he opened the door to the outer office, his ears were assaulted by a musical bombardment such as he had never heard before. "What is that? Who is that?" he asked the secretary he shared with the other studios in the suite.

"Your student, Mr. Jordan. He's been at it for nearly fifteen minutes. It's quite entertaining, once you catch on to what he's doing. It sounded like a most unholy racket at first."

Gregory stood still and listened. Within seconds, his trained ear picked up on the musical conversation that was taking place in the next room. What type of mind did it take to invent such a cacophony? A brief smile crossed his face before he walked through the door.

Crossing the studio floor, Gregory set his briefcase down before turning to stare at his pupil. The man was obviously enjoying himself, and his green eyes were sparkling with amusement. When Britt glanced up and caught Gregory watching him, he raised his eyebrows and finished out the line he had begun. Abruptly, he stood up.

"My apologies, Mr. Jordan. I was unavoidably detained."

"No problem. I'm finding these days that New York is best viewed from this angle, anyway," said Britt, nodding his head toward Gregory's window.

"Ah." Gregory walked over to the piano. Britt looked him in the eye. Never having smiled at his pupil before, the coach did not do so now. He did, however, reach out and touch Britt's neck. "Consciously relax these muscles, Mr. Jordan. They are suffering from the damage to your larynx." Gregory sat down at the piano. "Now take your hands out of your pockets and we'll begin."

"Phyllis, help me get a handle on this." Bob Johnson, Britt's agent, was pacing the floor of Britt's office in Los Angeles. "You say you're not sure that Britt's actually retired, yet you don't know if or when he plans to return to work."

Phyllis shuffled papers on her desk, looked harassed and flustered. "Sit down, you're making me dizzy," she said. Bob stopped pacing directly in front of her desk and stood there, running his hand through his hair. Phyllis continued, "I know the public is clamoring for Britt, but those of us who know him best can surely understand . . ."

"Understand! There's nothing to understand." Bob placed his hands on her desk and leaned forward. "A commodity like Britt can't afford to sit on his rump coddling his voice. It doesn't matter whether or not he wants to sing. He needs to be out there in front of the public. He needs to be on the talk show circuit."

"Bob," Phyllis tried to interrupt.

"He needs to write a book . . . Hell, I'll write it for him. I could get him on *Dancing with the Stars, American Idol . . .*"

This time Phyllis did interrupt. "Have you met Britt?" she asked sarcastically. "He wouldn't be interested in doing any of those things even if he hadn't retired."

"It doesn't matter what he's interested in! That's not my problem." Bob pointed a nail-bitten finger in her face. "My problem is that you're not telling me where he is."

Phyllis rolled her chair back a few inches. "Britt's just resting right now. He doesn't want to be disturbed."

"Disturbed! Let me tell you about disturbed." Bob wagged his finger at her. "I've got a movie producer on my ass day and night wanting to cast Britt as the lead in a major movie. What am I supposed to tell the man?" Spreading his arms wide, his coat opening to reveal his sagging belly, Bob shouted, "I don't even know where Britt is!"

Phyllis pushed her chair back another couple of inches. "Take a vacation before you have a stroke, for heaven's sake."

Bob snapped his fingers. "Do you know when this began?" he demanded. "He started losing it right when he met that woman."

Phyllis stood up, hands on her hips, her face contorted with rage. "Britt has had almost everything he cares about ripped out of his hands. His wife is the last bit of glue holding his mind together, and she's . . ." Phyllis stopped. Britt would fire her if she revealed anything about his situation. She pointed toward the door. "Get out, Bob," she said, her voice shaking. "When Britt wants you, he'll call you."

His face blotched purple with rage, Bob backed toward the door. "I'll find him myself," he shouted. "The hell with you!"

Britt came in from a morning sail in a mellow mood. Even this early in the day, he was finding there were too many speedboats and skiers on the water for sailing to be a pleasure. This morning, however, he had gotten on the water just after dawn, while mist still hovered over the water and the bass swirled and popped the surface greedily hunting breakfast. He had motored out to the widest part of the lake before killing the engine and letting the boat drift. The gurgle of water and the peaceful rosy hues of the morning sky had enticed him into letting go of some of his worries. Once the breeze finally began to stir, he had put the sloop under sail until boat traffic forced him to return home.

As soon as he set foot on the deck of his home, he was greeted by some interesting culinary odors. Peering through the French doors, he could see Dena in the kitchen chopping a roast of some sort at the butcher block. She was barefoot, wearing shorts, and her hair was pulled back in a ponytail. Soft tendrils of auburn hair had pulled loose from the ponytail and brushed her face as she worked. Her expression was content, peaceful. Glancing up, she saw him looking at her, and her face broke into a bright smile. Britt fell in love all over again.

As he stepped inside, she looked back down at her work, smiling, humming, "Happy Birthday to You." He crossed the room to stand beside her and helped himself to a chunk of roast.

"Mmm, what is that?" he asked.

"Pork shoulder," she answered, still chopping.

"Why are you chewing it up for us?" He pointed to her knife.

Her mouth twisted in amusement. "I'm making barbecue. That's how it's done. Check out the sauce on the stove."

He looked at the liquid simmering in the pot. So that was the pungent odor he smelled. He stirred the sauce, which looked and smelled like liquid fire. As he had seen Dena do, he lifted a few drops to his tongue with the handle of the spoon. "Yow! It bit me back!"

She nodded her head in approval. "Then I'd say it's about ready."

"Are you sure it's edible?" he asked, his mouth puckering.

"Well, of course it is. It's mostly vinegar and red pepper. You'll like it; I promise. I thought I'd cook a Southern meal for your birthday."

"What else are you cooking?" he asked, opening the refrigerator door and poking around inside.

"That's potato salad you just stuck your finger in," she said. "Ambrosia on the next shelf. And I'll chop slaw and do baked beans later."

He returned to his place beside her. When she didn't look up from her chopping, he bent down, his face level with the block.

251

"This is an awful lot of food for three people," he said.

She smiled slightly but didn't meet his eyes.

"Dena. Dena, look at me."

She just kept on chopping the roast, that mysterious smile on her face.

"Tell me you're not having a party for my birthday. Tell me you're not."

Her voice was soft as honey. "Whatcha got against parties, Britt?"

Panic began to rise in his throat. So far, hardly anyone knew where they were living. The less people who knew, the less likely someone, however innocently, would let it slip to the wrong person.

She glanced up and saw the strained tension around his eyes. "Relax. I'm not having a party." She tilted her head to one side. "I thought about it. Our lives have been so hectic, and almost none of my friends have met you. And we have this beautiful home, and it's such a shame we can't share it with anyone. But you've been so paranoid lately, I decided you wouldn't like it, and anyway . . ." A shadow crossed her face so quickly he almost missed it. ". . . I just decided against it." Her face brightened again. "But I have invited Charlie and Sue over for dinner, so we'll have a nice little choir to sing 'Happy Birthday.' Okay?"

Without comment, he opened the refrigerator door and poked around again. Then he peeked inside several cabinets.

"What are you looking for?" she asked.

"My birthday cake."

She chuckled. "I ordered a cake for you. Sue's bringing it this evening."

Disappointment pulled at his features. He bent down again so she could see.

Sputtering into laughter, she asked, "What's the matter?"

"Nobody has baked me a homemade cake since I was a kid. You're a mom, and I thought that was what moms did."

"You haven't had a cake in all these years?" she asked.

"Not a real one. Well, Darrell tried one time, but his was too pitiful to eat," pouted Britt.

"Well." She set down her knife. "What kind do you like?"

"Mom used to make one that was chocolatey and fruity. With nuts."

"With nuts," she repeated, her mouth twisting to one side.

"Don't get mad," he said.

"I'm not mad," said Dena. "I'm just perplexed because you usually turn up your nose at anything sweet, so I didn't think it mattered about the cake. Plus, I don't have a recipe like your mom's."

His face lit up. "So you'll do it?"

She shrugged. "Sure, if you'll get the recipe. I was going to help Bonnie clean the house, but she usually does fine without supervision."

Britt grinned. Bonnie, he had learned, supervised Dena when it came to housework.

Just minutes before their guests were due to arrive that evening, Dena ran upstairs to shower and slip into a knit T-shirt dress. Britt walked into the room just as she was walking out.

"You're going to have to take that dress off," he said matter-of-factly.

"Excuse me?"

"*Get naked, baby*," he sang raucously.

Dena crossed her arms. "I know it's your birthday, but really. We have guests coming."

With a grin, he reached under the bed and pulled out a wrapped package the size of a dress box. "I bought myself a present. Perhaps you'd like to open it for me."

She shook her head, smiling.

He opened it quickly and pulled out an emerald green dress. "What I want for my birthday is to see you in this dress. I like you in green." he said simply.

She let him zip her into it, watching in the mirror. The dress flattered her figure perfectly—scooped neck, fitted bodice, flowing skirt. When she started to turn to face him, he stopped her. "There's something that goes with it," he said. Looking back in the mirror, she watched in awe as he slipped a necklace around her neck. Emeralds and diamonds, to match her wedding band.

"Britt, you shouldn't have!"

"Yes, I should have, and I'm glad I did. You look beautiful and happy, and that's the best birthday present I could hope for." He turned her around and looked her over, taking his time. "I know it's hard for you to believe after the debacle of our honeymoon, but I actually have a few real friends scattered around the globe. Soon, when I don't have to keep you sequestered here, it will be my great honor to introduce them to my beautiful wife."

She was still kissing him thank you when their guests arrived.

Charlie could play guitar a little, but he had never played bass. After dinner, while Dena was making coffee and cutting the cake, Britt plugged up his electric five-string bass and gave Charlie a quick lesson. "Just practice those few notes," he instructed. "We're going to make music history tonight."

Seeing the dumbfounded look on his friend's face, Britt slapped him on the back and said, "It'll be easy. You play each note as a chord change. If you can sing bass, you can play bass."

While Charlie practiced, Britt drew Sue out onto the deck. He didn't waste time on pleasantries, but got straight to the point. "If I ask you a hard question, will you give me a straight answer?" he said abruptly.

"Um, I guess if anyone will, I will," Sue replied.

He nodded his head once, pleased with her answer, and proceeded. "Are Dena's friends shunning her because of me?"

"Why would you think that?" she hedged, not answering.

"It was something Dena said, or *didn't* say, this morning." He shrugged. "She said she thought about having a party, and then decided against it. In between those two phrases was something she didn't say. I thought you might know what it was."

"You're very astute," Sue commented. The silence was heavy between them. Finally, she offered, "If Dena had a party, everyone would come and be very cordial to you. I mean, nobody in town has even stood this close to someone as famous as you." She gestured back and forth in the space between them. "You're very rich and powerful, and it would be a big deal to meet you."

He turned away and rested his forearms on the deck rail. "I know all this . . . I've been me for a long time." With a sideways glance at her, he said, "I asked about Dena."

Sue sighed. He was like a bulldog when he got something into his head. "You have to understand about small towns, Britt," she said, relenting. "Everybody knew and liked Johnny Martin. People have been very protective of Dena since he died, and they expected her to marry—I don't know, if not one of them, then somebody like them. It was a big shock when she suddenly married you."

Britt's jaw worked from side to side, but he stayed silent.

"I guess her friends considered it an insult that she didn't consult any of them before marrying you. And now they feel like you're keeping her away from them."

Looking down at his folded hands, Britt asked, "And so they do shun her?"

"Shun is a strong word . . . I wouldn't go so far as to say that. I do think people have been cool to Dena lately, though." Sue put her hand on his arm, the first time she had ever voluntarily touched him. "People have a certain image in their minds about you. I overheard a couple of guys talking about you the other day. Remember that world-wide stunt you pulled three years ago?"

Britt smiled ruefully. "Eight countries in twenty four hours. I played half-hour concerts in every continent except Antarctica. Only I was actually working for thirty-six hours, with the time changes."

"Do you remember what you said when you stepped off the stage after the eighth concert?" she asked, her voice quiet, insistent.

The silence between them was painful. Finally, Britt shook his head. "I ran my mouth a lot back then. I don't recall saying anything memorable."

"These guys remembered it," said Sue. "According to them, you stumbled when you stepped off the stage. When a reporter asked if you were tired, you said, 'I have a slow drink and a fast woman waiting. I plan to be tired about this time tomorrow.'" Sue patted Britt's arm. "People can't help wondering about Dena's relationship with *the* Britt Jordan. They see your picture in the tabloids every week, and they think she made a mistake."

"And what do you think?" Britt asked in a low voice. His jaw was working from side to side again as he waited for her answer.

After a pause, Sue said, "I think Dena is very happy, and I know for a fact that she has no regrets about marrying you. But since you've asked my opinion, I'll tell you something. I think she would be a lot happier if you'd just tell her why you're being so paranoid."

Britt turned his intense gaze on Sue. "Has Charlie told you about the threatening notes?"

"Yes."

Britt let his hands fall to his sides. "Then you see where I stand. I'm trying to do everything I can to shield her from that lunatic. I'm helpless to do anything more for her, except for this one thing . . . I can protect her from being more afraid. She thinks I'm crazy, but at least she doesn't have to live with the awful images in those notes." He held out his hand for a handshake. "Can you understand that?"

Sue smiled in acceptance and shook his hand just as Dena tapped on the French door and waved them inside for birthday cake.

After they'd eaten dessert and talked for a while, Britt stood up. "Are you ready to rock?" he shouted to Charlie.

"We'll see," said Charlie, his eyes wide with skepticism.

Britt picked up the bass and began to play, untangling a complicated series of notes, his fingers flying down the neck of the guitar, and then tying them back together in a heart-stopping improvisation that lasted five minutes. When he was through, he handed the guitar to Charlie. "Okay, Duncan, that's how I want you to play it," he said, his eyes serious.

"Uh, in which century?" asked Charlie.

Britt laughed. "I was only kidding. Just give me the notes I showed you. The piano will tell you when to change." Sitting down at the piano, Britt launched into an untamed force of music that Charlie followed, hesitantly at first, and then more confidently when he caught on to the fact that Britt had deliberately made his part easy.

When Britt began to sing, his voice was raspy as always, yet noticeably deeper, more resonant, then it had ever been:

Daylight is hot—
Bare skin on the sand,
Raw wind in your face.
I mean, hot, baby.
A thousand chances to make it happen,
A thousand gifts in my hands
To do it all
Or do nothing at all.

Nighttime is hot—
Sizzling love in the air,
Wild music in your head.
I mean, hot, baby.
A thousand lights in your eyes.
A thousand words on my tongue
To say it all
Or say nothing at all.

Britt let the piano slide into a mellow minor key, softer, and he nodded at Charlie to cease playing as he sang:

But between the hot day
And the hot night
Is a place where the breeze is cool,
The words are sweet,
Your skin is soft,
Our hearts can meet.

He let the force of the music build again:

A thousand keys to open one door;
A thousand voices to speak one word.

The piano found the original rhythm and key, and Charlie resumed playing. Britt sang now with his eyes closed, sustaining the power of the music to the last note, even though his voice subsided as the words ended:

Daylight is hot—
There's no calm on the sea.
Nighttime is hot—
No peace for you and me.
Take a thousand roads to the place.
Open a thousand doors if you must.
Come there with me.
Come there gently with me.

The song ended abruptly. No one said a word. Everyone stared at Britt in awe, even Bonnie. Finally, Charlie humbly lifted the guitar strap from his shoulders and put the instrument down. "That was the most extraordinary thing I have ever heard," he said to Britt. "Thank you for letting me be a part of it."

"My pleasure," said Britt. "This song will net me the first Grammy I really deserve. I'll let you keep the award a while if you promise to talk to it every day. After that, it will have to go to my museum." He smiled as Dena joined him on the piano bench, giving him a huge hug of approval.

"You have a museum?" Sue asked incredulously.

"Of course. Don't you?" Britt's eyes sparkled with mischief as Sue shook her head. "I'll bet you do. Mine's in my mom's living room. Every award I've ever received is lined up in a neat row on her mantel."

"You . . . you gave your Grammys to your mother?" Sue sputtered.

"Why not? She made me practice, work hard, and stick to my goals. She made me *me*."

"She didn't let you play ball," Dena pointed out.

"That's true," said Britt with a grin. "The only fun thing she ever let me do was sail with my cousin on Lake Michigan. It was okay if I got shipwrecked and froze to death or drowned, just as long as I didn't break a finger playing ball." He shook his right hand as he added, "The world no doubt has been deprived of the all-time greatest short stop."

It was very late when the Duncans left to return to Deerfield. Dena walked slowly up the steps and paused to look down on her living room. Rustic timbers formed beams across the vaulted ceiling, and a massive wrought iron chandelier hung from one of the beams, its light still glowing beneath her. The rich hues of the green and coral sofas against the hardwood floor gave the room a classic look, as if it had jumped off a magazine cover. Yet it was home. She smiled as she watched Bonnie kiss Britt goodnight on the cheek. Her child was getting to be so tall that she didn't even need to stand on tip-toe to kiss him. Next week, she would be thirteen. With a sigh, Dena turned and walked into the bedroom.

When Britt joined her, she was wearing a bulky terry robe. He eyed the robe. "It takes a cold-hearted woman to do that to a man on his birthday," he said pleasantly.

"It's very late," she said softly.

"I can read a clock, Dena." He folded his arms and looked her over. "You didn't even get me a birthday present."

She chuckled. "I did. I told you, a man is making a model of Shirl for you. We need to go down to Beaufort soon and talk to him about it."

"Hmm." Britt walked through the sliding doors to the outside balcony without another word. When he looked back at her, Dena followed him.

"You're looking at me like a ten-year-old kid again," she said, drawing the robe tightly around her body.

"Maybe I feel ten instead of forty five," he said with a smile. He stepped to the rail and looked out at the lake. In a few seconds, he heard a low whistle from behind him. Turning, he saw that she had dropped her robe to the deck.

"Wow," he said. "That's some birthday suit."

She was still wearing the green dress.

"Wow," he said again, crossing the balcony to stand before her.

"How old do you feel now?" she asked.

"Old enough," he said as he pulled her close.

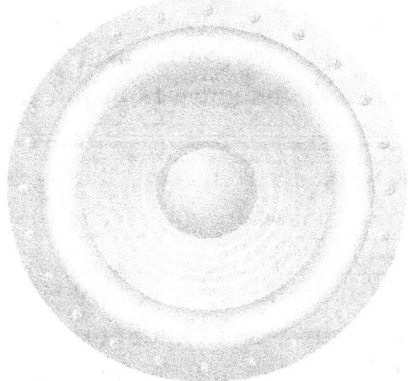

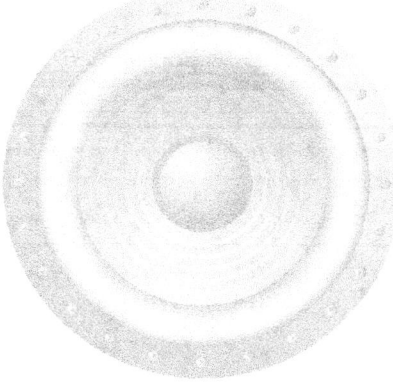

TWENTY-THREE

*W*ith Britt Jordan, you never can tell. Those exact words were going through Ron Edwards's mind as he followed Dena's car from the interstate highway onto a rural road near Lake Norman late Monday afternoon. Ron was a freelance writer, who was paid well for his insightful stories into the lives of the rich and famous. He had come to North Carolina at the request of Britt's agent, Bob Johnson, specifically to ask Britt for an interview.

For two months, since Britt's abrupt disappearance from the public eye, Ron had been trying to get an interview with the singer. Brick wall after brick wall had blocked his way. Britt had fired his manager. His publicist merely recited the party line: no interviews. And Britt's secretary had sweetly promised to move his name up on the list of calls for Britt to return. All the way up to number eight hundred seventy-five from, oh, around number two thousand.

Unexpectedly, Britt's agent had called Ron just two days ago, suggesting that Britt might grant Ron an interview if he could find the singer and make the request face-to-face. What Ron found shocking was that the singer's own agent didn't know where he was. Johnson had paid Ron a thousand dollars cash just to find Britt, promising him another thousand if Ron would tell the agent where the singer was hiding. Intrigued, and well aware that somebody would pay big money for a genuine story on Britt Jordan, Ron had agreed.

He had begun his search at the most obvious place: Britt's wife's place of business. That was how he discovered that she hadn't been seen in Deerfield in three weeks. During the three weeks prior to that, she'd only made one trip into town a week, Britt's bodyguard close by her side. Ron had a hunch that she and her child had remained fairly close to her business and her parents.

But you never know about Britt, Ron was thinking. Britt might not even keep his residence with his new wife. He could just as likely be in Australia. Still, Ron's instincts as a reporter told him it wasn't a coincidence that Britt had been pulling stunts all over Manhattan during the same three weeks that Len had been watching Dena. And then both of them had dropped from sight. Wherever Dena was headed today, Ron was pretty sure the trail would lead straight to Britt.

Not surprisingly, Ron had discovered that he wasn't the first reporter to try to reach the singer through his wife's office. What had changed, though, was that Dena had hired a manager out of Charlotte to run her paper. This new manager didn't have the same loyal, closed-rank mentality as the rest of Dena's staff, and he'd let it slip to Ron that Dena was in Deerfield that very day. In fact, the new manager was on his way out the door to meet her for lunch. And now, as Ron followed Dena's car in the late afternoon sunshine, he assumed that she was on her way home.

The thing was, Ron knew, if he did actually get the chance

to ask for an interview today, he couldn't even guess what Britt's reaction might be. Ron had done a killer cover story on Britt for *Rolling Stone Magazine* six years ago, and he was sure Britt would recognize him. But whether Britt would speak to him, hide from him, or shoot at him, Ron did not know.

Britt was an anomaly, nearly always a maddening man to try to interview. If he were in one mood, the interview could be rollicking good fun, with Britt jumping all over the place, making nonsensical, sometimes lewd, comments about his career and life in general. At other times, he could be so doggone intimidating that it was nearly impossible to get him to talk. In either case, a good, rational story about Britt was hard to come by.

Some reporters attributed Britt's mood swings to drugs, some to alcohol, and still others to artistic madness. After studying the singer, Ron had come to the conclusion that none of these theories were correct. For one thing, Britt's career had suffered none of the setbacks that chronically plagued musicians who dabbled in drugs. As to alcohol, from what Ron could tell, Britt scheduled drinking days into his calendar. The day Ron had interviewed Britt, the singer had been stone cold sober, tanned, and healthy-looking—very relaxed and very much in control.

There was something surprisingly lucid and honest about Britt, even when he appeared to be talking nonsense. And in the middle of their day-long interview, Ron had seen the man shift from one side of his mind to the other. Britt had done so consciously, easily, practically in mid-sentence. It was the most intriguing thing Ron had ever seen, almost like turning off one faucet and turning on another.

Ron had thought to himself at the time that some psychiatrist would be thrilled to get Britt's mind under a magnifying glass. Other people might think the rocker was insane, but Ron had concluded that he was one of the sanest people he'd ever encountered. Britt Jordan had nothing to prove to anybody. He could act any darn way he chose, and he quite frankly and intentionally chose to become a different person that afternoon than the one he'd been in the morning.

Ron doubted that Britt had changed, even if he'd chosen to hide himself in North Carolina, of all places. He was definitely well hidden, Ron realized, as he muttered directions into a mini-recorder in his pocket, at first in order to give them to Bob Johnson, and later because he was afraid he'd never find his way out.

Finally Dena's car turned off the narrow road, turning into a long driveway that wove through a thick grove of trees. Ron drove past the driveway, parked his car, and stumbled through the woods in the direction where Dena's car had disappeared. All he wanted at this point was to get an idea of the lay of the land before deciding on his approach. He came to a tall, chain-link fence. Following the fence to the driveway, he saw that it was connected to a wrought-iron gate through which a con-temporary, redwood home could be seen about seventy-five yards away, nearly hidden by the trees. He saw Dena cross the wooded lawn, stopping to pick a few flowers from a flowerbed in the one patch of sunlight, whistling as if for a dog, which Ron did not see. She went inside the house, and Ron looked at the home through his camera lens, not planning to take a picture, just noticing how the trees and shrubbery got in the way of a good shot.

A familiar husky voice behind him caused him to jump, his heart suddenly burning in his chest.

Britt was not in a pleasant mood as he stood hidden in the woods near his driveway, the Rottweiler by his side. Mid-afternoon, the police chief had called to tell him that another threatening note had turned up, postmarked this morning in Deerfield. The postmaster had sent it over to the chief. This one simply said, *It won't be long now.* "I don't know what this means," the chief had said, "but I think it's time for you to get Dena out of the country. This person is hanging close, and he or she is bound to slip up soon. If you can keep Dena away for two weeks, we may be able to get this thing wrapped up."

Later in the afternoon, Len had called to say that a car was following Dena from Deerfield. A quick check on the tags of the rental car revealed that it had been rented to Bob Johnson. Len had gotten a visual on the driver and reported to Britt that the guy wasn't Bob. It was Ron Edwards, a writer Britt had worked with a few years back.

This was a tricky situation. Ron was just a reporter looking for Britt, and he was certainly not stalking Dena or trying to kill her. But what was his connection to Britt's agent? Len could have Ron arrested, confront him directly, or run his car off the road. None of these tactics, however, would answer that question.

"It's your call," Len told Britt. "Depends on how badly you want to know what Bob's up to."

"Edwards is no threat," Britt had said tersely. "Let him come on in."

Now, Britt watched as Dena turned down the driveway. He heard another car drive past, and then pull to a stop. He didn't hear a third car, but he knew that Len and another guard had been following Ron. Neither he nor the dog moved while Ron wove his way through the woods, just a few feet away from them. The dog twitched when Dena whistled, but Britt narrowed his eyes at it and pointed a finger in its face. The dog stayed in place as Britt eased his way toward the man, watching him watch his wife.

He made his voice very low and distinct. "Why are you following my wife?"

Ron jumped, and then slowly turned and looked Britt in the eye. "Mr. Jordan. I'm Ron Edwards. I interviewed you a few years ago for *Rolling Stone*."

Britt didn't blink or register any recognition.

Ron continued in a hurry, "I followed your wife because there has been no other way to reach you. I very much would like to do another interview at your convenience. That's all I came here to say."

"Nothing else?" asked Britt. When Ron shook his head, Britt pointed a finger at the recorder in Ron's shirt pocket and held out his hand for it. He turned it on and held it to his ear, listening for a connection to Bob Johnson.

Ron looked away just in time to see Bonnie step out from behind the garage. She saw Britt, and a smile of delight crossed her face. As she walked closer, a ray of sunlight filtering through the trees caught her face, and she looked like sunlight itself. Ron raised his camera to his eye and opened his mouth to ask permission to snap the picture.

In that instant, Britt heard Ron's voice on the recorder mutter, "Don't come in here after dark, Johnson. I swear I may never find my way out." He looked up and saw Ron's camera aimed at his step-daughter. Britt's fist caught the side of Ron's face with all the weight of his love behind it.

Blood splattered the black iron gate just before Ron's head slammed against it, the lens of his camera cracking and falling to the ground in pieces. Staggering, grabbing an iron rail for support, Ron stared at Britt in disbelief. Blood poured from his mouth and nose. When he touched his nose with one hand and blood spurted between his fingers, he turned away from Britt, his face white. He gagged on the blood and spat.

When he turned back around, Britt had his shirt off, holding it out for Ron to use as a sponge. Ron snatched the shirt and held it to his nose as Britt looked on calmly, no remorse in his eyes. Finally Ron took the blood-soaked shirt away from his face and said in a voice that shook with anger, "Does the word 'lawsuit' mean anything to you?"

Britt snapped his fingers once and waited five seconds. "Does the word 'Rottweiler' mean anything to you?" he countered.

A massive dog appeared at his side. For that matter, so did two big men, one of them Britt's bodyguard. Ron looked at them all and spat once more. Something was going on here, something bigger than a retired rock singer hiding from reporters.

"There's a story here, Mr. Jordan." Ron's voice was thick from the blood. "When you decide you want to tell it, I'm your man. You know I'll be fair."

He walked past Britt on the side opposite the dog. Ten yards away, he stopped and turned around. "And Britt," he said, "I won't tell Bob Johnson where you are."

Britt nodded his head and tossed him the recorder.

Leaning against the gate, Britt watched as Ron walked up the driveway, still holding the shirt to his face. No one spoke until he was out of sight, and then the voice Britt heard was Bonnie's, close behind him.

"Britt, why did you hit that man? And who's this guy with Len?"

He looked into her eyes, which were wide with fright. In a soothing voice, he said, "A reporter found us again, sweetie. No big deal. Len brought another guy with him to make sure the reporter understands he's not welcome." He touched the combination to open the gate and slipped inside, the dog following. One arm around Bonnie, he started down the driveway, whispering to her, "Your mama is going to kill me. Maybe you should let me tell her about punching that guy in my own way."

When they entered the house, they could see Dena through the glass doors, sitting on the deck in a chaise, her feet up. Bonnie scooted past Britt and opened the door. "You're not going to believe what Britt has done now," she said before shutting the door with a giggle. "I didn't tell her," she said to Britt, her eyes sparkling with the joke.

He chuckled and went into the kitchen. After rummaging around, he came out of the kitchen carrying a bowl of ice and stepped onto the deck. He sat in a chair opposite Dena and put his feet up on either side of hers on the chaise, placing the bowl in his lap.

"What's the ice for?" she asked.

He didn't answer. The dog came up on the deck and gave Dena's hand a lick, and then stood at Britt's right side for recognition. Britt reached across with his left hand and rubbed the dog's cheek. With a single wag of her tail, Brandy trotted back into the yard.

Slowly, Britt eased his right hand into the bowl, burying it under the ice.

"What have you done?" asked Dena.

"I'm hot."

"He's lying," announced Bonnie, stepping onto the deck. "There was blood everywhere, Mama."

"Are you going to let me tell her, or what?" asked Britt.

Bonnie giggled. "Not if you don't hurry up."

"Blood?" Dena leaned forward, trying to see his hand under the ice. "Have you cut your hand?"

"No, but I wish I had." Britt said nothing more.

After a few seconds, Dena exclaimed, "I'm going to dump that ice on your head if you don't get on with your story."

Britt said in his most offended voice, "Since you put it like that, I'll tell you. I punched a reporter out front."

"A reporter? Oh, lordy, they've finally found us," said Dena. "He'll be back tomorrow with a telephoto lens."

"I don't think so. I know this guy, and he's a pretty decent fellow."

"So why did you punch him?" Dena asked, leaning back in her chaise.

Britt's mouth twitched.

"He was about to take a picture of me," Bonnie put in.

"Well, why didn't you just take his camera away?" Dena asked Britt.

He looked down at his hand. Good question. He couldn't explain about the fear and frustration that had been building in him since the threats had started . . . and he didn't want to tell her about how his agent had betrayed him.

Dena leaned forward again, reaching out to him. "Let me see your hand," she said.

"It'll be all right," said Britt, adjusting the ice with his left hand.

She sighed. "You really should go get it x-rayed."

"We need a vacation," Britt said abruptly. "That's why I punched the guy. I'm stressed out."

"Okay," said Dena. "When you get back from New York on Thursday night, we'll run down to Beaufort for the weekend and talk with the man who's building the model of Shirl."

"I mean a real vacation," said Britt. "Have you ever seen Italy's Amalfi coast? This time of year, it's—"

"Britt, you can't run off to Italy and give up your voice lessons now," Dena broke in. "You should have heard yourself sing the other night. It was fantastic! Stay focused, honey. The main things on your agenda right now are working on your voice and getting that hand x-rayed. We'll go on a long vacation later; I promise."

Britt studied her. Later could be too late. One way or the other, he would get her out of this house tonight. He took his hand out of the bowl and showed it to her. Already it was swelling, the middle finger turning purple.

She gasped. "Oh, Britt, what have you done? I'm driving you to the hospital right now."

"And then it will be on national news tomorrow that I'm fired up on crack and punching everybody in sight," Britt said quietly. "There's a private clinic near my apartment in New York. I'll go there tonight if you and Bonnie will come with me."

Dena looked from Britt to Bonnie, who jumped out of her chair.

"Can we go to the art museums?" she asked, her eyes dancing with excitement.

Dena looked back at Britt and didn't take her eyes from his face as she said in a quick voice, "Yes."

Britt stared back at her, his gaze just as intent. "From there, we'll leave for Beaufort. We can stay the week."

Dena studied him with concentration as Bonnie stepped forward and touched her shoulder.

"But my birthday is next week," said Bonnie in a small voice. "I wanted to have some friends over."

Her eyes still fixed on Britt's face, Dena said, "We'll do as Britt says. Go pack your suitcase."

"But it's my birthday," said her daughter in an even smaller voice.

Britt broke eye contact with Dena and turned to look at her. "I'll take you anywhere you want to go for your birthday."

"I don't want to go anywhere," Bonnie said stubbornly.

"Anywhere in the world," said Britt. "Paris. Rome. Tokyo."

Bonnie turned on her heel and fled into the house.

Once again, Britt met Dena's eyes. She was frowning slightly, her face taut with concentration. Then her head tilted slightly, and he spotted the perfect trust he'd seen that day when she caught him checking her car for explosives.

"I'm guessing you've heard something else from the lunatic," stated Dena. She leaned forward to lay her left hand gently on his injured right hand in the bowl of ice. "You go about things the hard way," she said in a very quiet voice. "If you would just tell me everything that's going on instead of trying to carry the whole burden yourself, maybe you wouldn't have to go around punching people."

Bonnie returned just then to stand beside them, her steps bold. To the child's credit, she didn't whine. "Did you say anywhere in the world?" demanded Bonnie.

"Yes," said Britt in relief. "Anywhere you want to go."

"Then I want to spend my birthday with my cousins in Tennessee. My daddy's people. All next week," Bonnie added for emphasis.

Britt blinked. Dena stood up quickly. "Then it's settled," she said. Her chin lifted as she looked at Britt. "We'll go to New York tonight, fly into Asheville on Friday morning, drive Bonnie over to Tennessee, and then fly from Asheville to Beaufort for the weekend before returning to New York for your next voice lesson. Any questions?"

"No, ma'am," said Britt meekly.

It was nearly ten when Britt turned the key in the lock and opened the door on the apartment he had kept hidden from Dena for so long. Lights, soft music, and fresh flowers greeted them.

"Wow!" shouted Bonnie.

The living room was sleek and sophisticated, with a more formal elegance than his home in Antigua. This was a room accustomed to black-tie parties catered by New York's finest chefs. The bar was centrally located and fully stocked, with black marble counters and gleaming brass fixtures. From the thick beige carpet to the plush butterscotch leather sofas to the abstract sculptures on pedestals, everything reflected Britt's distinguished taste. The lighting was perfectly directed from above to give it all a startling effect.

The view of the city through the floor-to-ceiling windows was astonishing. Dena and Bonnie both dropped their bags on the sofa and ran to the windows, where Dena began pointing out landmarks in the city. For a small-town girl, she had a remarkable sense of direction, Britt noticed.

"My appointment's at ten thirty," broke in Britt. "Let me show you to your rooms, and I'll get going."

Bonnie's room was quite practical, with two big beds and a private bath. While she unpacked, Britt and Dena walked hand-in-hand to his bedroom. He stopped and faced her, blocking the doorway. "Are you sure you can stand it in here?" he asked in a low voice. "There are three more bedrooms."

She smiled. "I'm prepared this time. I'm not a blushing bride anymore."

Britt's face relaxed. He pulled her inside and shut the door. "You weren't a blushing bride to start with. Do you think I can make you blush tonight? Ouch." He bumped his injured finger trying to embrace her.

She chuckled. "I doubt it. But I'll tell you what. When your hand feels better, I'll bet you breakfast in bed the next morning that you can't make me blush."

He looked into her eyes. "You're right, no doubt," he said.

Before he left to get his hand x-rayed, Dena and Bonnie cornered him in the living room, eyes sparkling. "We brought along a couple of housewarming presents," said Dena, producing from behind her back a recent portrait of mother and daughter. Britt stared at it for several seconds before taking it from her. "Thanks," he said, his voice more husky than usual. "That's exactly what this room needs." Carefully, he set it down in the center of his desk.

"That's not all," said Bonnie. She ran down the hall to her room and came back with a canvas, a bold abstract.

He considered it for a moment before speaking. "How did you know that I've searched the world for a painting just like that to hang right there?" He pointed to the wall near the foyer where a 1918 Feininger hung, one of few that belonged to a private collection.

Bonnie held her canvas in front of the Feininger painting for him to observe.

"You've got it upside down," said Britt, grinning at the face she made at him. "I've got to run," he told Dena. "Lock the deadbolts. I won't be gone long."

Two hours passed. Dressed in a long silk robe, her hair down, her makeup off for the night, Dena stood by the windows sipping hot chocolate. When the doorbell rang, she set the cup down and went to unlock the door. Glancing through the peephole, she was shocked to see Lori Sink standing in the hallway. Britt had assured her that the security in this building was failproof.

For a moment, Dena hesitated. It would be easy to pretend no one was home. Then the bell rang again, and she straightened her shoulders and opened the door. She stood in the doorway, one hand on her hip. Lori's eyes raked over her as if Dena had just crawled out from the sewer, and the young woman brushed past her and into the room.

"Where is Britt?" Lori demanded, making a circuit of the spacious living room as if expecting him to materialize from behind a sofa.

"He isn't here," said Dena, closing the door. She watched, puzzled, as Lori began a second circuit of the room. Stepping in front of the hallway that led to the bedrooms, Dena blocked Lori's path. "My daughter and I are here alone," she said in a crisp voice that carried only a hint of her Southern upbringing. "I will not have her disturbed. You'll have to see Britt some other time."

"I intend to see him tonight," said Lori, her face flushed with anger.

Dena folded her arms, her wedding band glittering against the deep maroon silk of her robe. "That may not be possible. Perhaps you would like me to give him a message?"

Lori's eyes swept Dena's body once more with contempt. "So you don't know where he is either." She gave a short laugh as she picked up the photograph of Dena and Bonnie, and then laid it facedown on the desk. "I can see why he wouldn't want to waste his time here with you and the kid." Lori went over to the bar and poured herself a short bourbon. Over her shoulder, she said, "I know he's in town. He came by my apartment earlier tonight, but I wasn't home."

Standing her ground, Dena said, "Then I suppose the best thing for you to do is go back home and wait for him there."

Lori drained the glass quickly and set it down sharply on the marble counter. Turning to face Dena, her face triumphant, she said, "Oh, he will be back . . . It's his apartment after all." When Dena's face failed to register surprise, Lori added, "Don't pretend you're not shocked."

Dena smiled politely. "Lori, I could care less. Now unless you would like me to tell Britt something for you, I don't know that you and I have anything more to say to each other."

Lori walked toward Dena, her hips swaying, her head raised. "Just tell him I enjoyed my little visit to your hick town today."

"You were in Deerfield today?" Dena asked, her voice pleasant, one businesswoman talking to another. "You should have called. I would have taken you to lunch."

Lori stepped closer, a swagger to her walk, her blue eyes ice, her voice threatening. "Oh, don't act like you don't know that I had lunch at your little hick police station. Two state investigators invited me, at your request, I'm sure." Her face was inches from Dena's. If she'd been hoping to force Dena to step back, it didn't happen.

"Then you've had a long day," Dena said in a quiet, firm voice. "It is time we both said goodnight."

Lori's breath, fired by bourbon, scorched Dena's face as she spoke. "I don't have to blow up your house to get Britt back. I have more persuasive ways, and I assure you, he remembers them well." She turned and strode toward the door. Dena joined her in the foyer. One hand on the door handle, Lori jabbed a manicured finger in Dena's direction. "You tell him he owes me big-time for that little trip to hell today. I'll be looking for payback real soon, or you'll be the one paying me back." With a flip of her blonde hair, she was out the door.

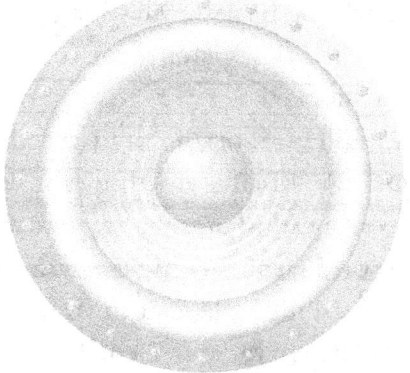

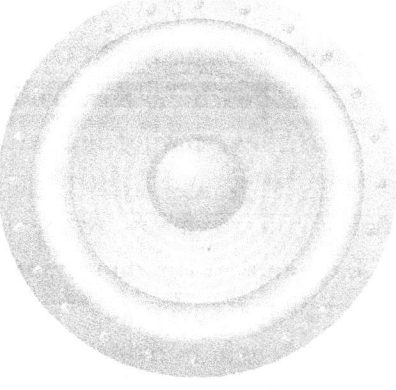

CHAPTER

TWENTY-FOUR

At three a.m. Britt was still awake, his bandaged hand throbbing with pain. Although the x-ray had indicated that he hadn't broken any bones, his middle finger had been jammed, causing damage to the joint. Not good for a pianist. The doctor had put a splint on the finger and immobilized it by bandaging it to the adjoining finger.

Unable to stand lying still any longer, Britt pushed himself into a sitting position. Awakened, Dena asked if there were anything she could do to help. "No," he whispered. She curled up against him, her soft feet touching his leg, and was soon breathing deeply again. Britt gently gathered her thick hair in his left hand and caressed it as she slept.

When he had finally returned from the clinic at about one o'clock, Dena had been waiting up for him, her eyes weary. She'd kissed his hand, murmuring over the visible swelling, and made him take the medicine for inflammation the doctor had given him. Then his wife had helped him undress, brushed his hair, and tucked him into bed as if he were a sick child. Remembering the many lovers he had brought to this bed, Britt acknowledged to himself that this was the single most remarkable event that had taken place here. A shudder ran through him. He would prefer not to think about anything else that had happened here.

Britt wished he dared take the pain medicine the doctor had given him. Dena had told him it would help him sleep, but he'd thrown it in the trash. Drugs had been his undoing in college, and Britt still had such a terrible fear of addiction that he rarely even took aspirin. Because he could control alcohol, in his way, he didn't fear it. Before meeting Dena, he'd sometimes deliberately pull a three-day drinking binge, emerging on the fourth as clear-minded as ever. Thinking back, Britt supposed that he'd used alcohol to escape from the reality of being who he was.

It was difficult to be Britt Jordan, living daily with the incredible music that bombarded his mind; the raw power that existed inside his soul; and the complicated, sometimes frightening schemes that his brain conceived, which he felt compelled to carry out.

But he had been mostly sober for exactly one year. Leaning forward, Britt fought the nausea that overwhelmed him every time he thought of what had happened in this very bed one year ago. He buried his face in Dena's hair and breathed in her clean scent. He should never have brought this sweet, trusting woman to this place. There were too many bad memories that could snag her like rusty nails.

Powerless to stop the flood of images, Britt finally gave in to the memories of that night last June. It had been a typical party. He could still hear the jazz music playing beneath the laughter and conversation of some sixty people, the clink of glasses at the bar. It was a social coup to be on Britt's list. One never knew who might show up: Clapton, Usher, Bon Jovi. The mood at Britt's parties was always electrifying. At this particular party, Lori Sink had not been in attendance, and Britt had been well aware that the guests were whispering about their recent breakup.

As was customary at these gatherings, Britt had amused himself by staring back at the women who were staring at him. Eventually, after he had stared with particular intensity at one young woman, she was drawn to his side. She had seemed a little afraid of him, he recalled, probably as intimidated by his wealth and the pure energy emanating from him as she was by his reputation. He had used his power and experience to his advantage, charming her into his arms and finally into his bedroom, the party still going on. No one would have raised an eyebrow—he was, after all, Britt Jordan, and he could do as he pleased in his own apartment.

Britt had locked the door and poured the young woman a drink from the wet bar in his bedroom. Soon it became apparent that she was even younger than he'd first thought, barely legal drinking age. When he began to undress her, it also became apparent that she lacked the sophisticated experience to which he was accustomed. Even with a few drinks in him, Britt knew better than to proceed, and yet he had. The stubborn ache in his groin at that point had been fueled more by a desire to be right than by a need for physical release. Just days after his breakup with Lori, he wasn't about to admit in front of his guests that he had chosen inappropriately.

Britt approached lovemaking with the same intense perfection of performance that he demanded of his music. He would give a heart-stopping rendition of himself each time. And he'd had years of practice to get it right, to master the art of making love for hours on end. Tuning a woman's body like he would a classic instrument, he could bring his partner to a fine, keen point of ecstasy, caress her body into surfing endless waves of groaning pleasure with him, and then break her with desperate ecstasy once again. His appetite for sexual perfection demanded a certain finesse and sophisticated knowledge from his partner.

The young woman he had chosen that evening lacked both. No doubt she had experienced the quick needs of a few fraternity boys, but she was in no way ready to be in Britt's bed. And he knew it, and he knew it was his fault when he brought her to a fast rush of pleasure from which she emerged ready to go back to the party. He knew he should have let her go and admitted his mistake. But he had persisted, determined to teach this girl what it took to make love. Not understanding, she had strained and floundered and finally laughed at him, thinking he was unable to complete his release. And when she laughed, he had pinned her down, and with fire and contempt in his eyes, he'd poured his hot pleasure into her with one hard stroke. Then he had sat up, turned his back on her, and said, "Now go get me that redhead in the blue dress. I'm not satisfied."

In that moment, the young woman had realized with humiliation that Britt's sexual needs were far beyond her knowledge or experience. And she had pleaded with him not to send her back out to the party, promising on her knees, tears in her eyes, to fulfill every desire he had, if only he would let her stay.

Disgusted, Britt had allowed her to stay in his bed, but he had drunk himself into a stupor to avoid dealing with her. When he had awakened the next morning, expecting her to be gone, he had found her in a coma instead, lying in a pool of vomit and urine, having taken a handful of her own Valium mixed with his Scotch. Even as he dialed 911 with shaking hands, he had thought to himself, *My God, Jordan. You have killed a girl young enough to be your daughter. And you don't even know her name.*

The young woman had lived to see another day, thankfully, but some of Britt's arrogance had died. Actually, a lot of it had died over the next several months, every time the memory brought him to his knees to vomit his self-loathing into a toilet. And he had handled it in his own way, by throwing himself into his work, saving the part of himself that he knew was worth saving: his talent. Held captive by the image of the half-dead girl in his bed and the screaming guitars that invaded every corner of his mind, he had erected a wall between himself and the life he had known—his vices, his acquaintances—and had started driving himself forward toward a destiny he could not comprehend. Until he'd met Dena. And she had from the first night seen something in him that was worth saving besides his talent. Clinging desperately to her and her love, sometimes he believed it was true. Sometimes he believed there might actually be a gentleman inside him worthy of rescue.

But it was mighty difficult to believe tonight, in this same bed, and it was a struggle to believe it every day, when he faced the reality that his presence in her life meant that someone wanted her dead. Dena rolled over at that moment, her hair slipping from his hand, and he reached for the lighting control behind him and brought soft light into the room. He watched his wife as she slept peacefully. Gently, he pushed her hair back in order to see her face. There was one thing more he wanted from her, and he doubted she would be interested in cooperating. He would like to have a child of his own. A child would mean that something worthwhile of himself besides his music would be left behind when he was gone.

Too exhausted to think of anything else, his hand still throbbing, Britt contemplated this desire until dawn finally came and Dena awoke. Seeing that he had not slept, she put both arms around him and laid her head on his stomach. "What is it, honey, your hand or your memories?" she asked, her voice soft.

"Both," he answered.

"It's time for your medicine," she said. "I'll fix some toast so you'll have something on your stomach. As for your memories," she sat up beside him, her right hand caressing his neck and shoulder, "whatever they are; it's okay. I love you, and I'm not going to stop loving you. All the good stuff between us is enough to drive out any ghosts hiding in this room. And that's the truth."

He met her eyes with a tired smile.

"Would you like me to shave you after breakfast?" she asked, rubbing his prickly cheek.

"You won't cut me, will you?" he asked, curious and apprehensive at the same time.

She smiled and left the room. Soon she returned with orange juice and four pieces of toast, hers loaded with butter and jam, nothing whatsoever on his.

He was just stepping out of the shower, a towel around his waist. "I'm not hungry," he said, eyeing the plate.

"You need something on your stomach. Don't you ever take medicine?" she asked.

"I'm never sick."

"It's a good thing." She pushed him toward the small table by the window overlooking the city. There he grudgingly took care of the business of eating toast and downing pills.

"Well, Dena?" he asked when he was through with his toast.

"Well, what?" She took a generous bite and wiped strawberry jam from her lips.

"Well, are you going to shave me?"

"What's your rush? The sun's barely up." There was good humor in her eyes as she spoke. But there was something wicked in her voice when she added, "You wait here while I get my tools."

It occurred to him that he should flee, but since he couldn't imagine why, he waited for her.

She returned with his gold-plated shaving tools and lathered his beard with shaving soap, the brush comforting against his skin. While the lather worked its magic, she combed his wet hair, humming to herself. Suspicious, he looked behind him to make sure she wasn't about to attack his hair with scissors. It seemed like she was up to something.

"Are you sure you know how to do this?" he asked. Britt practiced the art of shaving with a straight razor because he habitually let his beard grow to a three-day stubble. Also, it was manly fun. He couldn't imagine how Dena had come to be familiar with it.

"Relax," she whispered in his ear, and tilted his head back, exposing his neck to the blade. "I inherited my grandfather's razor. Johnny used to let me practice on him, just for the pure heck of it." With one expert, clean swipe, she brought the blade up his neck, across his jaw and to his ear. Flipping the lather off of it, she brought it firm against his neck once more and whispered, "Lori Sink was here last night. At midnight. She was looking for you."

He didn't even dare to swallow.

With agonizing precision, she sliced the blade upward again, not even hesitating at the angle of his jaw. Just at his cheekbone, she let him feel the keen edge of steel against his skin and whispered, looking into his eyes upside-down, "Do you want to know what she said?"

"No," he squeaked, trying to raise his head.

She caught his hair and pulled him back with a wicked

laugh. The front of her robe opened as she leaned over him; the blade was at his throat again, and her grip was strong on his hair. Sweat popped out on his forehead from the agony of it all.

"Actually, she didn't say much worth repeating," Dena said in a raspy voice, "except one thing." The blade made a slower course up his neck as she continued, "She said state investigators questioned her yesterday about the bombing at our house. Would you care to explain that?"

"No," he squeaked again. The blade was moving so slowly he could have sworn he felt each hair die a screaming death. "Okay, I'll tell you," he whispered. She finished out the stroke cleanly, but did not let go of his hair. "There was a note from the lunatic that mentioned 'wanting me back.' Considering her access to my car, I thought . . ." Dena's grip tightened on his hair. ". . . I thought it was possible that I was wrong about her innocence."

"And yet she marched right in this supposedly secure building. Are you happy she didn't murder me?" When he nodded his agreement, the blade returned to his neck, just beneath his Adam's apple. "Is that all you have to say about Miss Sink?" she asked. "Think carefully."

After a hesitation, he realized he couldn't lie without first swallowing. "No," he whispered. She brought the blade quickly up the center of his neck, his tender larynx absorbing the stroke, and across his chin to his lips. Then she let go of his hair and used her left hand to guide the razor around his mouth, her fingers sensuously firm against his lips. He could have stopped her at any time, of course, but she had just taught him something he had never realized: Fear could be quite erotic.

As she leaned over him to touch his neck once more, he whispered, "She left me about twenty messages yesterday."

She completed the next stroke with frightening speed, and

then said, "So is that why she says you stopped by her apartment?"

The blade was at his throat once more, and he didn't blink as he said, "She's lying."

"That girl needs closure, Britt. She's under the delusion that you're coming back to her. And would you care to explain why she says you own her apartment?"

Britt relaxed and didn't answer her immediately. He let himself enjoy his wife's expert hands on his face as she completed the job. When she was finished, she pressed a white towel to his face and held it up to show him that there wasn't a single drop of blood. And he slipped his left hand inside her open robe and helped himself to her warmth before he answered.

"You have my word as a gentleman, Dena, I did not go to her apartment, nor would I ever." When she raised her eyebrows at him, expecting a complete answer, he continued, "I gave the apartment to her as a gift, and when we broke up, I was too arrogant and lazy to deal with asking for it back. Literally, I wrote it off. If she'd bother to look at her tax bill, she'd see that it's not in my name anymore. I never intended for my arrogance to confuse her or hurt you."

Dena smiled and looked into his eyes. "Well, she is confused, and it's time for you to deal with it."

He looked away, the piercing sword of her love bringing him close to tears.

"As for me, I didn't say I was hurt," said Dena. "The mother in me was quite frustrated that I didn't have a flyswat to paddle her behind. That child is a brat!"

Britt laughed in spite of the lump in his throat. When Dena leaned down to kiss him, her lips deliciously promising his that once his hand felt better, she would be waiting for him, it was as if she had dropped an anchor into his heart. Finally, maybe for the first time, he felt it in the center of his soul: This woman wasn't going anywhere, no matter what happened.

"Now tell me," she said, only curiosity in her voice, "how did Lori know you were in town? And how did she get in here?"

He answered, "Her building is on the way to the clinic, and I exchanged a few words with the doorman, whom I haven't seen in a year. I should have known better. As to how she got in here, I have no idea, but somebody will get fired today."

"Don't do that on my account. I'm not afraid of her. But I do have one more thing to say," said Dena, brandishing the razor blade at his throat.

"Okay," he squeaked.

"I honestly think you should tell me one secret about this place." When she saw skepticism rise in his eyes, she added, "Whatever your ghosts are, they can't have any power over you once you let them out into the open. Just tell me one thing, and I'll bet you'll feel a weight lift from your heart."

He gave in, but not because he believed she was right. "Actually, there is something you should know," he said. "You have never questioned me about this, even though it's a matter of public knowledge."

"Your arrest for cocaine possession?" she asked.

"Yes. It happened in this apartment. And considering that I used to allow guests to use it at my parties, they might have had a case against me. But not this time." He was silent, his face tense.

"What happened?" she asked gently.

"My brother." He closed his eyes. Really, he didn't have to offer a further explanation but, drawing in a breath, he did. "Just for the pure hell of hating me, he planted cocaine in the apartment and called the police. I would surely have gone to jail if I didn't have the proof that the apartment had been occupied several times since I'd last stayed there. And my lawyers provided the D.A. with a long list of people who were willing to swear I never used the stuff. It never went to trial." He looked down at his right hand. "The reason I'm telling you this now is that I jammed the same finger against the side of his jaw then." Looking back up at her, rubbing his hand, he added, "I'm pretty scared about it this time. They told me at the clinic that I might always have trouble with this joint after damaging it twice."

She put her hand over his. "Did the doctor give you any instructions?"

"Yes. After two days, I'm supposed to take the splint off and alternate warm water with ice," he said.

"Then we'll do what he says, and we'll pray about it," she said. "Now do you feel better after spilling your guts?"

"Not really. Anything that makes me think of my brother just stirs me up and reminds me that Phillip is not done with me." Britt pushed back his chair, done with the conversation. "I need to make a phone call. Will you excuse me?"

"Certainly," she said. "I'll wake up Bonnie and fix her breakfast." She left the room, closing the door.

Thirty minutes later, Britt emerged from the bedroom fully dressed, a distracted look on his face. "I'm going for a walk," he said. "There are maps in the top desk drawer that will show you where the museums and galleries are. You and Bonnie have a good day."

"Should we meet for lunch?" she asked.

"No, I won't be back until later this afternoon, after my lesson."

"Aren't you afraid somebody will jump you?" asked Dena.

He started out the door. "New Yorkers never really look at each other on the street. I'll keep my hair down and keep moving. Lock the door." He was gone.

By mutual agreement, Bonnie and Dena decided to visit a local gallery that morning and save the museums for the next two days. When they returned home that afternoon, Dena put a roast in the oven while Bonnie perused Britt's extensive movie collection. Joining Bonnie in Britt's bedroom, Dena found her daughter watching a Britt Jordan video.

"Watch this, Mama," she said. "This is cool."

Dena raised one eyebrow and watched. There was only one word to describe Britt in this video: raw. She glanced at Bonnie and cleared her throat. "Does this confuse you, seeing him like this?" she asked.

"No. Why should it?" said Bonnie without looking up.

"Well, he doesn't exactly walk around the house looking like . . . like he does there."

Bonnie giggled. "Mama, I know Britt's full of bull."

"Bonnie!" exclaimed Dena.

"He is. He probably just walked into the place with the notion that that was how he wanted to be that day," stated Bonnie.

Dena fiddled with the DVD player for a few seconds so Bonnie wouldn't be able to tell she was choking back laughter. When she looked at her daughter, she kept her face stern. "He may well be full of something, but he is your step-father, and I insist that you show him respect."

Bonnie rolled her eyes. "I can't say anything without getting a lecture."

When Britt returned to the apartment that evening, Dena met him at the door. "Smells like home," he commented, kissing her. "What have you done all day?"

"Follow me." She led him to the bedroom. Bonnie was lying

on her stomach on the bed, feet in the air, chin in her hands, eyes glued to *The King and I*. The bedspread was quite rumpled, and the pillows were strewn all about.

"You two girls are disgusting," he said.

"I knew you'd be impressed," Dena said with pride.

"You've been eating in my bed." He brushed away a couple of crumbs with exaggerated horror.

"I know." Dena arranged a few pillows for him against the headboard. "We took your room captive."

"Shhh," said Bonnie, waving her feet in the air.

He straightened the spread a bit before sitting down next to Dena.

"How's your hand?" asked Dena.

He held it out for her examination without a word.

"Ooh. You need an ice pack on that, and it is past time for your medicine." She started to get up, but hesitated when the phone rang.

Britt reached behind him and answered it. "Hi, Darrell. What? WHAT!" His face went white and he left the room quickly, taking the cordless receiver with him.

Five minutes passed. Dena walked slowly into the living room. Britt was off the telephone and was standing by the window, a hard drink in hand. She slipped in front of him. He didn't look at her. "What is it?" she asked softly.

He drained the glass, then went to the bar and poured another. When he returned to the window and shifted to face her, she saw the pure pain in his eyes. He appeared to be trying to dilute it with alcohol.

Finally he spoke. "My agent and Lori Sink." He closed his eyes and drank more. When his eyes opened again, the pain was gone, as if he had swallowed it. He rubbed his chest as if the pain had lodged there.

Something had not yet been spoken. Dena stood in front of him, almost eye to eye, but he did not look at her. "What about them?" she asked.

He closed his eyes. "I woke my agent up this morning and fired him," he stated in a dead-tired voice. "Then I called Lori while I was on my walk and instigated an hour-long shouting match, which I won. Or so I thought." When he opened his eyes, the pain was raw and fresh.

"So?"

"So they've managed to join forces within the short space of eight hours. It seems as though they're writing a book on me, and they've already found a publisher. It's set to hit the shelves in six weeks. While I'm still a hot commodity, I suppose."

"Oh, Britt." She put both arms around him. He did not hold her. He drained his glass and tried to step away from her, but she kept a strong grip on him. "Why do you even care?"

"I care because I've been trying my damnedest not to be the man Lori Sink knew. I care because if you read it, you'll know Johnny Martin was wrong. I'm not an 'all-right guy.' Never have been."

"Look at me." Her voice carried the insistence only a wife could use with him. He obeyed, his eyes narrow, his mouth hard. "Since you brought up Johnny Martin's name, I'm going to tell you something I haven't dared say to you before." She waited for the line of his mouth to turn less severe. "I fell in love with you the night we met, but I didn't fall completely, crazily, head-over-heels in love until our wedding night. Would you like to know what you did that night?"

There was curiosity in his eyes now, and she continued, "You didn't insult my late husband by treating me as if I were too naïve to meet you half-way while making love. In fact, you very patiently and kindly treated me as if I were the one who knew all the secrets. I've trusted you with my whole heart and body ever since, and I always will." She put both hands on the cheeks she had shaved that morning. "I don't care what your agent and Lori Sink write about you. The real Britt Jordan is the one I hold in my arms at night."

A full thirty seconds passed. Britt's eyes searched hers as if hungry for truth. Then he sighed, his eyes closed, and he dropped his head to her shoulder. "I have a confession to make," he said, sounding like himself again.

"What's that?" she asked, stroking his hair.

"I have had nothing to eat all day besides that toast, and I don't hold my liquor well on an empty stomach."

"I can remedy the empty stomach," she said sweetly. They held each other, cheek-to-cheek. Both their cheeks were wet when he finally let her go.

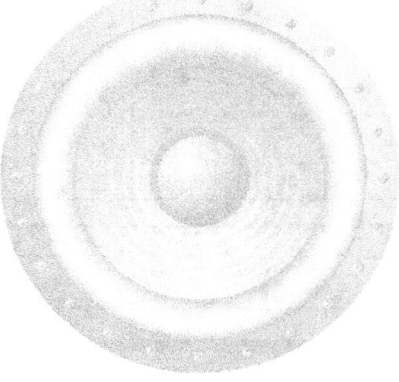

———CHAPTER———

TWENTY-FIVE

G regory Marcello looked up from the piano. "Mr. Jordan, I need to speak with you." He hesitated before continuing, "You may wish you end your coaching today."

"Why, Mr. Marcello?" Britt seemed genuinely perplexed.

"From this point on, you can work the vocal exercises on your own to achieve the range you desire."

"You don't wish to work with me any longer?" asked Britt.

"That's irrelevant," said Gregory briskly. "Have you listened to your voice?"

"Not lately."

"I've been recording you." Gregory stood up and walked to a cabinet and opened a door to reveal recording equipment. When he looked back at his student, Britt was staring at the microphone hanging from the ceiling and frowning.

Well aware of the legal ramifications that Britt was surely considering, Gregory said, "Don't worry, I'll destroy this in a moment. I only want you to listen."

Gregory had spliced together identical sets of exercises from the past couple of months that they'd worked together. When he played the recordings for his student, he could tell that the material from the first three weeks was painfully embarrassing for Britt to hear. But there was a slight improvement in the fourth week, and the change over the following three weeks was remarkable.

"I don't understand," said Britt. "Why are you suggesting that we end our association now?"

"If you go any further," Gregory said stiffly, "you will begin to lose the integrity of your voice."

"Sir?"

"The peculiar quality of your voice that has made you famous will be lost. When you sing, you will no longer be Britt Jordan to your fans."

Britt opened his mouth and shut it quickly. Gregory had a feeling that his student had stopped himself from saying something. Britt said instead, "Britt Jordan's voice is a part of rock and roll history. The name will be famous long after the singer is gone." He looked Gregory in the eye. "Don't concern yourself with my fans. I want you to push my voice as far as it will go. I want to know just how good it can be. Will you do that?"

Gregory looked him over. He had already pushed the man as far as he knew how, and he was stuck with the same confident man who had walked into his studio eight weeks ago. The only difference was that Gregory was beginning to understand the intensity he'd detected in Britt on that first meeting. Yes, he would be glad to push Britt Jordan's voice. If the singer wasn't afraid to explore his voice's limits, then Gregory most certainly wasn't. "Mr. Jordan, you have made a wise decision," he said.

"Hand over those tapes, Mr. Marcello."

Gregory's face twitched.

Friday morning, true to his word, Britt deposited Bonnie at her paternal grandparents' house to visit with her freckled Tennessee cousins. This involved flying into Asheville from New York and renting a car to make the remainder of the trip across the mountain into east Tennessee. On the way there, Bonnie snoozed, and Britt and Dena spoke little. His agent's betrayal weighed heavily on Britt's mind, and he knew Dena was feeling a bit nostalgic over Bonnie turning thirteen in a few days.

On the drive back to Asheville, Dena fiddled with the radio until she found a station playing classic rock. "We both need some cheering up," said Dena. "I know you'll hate this game, but play it anyway. Tell me the dirt on how you met each of these singers."

"You're right," he said pleasantly. "I do hate this game." Don Henley's voice was crooning on the radio. "But for you, I'll play. Let's see, Don Henley. I run into Don from time to time, but up until a few years ago I had never really hunkered down with him. One night, I decided we would become best friends. I found out where he was playing, which was only a time zone away, jumped on my jet, and walked on stage in the middle of his last set. When I took over the mic, the place went into pandemonium." Britt chuckled at the memory. "He was a good sport. Didn't boot me off his stage. We partied for two days solid."

Soon Stevie Nicks's throaty voice poured from the radio. Britt said, "Now there's a gal who hates my guts!"

"Why, because you wrote that song, 'Too Much Rhiannon'?"

"No, the song came later. We worked a benefit concert together once—well, a whole gang of singers did. I took it upon myself to tease her mercilessly about her Rhiannon song in front of everybody, just for the pure amusement of watching her hate me. I wrote my song a couple years ago, in case she somehow managed to forget the fact that she hates me."

As each new song was played, Britt had a story about almost every singer. "Britt," Dena finally said, "you haven't seen any of these people over the past year. What did you do for six months before you met me?"

Britt tensed, and then realized a blessed truth—his strongest memory of his bed in the New York apartment was of Dena and Bonnie watching movies amidst crumbs and rumpled covers. With a smile, he said, "I worked. I holed up in California and put together my last album while the promoters did a fast dance to get my tour booked by October."

"Why?" she persisted.

His mouth worked, trying to form the right words. "I was purging myself to meet you, my dear," he said primly.

A siren interrupted her laughter, and Britt realized too late that he was speeding. With an aggravated growl in his throat, he pulled the car over.

Without a word, Britt handed his license over to the patrolman, who smiled briefly in recognition, and then walked back to his car. Britt sat with folded arms, waiting. When the patrolman returned, he spoke not to Britt, but to Dena.

"Excuse me, ma'am. Are you Mrs. Jordan?"

"Yes, I am."

"Do you have a valid driver's license?" The patrolman was stooped over, peering in the window at Dena.

"Yes, I do," she said with surprise.

"May I see it?"

She handed it over. Again, the patrolman walked to his car. Dena and Britt sat and stared at each other. When the patrolman returned, he directly addressed Dena once again.

"Mrs. Jordan, you need to drive this vehicle now."

"Excuse me," Britt interrupted impatiently, "what's going on?"

The patrolman gave him a condescending smile. "Sir, I'm sure you're aware that this is your third speeding violation in this state this month."

"What?" Britt asked, looking up at him, trying to keep his voice level.

"I don't know how they do things in California," the man said, handing both licenses back to Britt, "but in North Carolina, you only need to be convicted on two of these violations to lose your license. If your wife weren't with you to drive, I'd arrest you today."

"There's been a mistake," said Britt. "I haven't received any other tickets."

"Yes, sir, you have."

"Could you tell me the dates of the other two violations?"

"One was the fifteenth," said the patrolman, "and the other was yesterday."

"You don't understand," said Britt. "I was in New York yesterday."

"Yes, sir. Sign here, please."

Britt complied.

"Thank you, Mr. Jordan. It's been a pleasure meeting you. I'll see you in court." He tipped his hat. "Mrs. Jordan."

Dena and Britt sat for a long minute after the officer left and stared at each other. "What is Phillip doing in North Carolina?" Britt finally said. "Not just with my face, but with my identification?"

Dena shrugged and shook her head.

"He's determined to send me to jail," said Britt. "I should have murdered him while I had the chance."

"Let's switch seats," advised Dena.

They stepped out of the car, and Dena walked around the back while Britt circled the front. Britt stopped halfway to the passenger's seat, clenched his fists, leaned back, and screamed long and loud. Passing cars swerved, the passengers staring at him with gaping mouths. When Britt got back in the car, Dena patted his knee in understanding.

"I guess that set me back a few vocal lessons," said Britt matter-of-factly.

They continued to sit by the highway, traffic blasting past. Britt rubbed his sore hand. "This has been a terrible week," he said. "I'm calling my attorneys from the plane so that they can get appropriately worried about keeping me out of jail. Then I'm going to declare this week over and start a new one. Maybe a new week will be better."

"Sounds like a good plan," said Dena, cranking the car.

They began their new week when they flew into Beaufort airport in the middle of the afternoon. "Tell me again why we're here," Britt said after they had settled into a rental car.

"You can't have forgotten," said Dena. "We need to talk to the artist who's building the model of Shirl I ordered for your birthday."

"We could have gone anywhere in the world, Dena."

"You'll like it here," she said cheerfully. "Look, we're crossing the intracoastal waterway."

Britt looked out the window. They were on an arched bridge high over Bogue Sound, and the sparkling water was busy with pleasure boats. "There are too many tourists here," he complained.

"Just ignore the tourists," she said. "Pretend they're invisible."

"I have a better idea." He rolled down his window and shouted, "Go home!"

"Do you feel better now?" she asked.

"Infinitely."

Their rented condo was on the sound side of Atlantic Beach, on a salt marsh. The place wasn't luxurious, but it was pleasant. While Dena unpacked, Britt prowled through the closets and drawers until he found a navigational chart and binoculars. When Dena joined him on the deck, he was spying on ships docked at the port in Morehead City.

"I love the smell of the sea," declared Britt. He drew in a deep breath. There was salt in the air, all right, and something else. With a noisy exhalation, he exclaimed, "This place is fishy."

Dena laughed. "You're sitting on a salt marsh."

He looked at the back of his pants, sending her into another peal of laughter.

"I mean, the building is on a salt marsh," she explained. "See the mud and grass below us? Ecologically speaking, you smell a gold mine."

He wrinkled his nose. "Well, at least it's good for something."

"Come on," she said, taking his hand. "I'll show you what it's good for."

She found clam rakes, buckets, and a rusty crab trap in the storage room. And after rummaging through the freezer, she came up with a bag of bait fish and took one for the crab trap. Handing a rake and bucket to Britt, she said, "Let's pretend we're on a deserted island."

This game appealed to him, and he threw all his concentration into digging in the mud for clams. After a while, Dena leaned on her rake and watched her husband. He seemed to be happy as a clam himself—his shirt off, his hands muddy, his eyes bright. He appeared to have forgotten all about his troubles and his sore hand . . . In fact, he seemed to have forgotten, for the moment, who he was.

Catching her watching him, he flashed a grin. "Better get to working, Dena. These clams are small, and I know how much you eat."

Chuckling, she resumed her job, staying close enough to him to hear his cheerful whistle. By the end of the afternoon, they had a fine mess of clams and eight crabs in the trap.

"Let's move to a deserted island," said Britt, surveying their catch and the fresh corn and green beans Dena had bought at the market.

Britt steamed the clams and roasted the corn on the grill outside while Dena sauteed the beans in butter and boiled seasoned water for the crabs. At the exact moment the first crab hit the boiling water Britt screamed mightily. Shocked, Dena dropped the second crab on the floor and had to chase it with tongs while Britt laughed at her through the screen door.

They ate on the deck in the evening breeze and waited for the sunset. The island faced the Atlantic south, not east, and the sun began to set over the waterway to their left, not straight across the mainland as Britt had expected.

"The sun is in the wrong place down here," he said.

"Are you lost again, honey?"

"Me? Lost? Impossible! I'm a navigational wizard. Somebody moved the sun. Who would do such a thing?" He walked over to the deck rail and rested against it, watching as the blue drained from the west and the sky became an upturned bowl of pineapple-orange fire.

Dena leaned on the rail beside him, watching his face as he

took in the light show with boyish fascination. He never seemed to tire of sunsets. She asked, "What are you thinking when you see a sunset?"

He shrugged. "I guess I just love beautiful things. If I'm thinking anything, it's that my sunset is the backside of someone else's dawn, which I find quite hopeful. Think about it."

She did think about it, her head tilted, smiling at him in admiration.

He smiled back. "What do you think about?"

"Thanks to you, from now on, I'll always see a sunset as the backside of my problems. When God says that what I perceive as an ending will become a beginning, it will happen."

He shook his head slightly, his eyes studying her face. Then with a deep sigh, he pulled her close and held her next to him as the evening grayed into night.

The next day, they rented a boat and cruised the backwater behind Shackleford Banks, navigating the tricky channels by means of the chart and binoculars. Eventually they arrived in Beaufort, windblown and hot. Hand-in-hand, they strolled the boardwalk, admiring the yachts that were docked there. Britt presented a different front when he was in public places—his sensuous, easy demeanor was replaced with a military crispness, and he wore his hair down and kept his eyes hidden behind dark glasses. This often allowed him to escape scrutiny. Today, although he drew a few stares, no one seemed certain enough of his identity to approach him.

They sat on a bench and watched a little girl, about three, hair tied in a neat red bow. She was intently studying the ice cream that was dripping down her arm and threatening to topple off the cone at any moment.

"Dena," Britt said softly, "would you—have you ever considered having another child?"

Her laughter startled a couple of gulls off their perches and made the little girl look up and frown. "I'm forty years old," she sputtered. The wishful look in his eyes silenced her laughter. "You're serious," she said incredulously.

He shrugged and looked away. "Never mind."

With her hand, she turned his face back toward her. "I never dreamed such a thing was going through your head. I'm sorry I laughed."

He brightened. "So you'll do it?"

"No! Good grief, that's the last thing on my mind." When his face fell again, she added, "Try to understand, honey. I did want another baby after Bonnie, but it never happened. I don't expect it to happen now, and at my age, I don't particularly want it to."

"Don't you love me, Dena?" he pouted.

"Yes, I love you. I just don't see a baby in our future, and I really would appreciate it if you would put this out of your mind."

"Okay," he said easily, but his smile was mischievous.

She pointed her finger at him. "I mean it. Out of your mind."

"It's out," he said, but his left hand was behind his back. She was pretty sure he had his fingers crossed.

Later that afternoon, they met with the model shipbuilder, who showed them the scale model he had begun of Shirl based on the photographs Dena had sent him. Britt filled the man in on the finer details of his ship. Then they walked to the Maritime Museum for a private after-hours tour. They were met at the door by a dignified lady who had clearly been brought up in the old school of Southern grace. She had refined bearing, a voice that was careful and cultured, and a smile that was cordial but not overly friendly. The evening light was mellow and warm when they stepped out of the museum over an hour later.

Marge Benson watched as the Jordans crossed the parking lot of the Maritime Museum. They were walking slowly and seemed to be having an intense conversation. Then Dena stopped and stood still on the pavement as Britt walked on without her. Marge locked the door. "I don't blame you, lady," she said aloud. "I wouldn't walk with him, either."

It had been a tiring day for Marge, and ending it by giving a V.I.P. tour to the likes of Britt Jordan had really topped it off. Settling into her desk chair, she reached for a butterscotch candy, and then picked up her phone and dialed a number.

"Hi, sis . . . No, it was even worse than I expected. Just terrible. I'm still shaking . . . Well, it was like I told you, who would think some big deal rock star would even be interested in boats? He made a mockery of all we stand for here. I started out by explaining about the museum's purpose and history. He just stood there with his arms folded and looked at the ceiling. Then all of a sudden, he bounced across the room and started looking at the spritsail skiff. Naturally, I stopped, thinking he must not be interested in the museum, and began describing the boat. Would you believe he had the audacity to look me straight in the eye and tell me to go back to the museum?

"No, his wife just stood in one spot and looked at him the entire time. She must have been as shocked as I was. She seems like she could be a lovely woman, if she weren't married to someone like him.

"No, they didn't drive up in a limousine. I don't know where they came from. As I was saying, though, he just stood still, and it didn't seem like he was listening to me at all. He walked around every boat, looked under them, did everything but crawl inside them . . .

"No, he didn't bother anything. The only time I saw him touch one was when he ran his hand down the Barbour craft and looked up and winked at his wife. As if a man like him would even know the difference between mahogany and fiberglass. He never did find out it was mahogany, because by the time I got to the boat, he was already across the room at the lifesaving exhibit . . .

"Well, what else could I do? I just kept talking, mostly to the back of his head. Once I got around to that exhibit, he had wandered off and was reading the whaling display. I don't know why I bothered to keep talking, but I did, because by then, his wife had begun taking notes. Whether it was on what I was saying or his behavior, I don't know.

"Finally, at one point, I did stop talking. I mean, I was completely fed up. He had been looking at the antique diving equipment with something that resembled interest, and so I tried to explain it to him. Would you believe he turned around and walked to the other side of the room to the Queen Anne's Revenge corner? I tell you, I was livid.

"Here's the odd thing. His wife motioned for me to keep talking . . . Well, of course, I did, but that was the most wasted breath I've ever spent . . . Yes, he's rude . . . No, I didn't get his autograph for Nicole. I was just happy to see the last of him. His wife had a few words with him after they left. If she's smart, maybe she'll drop him and look for somebody with some manners . . ."

Dena and Britt thanked Marge Benson for their tour and stepped out into the warm, sticky night. It was that yellow time of day before dusk falls. As they started across the parking lot,

Britt commented, "That was very interesting. The lady really knows her stuff."

"What did she say about the diving equipment?"

"Weren't you listening?"

"Actually, I was taking notes, but I may have missed something."

"And you call yourself a journalist?" Britt proceeded to repeat back everything Marge had said, almost word for word. Dena checked her notes to make sure.

"Now tell me, what did you find least interesting of everything you saw?" she asked.

"The Fresnel lens, only because I've seen one before."

"What did she say about it?"

"Dena, honey, do you want me to buy a tape recorder for you?"

"Just answer the question."

He repeated it back, word for word.

"Have you always been like this?" she asked.

"Yes, I have always been incredibly good looking," he said.

"I mean, able to absorb information when you don't appear to be listening."

"Oh, that. Mom used to spank me all the time for that. She said it was rude. Do you think Mrs. Benson thought I was rude?"

"Probably."

"I'll have Phyllis send her flowers."

He walked on, and Dena stood still on the sidewalk and stared after him. Britt's mind was amazing. Locked somewhere inside that head of his was every word he had ever heard, good and bad. Every concept, righteous and evil. Truths she had read to him from the Bible and lies the world spoke to him each day. Heaven and hell a brain cell apart.

Britt turned around and caught her scrutinizing him. "Are you going to spank me?"

She smiled. "Not if you buy me supper. I'm starved!"

Skepticism crossed his face. "Is there a place with a private dining room? Last time I counted, the tourists outnumber us."

"Just bring your pocketbook and follow me," she said. "I've spent enough time with you to know how these things are done."

Dena talked the owner of her favorite restaurant into sending a waitress out to their rented boat. A bit of extra cash changed hands, much to Britt's amusement. They ate in Beaufort Harbor in the fading light—a feast of homemade seafood bisque, fresh crab cakes, and hush puppies with a hint of onion. Their boat rocked gently in the wakes of passing boats. From the moored yachts came the sounds of evening activity, people hosing down decks, grilling dinners, and calling back and forth over cocktails. Twilight had fallen by the time Britt and Dena finished their dinner and eased away from the dock.

After a minute, Dena spoke above the growl of the motor, "Wait, I need a flashlight. The interior light doesn't work, and I can't read this chart by the running lights."

"Relax and enjoy the ride," said Britt. "I memorized the chart before we started out this morning."

He was telling the truth. What he would never tell her was that he was also following the lights of the boat ahead of them. Although he had reluctantly agreed to leave Len behind on this trip, two other guards had her in their sight at all times.

They made the most of their long night alone, washing the sticky day from each other's body, massaging away the aches and worries of the past week with concerned, loving hands. Britt rubbed Dena's feet last, taking his time, his warm hands gentle on her bare feet.

"What are you up to?" she asked fondly.

He flashed a dimpled grin.

"Please tell me you're off this baby kick."

"Of course," he said. "Sit back and enjoy being my wife for once. All you have to do is think about how much you are loved."

She did just that, a peaceful smile on her face. He whispered, "Let my love soak into your heart through my fingers."

When he stopped caressing her feet and took her face in his hands, her eyes were closed, that smile still on her lips. He kissed her deeply.

"I thought you said I didn't have to do anything," she murmured.

"I lied." As the soft hours of the night blurred together, he kept his eyes trained on her face, watching every expression, every nuance of pleasure. She didn't blush, and she never stopped smiling.

She was still smiling when she awoke the next morning, sunlight streaming in, the smell of burnt toast in the air. Britt brought her breakfast, sort of: fruit, toast, and sliced cheese. "You win our bet," he said. "You never did blush."

She blushed then and laughed merrily.

"I saw that." He touched her cheek. "You're going to have to pay me back."

"Now isn't this as good as the Mediterranean?" she asked.

"Yes. Let's buy the whole island and run the tourists off."

"Perhaps we should shoot for a smaller island," she suggested.

It was an idyllic day. Early, before the majority of the tourists made it to the beach, they ran beside the restless Atlantic, salt spray rising like fog in the morning light. They had fifteen minutes of bliss floating on their backs in a tidal pool until they were joined by two noisy boys armed with buckets and torturous intentions toward the lone landlocked crab that shared the pool with them. Britt rescued the crab and sent it scuttling into the surf, and then they returned to the condo before setting off in the boat again for a morning of fishing. At about noon a pod of dolphins surrounded the boat, playing hide-and-seek among the waves and slapping the water with their tails. Even the fish were biting. They ended the day on the condo's deck, enjoying the sunset once again.

Britt was grateful to spend this peaceful time with his wife. It almost helped him forget that there was someone out there who wanted to kill Dena. And that his brother was hanging way too close.

———CHAPTER———

TWENTY-SIX

B ritt stood on the deck of his home in the sweltering July heat, presiding over a smoking grill. His wife had mentioned wanting fried catfish for supper, and by golly, he had fetched her one from the cove and had set about to cook it, but by some means other than fried. With a tall glass of ice water in hand, he was tolerating the sticky Southern air as best he could. He looked up to see Dena leading an Iredell County deputy through the living room. Deputy Leon Stokes, or so the guard at the gate had announced. Britt couldn't imagine what the local sheriff's department could want with him, but he was determined not to let this man ruin his good mood.

Dena introduced the deputy and stepped over to the grill. "Will you take a look at that, Mr. Stokes?" She lifted the lid to reveal a whole catfish that was staring straight up at the deputy with both eyes, its belly spread out on either side. "Tell him no self-respecting Southerner would ever cook a catfish whole. He hasn't even skinned the thing. All he did was gut it and slap it on the grill."

"I'm telling you, that's how the Internet said to cook it." Britt slammed the lid of the grill shut and smiled at Leon. "Have a seat, Mr. Stokes. Can I get you anything to drink? My wife makes fine iced tea. I haven't learned to drink it yet, but I'm sure it's fine."

"Uh, no, thank you." Leon sat and stared at Britt, scrutinizing him closely.

Britt had a feeling that the man wasn't star-struck. He perched on the edge of a chair, facing Leon, and asked, "What brings you all the way out here this evening?"

"I need to ask you a few questions."

"Okay, shoot."

Leon squinted at Britt. He seemed perplexed about something. "Where did you go after you were released last night?"

Britt squinted back at Leon and didn't answer.

After a silence, the deputy said, "If you would prefer to do this down at the station, feel free to call your lawyer."

"Mr. Stokes," Britt began, keeping his voice level, "I have no idea what you're talking about or what you think I might have done, but my wife and I returned from New York yesterday evening. I only left the house once, to take my car for a spin. She hadn't been driven in over a week, which isn't good on a racing engine."

"Where did you go?"

"I went that way." Britt gestured over his shoulder. "And toured those little towns across the lake. Now would you please tell me what this is about?"

"Could you give me some idea of the time?"

"My husband was safely in bed with me at eleven o'clock, Mr. Stokes. Now what's on your mind?" Dena's voice was curt.

"And you would testify to that in court?" the deputy asked, his voice equally curt.

"Yes," she answered.

Leon narrowed his eyes, and Britt felt sweat beading at his temples.

"Mr. Jordan," began the deputy, "as you well know, when we released you yesterday, we allowed you to drive your vehicle home upon your promise that you would not be on the roads again pending your court date next week."

Britt clasped his hands together, elbows on his knees, and leaned forward. "So . . . you're saying that I was arrested yesterday?"

Leon frowned and glanced from Dena to Britt. "As I said, Mr. Jordan, we can do this in my office."

"Please, Mr. Stokes, tell me what happened. If I was arrested, why didn't it make the news?"

The deputy's frown grew deeper, and he cleared his throat. "You were detained, as you know, and we went to the trouble to keep it confidential as a *courtesy*." Leon spat the last word out, apparently done with being courteous.

Britt felt his throat constricting. "Detained for what?" he managed to rasp out.

Abruptly, Leon stood up. "Jordan, you may be crazy, but I'm not. I'll see you down at the station in one hour. Mrs. Jordan, will you show me out?"

"No," said Dena. "Sit back down, please. This is important."

Leon hesitated.

Britt growled low in his throat. "I'm going to murder him!"

The deputy's hand went to his gun.

Firmly, Dena said, "He's talking about his brother, not you."

"Your brother? You want to kill your brother?" Leon's voice was gruff. "Is there a reason for that?"

Britt looked Leon in the eye and kept his voice even. "Whatever he did to get himself detained yesterday, I can assure you that it was part of his scheme to ruin me. Phillip has my face. Now he's got my name. I don't know what he'll get next."

"Are you saying that it was your brother we held and not you?"

Britt nodded, still looking Leon in the eye.

"That's absurd. It ain't even possible. I don't find this joke one bit fun—"

Just then, Britt turned his head and placed both hands on his thighs and rubbed up and down, looking out at the lake. Leon stopped talking and stared at Britt's hands, then at his face in profile. "How tall is your brother?" he asked.

"A little taller than I am. He's also straighter." Britt gestured up and down with his hands.

"Do you mean he's more slender where you're more solid?" asked Leon.

Britt squinted at Leon.

"And not as tan as you are," stated Leon flatly. "What else is different?"

"He's younger than I am. His eyes are gray, and I'll bet he was wearing long sleeves." Britt gestured toward his sea dragon tattoo.

Leon whistled in admiration. "I wasn't there for the intake; but you're right, he was wearing long sleeves when I saw him. Okay, I believe you, Britt. I have to admit, I was confused as soon as I saw you. The man in my office yesterday hit me with a bully attitude right from the get-go. Your attitude, well," Leon cleared his throat, "is a little different. It's your hands, though, that are pretty conclusive."

Britt flexed his right hand and looked at it, broad across the palm where Philip's were slender with long fingers. "Yeah, tell me about the bully attitude. What exactly did Phillip do to get himself detained?"

"He was picked up before I came on duty, for driving erratically and speeding, with a trace of amphetamines in his system."

"I'll bet he claimed to have a prescription for asthma," said Britt.

"Yeap. Since that can be true in rare cases, and we never found drugs in his vehicle, we finally had to let him go."

"Next time check his hair band," said Britt, flipping his ponytail for emphasis. "He usually keeps a stash sewn into it. So, what did you come here to ask me? I assume something happened last night?"

"Yes, a hit and run involving a car that's the same make and model as the Jag your brother was driving."

The air suddenly seemed very still. Very muggy. Britt looked at his wife. The lines around her mouth were tense, and she looked away.

Britt sighed deeply and stood. "Was anybody injured?"

"Yes, but not badly. If word gets out that it might have been you driving, though . . ."

"I get the picture. Lawsuit and possible jail time if convicted. In theory, the only thing I can be convicted on so far is one speeding ticket."

"Speaking of speeding," said Leon, "what kind of car do you drive? You said it had a racing engine."

"A Monteverdi high-speed. Ever seen one?"

"I've never even heard of one."

"They're extremely rare." Britt said politely, "Come take a look at it."

They walked toward the garage. "You know," said Leon, "your brother had green eyes yesterday, same as yours. Contacts, I'm guessing?"

"Aaargh! That . . ." Britt sputtered a stream of garble that was not quite cursing.

"Uh, is that your way of cussing?"

"Yeah," said Britt. "Keeps me out of trouble with my wife, sort of."

"Women," muttered Leon.

Britt opened the garage door, and they stepped inside.

"Sporty little thing," commented Leon, walking around Britt's silver car.

"That's my baby," said Britt, running his hands lovingly over the hood. "Swiss body, Hemi engine." Britt slid into his car and started the engine for Leon's listening pleasure.

Britt raised the hood for Leon to inspect the engine. The deputy gave an appreciative whistle. Britt said, "On top of having a lunatic for a brother, there's another one out there who wants to kill my lovely bride. I have kept Dena away from this house for nearly two weeks hoping that the investigators would catch the lunatic, but it hasn't happened. I honestly don't know what to do next."

Leon rubbed his face, studying Britt. After a minute, Britt shut off the engine, and they left the garage.

"How fast will the car go?" asked Leon.

"Oh, a hundred and fifty or so. What makes her such a babe is the way she handles. I can do sixteen point three in a quarter of a mile. Phillip can shave over two seconds off that. I don't know how he does it. Faster reflexes, I guess."

Leon opened his car door. "I guess you know that we'll have to continue investigating the hit and run."

"Yes, I realize that."

Leon got into his car. "Tell me the truth, Jordan. You weren't in bed with your wife at eleven last night, were you?"

"Yes, as a matter of fact, I was." Britt let five seconds pass. "I took the car out after that, though."

Leon shook his head and laughed as he cranked the car. "Women." He started to close the door, averting his gaze as if considering something. Finally he looked Britt in the eye. "Does your brother know where you live?" he asked.

"Uh, no, hardly anyone does. The house is listed under the name of a holding company. Only one reporter has found us so far. You must have contacted the Deerfield police chief to find me."

Without breaking eye contact, Leon said quietly, "Britt, I think your brother followed me here."

"Damn," said Britt under his breath.

"A black Jaguar XKR-S convertible like his was behind me, at least part of the way. I assumed it was you, and I had no reason to give it another thought when I saw that you were already here."

Britt let forth a stream of curses that weren't garble.

Leon looked Britt over. "Is there something my department needs to know?"

"I'm pretty damn sure he won't be dropping by for a social call." Britt caught Leon's measured glance. "Whatever he's planning, I'm not scheming an actual murder, if that's what you're asking, Mr. Stokes."

Leon nodded, closed the door, and put the cruiser in gear. "Hope to meet you again under better circumstances." With that, he drove away.

As Britt watched Leon leave, he bounced up and down a time or two in an attempt to unseat the anger that had lodged in his chest. Even so, he entered his home in a less than jovial mood. He crossed the living room to stand behind Dena in the kitchen as she took baked beans and squash out of the oven. Looking around, he discovered that she had filleted the catfish and disposed of the carcass.

"You lied, Dena," he said matter-of-factly.

"I did not."

"You did."

"I told the exact truth."

"You said I was safely in bed with you at eleven," he persisted.

She chuckled. "You were."

"I was not safe. This untamed inch of yours gets the best of me sometimes." He kissed the back of her neck. "You lied," he whispered. "You implied I was back from my drive."

"I bluffed," she said. "I wanted him to leave you alone."

"You lied. Admit it."

"Britt," she said, her voice edged with exasperation, "if you said you went that way, then that's where you went." She gestured in the direction of the lake. "That's all I need to know, and it was enough for him. This thing is ridiculous, and I don't want you to have to go to court over it."

He argued, "You know you couldn't say in court that I was safely at home at eleven, which is why it was a lie."

"Let it go! We're not in court." Dena had continued working as she spoke, arranging the catfish fillets on a platter, sticking spoons in the beans and the squash.

Without another word, Britt turned on his heel, crossed the living room again and went out the door, slamming it hard behind him. He stood on the porch for several seconds, gathering the storm inside him into one hot, angry breath, which he released in a long, agonizing, gut-wrenching scream. He shook himself, turned around, and rang the doorbell. In a few seconds, Dena opened the door with a flourish.

"May I have a do-over, please?" asked Britt.

"By all means," she answered with a sweep of her hand, inviting him inside.

"My darling wife, the love of my life, please," he began, "please, never lie for me again."

"I apologize," she said. In a quiet voice she asked, "Why is this so important to you?"

He was silent for a moment. "My entire world is falling apart at the seams this year. You are my one constant, the one person I can trust."

"I didn't think, Britt. Do you want me to call Mr. Stokes and tell him?"

"No, I already did. You see, if the world has gotten so bad that even you have to lie, I want to find another one. Do you understand?"

"I do," she answered penitently. "But I don't think that's what got you all stirred up. Are you really worried about going to jail?"

He grunted a short laugh. "I wish that were all I had to worry about." He blew out a breath. "My loving brother has found us, apparently. I don't know what that means."

"Maybe it means that you'll have an opportunity to sit down and talk with him," suggested Dena.

"What a concept!" declared Britt. "To actually sit down and talk with your brother!"

Just then Bonnie came in from the deck. "I thought you wanted to murder your brother," she said. "Now you want to talk to him?"

"Yeah, sure, why not?" said Britt with a broad wave of his arm. "What the heck could it hurt at this point?"

Bonnie stepped into the kitchen and poked a finger into one of the catfish fillets. "The fish is getting cold," she said. "Let's eat!"

Putting one arm around Dena, Britt motioned for Bonnie to join them with his other hand. "Get over here, you purple-haired teenager," he said fondly.

Just a couple of months ago, Bonnie would have scooted giggling to his side, but today she sauntered across the room, making them wait. She had returned from Tennessee that morning, her sandy hair adorned with one shocking strand of purple. She was wearing a bit of purple eyeliner to boot. When Britt embraced both of them, she returned his hug with a brief but heartfelt squeeze, giving him a quick peck on the cheek as she backed away.

"Yuck, you're sweaty," she declared.

"Grilling catfish to culinary perfection will do that to a man," stated Britt. He watched her long-legged stroll back toward the kitchen, raised an eyebrow at Dena, and sighed simultaneously with his wife. Bonnie was a teenager all right.

—— CHAPTER ——

TWENTY-SEVEN

The very next morning, Dena came in from her small garden, arms loaded with fresh herbs and a couple of tomatoes, and stopped still in the living room. Her husband was asleep on a sofa, arms folded, one leg cocked up on the back.

She stood in place and looked at him. Never had she been around anyone who slept as little as Britt Jordan. Two hours at a stretch usually did it for him, and he rarely indulged in more than four in any twenty-four hour period. If he needed a nap during the day, he would usually go in the guest room and shut the door. To catch him in unguarded sleep was rare.

The fact that he was asleep, not just thinking, was evidenced by the rounder, more youthful appearance of his face. Even his firm jaw, so frequently clenched lately, was relaxed. In fact, this was the most tranquil she had seen him since, well since the first afternoon of their honeymoon, when they had toured the coastline of Antigua in his cruiser. Tears sprang to Dena's eyes. It seemed to her that Britt had given up incredible chunks of his life for her. And yet he appeared to accept the confines of his new existence with grace.

Lately Britt's habit had been to hold her at night until she fell asleep. Then he would slip out of bed, and go to work composing new songs. Strains of music, guitar or piano, filtered through Dena's dreams. At around five, he would come back to bed, sleep a couple hours, and be wide open the rest of the day, most of which would be spent scoring the music he had written the night before. Since he wasn't in his studio with a full range of equipment suitable for his task, he scored using a portable synthesizer and his laptop, a time-consuming operation. Besides being inconvenient, this system required him to retain huge amounts of music in his head until he could get it scored. Even so, he never complained.

Britt's eyes opened just as Dena was wiping tears from her cheeks. He immediately picked up on her mood and asked, "What's the matter?"

"Nothing. I was just happy to see you sleeping."

"While I decide how insulted I should be by that statement, come here." He patted the sofa. "I want to ask you something."

Indicating her armload of bounty from the garden, she proceeded to the kitchen. When she returned, he had made room for her by hooking both legs over the back of the sofa. As soon as she sat down, he asked, "Are you happy?"

"What? Of course I'm happy," she replied.

"You're happy-ish," he said, touching her still-wet cheeks. "Not what I wanted for you when I chose this house. I wanted to pick a place where you could thrive."

She took his hand in hers. "I don't know what goes on in that brain of yours sometimes. Please believe me when I tell you that I am very, very happy. If I'm not yet thriving, it's because I can't be fully sure that Bonnie is safe. Once that lunatic is behind bars, I promise to focus on thriving." When he smiled, his lips still relaxed with sleep, she continued, "In fact, I might thrive a little right now," and she bent down to kiss him.

Thirty seconds later, Bonnie's voice behind her announced, "Good Lord, what is it with you people? When I get a boyfriend, I don't want to hear one word. Not one word."

Dena buried her face against Britt's chest and held back laughter. Her daughter's statement seemed to require a parental reprimand, but honestly, she couldn't think of a single thing to say at the moment.

That afternoon, the vintage Chris Craft speed boat Britt had purchased in May was finally delivered. The motor, seats, dashboard, gauges, windshield, trim and lights had all been beautifully restored. He had saved the job of stripping, sanding, and refinishing the mahogany hull for himself. The first challenge, however, was to get the boat up the ramp and into the house's basement by means of the rusty winch-and-trolley system that the previous homeowner had not maintained. And Britt was determined to winch the boat up the ramp without cutting any of the precious tree limbs that afforded them privacy. It took all afternoon, a few muttered curses under his breath, and a lot of help from Bonnie, but he finally got the boat situated in the basement, steadied by a framework that would allow him to work on the hull.

While Britt and Bonnie walked around the boat, admiring it, a radio played in the background. Britt was telling Bonnie about all the work that would go into restoring the wood to its original glory when he heard his name spoken by the news reporter. The newscast was informing the world that Britt Jordan was under investigation for a hit and run accident.

Britt turned the radio off quickly. He looked at Bonnie, who was staring at him, her mouth twisted to one side. "I'm sorry," he said.

"Yeah, me, too," she said and reached inside the boat and blew the horn. "So when do I get to drive this thing?"

"Soon," he laughed, tweaking the purple strand in her hair. "Maybe next week."

Meanwhile, Dena had spent the afternoon at her desk in the den, pouring over stacks of paperwork, answering correspondence, and typing columns and editorials. She did not have much to say at supper, and she continued to work into the evening. At nine o'clock, she finally stopped and sat with her head propped in one hand, using the other to rub the back of her neck. Britt came to her at once and massaged her shoulders, not speaking. It wasn't until she reached for a tissue that he realized she was crying.

"I am so sorry," he whispered, pulling up a footstool to sit beside her. "My name has brought you nothing but embarrassment since the day you took it."

She waved him away and dabbed at the corners of her eyes with the tissue. After taking a moment to compose herself, she said, "This doesn't have anything to do with you, Britt. It's just all this work—" She gestured toward the stacks on her desk. "I've been away from the office so long that it's piled up." She spoke emphatically, her words tumbling out. "And look at this." She sniffed into the tissue and handed him a recent issue of her newspaper, which was covered in red ink. "These people can't even string together complete sentences if I'm not breathing down their necks. And that so-called manager I hired! Lord, don't even get me started."

He sat silent, studying her face for so long that she looked over the tissue at him with raised eyebrows. Very carefully, he said, "You know there is a solution to this problem."

"Not really. I know I could stay on top of my editorials better, but . . ."

"That's not what I'm talking about." He paused. "You could sell the paper."

"Sell it?"

"Yes, Dena. You could sell it."

"You want me to sell it?"

"At least think about it."

She sounded exasperated. "How long have you been walking around with this idea in your head?"

"It's not like that," he said. "It's your decision."

She reached for another tissue and blew her nose. "This is rich," she said flatly.

"No, you're rich," Britt said. "I've been waiting for it to dawn on you. I am wealthy, which means you are wealthy. You don't need the paper."

"We have a complete lack of communication." Her voice was muffled, and her shoulders were beginning to shake.

"Don't cry," he said. "I know how much the paper means to you. Just give it some thought. I swear that I'm not trying to control you."

She buried her head into her arms on the desk, her shoulders still shaking. It took several seconds for him to realize that she was laughing. He sat with his arms folded and mouth twisted, and when she looked up at his face, she started laughing again.

After a while, she collected herself. "Britt," she said, "we should have had this conversation a long time ago."

"Well, excuse me for not wanting to tell you what to do."

"It's my fault, really," she said. "I just assumed that you were okay with me continuing to work."

"So you don't mind? You'll sell it?"

"No, I can't do that."

"You can. It will be easier than you think." He started to reach into his back pocket.

She flipped her tissues into the trash can, her face annoyed. "If I could sell the paper, I would have done it when Johnny died. I don't even particularly like newspaper work. It was Johnny's paper, and it has fallen on me to keep it lucrative."

He blinked. "What do you mean?"

"I mean, it's not mine to sell. It's Bonnie's. It can't be sold until she's twenty one."

Britt stared at her.

"We should have talked about this a long time ago," said Dena. "We're both at fault."

"I don't understand this," said Britt.

"It's the way Johnny wanted it, the way he set it up in his will."

"Why in the hell would he do a damn stupid thing like that?"

"Britt." Her voice was flat.

"Excuse me." He ran both hands through his hair and took a deep breath. "Why did he do that?"

"For one thing, he never lived to see Bonnie's doodlings bloom into real art. It was his dream that she take his place at the paper one day." She didn't offer any other reasons.

"Why else?" he asked.

"What makes you think there's something else?"

"Because you said, 'for one thing.'"

"Oh, well . . ." She blushed. He touched her cheek with his finger. "Johnny left me pretty well off. Not rich by your standards, but well off." She paused before adding, "When they diagnosed his heart condition, he became obsessed with what would happen to me if he died."

She looked away, and Britt gave her a few moments to collect her thoughts. She had told him previously that she'd been emotionally unprepared for her first husband's death. Finally she continued, "He had this fear that I would marry somebody who was after his money, and I would wind up poor. Really, Britt, he was trying to leave Bonnie and me both with something we could count on. He didn't consider the possibility that I might marry Britt Jordan."

Britt chuckled and squinted his eyes, studying her.

"So that's it, then," said Dena, turning as if to go back to work.

"No, it's not," Britt insisted.

"There's nothing more to talk about," she said.

"Yes, there is. You yourself said that you don't like newspaper work. I'm not trying to run your life, but I can't stand to see you like this. Worse than happy-ish. Unhappy."

She lifted her hands palms up. "I'll just have to work harder. There's no other solution."

He leaned forward. "You've already hired a manager. Hire an editor."

"I've thought about it. To hire someone qualified would take most of my profits." She picked up a pencil and drummed it on the desk. "I'm not making as much money as Johnny did."

"Forget the profits; we're already rich. As long as you hire someone who can keep it afloat, the paper will still be a valuable asset that Bonnie can run or sell when she comes of age."

She smiled as if that angle had not really occurred to her. With a tilt of her head, she asked, "If I were to hire someone, then what would you expect from me?"

"Expect?"

"What would you want me to do with myself?"

He put his hands on her swivel chair and turned her around to face him. "Dena, get it through your head that I'm not trying to tell you what to do. Get a master's degree in horticulture. Start a tree farm. I don't care. Just be happy. That's all I want for you."

A sly smile crossed her face. "I don't think there's much money in tree farms."

"Money, money, money. That's all you think about." He grinned at her. She had rarely used his credit card. "You like having your own money, don't you?"

She shrugged. "Sure."

He reached into his back pocket once again, but this time he came out with his billfold. From it, he extracted a neatly folded check, which he carefully unfolded and looked at for several seconds. He was a very wealthy man. Jordan Enterprises owned the production company that produced Britt's albums, not to mention a wealth of commercial real estate, and the rights to all the Britt Jordan music and products. It took several managers, accountants, and tax lawyers to keep his assets straight. But nobody, absolutely nobody besides Britt knew the value of his offshore holdings. Dena did not have a clue how rich he was. And so it was a small matter to him when he laid the check on the desk in front of her. It was made out to Dena Jordan in the amount of three million dollars.

She stared at it. She blinked. She stared at it some more. She did not touch it.

"Uh, Dena?"

"Yes, Britt?"

"You're not mad, are you?" he asked. "You haven't said anything."

"Yes, I'm mad. You haven't signed it."

He grabbed the check and held it away from her, chuckling.

"You put that back!"

He did, trying not to laugh.

"What is this for?" she asked.

He put his hand on her arm, connecting with her. "Now don't be mad, okay? I've been carrying that check around every day, waiting for you to decide you wanted to sell the paper. Then I was going to buy it from you and let my lawyers worry about selling it, so it wouldn't be a burden to you."

She started to laugh.

"Now I just want you to have the money. Put it in your own account, so that you'll know you're wealthy, apart from me." Her laughter continued, and he shook his head. "What's so funny?"

"Do you mean you were actually going to pay three million dollars for that dinky paper?"

He nodded solemnly.

She laughed even harder. "I don't even own the building!"

"You don't?" He reached as if to grab for the check again. She smacked his hand, which made him laugh.

She pushed it toward him. "Now sign it."

"I will Monday, inside the bank," he said, refolding the check and returning it to his billfold. "Why was I worried that you'd be mad?"

"I can't imagine." She fanned her face, which was quite red. She stopped and pointed a finger at him. "Now, wait a minute. You're not getting a newspaper for your money."

"No, I'm not," he said smoothly, anticipating the way her mind worked.

"Well, what do you want for your three million dollars?" She batted her eyes at him.

He stood up from the footstool and leaned toward her, letting his hair brush her cheek. "I'll take whatever you have in mind, with one stipulation," he whispered. "I want it in hundred thousand dollar doses."

"Oh, really?" She turned away from him and shut down her computer. Then she stood, leaving her work, and tapped on Bonnie's door. "We're going out in the sailboat," she called to her daughter. "We'll be back in about an hour."

The door opened. "I thought Britt got a bunch of tickets for driving that boat without lights," said Bonnie.

"Then I guess we won't go far," said Dena. She took Britt by the hand and led him outside, down to the dock, and onto the sloop. She fired the single engine and steered the boat around to the cove beside their neighbor's house.

The sound of the sloop leaving the dock was drowned out by the big-cat roar of a supercharged V8 Jaguar engine at the gate. The man behind the wheel of the black Jag lowered his window halfway down. "Like my new ride?" he asked the guard.

The guard looked at him and began pecking the keyboard of a laptop.

"What's the problem?" Britt's distinct, husky growl was unmistakable.

"Well, sir, there's no record of you leaving the property." The guard reached for his cell. "I need to check . . ."

The window was lowered fully. "Look at me," the man commanded. "There's nothing to check." When the guard hesitated, he added, "I can fire you tonight or I can fire the other guy tomorrow. Your choice."

"I apologize, sir."

The gate was opened, and the black Jaguar drove through

and parked behind the garage, out of sight of the house. The big engine went silent.

On the lake, Dena cut the sloop's motor. The sound seemed to echo around the cove with more reverberation than it should. "What was that?" asked Britt. Several seconds passed with no sounds other than the lap of their wake against the shore on either side of them. "I guess I've never been in this cove at night." He checked the electronic depth-finder. "I'm going to drop anchor here. The keel's about on the bottom already."

With the boat situated, they sat in the cabin on the single berth, the hatch open to catch the moonlight, serenaded by a chorus of bullfrogs gathered in the marsh at the head of the cove. After a long, professional silence, Dena crossed her legs and said, "So, Mr. Jordan, would an hour-long kiss be a suitable hundred thousand dollar dose?"

He cleared his throat. "Yes, ma'am."

"I thought so," she said with a cool, business-like smile. She put her arms around him and leaned him back, her lips sweet, her strong hands warm against his skin. She kissed him tenderly, with gentle murmurings of love; she kissed him with fervor, hot promises in every practiced stroke of her tongue; and then she kissed him with jealous, fierce passion that drenched them both in sweat. By Britt's estimation, about a sixty thousand dollar dose had been administered, and he wondered if any man had ever passed out from a hundred thousand dollar kiss.

Suddenly, in one quick movement, she pulled away from him and said, "Oh, pfftt."

It took one half-second for him to realize that she had just cursed and another to recognize the flashing blue light reflected on the mast above them.

"You stay put," she said and stuck her head up through the hatch. "Is there a problem?" she called to the lake patrolmen.

"Are you Mrs. Jordan?" one called back.

"Well, who else would I be?"

The patrolmen pulled up alongside them. The one driving the boat called out to her over the motor, "We told Mr. Jordan that we would impound this boat if we found it on the water again with no lights. We're going to have to tow you in."

"I don't think so," she said firmly and stepped up onto the deck, raised the anchor, and started the motor. She backed away from them and steered toward her own dock before they could stop her. When she got there, she leaped onto the dock and threw the tow rope to the patrolmen. "Happy impounding!" she shouted.

Britt's head popped through the hatch. "What are you doing?" he yelled.

"That'll teach you to fix your lights!" she shouted back. "I'll pick you up at the marina." She waved and blew kisses as if he were going on a cruise.

Her laughing face was quickly hidden in the darkness as the distance grew between them. Britt watched as Bonnie stepped from the shadows of the dock, her shoulders slumped, and put her arms around her mother. Dena started waving both arms, trying to flag the boat down. Something seemed to be wrong, but he couldn't imagine what. He yelled several times for the patrolmen to stop, but either they couldn't hear him or they ignored him.

The boat had disappeared from sight and the night was once again quiet as Bonnie's sobs subsided to hiccups. "I'm not going back in that house until Britt comes back," she said. "Phillip scares me."

"Come on inside with me," said Dena. "Phillip won't hurt you."

Bonnie grabbed her mother's arm. "Stay out here with me. Maybe he'll go away."

"I can't do that, honey," said Dena. "Phillip is my brother-in-law, and besides, I don't want him to leave. Whatever he's doing here, Britt needs very badly to talk with him."

Stepping into the house, her arm around her daughter, Dena looked around for Phillip, who had evidently shown up within minutes of her departure with Britt. She wasn't sure how he'd managed to get past the guard, but Bonnie had let him in when he rang the bell because she'd heard Britt say that he wanted to talk with his brother. She had sat alone on the dock, crying, waiting for their return. Now Phillip was nowhere to be seen, however.

Dena called his name. A few seconds passed before he appeared in the doorway of the upstairs guest room. His face broke into a charming smile.

"Dena, how good to see you," he called down.

She stared up at him.

"Please forgive my curiosity. Your home is lovely. I couldn't wait another minute for the grand tour."

He started down the steps as she continued to stare at him.

"Where's Britt?" he asked as if he were inquiring about a dear relative. "Your daughter said that the two of you had gone for a sail."

"Uh, he's seeing about getting the boat fixed," she answered carefully.

"Oh, yes. Britt and his boats—it's always something. What has he named this one?"

"He hasn't," she said.

"Ah, so she's being coy, and won't tell him her name?"

Dena laughed shortly. "That's right. Now if you'll excuse me for just one minute more, I need to tuck Bonnie into bed. Can I get you some iced tea?"

"I'll get myself a glass, if you don't mind," he answered politely. "Just take your time. How long do you think it will be before Britt gets back?"

"I don't know. It could be quite a while, I'm afraid."

Dena kept her arm around Bonnie until the bedroom door was shut behind them. Bonnie didn't say a word as she changed into shorty pajamas and jumped into bed. She frowned when Dena kissed her goodnight and said only three words. "Lock the door."

Dena slipped into the den and dialed Britt's cell, only to hear it ring inside the top desk drawer where he'd left it. Drumming her fingers on the desk, she dialed the marina. No one answered. She felt as though Phillip was up to no good, but she also felt that the brothers needed to talk. Her best option was to try and keep Phillip here until Britt returned. Composing her face, she left the den and found Phillip in the living room drinking iced tea. "Good tea," he said. "I'll bet Britt won't drink it."

"No," she said with a chuckle. "Southern tea is too sweet for his taste." It was odd how Phillip knew Britt so well, and yet didn't know him at all. "May I take your jacket?" asked Dena.

"No, I'll keep it on." A hard look flickered in his gray eyes before disappearing. "So, how is life as Britt's wife?"

"Well, it gets interesting at times," she said lightly.

"I can imagine." He laughed politely. "I can imagine."

They chatted for twenty minutes, careful small talk, before

he stood up. "Tell Britt I'm sorry I missed him," he said.

"Stay, Phillip. He'll want to talk with you."

"No, I really need to go." He headed for the door.

"Where can he reach you?" she asked.

"I know where to reach him, so there's no need to worry." Again, that hard look flickered. "See you, Dena." He gave her a formal peck on the cheek and was gone.

Dena stood at the door and watched him drive through the gate in a slick black Jaguar.

She was waiting for Britt when he returned in a cab, very late. "I am so, so sorry," she began.

"I hope you have a good explanation for not coming to get me." He sounded a bit miffed.

"Phillip was here. Bonnie was all torn up, and I didn't want to leave her here."

"What did he want?" he asked with a frown.

"He refused to say. I tried to get him to stick around, but he insisted on leaving."

"Did he give you a number?"

"No. I asked, but he wouldn't," she said.

"How did he act?" Britt's eyes were beginning to narrow.

"Unusually sociable. Downright charming, in fact."

"Charming?" Britt began to look around the house. "Exactly what did he say that was charming?"

"Oh, you know, small talk. I did my best to keep him talking until you got here, but there was nothing I could do to keep him from leaving."

Britt scratched his head. "I don't like this." He went into the kitchen and came out with a beer. "I don't like this at all." He opened it, took one swallow, and set it down. "Did he do anything unusual?" he asked.

"Nothing besides being nice."

Bonnie came out of her room, yawning. "Is it safe out here now?" she asked.

"Of course, it's safe." Britt sounded impatient. "What did you do before your mother got back?"

"I sat out on the dock and waited for you," she said in a small voice.

"Do you mean you left him alone in this house?" Britt shouted. "For how long?"

Bonnie started to cry and ran into her room, shutting the door without answering.

"How long do you think he was alone in here?" he asked Dena through clenched teeth.

"Britt, there's no call for you to act like this. If you want to shout at somebody, go yell at the guard who let him through the gate."

"How long?" He took another swallow of beer.

"Maybe forty minutes." Her voice was thick with anger.

"Damn!"

"Don't you . . ."

"Shut up, Dena. Where was he when you came in?"

She didn't answer. She lifted her chin and glared at him for the first time in their marriage.

He slammed the beer down. "I asked you a question."

"The guest room," she hissed.

He took the stairs to the guest room two at a time. The room could not contain the cursing and banging that followed.

"Britt, I am not listening to this," she shouted.

"Then take Bonnie and get out," he yelled back.

She could hear Bonnie sobbing as soon as she opened her bedroom door. "Pack a bag quickly," Dena said. "You're going to

Grandma's house for the night." She closed the door and walked back to the living room, where she looked up at the guest room.

Britt appeared on the balcony, rage pouring from his body, as real as sweat. "There's your nice, Dena." He held up a plastic baggie by one corner before dropping it inside a pillowcase. He tossed the pillowcase down to her, and she caught it. "There's your charming." She looked inside it and closed her eyes. The baggie contained a fine white powder. "I want you out of here," he said. "It's not safe."

She forced her voice to remain calm. "I'm taking Bonnie to Mother's. I'll be back in a few hours."

"Don't come back," he said as he ran down the stairs and into the basement.

Dena sent Bonnie out to the car with her bag, and she was waiting by the front door when Britt ran up from the basement, crashing the door against the wall as he opened it. He stopped when he saw her. It was as if his mind had already filed her away at her mother's.

"I'll be back." She slipped quickly out the door and closed it behind her.

He jerked open the door before she was down the front steps. "Don't!" he shouted.

She continued across the yard without looking back.

"This is between me and my brother," he growled. "Stay out of it."

She didn't look back until she reached the garage. Then she turned and looked him in the eye, even with the darkness and distance separating them. "I'll be back," she said. She flinched as the front door was slammed shut.

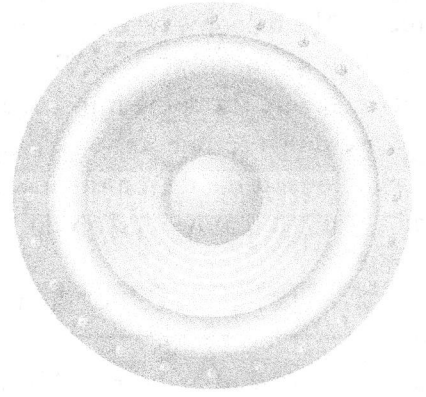

CHAPTER

TWENTY-EIGHT

ights blazed from every window of the house. It was two a.m. Dena slipped from her car and closed the door quietly, and then stood there and stared at her home for a long moment.

Her father, awakened after midnight by his daughter's resolute pounding on his door, his frightened granddaughter in tow, had begged her not to return, practically ordering her to at least wait until morning and allow him to accompany her. She was resolute. She was unquestionably returning, she had told him, alone, tonight. What she did not tell him was that she doubted that Britt's anger had reached its boiling point yet.

She stepped inside her house and did not take a step farther, shocked by what she saw. Her living room was in shambles—it was as if some giant hand had turned the room upside down twice, shaking it like a snow dome. She closed her eyes and took several deep breaths before venturing farther. Only when she reached the center of the room and looked around for several seconds did it become apparent what had happened. Britt had methodically taken the room apart.

Every end table and both coffee tables were upside down, the drawers out, the contents of the drawers strewn on the floor. Every lamp was on its side, the bottom pried off, cords dangling like exposed guts. Every chair was upside down, the seats removed, the foam padding lying naked because all the cushion covers had been unzipped and cast aside. Both sofas were resting on their backs, the cushions removed in the same way, and the dust coverings had been slit along two edges on the undersides and pulled back to expose the wood frames and coils. The patterned rug that had been in the center of the room was rolled up to the side. A console had been pulled away from the wall, and every drawer had been pulled out and emptied and stacked in a pile. Across the room, beside the French doors, every plant had been pulled from its pot, the pots stacked, the plants left prone in a heap on the floor, roots pitifully exposed, dirt covering the hardwood floor. Every curtain had been removed from every window—the rods were in one pile, the curtains in another, and the wooden valances in a third. Looking up, she could see that the four light fixtures that illuminated the balcony had been removed from the wall, leaving exposed rectangular holes in the wallboard. More guts.

All of this, destructive as it appeared, had been methodically and rationally carried out according to some plan in Britt's strange mind. Deliberation and control were evident even among the chaos. The point at which he had lost control was just as evident.

On one wall of the room was an entertainment center and bookcase that ran ten feet long. Apparently, Britt had started to take it apart by removing the drawers that held his stereo components, as the drawers and components were in a neat stack. Then he must have removed the television set and, using a drill, he'd taken off the pocket doors that hid the television. At some point in this process, he had evidently cut his hand, as there was blood on the cabinet, on the pocket doors, and a small dark pool on the floor. The pain must have fueled his temper, already scalding, and he had begun flinging the books off the shelves, his blood splattering the hardwood floor and the wall, anywhere a book hit. The books now lay in an unholy mess, covers open, pages bent, some covered in his blood. She bent down and picked up a Bible and placed it carefully on a shelf. Otherwise, she didn't touch anything.

A door slammed upstairs, and Dena looked up. Britt strode from the guest bedroom across the balcony above her, every step emphasizing the anger in his soul. He did not look down, and she did not call out to him. He entered the master bedroom, and soon she heard his voice on the telephone asking what time Leon Stokes came on duty. She heard him leave his name and number, and then a curse and a ringing crash indicated that he had slammed down the receiver. Without a pause, he came out of the room, crossed the balcony again, and began to run down the stairs. His jaw was clenched and his eyes were pinched narrow, nearly shutting off the anger that boiled within. There was barely a break in his pace when he saw her standing there, and he didn't even glance her way as he turned the corner and continued on down the steps to the basement.

It would be difficult to say what she had expected from him. More shouting? Ultimatums? Certainly an argument. That he didn't even acknowledge her presence felt like an icicle slicing down her spine, splintering into slivers beneath her skin. Her entire back stung as if she had been physically struck. She rubbed her neck and didn't move from her spot in the middle of the floor.

Ten minutes passed. There was a commotion in the basement, punctuated by the ring of metal on the concrete floor and more cursing. She stayed right where she was. It was the sound of horns blasting at the gate and simultaneous shouts from the lake that finally caused her to move, jumping in one place, not knowing which way to turn. She took one step toward the door and was thrown off by Britt's voice filtering up the stairwell, loud enough to fill a coliseum, "Stay put, damn you. I told you to keep out of this."

Rage spilling from his every movement, Britt ran up from the basement and jerked the front door open. She could see the blue flashes from the patrol cars' lights reflected on his face. His fist hit the switch to activate the gate even before they shouted for him to do so. He looked back at Dena and with one gesture motioned for her to move to the piano.

Four car doors slammed in the driveway and the alarm system screamed that deputies had stepped onto their dock from a boat. Just as Britt shut off the alarm, four deputies clamored through the open front door.

Dazed, Dena settled on the piano bench and found an orderly detail in the midst of the chaos: Britt's wedding band lay peacefully on the piano on top of a folded sheet of paper and a neatly folded check. Blinking back tears, she slipped all three things into the pocket of her shorts, understanding that this was the reason he had sent her to the piano.

The sight of the room stopped the four deputies in their tracks, just as it had Dena. While the other three stood still in confusion, Leon Stokes himself walked across the room and opened the back door for the two deputies who were pounding on it.

"Take your boat and leave," he told them crisply. "You're not needed here."

"What?" they asked, craning their necks to look past him into the room.

"You heard me. Just get out of here." Leon shut the door in their faces and turned to look at Britt, who was standing beside him, arms folded. "What in the hell?" he asked.

One of Britt's hands rose in a sharp movement, palm flat. "You tell me something." His voice was very low and distinct. "How did you get this search party together so fast? My brother couldn't possibly have called you before eleven thirty."

Leon looked him in the eye. "They got me out of bed at one o'clock to take care of this." He paused. "We already had the warrant." He didn't offer an explanation. Leon and Britt stared at each other for several seconds as the three other deputies shuffled uneasily. Finally, Leon spoke. "You say your brother made the call?"

"Laid the bait and made the call," Britt said. "If you check into my record, you'll see that this exact thing happened to me before in New York."

Leon nodded once. "That arrest on your record combined with the speeding incident caused them to issue the warrant. If you had so much as sneezed backward, somebody was ready to hand it to you to wipe your nose. The warrant was in place before I met you." Britt raised his eyebrows. "And yes, I looked into that arrest in New York. There's no mention of Phillip having been arrested after you were cleared."

"I was too stupid to turn him in. I thought that beating him half to death would teach him not to try it again." Britt raised his clenched right fist, still visibly swollen from the punch he had thrown two weeks ago, the thumb newly bandaged. "I was wrong."

Leon sighed, considering, and motioned for two of the deputies to go outside and wait. "Okay, Britt, what have you got?"

Britt gestured for Leon to look on top of the bar that separated the living room from the kitchen. The deputy walked over and looked. "Five bags," he said, "maybe a gram each. Enough to get a conviction for intent to sell." He gave Britt a sidelong look. "Where did he get that kind of money?"

"God, I don't know," Britt said, his voice defeated for the first time. "He's probably accessing my bank accounts now."

Leon said, "We were told to look for six."

Britt ran both hands through his hair and looked around the room, muttering to himself.

"You don't appear to have searched the kitchen," Leon pointed out. "Why not?"

"I thought I had it all when I called you a few minutes before you got here." Britt's voice was terse.

"You called me?"

"Yes."

"Did you leave a message?" asked Leon.

"Just my name and number."

"That should help when I try to explain this to the D.A." Leon scratched his head. "Still, you left the kitchen. Why?"

Britt folded his arms again. "I don't use cocaine, but people who do don't store it in the kitchen. It looks too much like—I don't know, baking powder or something."

"Still . . ." said Leon.

Dena stood up and walked past them. If Phillip had hidden a bag in the kitchen after her arrival, he had done it quickly, without any unexpected clatter. She opened the refrigerator, took out the tea pitcher, and emptied its contents into the sink. Only tea. She pulled the ice tray out of the freezer and dumped it into the sink. Only ice. "He fixed himself a glass of tea," she explained, still holding the freezer door open.

Britt moved into the space beside her. He didn't touch her, but she stepped aside as quickly as if he had pushed her. One whack against the icemaker with his fist produced the sixth bag.

One of the deputies who had been sent outside stuck his head in through the door. "Are you ready to start?" he asked.

"Start? You idiot, it's already finished. Just wait outside." Leon snapped on a rubber glove to pick up the bags and drop them into an evidence bag. "Let me take a quick look upstairs for my report," he said. "You'll need to come down to the station with me and wait for the rest of the world to wake up. The sheriff and the D.A. will both need to hear the complete story from you in the morning. Of course, you have the right to wait until your attorney is present."

"I have two en route from California as we speak." Britt's voice was flat and final.

Leon took less than a minute to tour the upstairs. "Beats any damn thing I ever saw," he muttered to the other deputies.

Britt didn't look at Dena as they waited downstairs. When Leon motioned for Britt to leave with them, however, he turned and gave her one lingering look. It was neither kind nor angry, yet its intent was obvious. She should not have returned. Had things gone differently, had Leon not been with the search party, both of them might have been arrested, despite the precautions Britt had taken. Car doors slammed, and Britt was gone.

Dena looked around once again, overwhelmed by the task of putting her home back together. She entered Bonnie's bedroom and resolutely shoved the mattress back onto the box springs, replaced the sheets, and sat down on the edge of the bed. Removing the contents from her pocket, she laid the ring and check carefully on Bonnie's upturned nightstand and unfolded the sheet of paper.

It was a note, hastily scribbled in large, shaky letters that only vaguely resembled Britt's normal, orderly handwriting. It read:

> *Dena, if you don't want to stay after this, I'll understand. Keep the money. Keep all my money if you want it. Ask your father what I mean. Leave this house and my name. You're not safe with either. Len will take you anywhere you want to go.*

She read it twice, and as she did so, she felt the ice in her back melt and dissolve away. She didn't understand this twist in Britt's mind or what her father had to do with it, but one thing was clear . . . She had been right to come back. Slipping into bed, still in her clothes, she hugged Bonnie's pillow and inhaled her daughter's scent. She was too tired to cry or pray, and she soon fell into a hard sleep.

It was six thirty when Dena awoke the next morning, and birds were chirping and soft light was streaming in through the window. She didn't exactly feel refreshed, but she did feel stronger. She arose immediately, determined to have her home back in order when Britt returned. That he might not return at all was unthinkable.

She went straight into the living room and without surveying the mess at all, she started tackling it, one table, chair, and bookshelf at a time. What she could not do—like lifting the television and the heavy window valances—she left. She did rehang the curtains, with a great deal of strain and two broken nails. And she scrubbed her husband's blood from the cabinet and floor, and began the process of removing the splatters from the wall. It was while she was repotting the plants, her stomach growling, that it occurred to her it was past ten o'clock and she had not yet called her father.

Her father was nearly frantic with worry when she reached him. He had been on his way out the door to come check on her. In a few words, she explained the situation and tried to reassure him that she was safe. She did not mention Britt's note.

The next fifteen minutes were spent trying to soothe and comfort Bonnie. Her inability to reach through the telephone lines and wrap her arms around her daughter was frustrating, but Dena was determined to stay at home and face whatever mood Britt brought with him.

Only after the room was back to normal and she had arranged bowls of fruit on the bar, sliced vegetables on a tray in the refrigerator, and fresh flowers from her garden on every table in the living room did she stop to eat breakfast, shower, and change clothes. It was while she was putting her bedroom back together that worry set in. What if Britt was charged? Today was Sunday, so would he have to wait until Monday for a bail hearing? What if he left the country, just called his pilot to come and get him? He was always talking about going to Europe. Wait . . . that didn't make sense. Surely he wouldn't leave without saying good-bye first. But you never could tell with Britt. He didn't think like other people.

Dena needed a break. She walked onto the upstairs deck and looked out at the lake, tears streaming down her cheeks. Eventually she noticed that the dog seemed unusually interested in a boat on the water. Wiping her eyes, she moved to get a better view of it through the trees. Nothing out of the ordinary, just an outboard with somebody fishing. She called to the dog, but Brandy barked once and continued to watch the boat.

Lost in thought, Dena didn't notice when the person on the boat picked up binoculars and tried to get a good look at her through the trees. She would never know that there was a high-powered rifle at the person's feet. She was accustomed to the boat manned by two guards that kept watch on her home, and so she did not notice when the guard boat passed between the fishing boat and the house. The binoculars were quickly put down and replaced with a fishing rod. Nor did she notice when a guard called out, "How's the fishing?" and a deep, flat voice answered, "Not bad."

Still feeling worried, Dena returned to tidying her bedroom. In the middle of the afternoon, the front door slammed. "I'm up here, Britt," she called down. There was no answer. She heard him open the refrigerator door, and then she heard him bang down into the basement. Soon the sound of an electric sander could be heard, muffled by the distance. Evidently he was working off his rage by tackling the refinishing of the Chris Craft. At least he was home.

About an hour later while she was working in the guest room, she heard a crash from the basement followed by a stream of curses. She went back outside on the upper deck. This time, she paced and prayed. When she returned to her task in the guest room, it was with fresh resolution. Britt had to wrestle with his anger and his hatred for his brother on his own. There was nothing she could say to him that would help. She wouldn't speak to him again until his battle was over.

When it was time for supper, Dena went to the kitchen and checked on the tray of vegetables. A handful was missing—it was evidently all Britt had eaten for lunch. She replenished the tray, added sliced cheeses, and started to make a peach pie. Britt banged up from the basement, stopped in his tracks when he saw her, and then continued upstairs. Without looking him in the eye, she kept working quietly.

Dena realized that to a casual observer, the situation might have appeared abusive: the explosive, seething husband and the quiet, subservient wife who was eager to please him. In reality, she was here by her own choice, and she was not at all afraid of him.

Britt continued to sand the hull of the boat until midnight, nine solid hours of noisy, hard work. Without taking a break, he began to apply marine varnish. Just yesterday, the job would have given him pleasure, watching the mahogany come alive under the finish. Tonight he attacked the job, not out of pleasure, but out of a desperate need to do something besides track down his brother and murder him. Watching his hand shake as he wielded the brush, he imagined what he would like to do to Phillip with his bare hands. It was not a pretty picture, but going over and over it in his mind gave him some satisfaction. His neck was beginning to ache from clenching his jaw, but he made no attempt to let go of any of the anger and bitterness. Hatred was too real and necessary a thing to him, coursing through his veins, a boiling liquid. There was a loud, ugly racket going on in his head, but it wasn't music this time. He had been able to drown part of it out with the sander, but now there was only the hum of the two exhaust fans at the door and the racket in his head. He worked until he was finished with the hull, leaving the topside for daylight. Too many bugs were being attracted by the light. That was what was wrong with the South—too many damn bugs.

Leaving the fans running, he stomped upstairs and went into the kitchen. It was two a.m. How long had it been since he had slept? His hand ached, and he knew he should take his medicine for the swelling. A note from Dena reminded him to eat something first. With a sigh, he spooned some of the peach pie she'd made onto a plate, frowning at the sticky goo. Too many bugs and too much damn sugar.

He sat on the sofa and ate the pie and took the pills and looked up at his darkened bedroom. What kind of stubborn madness had brought Dena back to this house in the middle of the night? She should have been frightened of him; she should have stayed away from his blind rage.

And yet he had known she would come back. And the fact that she was here, and had *remained* here, was what was anchoring him to this place. There was no other reason for him to stay in this hot, buggy, sugar-infested state. One speeding ticket. As his lawyers had assured him and the D.A., it was the only thing Britt could be convicted on. Ha! Would the state of North Carolina come to London after him for one speeding ticket? He didn't think so. Were it not for Dena, he would be there now, letting his British buddies pour enough alcohol down him to drown out the god-awful racket in his head.

Dena. What kept her here? What had made her put their home back together single-handedly? She should be angry at him or hurt or afraid. She did not appear to be any of those things, although he could not exactly determine what her mood was. And he was confused by her silence.

Britt sat on the sofa with his arms folded and cursed his brother until dawn.

—————CHAPTER—————

TWENTY-NINE

Hungry eyes watched Britt. He stood in the darkness on the boat dock on Monday night, the dog by his side. Brandy growled at the canoe on the water until Britt snapped his fingers for her to hush. He leaned against the rail, staring at the reflection of moonlight on the black water. Lost in the blackness of his own mood, he couldn't feel the eyes that greedily caressed his body from a distance. He did not know that those same eyes had watched for Dena from a certain point on the road this morning through a rifle scope, hoping to see her car come around the curve. Or that they had later spotted Dena from a pontoon boat that afternoon while she was digging about in her flowers, half-hidden by tree branches. Dena had walked down to the dock once, a nice, clean shot, but by then two men in a bass boat had begun trolling back and forth between the pontoon boat and the dock. The men had seemed more interested in staring at the pontoon boat than in their fishing, and the pontoon boat had left.

Now, at midnight, Britt turned from the dock, reset the security sensors, and went inside the house. The canoe paddled away quietly. Never mind. There was a better way to kill Dena than from the water. It might take a little longer, but Britt was worth the wait.

Monday had been spent in a kind of a silent dance between the Jordans: Dena working in the yard, Britt working in the basement. Dena did not speak one word to him the entire day, but once, when he came upstairs for food, she had smiled a sad, sweet smile at him that had nearly stopped his heart. In fact, a raw pain had lodged around his heart as the day wore on, and he wondered how it continued to beat inside his chest against the hard edge of that pain. Britt's need to work was desperate, the only distraction that could keep him from murdering his brother. The satisfying image of his hands killing Phillip remained fixed in his brain, a videotape stuck on pause. And so he had worked on the boat for eighteen hours straight, the hatred in his soul intensifying the physical pain in his chest.

There was nothing more Britt could do to the boat tonight, but he had to do something. His anger had become a molten pain within him, and if he let it explode, it would surely scald Dena. It was important to him to protect her from that. Perhaps tomorrow she would speak to him again.

Despite the late hour, Britt undertook the task of wrestling with the window valances. He lifted the television back to its place inside the entertainment center and reconnected the stereo components. This did not take nearly enough of the dark hours of the night, and after he was done, he paced the house restlessly, a trapped animal. Britt was afraid to sleep. He was terrified that the image of his hands on his brother's throat—squeezing until Phillip's heart stopped and blood poured out of his mouth and the flesh turned black beneath his fingers—would become a nightmare that would seize his own heart and stop it.

At three a.m., Dena was awakened by the sound of Britt's Monteverdi roaring up the driveway. Three hours later, she sat on the deck in a silk robe, sipping coffee, watching the mist rise from the lake in the rosy light of dawn. She thought she heard the sound of a racing engine on the road above the house, a sound she had waited three hours to hear. No car turned down their driveway. She sighed. Surely Britt would return. Surely he was not out tracking down his brother. Of course, today was Tuesday, the day he normally left for New York for his vocal training with Mr. Marcello. But surely he would say good-bye before he left.

Just as she was bringing the cup of coffee to her lips, a chainsaw fired up beneath the deck. She nearly dropped the cup, the coffee spilling down her robe. Jumping up and running to the edge of the deck, she leaned over. There was Britt, chainsaw in hand, enveloped in blue smoke, attacking a few low-lying branches over the boat ramp. Evidently, the launching of the Chris Craft was imminent. Had he slept? Was he sane? Where was his car? When he looked up at her, she gave a small wave and went inside to wash the coffee stain from her robe. Later in the day, she discovered that his car was just outside the gate, as if he had coasted from the road.

The entire day passed. Britt sanded the cured finish furiously by hand with a fine grain buffing powder. Dena's concern grew by the hour. If he had forgotten his appointment with Marcello, then his state of mind was worse than she had imagined. She could not even picture what anger, harbored for so long, would do to a man.

At about five o'clock, Britt called her name for the first time in three days. "Dena! I need you!"

She hurried outside. Britt gestured to one side of the boat ramp. "Stand there and watch for me. I've barely left clearance for the boat to come down. Raise your hand before a limb scratches the finish so I can stop the winch." His voice was rough. She could see that he badly needed a shave.

It sounded like a simple enough task, but it was nerve-racking. The new finish was beautiful, sanded to a fine luster, and she anticipated an angry reaction from Britt if it were scratched. Slowly the boat was lowered down the ramp, the cables taut, winches groaning. Twice Dena stopped Britt and moved a branch aside for the boat to continue. Both Dena and the machinery were relieved when the boat finally settled in the water.

Britt boarded the boat at once and fired the twin inboards, listening to the motors. Dena turned and headed toward the house when he didn't motion for her to join him. From the living room, she watched as Britt sped away in the boat. She dabbed at her eyes with the hem of her T-shirt and stuck her hand in her pocket, feeling his wedding band, which she had kept safe for three days. It had hurt when he jumped in the boat and fired the engines without a backwards glance at her. She could only hope the wind and the power of the boat would blast away some of his anger.

It was late when he returned, and she was in bed reading. He hated to disturb her peace with his disquiet, but he needed a shower and a shave badly. He eased into their bedroom. She looked up without speaking. Since she didn't speak, he didn't either, and he slipped into the bath, took his shower, and put on fresh clothes. He looked at her for a long moment before starting out the door, not knowing where he was heading.

She spoke for the first time. "Stay, Britt." She patted the bed beside her. "You must be exhausted."

"I am," he said and stood looking at her another moment.

"A package arrived from your mother this evening," Dena said. "She called twice tonight to make sure you opened it. It's on that chair."

She didn't say another word. He picked up the package and sat down in the chair. More time passed before he opened the package, glanced at the contents, and then read the card. He did not lift anything out of the box for Dena to see.

He muttered, "I swear, Mom, you're even crazier than I am." Then he leaned his head on his hands, elbows on his knees. Several more minutes passed before he moved, finally coming to his place beside her in the bed, not undressing, not speaking. She switched off the light. In the darkness, he reached for her hand, and it was as strong and warm as he remembered. Neither of them moved, afraid of disturbing the other, until both finally found sleep.

Sleep did not last. Sometime after midnight, Britt sat up suddenly, his breath short and ragged, sweat pouring from his body. He rubbed his chest, his heart banging, tight with pain.

"What do you want me to do?" Dena asked.

"Get—my—brother—out—of—my—head!"

She wrapped her arms around him.

"I've got to do something, Dena." He was unable to draw a deep breath. "I've got to do something. He's choking the life out of me. I imagine myself pounding his face, over and over, but I look and it's my face. It's my blood. My heart I'm ripping through his throat." He began to shake, his throat choked shut. "I can't do it anymore! I'm killing myself, not him. If I don't stop it, I'll die. I don't know what to do. I can't even think over this racket in my head. Tell me what to do, Dena."

She touched his swollen right hand. "Can you play?"

"I don't know," he whispered. "Maybe."

"Go," she said. "Pour the noise in your head into your piano. Then listen to your own heart. I can't tell you what to do, but I can promise that there is an answer, prepared just for you, if you'll only listen."

Feeling oddly alone, he got out of bed and left the room. He walked down the stairs, looked up at their room, then down at his piano waiting for him. Moonlight seemed to be caught between the two, peaceful, a marked contrast to his own spirit. He slowly moved across the room in the semi-darkness, rubbing his chest, and sat down at the piano. She seemed foreign to him somehow, like a woman he had never touched. He wasn't sure that she would welcome the passion he was about to pour into her. After rubbing the sweat from his hands onto his shorts, he touched the keyboard.

The piano resisted at first but finally gave in to his touch, which was urgent, demanding. Pieces of anger and bitterness began to break from his heart as he poured his agony into the instrument. It was music meant to be played only once, carrying the fever within the musician away forever, a melody that would not be remembered by Britt or Dena later.

The music flowed out of him for what felt like hours, and the silence that it left behind lasted even longer. Britt did not move from the piano—he just sat there with his head in his hands. The last pieces of anger had cut through his soul, searing his chest with hot pain that subsided slowly. Now only his hand hurt. And finally, even that pain subsided. He rubbed his hand. It was no longer swollen.

"Dena!" he shouted.

"Yes, Britt?" Her voice was soft, floating down from the balcony above his head.

"I know what to do," he said urgently. "I have to do it now. Come with me. Bring the box Mom sent."

She did it quickly, as she was already dressed.

"Right now. It has to be done now, while there's no pain." He rubbed his chest. "If the pain comes back, it will be too late."

He took her by the hand and pulled her toward the dock. A haze hung over the lake like a curtain in the moonlight expecting to be parted.

"You've got to take me out on the lake," he said. "Get me so lost that I don't know where I am." They boarded the old Chris Craft, and he fired the engines.

"What if I get lost?" she asked. "I'm not as familiar with the lake as you are."

"You won't," he answered. "Just don't run over anything in the dark."

She idled away from the point and eased the throttle forward. He sat with his eyes closed, the box in his lap. After several minutes, she asked, "Are you lost yet?"

"No. There's an island right there." He pointed, his eyes still closed.

Thinking to confuse him, she started to circle the island.

"Don't run over that . . ." A sudden whump that halted the boat interrupted him. ". . . mud bank."

"Sorry." She backed off the mud, the hull grinding on the sand.

"This isn't fiberglass, Dena," he said with a chuckle. "You've got to be careful. I can drive better with my eyes shut."

Finally, after twenty minutes of riding in circles, he declared that he was lost. "So am I, Britt," she said. "We'll have to wait until dawn to get home."

"Surely not." He stood up, his eyes still closed, and extracted a rock from the box.

A rock. Dena cleared her throat, but she asked no questions.

Feet planted apart, he tossed the rock in the air and caught it with one hand, again and again, swaying with the rhythm of the boat's wake

Finally he spoke. "Everything I felt against my brother, I put into this rock. It's not because he deserves it; it's because I don't want to feel it anymore. I forgive you, Phillip." As simple as that. He flung the rock in an arc into the air, and it disappeared into the mist. They both heard it plop into the water, but even Dena, who was watching for it, did not see where it fell. "Now take me home," he said.

She fired the engines and he felt the boat make a wide one-eighty. He fell asleep before she had the boat on plane.

When he awoke, it was to a gray dawn. Apparently Dena had given up on finding her way home in the dark and had anchored and waited out the night beside him in the boat. He stared hard at her until her hazel eyes opened.

"You didn't leave me," he said.

"No, Britt." It was a whisper; she was hoarse from the damp air. "That's not how it works." She reached into her pocket and pulled out his ring.

He took it from her and slipped it back on. "Would you still do it again?" He looked at the wedding band on his finger as he asked this.

"Yes."

He was silent for a minute. Then he looked her in the eye. "I don't know what to say. I'm embarrassed even to ask you to forgive me."

In a heartbeat, she was in his arms, her lips warm on his. He had never known forgiveness could taste so sweet.

"You put me to shame," he said quietly. "I'm not worthy of your forgiveness after all I've put you through." He held her close. Only when she began to cough did he realize that she was shivering from the cold.

"What have I done?" he asked. "Now I've made you sick on top of making you miserable for three days."

"You know what day it is?" she asked in surprise.

"Of course; it's Wednesday."

"Why didn't you go to New York yesterday?" she asked.

"I wasn't about to leave until you spoke to me again. Why wouldn't you talk to me, Dena?"

She stroked his hair lovingly. "Would you have listened to anything I said?"

"Probably not," he said humbly. "I'll listen now."

"First explain to me about the rock," she said.

"Oh." He rubbed her arms, trying to warm her. "According to Mom's note, my father buried it under a tree while I was in the Army. It was his way of putting the past behind him. Evidently, he was going to dig it up and give it to me when I came home to prove that he'd forgiven my rebellion. Of course, I never did go home until it was too late." He paused. "The rock is gone forever now, impossible for me to reclaim. And so is my hatred toward Phillip."

There was a silence. The mist began to lift as the sun rose above the trees to the east. In the light of a new day, she looked at him in wonder.

"Do you know how God forgives?" she asked him.

"You're about to tell me."

"As far as the east is from the west," she said softly. "He forgives that far, with no limits, and as impossible to reclaim as that rock."

"Hmm," was his only response. "Let's go home and get you warm and dry. I've got to call Bonnie, which will probably be the hardest phone call I'll ever make. Do you think she'll forgive me?"

"Eventually," said Dena, "if you're patient."

He sighed deeply and moved to raise the anchor.

CHAPTER

THIRTY

"Head up. Head up. Too much luff."
Britt's terse words were clipped.

Acting as the helmsman of Britt's sloop, Charlie Duncan steered close into the wind, his eyes as much on Britt as they were on the sails. This was his third sailing lesson, and he was trying hard to master the skills Britt had taught him. Trying to please Britt.

During their previous two lessons, Britt had been equally short with his words, but Charlie had soon figured out that his friend's mood was actually quite affable. Britt had slouched against the gunwale, squinting into the sun as he watched the sails, grinning at Charlie from time to time. Sailing in general—and Charlie's attempts at sailing in particular—seemed to offer him pleasant amusement, and Charlie had felt at ease.

But not today. Today Charlie felt he was imposing on Britt, but since he was there at Britt's invitation, he felt awkward suggesting they end the lesson. As the July sun beat hot on their backs, Britt stared darkly at the water, his eyes narrow. He barely glanced at the sails, his quick instructions coming from instinct and from listening to the sails. Not once did he look at Charlie or flash a grin in his direction. Today Britt seemed displeased with something, and frankly, Charlie found him intimidating.

That is until Charlie saw Britt's hand shaking when he let go of one jib sheet and reached for the other. He stared at Britt with unmasked concern, the sloop stalling, and Britt looked up with a frown. Their eyes met, and Britt looked away.

"Are you all right?" asked Charlie.

"Me? Hell, yeah. Why wouldn't I be?" Britt stood abruptly and dropped the jib with quick motions. "Steer me over to that pontoon boat." As Charlie did what he was told, wondering whether he was about to be left stranded, Britt crammed his hair under a baseball cap. "Steady. Hold your course." Britt lowered the mainsail, and the boat drifted alongside the pontoon.

Grabbing the boat's rail, Britt grinned at the half-dozen passengers enjoying the sun and a few beers. "Anybody got a cigarette I can bum?" he asked politely.

One woman gave him an appraising stare, winked, and said, "Sure. Trade you one for an autograph."

"That'll require a light to be an even trade," rejoined Britt smoothly.

The woman plundered her bag and came up with a pencil, someone else produced a paper towel for Britt to sign, and the exchange was made. Britt shoved off and returned to his seat. While Charlie raised the mainsail in an attempt to get the boat moving, Britt dragged slowly on the cigarette, his eyes closed.

Eventually Britt removed the cap, shaking out his hair with a sheepish shrug in Charlie's direction. In a low voice, he said, "Considering that I have no idea what my insane brother will do next, my wife is still in danger, and my step-daughter is afraid of me, I'm doing all right." After a pause, he added, "And did I mention my agent and Lori Sink, who both hate me now, are writing my unauthorized biography? Oh, yeah, and I'm still facing a federal indictment for cocaine possession."

Charlie watched Britt out of the corner of his eye as the sail began to fill. Britt smoked deeply, his eyes still closed. The next time he spoke, his voice was so low Charlie wasn't sure he was meant to hear it. "And one of my many mistresses calls to me." Britt smoked the cigarette down to the filter before he opened his eyes and held out a steady hand in Charlie's direction, palm down, to prove that the nicotine had done its job.

"Talk to me, Britt," said Charlie.

Britt squinted at him, his head cocked to one side. "Ever been addicted to anything?" he asked.

Charlie shrugged. "Don't know that I have." With a short laugh, he added, "Maybe Sue's brownies."

"What did you do about it?"

"I asked her to stop making them," said Charlie.

Britt appraised the other man for a long moment. "You live an enviable life, my friend," he finally said.

Charlie met Britt's eyes. How odd that Britt Jordan, of all people, would say that.

Britt studied the filter before discarding it. "Twenty five years ago, I was addicted to a variety of weeds. My father kicked my ass into the Army instead of a rehab center. Cleaned me up just as effectively." The sail beside his head luffed. "Sheet in." Britt stood up and didn't speak again until he had the jib flying.

When he returned to his seat, Britt squinted up at Charlie once again. "Tell me, have you ever been to one of my concerts?"

"Yes, I have," said Charlie. "It was a few years ago, before I met Sue. You were phenomenal!"

Britt closed his eyes and rubbed his chest. His jaw clenched, and he muttered, "The spotlight, it seems, is the strongest addiction of all."

"I can see how that would be true," Charlie said quietly. "It was obvious to anyone who saw you on stage that you loved it."

"Loved it, absorbed it, needed it, drew my life from it. Hold steady—you've got the right of way." After a weighted silence, Britt looked Charlie in the eye and spoke in the voice that millions of people had paid to hear. "Music is my soul; rock and roll is my blood; and the crowds are the air I breathe. The stage was a lovely mistress, but she was killing me, so I walked away from her. It was easy enough at the time, but it's been over three months now, and I need a fix in a bad way."

"So what are you going to do?" asked Charlie.

"Hold my own course steady for now. That's all I can do. I'm sick of her, and yet she calls to me. She wants to consume not only me but my Dena as well. I'm in a cold sweat now just thinking of how much my fame has threatened my wife. I can't go back, but some days it's damn hard going forward." Britt studied Charlie, rubbing his face with one hand. "I don't suppose you can connect with anything I've said."

"Maybe not," said Charlie, "but I can sympathize. And I can pray for you."

Britt held out his still steady hand and pointed his middle and forefinger at Charlie. "So there you go. Whether you'll admit it or not, you do have an addiction. Religion."

Charlie met Britt's eyes. "And do you think Dena is addicted?"

Britt looked away. "No. She is kind and tenderhearted and forgiving. Like that guy in the Bible who was shipwrecked."

Surprised, Charlie asked, "Do you mean Paul?"

"Yeah. Shipwrecked and beaten—I can relate to that."

With a chuckle, Charlie said, "I hate to burst your bubble,

Britt, but Paul had innocent blood on his hands and was pretty proud of it, until, well, until he wasn't."

"Was this before or after he was shipwrecked?"

"Before. And the people who beat him were, ironically, happy when he was a murderous bully and not happy when he changed."

Britt folded his arms across his chest and looked darkly at the water. "So being shipwrecked is hopeless."

"Not necessarily," said Charlie. "Can I ask you something, Britt?"

Britt shrugged.

"Do you believe in God?"

Britt glanced at the sails and eased out the jib sheet. When he spoke, his eyes were on the water. "I think if there is such a thing, it has nothing to do with me." He looked back at Charlie, a challenge in his eyes.

Charlie met his challenge squarely. "Fair enough." He held Britt's gaze unflinchingly. "But what if life's mysteries can't be explained in any other way? Talent. The love of a woman. Forgiveness. They're all a mystery to me." Charlie squinted at Britt. "The fact that you found Dena. Maybe even the fact that you've survived all your escapades."

"Luck," said Britt, rubbing his chest.

Charlie looked at Britt's tanned hand against his chest. That hand had enough talent to grab the world by the throat, yet it could do nothing to assuage the pain in the man's heart. "What if there was someone big enough," said Charlie softly, "to pull you out of the shipwreck and hang with you, even when you're beaten?"

Britt stood abruptly. "Take me home, skipper. I have a better way to chase my demons." He grinned at Charlie. "What do you know about carpentry?"

"I do all right for a jackleg," said Charlie with a slow smile.

"Good enough. We're going to build a studio onto my house. Me and you. Starting today." Britt stepped agilely onto the foredeck as Charlie brought the boat about.

"We are?" asked Charlie.

"Yeah. Work is my religion. And besides, you said you wanted to repay me for these lessons." He watched with pride as Charlie executed the maneuver of turning the boat smoothly. "Damn, Charlie, you're getting good at this." The familiar boyish mischief shone in his eyes. "Learning that move ought to be worth some carpentry help. Whadaya think?"

The grand jury would be meeting in August to decide whether or not to bring an indictment on the cocaine matter. Because of the publicity it had generated, the world now had a general idea where Britt was hiding. Very soon, reporters had his location pinpointed exactly.

But for one detail, Britt would have happily packed up his family and moved to Australia the day the first reporter stepped onto his dock, setting off the alarm. That detail was Bonnie. She had very little to say to Britt since the night Phillip had invaded their home. As the humid weeks of July ground forward, the possibility of an indictment as depressing as the gray haze overhead, all of Bonnie's energy was funneled into her art. She worried for hours over fine details that couldn't be seen more than a foot away from the painting. Few friends called, and she never asked for permission to spend the day with anyone. The only thing that seemed to cheer her up was the progress of the new studio, which Britt had promised to share with her. Dena and Britt both agreed that dodging reporters was preferable to upsetting the child with another move.

And so they remained in their home on the lake. Besides the guards on the water, now guards openly patrolled the property, the Rottweiler frequently pacing beside them.

To provide a distraction for Bonnie, Dena asked the tutor she had hired to start coming to their home three days a week. The plan was for this man, Marvin Stancell, to teach Bonnie advanced studies in English and history in addition to the art training. Bonnie would continue to attend public school for math and science.

On the last day of July, Mr. Stancell approached Dena as she was preparing supper in the kitchen. "Mrs. Jordan, we have a problem with your daughter," he said.

Dena looked up, startled. "What's wrong?"

"She goes into a panic every time I mention school starting." Marvin's eyes were kind beneath his white hair.

Drawing in a deep breath, Dena said, "Define panic."

"This morning she began to hyperventilate. I don't think she was faking it."

"Of course not; Bonnie has always been very straightforward." Dena frowned and put a hand to her throat. "Or she has been until the last few weeks." She looked at Marvin. "Is she that afraid of being with the other children?"

Marvin nodded. "Yes, I think so. After all that's happened with Mr. Jordan, I think going to public school will be too much pressure for her at this time." He hesitated, stepped forward. Tactfully, he added, "You do have the means to hire a tutor for math and science."

"Thank you, Mr. Stancell. We will definitely take action at once."

Marvin cleared his throat. "One more thing. I have a granddaughter in Charlotte who's about Bonnie's age. I think they would have a lot in common. Perhaps I could bring her with me one day next week."

"That would be nice," said Dena. "You're very kind to take such an interest in Bonnie."

"She's quite a special child. I don't like to see her hurting."

"Neither do I," said Dena softly. As soon as Marvin left, she made a few phone calls and soon had a stack of papers in her printer, which she studied until Bonnie and Britt came in for supper.

That evening she approached Britt. He was sitting at the desk scrutinizing his monthly business statements.

She tapped the papers in her hand until he looked up. Abruptly, she asked, "What was your best subject in school?"

"P.E." He flexed his biceps for her inspection.

"Besides that?"

"Chorus."

She sighed in exasperation. "I mean, a real subject."

He shut one eye and looked at her. "Tell me what you want me to say, Dena, and I'll say it."

"Specifically, how were you in math?"

"I always made A's in geometry," he said. "Aren't you proud?"

"What about algebra?"

"Algebra. Well." There was a long silence.

Shaking her head, Dena turned on her heel and left the room. In a minute, she was back. Once again, she stood in front of him until he looked up. "Tell me again about you and math."

He indicated the printout in his hand. "I can read a balance sheet as well as a navigational chart and a blueprint. Do I get a diploma?"

"Maybe." She pulled a sheet from the stack in her hand and handed it to him. "Tell me the answer to the first problem."

"Algebra. Hmm." He studied the sheet for a second. "X equals eleven. Easy."

"How did you know that?" she asked.

"Any idiot can look at that and figure out the answer," he said.

"This idiot can't. It took me five minutes."

"I apologize. Are you going back to school to learn algebra?"

"No." She pointed at the paper again. "Tell me the answer to that one."

He squinted at the figures. "This one's a little trickier, but N=353-X."

She flipped the papers over and exclaimed, "How can you do that in your head?"

He shrugged. "I just can."

"Could you always?"

"Yes."

"Then why didn't you say you made As in algebra?" she demanded.

"Because I made Ds. I refused to write the formulas out, so they barely passed me, even though I always had the right answer."

Once again, she handed him a paper. "Take a pencil and figure this one out. Put in all the steps."

"I'm busy," he said in a deliberately rough voice.

"Humor me."

He sighed and worked the problem quickly, beginning with the answer, and then working his way backwards.

"Britt, you just worked the problem backwards," she pointed out.

"So? Flunk me."

"Are you able to work it forwards?"

"I—don't—need—to," he said distinctly.

She was not put off. "What if you were going to teach someone else how to do it?"

"Honey, do you want me to teach you algebra?"

"No, I want you to teach Bonnie."

"Bonnie's doing fine in school," said Britt. "You're the one having trouble."

She looked him in the eye. "You and I are going to tutor Bonnie in math and science."

He scratched his head. "Why?"

"Because Mr. Stancell says she's in a panic about returning to public school."

Britt's face tightened. "Because of me."

"It's just for now, until she's feeling more confident." Dena patted his shoulder.

"Sure, I'll do it," he said with enthusiasm. "I'll do a good job, really, I will."

"Will you teach her to think forwards instead of backwards?"

"I'll teach her both ways. It will be the best thing that ever happened to her brain." He was silent for a moment. Humbly, he said, "Thanks for having faith in me."

She smoothed his hair with her fingers and kissed him. "I do. Now and always. Let's go tell Bonnie our plan."

The grand jury met three days later. Dena and Bonnie stayed close to Britt all day. When he went outside, he was harassed by reporters shouting questions from boats out on the lake. When he came inside, he paced the entire house, too agitated even to play his piano. For a long hour, he poured his restless fever into his guitar, pulling wave after wave of brilliant sound from the instrument that sent Dena scurrying for ear plugs. Nobody could make a guitar talk quite like Britt could, the music flowing straight from his heart through his sensuous fingers.

And then the house went silent as they all waited for the phone to ring. Britt's lawyers had assured him that, even if an indictment came down, the court could never get a conviction. They had Dena's statement on their side as well as an entire sheriff's department that doubted his guilt. Britt's fingerprints were on none of the bags, since he had very carefully collected them, but there was one clear print on the bag found in the freezer. Once they proved that the print belonged to Phillip, his lawyers said, Britt would be cleared.

Of course, Phillip had vanished.

Late in the afternoon, the phone finally rang. Britt listened intently, the receiver to his ear, his face not registering the news as Dena and Bonnie paced anxiously in front of him. He hung up the phone and let several seconds pass before he spoke. "It's over," he said quietly.

While Dena hugged him, laughing and crying at the same time, Bonnie disappeared without asking a single question. Knowing she had gone to her studio behind the garage, they left her alone. Eventually, she returned, carrying a large canvas, which she set on an easel in the living room.

Bonnie stood back and looked at it, arms folded. Britt and Dena joined her, heads tilted as they studied her work. The painting was a mess, actually; still wet. Gone were the dark, subtle colors, the minute details of the past few weeks. The canvas was covered with great splatters of the brightest colors in Bonnie's palette. No one spoke for a minute.

Britt tilted his head farther. "It's upside down," he said.

Bonnie tilted her head against his and they stood and viewed the painting, their heads together. Then she stepped forward and turned the canvas around. "Let's eat. I'm starving," she said.

Britt closed his eyes and smiled, still standing in the middle of the living room. He stayed in that position a long while as Dena and Bonnie clattered about in the kitchen, their voices better music to him than any he could ever make.

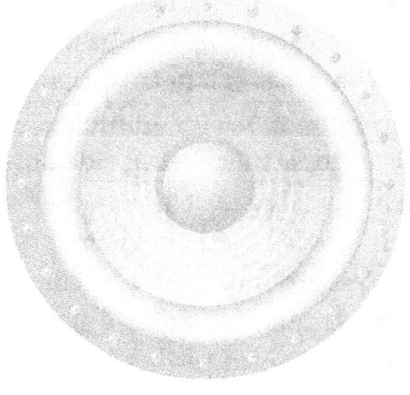

CHAPTER

THIRTY-ONE

Britt ran up the steps from the lake, banged into the house, and literally skidded to a halt on the hardwood floor in the living room. "I have forgotten something," he muttered to himself. He flipped through the calendar on his cell phone. September sixth. There was something important about that date, something he was supposed to remember, and the day was nearly over. He flipped through some papers on his desk, opened and shut several drawers. He telephoned his secretary, who seemed befuddled. She had no idea of the date's significance either.

"Are you sure?" Britt insisted.

"Britt," Phyllis said firmly, "there's been nothing on your schedule for months. I'm as busy as ever just telling people they can't see you. If you had an appointment, I would have synced it with your calendar."

"Am I going crazy?" asked Britt.

"Maybe not," responded Phyllis blithely. "You always did have a habit of remembering only the things you want to remember."

"But this is important. I'm sure of it. And I have a strange feeling I'm going to be in big trouble if I don't remember it soon."

He hung up and started searching through the house, not sure what he was looking for, just hoping that something would jog his memory. On went the television and then off again. He fiddled with the stereo, played a few notes on the piano, rambled through drawers, and took a few books off the shelf and flipped through them. Surely something would help him figure it out.

Back he went to Dena's desk, where she kept a daily calendar. September 6. She had made no notations for this date. The calendar had a poem or something printed on it:

And hope does not disappoint us . . .

It was a Bible verse, more likely. No help there. He returned his cell phone to its place in the top drawer, slammed the drawer shut, and ran upstairs without missing a beat.

"Dena," he began before he reached their room, "I have forgotten something."

"And what have you forgotten, Britt?" She was sitting in bed, reading.

"Well, if I knew what it was, it wouldn't be forgotten, would it?"

She raised one eyebrow at him.

He continued, "It's something important. Somewhere I'm supposed to be; something I'm supposed to do; somebody I'm supposed to see. In fact, I think I should be doing it right now."

"Have you checked with Phyllis?"

"Yes, but she doesn't know. It must be some appointment I made myself and didn't write down."

Dena chuckled. "I told you that you were going to get into trouble talking on the phone in the middle of the night. Who were you talking to at four a.m. three mornings ago? I've never heard you laugh so hard."

"Could have been anybody in the world . . . I don't remember right now. It might have been Charlie; he's a funny guy at four a.m."

"Charlie? Don't tell me you've been waking poor Charlie up in the middle of the night!"

"Of course not. Sometimes he gets up early and sends me a text to see if I'm still up. But you're right. I probably promised somebody I'd do something, hung up and went to bed, and forgot by the time I woke up. I'm sure somebody is mad at me or is going to be. I apologize in advance, in case it's you." He stood at the dresser and brushed his hair. "September sixth," he muttered.

"Oh," said Dena. "You've just got today's date stuck in your head because Bonnie has been talking all week about going to Charlotte for her sleepover with Mr. Stancell's granddaughter."

"I knew about that. This is something different, something I'm supposed to be doing."

He had started to undress as he said this last thing, and he looked up to see Dena watching him, smiling. "What?" he asked.

"I just like to look at you. I think you look the best you ever have."

He glanced down at his torso. He had married her in the middle of a tour, which always took a few pounds off him. Over the summer, he had gained that back, plus maybe five pounds extra. "This is important," he scolded. "I'm trying to concentrate."

One eyebrow went up again, but the smile did not leave her face.

He didn't blink. He reached inside his closet and pulled out a pair of dress pants, hand-stitched by an Italian tailor to fit him perfectly. "Do you know what we haven't done lately?"

She looked him over as he put on the pants. "Gone to bed

wearing our best clothes?"

"Danced. We haven't danced in a long time."

"I thought you were trying to concentrate."

"I am." He held out his hand toward her. He didn't put on a shirt.

She looked him over. "I'll be delighted to dance with you, Britt Jordan. Just let me put some clothes on."

"Wear that dress." He opened her closet, and then shut it again immediately, shaking his head at the disarray. "If you can find it. The pink one you wore on our honeymoon."

"Don't worry; I'll find it."

He ran downstairs and popped a CD in the stereo. Jazz, plenty loud. They had the whole house to themselves. When he turned and looked up, she was already on the balcony, wearing that dress. Tonight, she looked more stunning than outrageous, her shapely body waiting for his arms alone.

Britt ran up the stairs, and then stood there for a moment, just looking at her. He rubbed his chest where his heart was doing funny flip-flops, amazed by her beauty, amazed by the simple wonder of her love for him. Charlie was right—the love of a good woman was a mystery too great for the human mind to fathom.

He stood still, twisting his wedding band. She crooked her finger at him and started walking toward him. When he met her halfway, he took her in his arms, feeling her hands warm against his bare skin. Whispering in her ear, he said, "I have yet to collect on my three million dollars. Will you dance with me a long time, maybe a hundred thousand dollars' worth?"

"Of course," she said softly. "You know I will."

They danced far into the night, often moving to their own rhythm instead of that of the music playing below. Much later, as he kissed her on the balcony with the music still playing, his hands tangled in her hair, his heart pounding at the sheer loveliness of it all, he wished, without quite verbalizing it, for somebody to explain to him what hope would look like for a man like him.

The next day, Dena was cleaning the house, not her favorite occupation. Bonnie was spending the weekend in Charlotte with her new friend, and Britt had taken the Monteverdi out for a spin.

Just when she was mopping the kitchen floor, the doorbell rang. Odd. The few visitors they had were always announced by the guard at the gate.

Without putting her mop down, Dena went to the door and opened it. There, on her doorstep, stood Mark Blue, one of the great names among all the great British rock and roll stars. Tall and lanky with unruly black hair and piercing blue eyes. Shirt unbuttoned to reveal a mass of chest hair. A cigarette hung from his lips, and his roguishly handsome face peered at her through a blue haze. She blinked twice and stared without speaking.

"Allo, miss, is this Britt Jordan's place?" he inquired.

She nodded.

"Well, is 'e here, then?"

Finally finding her voice, she stuttered, "Uh, no. He'll—uh—he'll be back shortly, though."

There was a silence as he continued to stand before her. Finally, he said, "Do you think I might come inside or am I to wai' on the doorstep?"

She shook her head quickly. "Of course. I'm so sorry." Stepping aside, she gestured for him to come in.

He took one step inside the doorway and peered at her curiously. "Miss, are you sure he remembered I was coming?"

Dena glanced at her left hand holding the mop. She had taken off her wedding band before beginning her chores. There she stood—no makeup, her hair tied up with an orange scarf, wearing the slouchiest outfit imaginable. For all she knew, she had dirt smeared on her face.

In a country drawl, she answered, "Oh, that Mr. Britt, he don't never tell me nothin.' You just come right on in and have a set-down here. Will you be staying all night?"

"I had though' I might, but . . ."

"Well, of course, you will, now, that's all there is to it. I'll just get your bags in and send that big ol' long car on its way."

"Are you sure, miss?" he asked.

"Why, sure, I'm sure. Mr. Britt, he'll be back real soon."

"And Mrs. Jordan?" Mark Blue persisted. "Is she here? It could be an imposition, if Britt forgo' to tell her, too, don't you see?"

"What I see is that you need to just set right down here and take a load off. What are you doing in these parts, anyway?"

"I had me concert in Charlotte last night. Britt said 'e migh' come join me, you know, slip on stage at the end like 'e used to do in the old days, and then lift a few with the lads after. I hoped 'e might actually do it, even though they say 'e's retired and all. Britt did insist tha' I pop around today, for sure, and told me which limousine service to call."

"I see," said Dena. Putting her mop away, she ran out to the limousine and retrieved his single bag. Lugging it up the steps to her front door, she muttered, "I am going to murder Britt Jordan."

Mark was seated on a sofa, looking around her living room. Politely she asked, "May I get you a drink before I put this in your room?"

"Sure, miss. Scotch."

"Mr. Britt, he—uh—he don't pay me to mix drinks. How

about I get you some nice, country water?"

He raised one eyebrow at her, and she raised one back at him. "Oh second thought, I'll wai' for Britt," he said.

"You do that." She was halfway up the steps with his suitcase when she heard his voice behind her.

"Miss, where does Britt keep his instruments? I migh' play a bit, you know, while I wait."

She turned around and looked him in the eye. "Britt's guitars are in that closet." Her flat country accent was gone. "Help yourself, Mr. Blue," she said in her normal voice and headed on up the stairs.

Not many minutes later, the Monteverdi roared down the driveway and screeched to a halt. Britt had remembered what he'd forgotten. He could hear the sound of a guitar as he ran up the steps, and he muttered, "Ho, boy. Dena is going to murder me."

Mark stood up immediately. "Britt Jordan, my friend, my man. I though' you had forgotten me."

"Mark, welcome, welcome. Look at you. You look great, man."

"I feel great. And you—you've never looked better. Didn't I tell you a few years ago you should ge' yourself a wife?"

"You did," agreed Britt. "That was about three wives back for you, too, wasn't it?"

"See? I took me own advice and look where it's gotten me."

Britt looked him over. "Waist deep in alimony?"

"Well, that, too, of course. That's just par' of it. But I'm happy. The third Mrs. Blue has made me about ten years younger than I was last year."

"And a bit thinner on top I see." Britt rubbed his friend's head.

"Wha' I've lost on top, you've put on in the middle, Britt, old boy." Mark tapped Britt's mid-section with the back of his hand.

"I know," said Britt, rubbing his stomach. "Dena's cookin', I guess."

"Say tha' again?"

Britt raised his voice. "I said, my wife, Dena . . ."

"I heard wha' you said," Mark broke in. "I want to hear you say cooking again. 'Cookin,'" he parroted. "You're turning into a Southerner, boy." Mark laughed raucously.

"Oh, man, say anything, insult me any way, just don't call me a Southerner." Britt chuckled and looked around. "Speaking of my wife, where is she?"

Mark sat down and laughed even louder. "You can't even keep up with your own woman. I just go' here, and already you're asking me where she is. Well, don't ask me, because I 'aven't seen her."

Britt frowned. "Who let you in?"

"The maid."

Britt scratched his head and looked upstairs toward his room, his brow puckered. "We haven't got a maid."

At this, Mark doubled over and hooted with laughter. "You're a dead man, Britt Jordan," he sputtered. "You forgo' to tell her I was coming, and now she's going to kill you for sure. I 'ope Rover's go' a big house because you're going to be sleeping with 'im."

"Your warm-hearted understanding is deeply appreciated," said Britt with drama.

"You're quite welcome. I can't wai' to see you charm your way ou' of this one."

"I won't have to."

"Oh, no?" Mark pointed a long finger at Britt, a lopsided grin on his face. "I'll wager a hundred American greenbacks that she'll be calling your ass up those steps any minute now to give it a good chewing over."

"No, she won't," Britt said with a smile.

"Of course, she will. You deserve tha' and worse."

"That's true, but she won't say a word to me."

"Ha! And you think you'll walk away from this withou' a scratch? Never happen."

Britt folded his arms. "I didn't say she wouldn't get me back. I just said she wouldn't say a word to me. You'll see."

Mark reached for Britt's guitar, making the instrument scream and laugh at Britt with high, quick notes. Then he switched to a blues rhythm and asked, "Where's the telephone? You need to call a florist." Deep, resonant notes rocked through the house, emphasizing the desperation of Britt's plight. "Better yet, call your jeweler. Diamonds may ge' you off the hook." The guitar laughed at Britt again. "Or 'ave you tried cash? Tha' used to work with my second wife well enough."

Britt chuckled and started toward the kitchen.

Mark jumped to his feet and put the guitar down. "Finally! I've 'ad to sit here in a drought waiting for you."

"I'm surprised Dena didn't offer you something, even if you did insult her by calling her the maid."

"Insult her? Now you're blaming this on me." Mark shook his head, his long hair waving. He was enjoying Britt's domestic quandary. "Anyway, I'm the one who was insulted. She tried to make me drink water. Imagine that!"

Britt laughed and poured a glass for himself. "You ought to try it some time. It's not half bad."

"Well, you 'ave your water, then, and point me toward the bar."

Britt passed one hand over his face. "I hate to tell you this, Blue, but I don't have a bar."

"Well, what 'ave you got, then?"

Britt opened the refrigerator door as Mark peered over his shoulder. There were three beers and a half-bottle of wine. Mark's head dropped to Britt's shoulder, and he let out a dramatic wail. "You did forget me. You didn't just forget to tell the missus, you plain forgo' I was coming."

Britt's face twisted with chagrin. "I'm sorry, man. It's been one heck of a summer."

"I though' the courts turned you loose."

"They did," said Britt, "but that's not all that's been going on." In a low voice, he explained, "There's a trigger-happy lunatic out there."

"You do attract the bullets, don't you?"

Still speaking quietly, Britt said, "This lunatic wants to kill my wife."

Mark whistled. "That would rattle your brains a bi' wouldn't it? I'm surprised she didn't pack and leave."

"You don't know Dena," said Britt. "You'll see." He stood on tiptoe and pulled a glass jar from the back of a cabinet. "I do have something here that might interest you." He held it up to the light for Mark's inspection before pouring an inch in a glass and handing it to Mark.

Mark swirled it, inhaled its aroma, sipped, and immediately started coughing. "What is that?" he sputtered.

"Cough medicine," answered Britt seriously. "It works every time."

Once again, Mark held the jar up to the light. "Is this what I think it is?"

"Yeap. Pure moonshine. Here, you're taller than I am. Push it to the back of the cabinet for me."

"Rationing it, are we?"

"Yeap. Cough season is coming up."

"And you? Won't you be joining me?" asked Mark as he shoved the jar back into place.

"Uh, no." Britt rubbed his chest. "Gives me heartburn these days."

Mark tapped on Britt's chest. "Alo? Is Britt Jordan in there? I say, are you in there, Britt?" He grabbed his host by the throat and shook. "What 'ave you done with him? You've killed him, you imposter!"

Britt laughed heartily and drew his guest out to the new studio that he and Charlie had almost finished framing. He explained his plans for bringing all his equipment from California and giving the sunniest corner to Bonnie. They reminisced over past escapades and practical jokes they had pulled on each other before returning to the living room.

"So, Britt," Mark was saying as he returned to the sofa, "it's too bad you didn't remember to make the show last night. We'd 'ave given the room qui' a shock, you know."

"I know." Britt was looking up at his room.

"Wha', you're getting nervous now, are you?" inquired Mark.

"No. I was just thinking that she's made you sweat for long enough. She'll be down in a minute."

"Me sweat?" Mark splayed a long hand on his chest. "I've go' nothing to sweat about. You, mate, are the one in trouble."

"Do I look like a worried man to you?" asked Britt with a sly grin.

"You look like a man about to ge' 'is ass chewed. Anyway, you missed a grand time after the show. We all drank to your memory. One of the lads brought this marvelous chick who was terribly disappointed you didn't come, you know wha' I mean?"

Britt smiled slowly, still watching his door. "Sounds like I didn't miss a thing."

At just that moment, the door opened. The men saw a lovely, elegant woman step out and cross the balcony. She was wearing a flattering emerald green dress, which revealed her long tan legs and gorgeous figure, and her hair was pinned up in a sophisticated twist. She looked down at the two men coolly, without smiling.

Mark stood up and nudged Britt. "Move over, Rover. It's going to be a long, cold night," he whispered.

Dena walked down the steps slowly and regally, her head held high. As she crossed the room, she looked at both men with narrowed eyes. When she reached Britt, she cut her eyes sideways at him. "Britt," she said levelly, her voice cool and refined.

Mark took a sip of his drink, expecting a show.

". . . How lovely of you. You've bought me another rock star for my birthday. You know how I love them." She walked straight past Britt and extended her hand to Mark.

Mark tried to swallow his sip of burning liquid, but he couldn't. He began to choke, his face turning red as he did his best to keep from spitting out the liquid.

Britt winked at him, kissed his wife on the back of the neck, and then dropped his head to her shoulder.

"You've got me," Britt said humbly. "I apologize."

Sweetly, Dena said, "Welcome to our home, Mr. Blue." She rubbed Britt's cheek with her hand. "I'm sorry to keep you waiting. I had to go fire our maid." And then she leaned against her husband and laughed the merriest laugh Mark had ever heard.

"See, I told you she wouldn't say a word."

Mark pointed a finger at Britt, thought a moment, then said, "But she did just kill you, right?"

"Actually, I think we're both dead men."

The evening grew late; the scent of Dena's jambalaya and apple pie still hanging in the air from dinner, spicy and homey. Dena and Britt sat on a sofa, her bare feet propped in his lap, and candles illuminated the room. The conversation turned mellow, Mark's mood aided by another dose of Britt's cough medicine, the half-bottle of wine, and a joint he had smoked on the dock after dinner while Britt helped Dena clean up the kitchen.

Mark turned to his friend. "This is an odd life you've chosen, Britt. No booze, no mates around you. Don't you crave the city lights?"

Britt looked around his home and at his wife's smiling face. "City lights are highly overrated," he said. "But someday soon, when we don't feel the need to stay so well-guarded, we might venture out in public once in a while." He pinched Dena's big toe. "Would you like to attend a premiere with me, dear?"

Dena shrugged. "Why, sure, Britt. It might be fun one time, mingling with the big shots."

Mark shook his head. "See, that's wha' I mean. 'Venture out,' 'one time.' You're holed up here in the country like a hermit. How long do you think you can live like this? Where do you see yourself twenty years from now?"

"Twenty years." Britt rubbed Dena's feet and smiled. "Twenty years from now, we'll be the best-looking old couple on the block."

"Still living here?"

Britt shrugged. "I see myself back in the Caribbean, sailing, at least part of the year." With a tilt of his head, he added, "Or as much as Dena can stand it." He looked at Mark. "What about you?"

"I'm asking you."

"Twenty years." Britt repeated. "Bonnie might have a couple of kids by then. I shall sit with my grandchildren on my lap at sunset and sing songs of the sea to them."

"Music," said Mark. "That's wha' I'm wanting to know. Will you sing again, Britt?"

"Yes."

"So, you've go' your voice back?" asked Mark.

"No. Britt Jordan's voice is dead. I've murdered it."

"I'm terribly sorry to hear that," Mark said. "Wha' will you do?"

With conviction, Britt said, "Come Monday, I'm going to toss aside everything I've worked on this summer and start something new."

"Are you sure, Britt?" Dena asked. To Mark, she added, "What he has written this summer is the best work he's ever done."

"And the work I'm going to do this fall will be better yet," said Britt. "I've decided that the music I've been writing is transitional. I need to cut myself loose from it and jump right into the middle of something new."

Mark looked at Britt. "Would you let me look at wha' you've been writing? Just ou' of curiosity."

"Sure." Britt stood up and went to the wall cabinet, unlocked a drawer, and pulled out a file folder. He handed Mark sheets of paper with lyrics written in Britt's neat hand. Chord changes were penciled in, but no melody line.

Mark looked through it, frowning, then selected one sheet and picked up Britt's guitar. He ran through the chords, still frowning. "Britt Jordan did not write this," he finally announced.

"Yes, I'm quite sure he did," Britt said.

"No. This is no' raunchy enough to be Britt's." Mark pointed his finger at Britt and said to Dena, "This man is an imposter. I hate to break your heart, bu' you 'ave not married Britt Jordan. Call your FBI and get his fingerprints checked."

Dena and Britt both grinned. Mark let the chord changes roll beneath his fingers. "Well, are you going to give me the melody," he said, "or am I to si' here all night doing this?"

"I'll do you one better. I'll sing one for you." Britt reached for the folder and pulled out the song he had sung the night of his birthday, the one he'd claimed would earn him a Grammy, and handed it to Mark. Then he sat at the piano and launched into the song.

He was only six measures into it when Mark yelled for him to stop. He stood up and stared at Britt. "Who the hell are you, man?"

Britt chuckled and began the song once more, nodding for Mark to join him on guitar. Music filled the house until the song's end. Mark let a few curse words fly.

"What's wrong with you?" he shouted at Britt. "You should be recording that now. Immediately. Where did you ge' that voice? I want it. Cough it up, and I'll buy it."

"The voice isn't for sale, but the song is," said Britt. "Are you interested?"

"Yes. Hell, yes. Will you sell any of the others?"

Britt carefully stacked the sheets in the folder. "Yes. My lawyer will contact you next week with a figure. Scored sheets will be available then."

His eyes locking with Britt's, Mark took the folder from him, pulled out the song Britt had just sung, and folded the sheet. Deliberately putting it into his pocket, he said, "I'm no' giving you a chance to change your mind on this one. It belongs to me, now, no matter what the price." He waited a moment for Britt to react. When he didn't even blink, Mark added, "You, Mr. Jordan, 'ave just made the biggest mistake of your career."

"No, I haven't," said Britt. His smile was confident and unperturbed. "My best work has yet to be written. I know that for a fact. Monday, I'm off on a new tack."

After Britt settled onto the sofa, his left arm around Dena, Mark leaned back in his chair, stretched his long legs in front of him, and said, "Okay, so we go' that question settled. In twenty years, you're going to be the undisputed god of rock and roll, still singing phenomenal music with that bitchin' new voice, and you can live any damn place you like. So let's ask a new question."

Dena raised one eyebrow at him.

"Excuse me, Dena. I forgo' me manners. Okay, Britt, here's another one for you. What's one thing you migh' do with a lo' of people you would never do with your wife?"

"Play poker," Britt answered so swiftly and seriously that Dena and Mark both laughed.

Mark turned to Dena, a challenge in his voice. "Now, it's your turn, pretty lady." Dena's eyes met his squarely, and Britt's jaw worked ever so slightly. Mark cleared his throat and paused. If he had meant to say anything impudent, he backed down. "Ah, yours is an easy question. Just tell me one place you would never go with Britt Jordan."

"A tattoo parlor," she replied without hesitation.

Britt grabbed both arms and gasped in mock horror. "What! You don't like my tattoos!"

She lightly touched his right forearm, tracing the finely detailed ink, and said, "This one reminds me of Britt's deliberate, meticulous way of taking care of things. Well, as long as he remembers what he's supposed to do," she added with a chuckle.

Mark hooted with laughter.

She moved his fingers from his left arm and kissed the center of the dragon tattoo. "This one is an exquisite work of art, *but*," she added with emphasis, "I don't see it."

"Wha'?" asked Mark. "You mean you don't get it?"

"Oh, I get it," replied Dena, tracing the design with her finger, from the image of Britt's ponytail through the sea dragon, ending with the imperiled comic heroine. "I just don't see it."

When both men stared at her, puzzled, she went on to explain, "As amazing as it is, it represents Britt's former life. I'm not naïve, but to my mind, Britt's real life didn't begin until we met." She was looking at Mark when she said this, and she didn't see Britt grab his hair. "When we're together," she continued, "just the two of us," she said in a sweet, melodic voice, glancing sideways at her husband, "I don't see it. Literally, it doesn't exist for me. And so it would be silly for him to go get another one," she finished.

"Aargh!" Britt leaned forward, his arms across his knees, and buried his face in his hands.

Dena patted him on the back. "Don't take it so hard," she said.

Britt didn't move. A loud metallic clank, like a heavy vault door opening, had reverberated through him at Dena's words. Then there was silence. Tense, Britt waited with dread for whatever racket would fill the silence. He expected the screaming music that had tormented him last year to blast through the open door in his mind.

Instead there came a whisper, so slight it was really not even a voice. The whisper said,

So you want to know what hope looks like? Start with your wife's smile.

Dena's hand was still around his back, and she whispered in his ear, "Are you all right?"

His head came up with a jerk, his eyes bleary, and he said, "Yeah. Yeah, I'm all right. I just need some air." He stood abruptly and started for the deck, rubbing his chest. Just as abruptly, he turned and came back, kissed her fully on the lips, and said, "Really, I'm all right."

And he went to stand on his deck, breathing in the crisp night air, trying to figure it all out. For the life of him, he didn't know what the whisper meant, but it had something to do with his tattoo. He was sure of it.

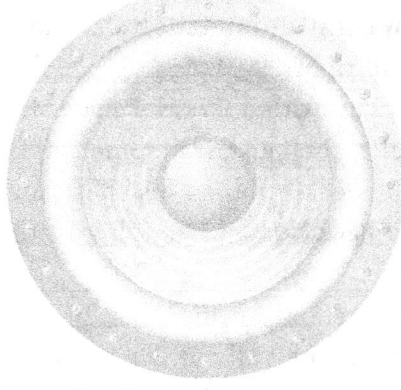

THIRTY-TWO

After Mark Blue left the next morning, Dena went for a run around the property, joined by the dog and paced by one of the guards. The security detail didn't like for her to be this close to the fence line, but Dena insisted that she needed the fresh air and exercise. She might even go for a swim this afternoon, which really would send them into apoplexy.

Just as she was starting her second lap, approaching the neighbor's property, the dog broke away and ran barking toward a figure that was walking around the neighbor's back yard. "Brandy, come!" Dena ordered.

The dog paused, looked over its shoulder at Dena, and then took off running again when the unidentified person whistled. Instead of attacking the person, however, the dog approached with a wagging tail.

Dena jogged closer to get a better look. With the distance and shadows, all she could tell was that it was a young woman, a blonde. As she came closer, however, a sick feeling hit her in the gut. She stopped and motioned for the guard to come closer.

"What is that girl doing here?" she asked.

"She works for the neighbor's cleaning service. She's bonded, and all her references checked out. Why, do you know her?" answered the guard.

"Uh, yeah," answered Dena. "Just hang back; I've got this." She approached the girl with one hand on her hip. "Rhiannon," was all she said.

The girl looked from her to the guard and back again. "What, are you going to get me fired from this job, too?" she asked.

"I just want to know what you're doing here. I don't think it's a coincidence that you're in our backyard again."

This time the girl looked pointedly at the dog before returning Dena's gaze. Otherwise she didn't respond.

"So you found us through our dog, how clever. That doesn't answer my question. Why are you here?"

"I like to clean, and I'm damn good at it. I was doing a good job for you, too, before you fired me."

Distinctly, with the voice inflection that Britt used so often, Dena said, "Why . . . are . . . you . . . here?"

"What's it to you?" responded the girl with a flip of her blonde hair. When Dena made no comment, Rhiannon said, "Look, I've got to get back to work. Keep your man in your own yard if you're afraid I'll steal him."

Dena watched the girl turn on her heel and walk smartly toward the house without a backward glance. With a click of her tongue to summon the dog, Dena turned toward her own home to see the guard looking on warily. As she approached him, he asked, "Is this a situation I need to take care of?"

"Make sure she leaves on time today, please. I'll let Britt handle this . . . situation, as you called it." When the guard paced alongside her, she added, "Thanks for the run. I'm going in now," and she walked on without him.

Really, she didn't want him to see how upset she was. What was it about that girl that got under her skin? As she came closer to her home, she heard two men talking, Britt's hearty laughter, and the resounding, rhythmic clang of a hammer hitting a nail. Charlie was here helping Britt finish the framing of the new studio. Shoot, she had wanted to tell him about Rhiannon and get it over with.

As she gave the dog a good-bye pat on the head and walked in the house, the sick feeling in her stomach gave way to a sense of dread. Oh, how she dreaded telling Britt! She would have to confess to him that she had, on two occasions, withheld the minor detail that Rhiannon had the key to their home in Deerfield. Britt would see her omission as a lie. It wasn't his anger that she dreaded—it was his disappointment in her.

In her defense, she had merely been protecting him from yet another star-struck fan. In retrospect, Dena realized that it really wasn't her job as a wife to be his guardian, protecting him from life's troubling details Even though it was virtually impossible that the girl could be the lunatic—she had neither the key to Britt's car nor the security code to the house after the system had automatically reset itself—Britt would want to have her questioned. He would definitely want her removed from the property. Unfortunately, her confession would have to wait until after Charlie left this evening.

Late evening, the shadows deep, twilight descending. Britt straightened up, hammer in his hand, and waved as Charlie's car passed through the gate. Charlie was a good friend for helping him with the framing, not to mention listening to Britt's latest concerns.

Another note had arrived from the lunatic today, this one hand delivered by Len. This note had been found outside the fence line, on the far edge of the tract of forest he had purchased as a buffer to the east of the house. And something about this note, brought to him as a physical piece of paper rather than an image on his cell phone, jogged his memory. The note simply read:

Britt, I'll be in your arms tonight.

Nothing threatening, on its own. But holding it in his hands, seeing the color of the paper and the girlish curly-q lettering, brought back the memory of the night he'd found that note in his undershorts. Could the girl Dena fired possibly be the lunatic? It seemed doubtful, but Len had asked the Deerfield police chief to check her out. Word had come back just an hour ago that she had moved to Statesville, but when Len went there with a deputy, the residence was empty. It was troubling to say the least.

Now Len was stuck in a traffic snarl on the interstate, and Britt was stuck hammering, at least for the next few minutes. He had gone upstairs a few minutes ago to show the note to Dena, but she was in the shower.

"Call me when you're dressed," he had shouted over the blast of five shower heads. "We need to talk." And after tucking the note inside the valet box on the dresser, he had returned to hammering.

Just a little more bracing, and the framing would be complete. On Monday a contractor's crew would be coming in to finish building the studio that Britt and Charlie had begun. The hard, physical work and camaraderie with Charlie had been good medicine for Britt, but it was time for him to get back to his real work. Come Monday, he was off on a new tack with his music, something which tapped into the poetry that he could feel building inside of him.

And it was past time for him to reveal to Dena the nature of the threats that had made him so crazily protective of her all summer. If she could verify that the note found today was indeed the work of the girl she had fired, then maybe the suspended life they'd been living could finally come to an end. Maybe they could actually begin living the real life his family deserved.

With his ear tuned to listen for Dena's voice, his body bent forward at the waist, Britt drove one of the final nails: bam-bam-bam-click-bam. He froze. What had to be the most hopeless sound in the world—the metallic snap one hears when a round is chambered in a semi-automatic firearm—had come from directly behind him. He drew a deep breath, slowly raised himself to a standing position, and turned toward the sound.

"I thought that would get your attention," she said. She was holding the handgun close to her body, steady.

"So it is you," he said.

Upstairs, Dena pulled on jeans and a soft cotton shirt. She had a need for comfort tonight; she could use all the help she could get when she made her confession to Britt. With a sigh she left the bedroom and stepped onto the balcony above the living room.

"Britt," she called down the stairs, "I'm ready."

In a rough, forceful growl that blasted through the house, he called back, "I'm busy!"

What in the world? There was a threat in his voice. Not even on the awful night of Phillip's invasion, when Britt had snarled at her in white-hot anger, had she felt threatened. She put a hand over her pounding heart, drew in a deep breath. Could he have intended a warning instead of a threat?

Where was Bonnie? Where was she? In her room or her studio behind the garage? There was a panic button to summon the guards in the bedroom, but none here on the balcony, and she needed to know where Bonnie was. Carefully, she took two more steps and leaned over the balcony rail. From here she could see Bonnie's room. The door was shut, but light slanted out from the crack under the door. She could hear no sound from Britt or Bonnie.

If Britt's intention had been to warn her, then no response might be construed as odd if there was an intruder . . . It could put them in more danger. And so she took two steps back and called down, keeping her voice a sweet sing-song, "Okay, sweetie, whatever you say."

His voice roared back, "Just shut up and put that money back like I told you!"

Dena rushed back into the bedroom. Money, what money? What was he trying to tell her? In a panic, she looked around the room, nothing registering. Slow down and think. Britt sometimes kept a few bills in the valet box on the dresser. She flipped the hinged lid open and immediately spotted the note, recognized the curly-q script: *Britt, I'll be in your arms tonight.* Even though she had no clue what the previous notes might have said, she knew one thing: The girl was in their home. Dena's family was in danger, and it was her own fault.

With a shaking hand, she hit the panic button and looked out the window, expecting to see two guards sprinting across the yard. She saw no movement, and she wasn't sure what that could mean. Would they approach the house stealthily? Was the alarm system not working? Had the guards been diverted elsewhere? Or, worse, disabled?

Assuming the system was operational, the call would also go to the local law enforcement, and Len, no matter where he was. She grabbed her cell phone in her right hand, pushed a button to begin a text to Len, and reached for her mobile tablet with her left hand.

She was holding the pistol in her right hand, relaxed, steady, the barrel pointed right at Britt's chest. Steady, but not steadied. She didn't intend to shoot at the moment, it would seem, but there was a round in the chamber. Britt couldn't risk any sudden movements just yet.

"Of course it's me," she said. "Was there ever any doubt?"

Britt swallowed and felt cold sweat form on the back of his neck. A thousand thoughts formed in a tangled knot in the center of his brain, and they began to spin out, one by one, like a ribbon of ticker tape before his eyes:

Where is Bonnie? What is this girl's name? Where are the guards? Something about one of my songs . . .

Just then the girl whistled, and the Rottweiler trotted over and sat on its haunches, looking from one master to the other. It growled into the space between them, perceiving a threat.

The girl said, "What did you just do? That thing with your eyes? Do you think you can plan some sort of escape?"

"Uh, no, not at all." Britt tossed the hammer out into the yard. He slouched a little, as he might for the cameras, right hand on his thigh, left fingers touching his hip. "It's something I do. You'll get used to it."

"Oh, I intend to get used to a lot of things," she said, and she stepped closer.

Timing is everything. Where are the damn guards? I have to stay alive. This girl has no idea . . .

At that moment, Dena called down the stairs that she was ready. Summoning every trick he had learned on stage, he growled, "I'm busy!" And quick, while he still had eye contact with the girl . . .

Timing is everything.

. . . he turned on that dimpled grin, the one *People Magazine* had labeled "heart-stopping," and he put one finger to his lips. "Shhh."

Listen, Dena, listen to my voice. Follow the protocol. This girl has no idea . . .

His wife's sweet voice floated down, melodic and submissive. Oh, she got his message, all right, and he yelled a direct order to put the money back. Dena would get that too.

The girl opened her mouth to speak, and he tilted his head fifteen degrees, a charming angle, and put his finger to his lips again. And winked.

She whispered, "Code? Really?"

He whispered back, "No, really. We're not that smart around here. We rely on fences and guards."

In a normal voice, she said, "Forget the guards. I took them out already."

It will take the guards on the water four minutes. How far out is Len? Where's Bonnie? What does hope look like? Start with my wife's smile. This girl has no idea . . .

"You've been planning this for a while," he said.

"Oh, yeah. When it became obvious you weren't coming after me."

"Sorry about that. I've never been too dependable."

"And you've been with that whore upstairs about as long as you have with any woman. You must be sick of her by now."

"Yeah, they do tend to come and go."

Keep this girl off-balance. Start with my wife's smile. The first moment I saw her. Her lovely laughter curling like a ribbon around me and Mark Blue last night. This girl has no idea . . .

"Is that what you think I'll do? Come and go? Because I won't, you know," she said.

"Just what is your plan, babe? You're the one with the gun, so how's this going to work?"

"My daddy says you were just a grunt in the Army. Me and this gun might promote you, depending on how helpful you are in eliminating that bitch."

"Well, I'm already at least a major around here. How about I make you field lieutenant?"

"We'll see," she said, and she stepped closer, put the gun to his head, and slid her left hand to his crotch.

Britt snapped his fingers to summon the dog. Brandy growled once but stayed put. Cutting his eyes to the left, he saw the girl's finger move off the trigger, and he stepped back. "I feel exposed out here," he said. "Come on, babe, let's go inside," and he began moving toward the open window, a portal between the framed-in studio and the den.

Dog might be a problem. Three-and-a-half minutes. My wife's smile has captivated my heart for eight months and twenty-two days. What's next after her smile? Gratitude.

"Stop!" shouted the girl.

Britt stopped and rubbed his chest, where the weight of gratitude had descended so sharply, it hurt. When he turned to look at the girl, she was in firing position, both arms outstretched, shooting hand steadied in her left palm. He cocked his head at her. "You can't take over a house from the outside, you know. Come on." When she hesitated, he raised both hands. "No tricks; I promise." He stepped closer to the window. His method of coming and going through the portal had been to grab the window on each side and launch his body through, feet-first.

I've been blind for two hundred and sixty-five days. My wife is a gift. Not luck. This girl has no idea who she's dealing with here. She has no idea. I will go to the depths of hell if that's what it takes. She has no idea.

Britt sat on the window sill and awkwardly swung his legs through. When he stood and looked at the girl, she relaxed her stance and followed him through, steadying herself with her left hand. She kept the gun aimed at his chest. Moving slowly, arms raised, Britt took a couple of steps back. From here, through the open door of the den, he could see Bonnie's door. It was shut, and light was streaming through the crack under the door. Not his first choice, but at least he knew where she was.

Dena's mobile tablet had an instant message feature. To Bonnie, she typed, "Stay put," and to Len, she texted on her cell phone, "Threat inside where r u?"

Len's answer came back at once, voice-to-text, "Three mints out. Protocol."

Three minutes. A lifetime. Of course. Protocol. It was the message she should have given to Bonnie in the first place.

Just then Britt's voice roared through the house, "Get down here now, bitch! Now!"

She messaged Bonnie, "Protocol," and she texted Len, "Bonnie in room." Then she locked the door, switched off the light, and headed for the outside deck.

Downstairs in her room, Bonnie was engaged in a normal activity for a thirteen-year-old girl. Ear buds in, she was listening to music, plenty loud, while messaging her new friend in Charlotte with her left hand. With her right hand, she was penciling algebra formulas. Every step, no smudges. Britt was schooling her in thinking intuitively, with much patience and humor. He had no humor or patience with the written lessons, however; for those he demanded perfection.

She was typing, "Britt is so anal," to her friend when a message popped up from her mother, "Stay put." What the heck did that mean? She flipped the ear buds out in time to hear Britt's voice, thirty feet away, roar a command for her mother to get downstairs.

Using both hands, she typed to her friend, "Crap. Step-dad gone crazy again. Gotta go."

"What r u going 2 do?" came back from her friend.

"Get in his face," Bonnie replied before standing up and marching toward her door. Her hand was on the door handle when, behind her, the laptop buzzed. She took two steps back to see the screen, which read, "Protocol."

"All right," she said. "You want to know my plan? You're going to help me eliminate that bitch, and then I'll be in your arms forever, just like in the song."

What song? What is this girl's name? Water guards can get to Bonnie in two-and-a-half minutes and Dena in another thirty seconds. I have to stay alive for three minutes. Two hundred seventy-three million dollars will not bring back my wife's smile if I die.

"One more thing," she said. "The only way the brat lives is if you help me. And you'd better hurry. I'm guessing those guards you keep on the water will be heading this way pretty soon."

"Hey, you don't need to convince me. Watch this." And he bellowed a command for Dena to come down, now.

"Does that work with her?" she asked, backing toward the door that led out of the den, near the bottom of the stairs and closer to Bonnie's room.

"Sometimes." Britt began moving, too, keeping his body a measured distance from hers. He reached the doorway first as she pivoted, following him with the gun. "Let me," he said. "I want to see her face."

Something on her body buzzed, and she reached into her back pocket with her left hand, coming up with her cell phone. The gun remained pointed at his chest as she glanced at the screen. "Stay put? Protocol? So you do have codes around here."

Timing is everything.

He fixed a hard glare on her, held her eyes with his. "You went behind my back; you're not fit to serve under me."

"You'd better believe I'm more fit than your wife," she spat back. "She's so stupid, she doesn't even lock her tablet."

"So you cloned her tablet's SIM card. But the security code reset only went to her cell. How did you . . ."

"Easy. I called your hotshot security people and had the tablet number added to the list. Just had to answer three simple questions. Want to guess what your genius wife chose as one of the questions? The name of her dog. And she didn't even own Brandy then."

At the sound of her name, the dog barked but stayed outside.

This girl must have stolen the car key from the locked kitchen cabinet and copied it. She's good. I may only have two minutes to live. Hope. My wife's smile. Gratitude. Then what?

"Haha," growled Britt. "You just got promoted to captain. Congratulations!"

"Step aside, major," she said, gesturing with the gun. "I'm going to be the first to see her face." She kept the pistol aimed at his heart as they swapped positions. Now she was in the doorway, and he was in the den. He stepped close, crowding her.

Forgive yourself. That other girl wasn't too much older than this one. Who do you think you are that you can refuse forgiveness? God?

"She's not coming down," she said, and she put the gun to his head again. "I've waited two years for you, ever since you wrote that song for me, and now I'm not even sure that I can trust you."

"Trust this," he said, and he kissed her.

She kissed him back, but she didn't take the gun away. Her finger stayed steady on the trigger.

One minute, maybe a little more. One way or the other, Britt Jordan will cease to exist tonight.

His hands gripped the door on each side of his body.

At the top of the road, Len switched off the motor, coasted off the pavement, jumped out of the car, and sprinted to the gate, punching in the code. Leaving the gate open for the law enforcement officers who were about a minute behind him, he headed for the north side of the house at a dead run. No lights were on upstairs; downstairs, dim light filtered out from the living room lamps, which had been set on automatic timers. He caught a glimpse of Britt silhouetted against that low light and kept running.

Britt's rules: The first protocol was to secure Bonnie. No matter the circumstance. Len rounded the northeast corner of the house and saw two guards sprinting across the yard from the lake. At his signal, they fanned out, guns drawn, one headed toward a living room window and the other toward the back deck. He reached the bay window on the north side of Bonnie's room.

Good girl; she had opened the center window. Though this wasn't a requirement—Len would have crashed through to get to her—it made a stealthy extraction possible. He tapped three times on the side glass, and she popped up from her hiding place underneath the window seat and dove headfirst through the window and into his arms. Britt had made them practice this maneuver a dozen times.

Running uphill toward the gate, Bonnie in his arms, Len covered ground as easily as he had downhill. Peering back at the house over his shoulder, Bonnie must have gotten a good look at Britt's silhouette, because she whispered, "What is Britt doing? Why is he . . ."

"Shhh," said Len. "He's been keeping you safe, and now he's trying to keep that girl alive." He deposited the child with the female officer who was running down the hill toward him, directed three more officers toward the south and east sides of the house before running back toward the north side.

Britt's second protocol was to secure Dena. No matter the circumstance. Dena's room was dark, and the ladder had been lowered from her outside deck, but she was nowhere to be seen. Len was not surprised.

Just as Len started up the ladder, hand over hand, Britt's voice, with enough force to echo through the whole cove and halfway across the lake, blasted into song. Springsteen's "Cover Me." It was Britt's signal to stand down.

"Dammit, Britt," muttered Len. "I could have taken that girl out by now. She wouldn't even know what hit her." He hauled himself over the rail and onto the deck, finally catching sight of Dena. She was standing with her ear pressed to the closed bedroom door. "You know the protocol," Len whispered, crossing the room in three easy strides.

"That girl was capable of setting a bomb in our home," she whispered back. "Britt's life may depend on me. Please help."

With a nod, Len put his left hand on the door knob and positioned Dena behind him with his right. Within seconds, Britt's voice floated up, distinct spoken words, "Dena, sweetie-pie, it's over. Come down."

"That girl has no idea, does she?" whispered Len as he began to open the door.

The girl stepped back, the gun pointed at his head. "I want your hands where I can see them."

"Of course." He dropped his hands from the door frame to his sides. "Now bring that tongue back over here. I was barely getting started."

"You start fast, don't you?" Never taking her finger off the trigger, she stepped toward him again, the gun at his temple, her left hand at his crotch. "So you're capable of performing with a gun to your head. Can you sing at gunpoint? I want to hear you sing that song to me."

Oh, you have no idea what I'm capable of.

The sound of crickets filtered in from outside.

"What was that?" she asked.

"Crickets. We're overrun with them here."

Bonnie's safe. Thirty seconds to Dena.

He started to step back, but she tightened her grip on his crotch. "I don't believe you," she said. "The guards are here, aren't they?"

He relaxed into the door frame, right leg crossed over his left, right shoulder slouched against the door frame, left hand resting easily against the frame. The picture of insouciance.

"Just you and me and the old gal upstairs," he said, and he flashed that dimpled grin. "Now let me tell you a secret. I'm sick of Britt Jordan songs. Just between you and me, they're damned wimpy. A smokin' hot woman like you deserves a hot song, maybe one of Springsteen's. Like this." With no more warning than that, he blasted the first line of "Cover Me" at stadium volume into her face, the notes deep and rich, the words brash and hot with his breath.

She jumped back into shooting position, left palm under her right hand. "Shut up!" she screamed.

Not taking his eyes from her face, he sang the second line with intensity, his face pulled into the glare that had forced a million fans to swoon, and she stepped back another half-step.

Perfect. Now stand down, boys. I've got room here to work.

He stopped singing, shifted his weight onto his left leg, and then gripped the door frame with his left hand.

"Somebody's going to die! If they shoot me, you're dead!" she screamed.

"Nobody's going to shoot you," he said calmly. "Let's get that woman down here and end this thing. You've got me so hot I can't stand another minute without you."

If Dena followed the protocol, I'm dead. I'll bet two hundred seventy-three million she didn't. Thirty-five degrees to the girl's

406

left, twenty-two degrees above horizontal.

"Dena, sweetie-pie, it's over. Come down."

The bedroom door opened above them. He could hear the metallic rasp of the latch scraping the plate. His wife's low, melodic voice carried nicely down the stairs, "Of course, Britt. You know I will." There was the scuffing sound of a footstep close to the top of the darkened stairs.

The girl kept her eyes on him, the gun trained in his direction.

He looked up the stairs and smiled at Len's big figure crouched low in the shadows, crooning, "Well, hello, darling, we've been waiting for you."

The girl was fast as she pivoted her body toward the stairs, swinging the gun in an arc. Britt's body was already in motion; he pushed himself from the doorframe and launched off his left leg, swinging his right leg right and high. His foot caught the weapon as she swung it to the precise angle he'd predicted: thirty-five degrees by twenty-two. Her finger was on the trigger, and the pistol discharged one round that struck the stairwell to the left and beneath Len's body before the force of his kick knocked it from her hand.

The gun was still spinning in midair when Britt twisted sideways on his descent, shoving the girl with his left foot before landing agilely on his right foot. With a bounce he launched forward and followed the girl's body to the floor, covering her body as the weapon clattered and spun on the hardwood. No more shots were fired. The boom Britt had been anticipating came in the form of a crash of glass and splintered wood, which signaled the arrival of a guard through the living room window.

Britt kept the girl pinned to the floor beneath him as she twisted and screamed his name. Still bucking and twisting, she spat viciously, "I felt you . . . I know you were hot for me."

"Timing and practice; that's all you felt, kid," Britt growled into her ear. Len dove into the space between them and put his big hands on her shoulders, holding her down as Britt pushed to a standing position. "And by the way, how do you think I got from point A to point B on stage? I didn't exactly levitate from floor to amplifier."

"Britt! I trusted you! I would have loved you forever! I would . . ."

"Quiet!" barked Len. "He just saved your life, idiot."

Within seconds they were surrounded by two guards and three officers, and Britt backed out of the circle, breathing hard, his eyes searching for his wife. In a heartbeat, she was in his arms, and he pulled her into the den, away from the girl, and collapsed against the wall, holding her tightly. He let out one long groaning exhalation. Relief. Exhaustion. Hope. All three expressed in a single groan.

He realized Dena was shaking in his arms. "I'm so sorry, so sorry. This is all my fault," she sobbed.

"Shhh. I don't want to hear it."

"But it's my fault. If only . . ."

"Hush!" Still adrenaline-revved, his voice was sharper than he'd intended. She put her cheek against his, and he could feel the warmth of her tears. He drew a deep breath, released it, and felt his heartbeat slow. "It's over," he whispered. "Let it go. All I care about is that you're here. You're safe." He held her tightly, rocked back and forth a little. From the living room, the girl kept screaming his name, over and over. "Tell me that girl's name again," he whispered.

"Rhiannon."

"Stay here," he said, and he let go of his wife and stepped back into the living room. "Rhiannon," he called. "Look at me. It's over. I did not write that song for you, and you will never see me again. But listen to me; you need help, and you'll get it. I promise you that."

"Go to hell!" screamed the girl.

"Just spent four minutes there and don't plan on going back," Britt muttered as he returned to the den and pulled his wife close once again.

Len came into the room, stared at Britt a long moment, and shook his head. Finally he said, "You are one more gutsy son of a . . ."

"Britt!" Bonnie ran across the room and sprang into his arms with such energy she nearly knocked him off his feet. He looked at Len, his arms around his family, barely able to breathe for the crush of emotion that swept through him, and he whispered, "No guts, Len. Just this. Just something to live for."

Outside, the dog barked once. "Ambulances are here," said Len. "I need to check in on my men." He paused. "In case you haven't noticed, that is one useless watchdog."

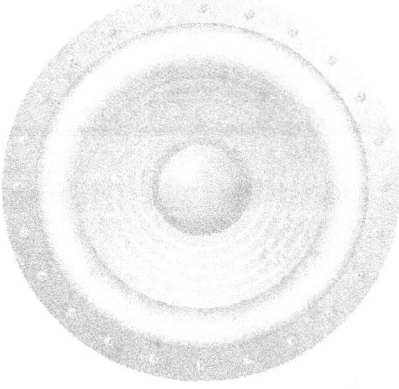

———CHAPTER———

THIRTY-THREE

D ena could hear birds beginning to chirp and twitter outside, and she opened one eye to view the gray pre-dawn light through her living room windows. She heard Bonnie wiggle and stretch, and in the dim light, she saw her daughter extend one arm over her head. Dena grasped Bonnie's hand, and their fingers intertwined, squeezing tightly. She doubted her child had slept much more than she had.

Britt was asleep between them on the sofa, his feet on the coffee table, his right arm around his wife. On his left, Bonnie's long legs stretched over the sofa arm, her head on a pillow on Britt's lap, snuggled beneath an afghan and Britt's hand on her left arm.

The little family had wound up on the sofa last night as investigators came and went, asking the same questions over and over again. Bonnie had told her end of the story with detail and a bit of dramatic flair. Dena had answered all the questions she was asked, giving little insight into what she had been thinking or feeling throughout the ordeal. And Britt had told them what they already knew, and no more.

They were told that the two missing guards had both been shot with tranquilizer darts designed to take down large animals. The guard who had paced Dena on her run was recovering in the hospital. The other one, who must have been shot seconds after Charlie passed through the gate, was in critical condition.

Someone had brought them food, and someone else had boarded up the broken window. When the last officers finally left, Britt seemed disinclined to move from the sofa, and neither his wife nor his step-daughter had wanted to leave his side. Just before piling a sofa pillow onto his lap and snuggling under the afghan, Bonnie had whispered to Britt, "I saw you through the window. Thank you. I'm glad Rhiannon didn't get shot." He had kissed her cheek, breathed in deeply, laid his head against Dena's, exhaled a long breath, and fallen asleep.

And thus they had remained in that tableau until four a.m., when Britt had eased his body from the sofa, his sleepy family rearranging themselves in his absence. Dena had heard him talking on his cell phone outside, his voice low. It was a short, one-sided conversation, which meant he had probably called Darrell. He'd returned after a few minutes, and everyone had settled back into their former positions.

"Have you been asleep this whole time?" she'd whispered.

"Couple hours. I've had some thinking to do," he had answered, and he had breathed deeply and gone still once more.

Now, in the pre-dawn gray light, probably not yet six o'clock, she assumed he was asleep, although it was hard to tell with Britt. Bonnie wiggled some more, still holding her mother's hand, but Britt made no movement.

Into the stillness, from outside the front door, a car horn blasted. Britt jumped and began disentangling from his family. "I fell asleep! I'm late!" He stood up just as Len entered through the front door. "Tell them I need two minutes," he said to Len, and sprinted across the living room and bounded up the stairs.

Dena touched her sleepy daughter's face and followed him upstairs. He was packing a duffel bag: jeans, a couple of T-shirts, undershorts. Strange. She had never seen him pack before—wherever he had gone, everything he'd needed had been waiting for him.

"Where are you going?" she asked.

"There's something I need to do."

"Well, what? Where? Why now?"

"It's just, I've just, I've got to go," he said. He glanced at her face and said, "Hey, you're the one who said I didn't have to tell you where I went or why, as long as I wasn't deceptive."

"I didn't mean it," she said. "And you are being deceptive."

"No I'm not. I'm telling you quite truthfully that I'm going somewhere private." He went into the bathroom and came out with a travel kit, which he dropped in the bag. "Gotta run," he said, and started for the door.

"Wait! When will you be back?"

"Not sure. A week, I think."

"Britt, wait! Can't you go later? We've all been traumatized, and we need you here."

He turned in the doorway, and said, "Len will be here," and kept moving.

"Not exactly the skill-set I had in mind! Stop a minute!" When he returned to the doorway, she said, "So what chapter is this in your marriage manual? Because I'm not liking it so far."

He smiled. "This is the chapter where the groom has done all he can for his lovely bride, only to realize that one more thing still needs to be done. Gotta go."

"Come back here! Aren't you forgetting something?"

This time he stopped short in the doorway, but he didn't

smile. "I would never forget. But after what I had to do last night, I need to purge myself before I can kiss you again." He kissed his palm and held it up to her, his way of blowing a kiss. And then he was gone, running down the stairs and out the door with a bang.

Dena followed him as far as the balcony rail, and stood looking down over her living room. Still on the sofa, Bonnie gave a fist pump and said, "Yes! No homework!"

Britt stuck his head back in the door and said, "Bonnie, I'll be emailing you your assignments." The door slammed, and that was it.

"Crap," said Bonnie.

"I don't like you using that word," Dena said with so little conviction that Bonnie barely bothered to roll her eyes. From outside, reporters on the lake caught sight of Britt making his dash to the waiting car, and their shouts were soon joined by more cries from reporters outside the gate. Apparently their ordeal had already made national news. Within seconds, four doors slammed on a vehicle that had just pulled in. She heard the tailgate being dropped on a pickup truck, and men's voices conversing. She heard the sound of heavy objects hitting the concrete floor. Soft Hispanic voices and a loud curse in a deep Southern voice. The contractor's crew had arrived to finish Britt's studio.

She sighed and looked down at Len, who was standing at the foot of the stairs staring up at her. Then she glanced over at Bonnie and smoothed the seams of the wrinkled cotton shirt she had worn all night. The monotonous beep-beep of a delivery truck backing down the driveway came next. A compressor fired up. Evidently pneumatic equipment was going to be involved in the construction. As she looked back at Len, who was still staring at her, she gripped the balcony rail with both hands.

"Bonnie," she said in level voice, "do you remember how to open the safe in the den?"

"Yes," the child answered, a question in her voice.

"Then please get our passports out and bring them to me. And run down to the basement and bring up two carry-on cases."

"Where are we going?" Bonnie appeared to be more perplexed than excited.

Dena folded her arms and looked at Len. "Wherever the first plane out of Charlotte will take us. Madrid. Paris. Rome. I don't care." She cut her eyes to Bonnie, who stared back at her, her mouth a round bud of astonishment. "Britt may have abandoned us, but his credit card hasn't. I'll go check the flight schedules and first class availability." She turned on her heel and started for the bedroom.

"Ma'am?" came from Len. She stopped but didn't turn around. "Mrs. Jordan? Dena?" His voice was insistent and yet entreating. She half-turned and looked at his up-turned face. "You don't have to do that, you know."

She blinked. Put a hand to her heart. Those were the exact words Britt had spoken the night she met him, when he was telling her that a room had been provided for her.

When she stepped back to the balcony rail, Len said softly, "Britt is flying commercial; that's why he was in such a hurry. He left the Gulfstream for you." He paused as she took this in. "Eddie will fly you anywhere in the world you want to go. And it would be my honor to accompany you. If that's what you would like."

Bonnie came back from the den, the passports in her hand. "Where are we going, Mama?"

Dena looked at Len, waiting for him to speak. He cleared his throat. "Ma'am, Britt thinks you might especially enjoy Rome at this time of year. There's a suite waiting for you, if you wish to take advantage of it."

She swallowed. "And what if I prefer Milan?"

"Then accommodations will be ready for you by the time you arrive."

Of course they would. Britt. She shook her head. The choice was hers; he wasn't forcing her to go to Rome. But why would she refuse? Her husband had thought this through, probably down to the last detail, and only to make her happy.

"Rome it is, then," she said. To Bonnie, she added, "On second thought, forget the suitcases. You'll only need your backpack. We're traveling light."

While Dena and Bonnie were enjoying their time in Rome, Britt was feverishly tackling two projects at once, working twenty hours a day. One of these projects involved Ron Edwards, the journalist who had sought him out for an interview and received a punch in the face instead. On the morning he left his home in such a rush, Britt had contracted Ron to write his authorized biography, *Britt: From Profane to Profound*. Ron would be allowed to write whatever scorching history of the singer's life and career he chose on one condition: The story of the past fifteen months of Britt's life would come straight from Britt's mouth.

He had begun his story by telling Ron: *The real story of Britt Jordan, the only one that matters, begins in a Manhattan apartment, with a half-dead girl in his bed.*

CHAPTER

THIRTY-FOUR

She was standing in the exact spot in their bedroom where he had left her just a week ago, surrounded by the radiance of candlelight. She was just standing still, wearing a simple sheath dress, her hands behind her back. Her lips parted when she saw him. Surprise? He didn't think so. He had a feeling her heart had told her the exact minute he would return.

He dropped his duffel bag and stared at her. She was the most precious thing in the world to him, and yet, although he was a poet, he did not possess the words to tell her. His eyes took in every detail: the new highlights in her hair, the European polish to her skin, the flattering lines of the dress she had no doubt purchased in Rome. None of it was essential to her beauty, by his assessment, but he liked it. She smiled beneath his scrutiny, that same disarming smile that had stopped his heart the first instant he saw her.

Closing his eyes, he thought of the words he had spoken to Ron Edwards: *The first hundred eighty-nine days in this story are like viewing eight millimeter film set to forty-eight frames per second. Freeze frame on the half-dead girl, then start the film rolling. All you'll see will be hopeless flashes of a face on the screen, hard to tell who the character is or where he's heading. Not much of a plot, just forward movement toward nothing. And then, freeze frame on day one hundred ninety. That was the night I was stopped in my tracks by a woman's smile.*

He felt her move toward him, bridging the space between them. With a slight movement of his hand that did not touch her, he stopped her from coming closer. He opened his eyes and saw her hand move toward his head, felt her fingers on his scalp as she combed them through his hair.

"Nice," she said. "What brought this on?"

He had cut his hair shaggy-short and darkened it in random streaks. "Just something I needed to do," he said, and he removed the dark-framed glasses he was wearing.

"Do you need those to see?" she asked. "You have been squinting lately."

"I can see you plenty well." Sweat beaded on his temples, and he licked his lips. He was in a lot of pain. "But yes, they are prescription glasses. I also have contacts, which I'm not yet used to wearing."

Her finger traced the angle of his jawline, now emphasized by a sharply contoured beard.

When she didn't comment, he smiled. And then he removed the linen jacket he was wearing, under which there was no shirt.

He watched her smile open into a shriek and the sweet welcome in her eyes darken into horror. She jumped up and down in place, covering her shrieks with her hands, tent-like over her mouth and nose. Then she took her hands away from her face and screamed a serious, deliberate scream that made him proud. "Britt, what have you done? Britt!"

His sea dragon tattoo was gone.

"I never said I didn't like your tattoo. I never said that! What possessed you to do such a thing? *Britt!*" Her words rushed from her lips in a torrent, her voice husky from the scream.

He chuckled. "I didn't do this because of what you said. Well, sort of, but not exactly."

"Then why?" she demanded. She covered her mouth with one hand again, absorbing the shock of what he had done. His arm appeared to be horribly scarred. A part of his history was gone forever. When he didn't reply, she said without malice, "You are insane! You really are. I've always suspected it, but this confirms it. Admit it. Admit you're insane."

"Actually, I'm probably the most sane person in the universe right now."

"I can't believe you did this! Why didn't you tell me?" She took his arm in her grasp, her strong hand incredibly gentle. As she bent to examine his wounds, he could see tears spill from her eyes and glisten on her cheeks in the candlelight. He had never loved her more. "How?" she asked. "Does it hurt as bad as it looks?"

"Three different lasers so far," he answered. "My tattoo is completely gone, but I'll have to go back to Dallas for more treatments to remove these scars. And yes, it hurts. I had the finest tattoo in the world. It was quite an ordeal to make it disappear."

"What's under the bandage?" she whispered.

He swallowed. What was under the bandage was a blood-red wound that burned intensely. "There was so much detail and strong color in the center of the tattoo that they decided to remove it with surgery and patch up the hole with skin grafts. They tell me there will barely be a scar when it's over."

Still examining his arm, she said, "This is . . ." she hesitated,

". . . extreme, even for you. I don't understand. Why did you do this? Your tattoo was part of you. It was part of who you are."

"I know," he said softly. He didn't say anything else.

"Will you tell me? Please?"

"Yes. I'm just not ready tonight." He wanted to make sure he got the words exactly right. In three weeks, Ron Edwards's book would go to the publisher. He had told Ron: *Britt Jordan's story ends two hundred sixty-five days after my wife's smile captured my heart. It ends on the night a young girl pointed a gun at my head.* He had given Ron the bare bones of his family's ordeal on the night Rhiannon had invaded their home, but there was a lot more to be said, and he was still working out how to say it. "Three weeks," he whispered to Dena. "I will tell you everything that's been going on in my heart since June of last year. I promise."

Skillfully, he unzipped her dress, and it fell to the floor. She was wearing nothing underneath. He stared at her as if seeing her body for the first time. "Dena, my wife, you are exquisite," he said.

She smiled. "We can't make love tonight. I'll hurt your arm. And where did they take the skin grafts?"

"From the inside of my thigh," he answered with a grimace.

Shaking her head, still smiling, she said, "Really. You need time to heal."

"Trust me," he murmured. "I thought of nothing else on the plane. I know just how." He took her right hand in his left so she couldn't touch his arm, and kissed her long and lovingly. It was a kiss that told her more than he was glad to be home. The kiss thanked her for being strong yet gentle, accepting yet uncompromising. His whole being delighted in thanking her for rescuing the gentleman inside him.

They did come together as husband and wife that night, slowly, gently, holding hands. When it was over, Dena began to cry.

"What have I done to make you cry?" he asked.

She shook her head and didn't answer.

He kissed her tears away and allowed himself to relax toward sleep. There was much work yet to be done, but for now, the only place he wanted to be was here, holding his wife's hand. Something else he had told Ron Edwards: *My friend Charlie raised the question of how we can explain life's mysteries. How can I explain that a guy like me was lucky enough to find the one woman who could stop his heart and then rescue it? I can't. There's no explanation. And if it didn't depend on me, on whatever luck or charm I could muster up, then what, or whom, did it depend on?* He was almost asleep when he heard her whisper, "I'll tell you in three weeks."

Britt did not sleep the night before Ron's book went to the publisher. He paced the house, stalking the words that would perfectly finish the story of his heart. Finally, at three a.m., he sat down at his piano and began to storm his way through Beethoven. Bonnie soon appeared in the doorway of her room, grumpily suggesting he switch from music to art, because it was quieter. He shut the piano and lay down across the top, scribbling words that had swirled through his mind for three weeks. By dawn, he had the final concise paragraphs typed into the computer, and he e-mailed them to Ron.

Today was the day he would lay bare his heart for Dena's inspection. After tapping on Bonnie's door to wake her up, he made a banana milkshake, her favorite breakfast, and left it in the refrigerator for her. Bonnie would be occupied all morning by her tutor, Marvin Stancell. Then he quickly made toast, sliced some cheese, and poured juice, a quick breakfast for Dena. He was anxious to talk to his wife.

As an afterthought, he ran outside and picked a few flowers. All that was blooming in Dena's garden in October were a few asters and marigolds. He didn't know what they were—he just crammed them into a vase and hurried upstairs with his tray.

Dena was up, as he'd expected, dressed and smiling. "I have some things to tell you," he said, coming closer with the tray.

She smiled and nodded. "Me, too," she said gently.

Britt set the tray down on the breakfast table and held the chair for her to come and sit. She did, and almost at once began back-pedaling, pushing the chair away from the table, waving one hand at the tray and patting her cheek with her other hand. "Get those marigolds out of here, Britt," she hissed, "they're taking my breath."

Caught off-guard, he froze until he saw how pale her face had become. Hurriedly, he grabbed the tray and carried it out of the room. "Bring the juice back," he heard her say.

When he returned, she took the juice from him and held the glass up to one cheek, still patting her other cheek. "Whew," she said, "that took me by surprise."

"What?" he asked innocently.

"Those marigolds. The odor nearly made me sick." As he peered at her anxiously, she smiled. "I'm okay. Really." She took a sip of juice, screwed up her face, and set the glass down quickly, fanning herself with one hand.

"Dena, are you all right?" he asked. "Should I call a doctor?"

She laughed. "No, silly. I'll be fine. Just give me a minute until the marigold fumes leave the room. Honest; I'm okay."

He sniffed. As far as he could tell, the fumes had left with the marigolds. The color was returning to her face, but she was still fanning. He wasn't sure what to do.

She solved it for him. "I know we've got some important talking to do today," she said. "I'll ask Mr. Stancell to stay a little later with Bonnie, and we'll take a lunch out on your boat. Meet me on the dock at ten thirty. That should give us both ample time to pull ourselves together."

"Okay," he said meekly. Once he had held enough power in his hands to make fifty thousand people dance and shout. Now he was at the mercy of one woman's sudden aversion to marigolds. "I'll go sailing for a while."

"You do that," she said, and she shooed him away.

After Britt was gone, Dena stood at the mirror, laughing ruefully at herself. Her heart had been telling her for three weeks that she was carrying his baby; this morning, before he came upstairs, a home test had confirmed it. She was not far enough along for morning sickness to set in, but those marigolds had sure jolted her stomach. Putting one hand over her still-flat belly, she studied her reflection. She was forty years old—almost forty-one. She had not expected or even wanted a pregnancy. And it was a bit frightening to imagine raising a little Britt. But her husband would be thrilled. And she would welcome his child; yes, indeed, she would.

Since they would be going out on the lake, she changed into a pair of shorts and a cotton sweatshirt and pulled her hair back into a ponytail. Once again, she studied her reflection as she tied a green ribbon in her auburn hair. Really, she didn't look forty. And she was just as healthy as she had been when she carried Bonnie. She wasn't thrilled about being pregnant, but she looked forward to having her husband's child. Smiling, she packed a pair of shorts and a sweatshirt in a bag for Britt. Knowing him, he would be so excited he might jump overboard.

The house was quiet, too quiet. Where were Marvin and Bonnie? She went downstairs. Bonnie's books were lying open on the desk in the den, where they usually worked on English, and they weren't in the new studio. Perhaps they had gone outside.

There was a fresh chill in the October air when she left the house, and clouds were moving in fast over the lake. She thought she heard a sound coming from Bonnie's old studio behind the garage, and she headed in that direction.

The gate at the end of the driveway was standing wide open. Next to Marvin Stancell's Cadillac, in the grass beside the driveway, sat a black Jaguar like the one Phillip had been driving the last time she saw him. The keys were in the ignition. She felt a prickle of apprehension. Even though they no longer relied on the constant presence of guards, that gate was supposed to remain closed.

On the water, Britt sailed his sloop, enjoying the crisp air, the blue sky, and the tug of the lines in his hands. Overhead, a flock of gulls, stranded inland by some forgotten storm, made their noisy way across the lake. The sound reminded him of the sea. He missed the Caribbean. He missed his ship!

Suddenly, the whole day seemed to change in tone. The air grew colder, the water grayer. Clouds began to push across the sky. Glancing at his watch, he realized that it was nearly ten o'clock. He brought the boat around and headed home. Soon he would tell his wife why he'd had the tattoo removed. Already, it was just a memory; anyone who didn't know him could look at his arm and never guess it had been there. The treatments he had received over the past three weeks had smoothed away the scars, and the skin grafts were healing nicely. At this point, his arm looked like it had been burned, as the fresh skin was still pink and a little raw. In six months, he had been told, there would be very little trace left.

Within sight of the house, he was hit by a desire, a need—no, more than that—a panic, to write a song. This morning he thought that he'd wrapped up the story of his life with the e-mail to Ron, but now, it seemed, there was one more thing he needed to do. Overwhelmed by the urgency to do it now, he lowered the sails and dropped the anchor.

With the melody flowing through his brain, as sweet as a baby's whisper, he caught the words on paper. They were gentle words, unlike anything Britt Jordan had ever written:

Some hearts lie.
Some hearts cry.
Some hearts burn.
And others yearn.
Few hearts will stay.
Most go their own way.
Fewer still know how to love.
And my heart, yes, my heart, was all the above.

Some hearts are cruel.
Some hearts are dual.
Some hearts are crazy.
And others are lazy.

Few hearts will dare,
Most don't really care.
Fewer still will die for love.
And my heart, yes, my heart, was all the above.

But there's a higher ground to love and life
A place where the heart is set free
A place where a heart can begin again,
A place only you could show me.
And there's a higher voice and a deeper song,
Only an humble heart hears.

Now my heart can face
Your heart of grace.
And my heart lives
Because your heart gives.
Few hearts will show
Forgiveness, I know,
Fewer still ransomed by love.
But my heart, yes, my heart, is all the above.

No sooner had he penned the last word than a sound reached Britt's ears. A sick feeling in his belly, he stood up. The sound was a familiar one: his home's security alarm. Britt fired the single engine, sliced the anchor rope, and steered the boat toward home. The wind had picked up, slinging spray into his eyes, as he faced the gathering storm.

Dena crossed the lawn, her arms folded against the chill. She entered Bonnie's former studio through the French doors Britt had installed. Marvin and Bonnie weren't there. This was very odd. And where was Phillip, if the Jaguar belonged to him?

Standing in the doorway, looking out across the lawn, she felt a sudden draft behind her and started to turn around. A familiar voice spoke, "It's been a long time, Dena." Startled, she looked behind her to see the door, which connected to the garage, open to reveal the figure of a man.

"Phillip." It was all she could say. She faced him, feeling sweat form on the back of her neck in spite of the chill air.

"I thought no one was home." He said this dully. "I didn't see a sailboat, so I decided to hang around until Britt showed up."

Carefully, she asked, "How have you been?"

"Huh!" He moved from the doorway and closed the door behind him, shutting off the draft coming from the garage.

She wanted to close the French door too, but the open door seemed to make the tiny room larger. As he stood looking past her through the door, she looked him over. Phillip had lost the weight Britt had gained. He looked older than Britt, his cheeks hollow, his gray eyes dull. In fact, she noticed his jacket seemed to hang loosely on him.

"Phillip, have you been eating?"

"Eating?" The question seemed to irritate him. "Hell, yes, I've been eating."

Dena became aware that Phillip was not looking her in the eye. The sweat on her neck ran down her back, meeting the cool air flowing through the open door, and she shivered.

"Shut the damn door if you're cold, Dena. I'm not going to bite you." Phillip's voice rose with increasing irritation.

"I'm sorry; where are my manners?" Dena said soothingly.

"Come on in the house and wait for Britt. He'll be home very soon."

"Ha!" There was an edge to his voice. "My brother does not want me in his house."

"You're wrong, Phillip."

"Don't tell me I'm wrong. Don't. And don't take on that condescending attitude with me. I can't stand it."

Phillip seemed to be growing more agitated by the minute. Dena desperately hoped to hear Marvin's voice or Britt's cheerful whistle. She shivered again.

With a curse, Phillip spanned the few feet that separated them, reached around her, and slammed the door shut. He didn't back away the same distance, standing uncomfortably close to her instead. For the first time, she saw that his hand was trembling. She looked again at his dull eyes, his loose jacket, and realized that her husband's brother was sick. Very sick.

"Phillip," she whispered, "Britt loves you."

Phillip released a stream of curses.

"He loves you more than you could guess. He has forgiven you."

The man's fist hit the work table behind her, sending brushes scattering, causing her to jump. "I don't want his damn forgiveness," he spat. "That's what I came here to tell him."

"Phillip, you . . ."

"Just shut up, Dena. I've kissed that son of a bitch's ass for the last time. Did you know he finally had one of his lackeys track me down last week?"

She shook her head slightly.

"I've been waiting for weeks for him to find me, waiting with a gun to blow his head off before he could kill me."

Dena shivered again and hugged herself tightly.

"But guess what his lackey showed up with? A letter! His gracious highness, King Britt, has forgiven his shitty little brother. Wants re-con-cil-iation." He slung the word in her face, his breath hot on her skin. "Why the hell would I want to reconcile with him?"

Very softly, she said, "Because he's your brother."

"Yeah, right. Some brother." He pointed his finger in her face. "I'll tell you what he wants. The whole damn world loves his ass, except for me. And that gripes his over-stuffed ego. He thinks he can force me to idolize him."

"I don't think Britt wants anything from you except to be your brother." Dena was trying hard not to back away from him.

"Try asking me what I want," he demanded.

"What do you want, Phillip?"

"I want him to leave me the hell alone!"

She backed up a step.

"I hate my brother! Imagine the insult when I looked in the mirror last year and discovered that I look exactly like him." Phillip's eyes burned with a destructive fire. "What do you think that does to a man, to have the face of the brother he hates? Huh? Answer me!"

Dena took another step back, and found herself against the door.

"Yes, I hate myself. I loathe myself as much as I do my brother. I tried to kill that hate by destroying him." For a long moment, the only sound was his raspy breathing. "I stole money from one of his accounts to buy the dope to put him in jail. Did he tell you that?" She shook her head. "I assure you, he figured it out. Britt's got every cent of his money memorized. It would have been pure poetry to send his ass to jail with his own damn money. But he bought his way out of that one too. Britt and his damn money. He used his money to buy my son. Now my own boy won't speak to me, but he thinks Britt is the king."

Phillip yanked the shoulder of his jacket down to reveal his upper arm. There blazed a tattoo nearly identical to the one Britt had just removed. Dena gasped in horror.

"Yeah, you get the picture." His voice was flat; his eyes were narrow slits. Sometimes Britt spoke in that tone, set his face in that same mask. But she had never, ever been afraid of Britt. She was terrified of his brother. "When I couldn't destroy him by sending him to prison to rot, I decided to replace him. Blow his head off when he came after me. Nobody but you and Mom would know the difference. I could shut Mom up. And you . . ."

He took a step toward her. Dena's hand went for the door, and she started to open it.

"Don't turn your back on me," he spat. "I'll tell you when this conversation is over."

"It's over now," she said, and she took one step outside.

She didn't have time to break into a run. He moved more quickly than she anticipated, grabbing her from behind, wrapping his right arm around her neck. "Don't worry, dear sister-in-law. I had big plans for you and me, but I changed my mind. I don't hate myself that much." He laughed a low, wicked laugh, his breath hot and sour against her cheek. "If I killed Britt, I would destroy myself, and he's not worth it."

She relaxed against him and tried to think calmly. Britt had told her Phillip's reflexes were quick, but surely if she waited for an opening, she could kick him and get away. His tongue dug into her ear, and she gasped in disgust.

"So you're horrified to be next to me," he said. "I can tell you things about that great husband of yours that will horrify you worse than having my tongue in your ear." He jerked her body hard against his and hunched against her in a raw, nasty gesture. "You put on a show of being an innocent priss," he growled into her ear, "but I know better."

Dena caught sight of Britt's boat on the water, only two hundred yards away. "All I have to do is scream, and Britt will be here," she said, trying to keep her voice steady. "That's his boat over there. Please let me go."

"Ha!" He jerked her head back by her hair. His lips against hers, he snarled, "Are you afraid that your precious husband will think you've switched brothers if I stick my tongue down your throat?"

No! she wanted to scream as his open mouth forced itself against hers. *I'm afraid he will kill you and destroy my family!*

Just then, Marvin Stancell's voice could be heard close by. Phillip stared hard into her eyes, mocking her. Then, with a curse, he pushed her away so roughly that she stumbled and fell, sprawling face down on the ground.

"I've said all I came to say." His voice was flat and cold. "Pass the message along." He turned away and strode back through Bonnie's studio into the garage. She heard an engine start and the familiar roar of a car as it went up the driveway.

By pure strength of will, Dena did not cry. She slowly pushed herself from the ground and was just standing up when Marvin and Bonnie turned the corner of the garage.

"Dena, what happened?" Marvin asked, taking her by the arm.

She pushed him away and brushed herself off, not looking at either of them. Deep within her body, she could feel a tremor begin.

"Bonnie and I were photographing the lake in the changing light for her next project. We walked up the road where the view is better. I forgot to close the gate . . ." Marvin began.

"Listen," Dena interrupted. The tremor within her was growing, and she felt that she only had the strength to speak a few words. "Go turn on the alarm on the dock. When my husband arrives, tell him his brother was here. Tell him Phillip is very sick.

Britt needs to call the sheriff and have him committed." Her voice was a rough whisper. "I don't want to talk to Britt until I have a few minutes to pull myself together. Just tell him I heard the car turn right at the top of the hill. The sheriff should be able to catch him on the interstate. Then please leave for the day."

Leaning heavily on her daughter, she walked across the lawn and up the steps, her hand spread flat across her belly. Once inside, the tremor within her exploded, and she began to shake violently just as the alarm on the dock started to scream and rain started to fall outside.

"Mama, what's wrong?" Bonnie cried, her voice filled with fear.

Dena could not speak. She dropped to her knees beside the sofa and prayed desperately, her daughter's arms around her. She heard Britt's boat return, she heard a car start and turn around on the grass before roaring up the driveway. In her heart, she had known Britt would go after his brother himself.

Dena lay down on the sofa, still shaking, and Bonnie brought a quilt over to cover her. She sat by her mother's side and stroked her face until the shaking subsided. Dena would not cry. She lay perfectly still, her feet propped up, and willed her body to protect her baby. One hour passed. Two. There was the sound of a car at the gate, and then a horn. It was not Britt.

Bonnie looked out. "It's the sheriff's car, Mama," she said. Dena nodded and sat up, and Bonnie activated the gate. Dena smoothed her hair but did not stand when Leon Stokes entered her living room.

"Hello, ma'am." Leon's voice was very low. He looked into her eyes for a long moment before looking away. "There is no easy way to put this, so I'll just say it. Your husband was killed in an accident a little over an hour ago. His car skidded and went off the road in a curve."

Dena did not flinch. "Are you sure it was him?" she asked.

"Uh, yes, ma'am. I checked everything out myself."

"What car was he driving?" she persisted.

Leon shook his head at her attempt to bring her husband back. "That fancy Swiss race car of his. I'm sorry, ma'am, but there's no mistake. That brother of his showed up in his Jag a minute after I did. He identified the body. Coldest man, coldest gray eyes I ever saw. Just stood there with his hands in his pockets in the rain and never shed a tear." Leon shuffled his feet. "I'm sorry."

"Did you arrest him?" Her whisper was barely audible.

"What? Uh, no. To tell you the truth, he left before I even remembered he's still wanted for planting that cocaine. But don't worry; now that we know he's back in the area, we'll get him." He stood in front of her, fidgeting uncomfortably. "Um, is there anything I can do for you, ma'am?"

She shook her head. She did not cry.

After Bonnie saw Leon to the door, she sat on the sofa, and Dena lay back down, her head in her daughter's lap. "I don't understand, Mama," said Bonnie. "Why did Britt . . ."

"Shhh. I don't know."

"What's going to happen?"

"I'm not sure. We're going somewhere, I think."

"Where? To a funeral?"

"I don't think so. Somewhere warm, I believe. Why don't you go organize your books and art supplies for travel? I need to rest." After Bonnie left, Dena spread her hand once more over her belly and felt an incredible sense of peace. *Britt's little fella's as determined as his daddy,* she thought. *I believe he's going to stick around.*

She drew in a deep breath, as she had seen Britt do, and let it out slowly. She felt herself drawn into a deep slumber. What awakened her was not a sound or a movement. She was awakened by the pleasant scent of bay rum.

Without opening her eyes, she reached out her hand and rubbed the top of his head. He was sitting on the floor, his back against the sofa. "I'm so sorry, Britt," she said. "So sorry." She heard him sigh deeply. There was no response. "Are you all right?" she asked.

"Not really. But I'm trying to be realistic. It was not going to end well for Phillip, no matter how badly I wanted things to be better. This has been a long time in the making."

She rubbed his head a while longer. "He was very sick, physically and mentally today," she said. He didn't reply to that, and there was another long silence. "What are you going to do about his funeral?"

"Mom's already handling it. Private ceremony. Ashes scattered. My nephew Marcus is good with it. The truly sad thing is, there's nobody besides us who will even miss my brother." After another silence, he said in a choked voice, "Britt Jordan is dead. Has been for a month. Now it's official."

She opened her eyes. Tears were running down his cheeks, and she saw him pop the contacts out of his eyes and fling them aside. She liked the glasses better on him anyway. The contacts made his eyes appear gray in certain light.

"What is your plan?" she asked softly.

By way of an answer, he pulled out his cell phone, clicked to a screen, and handed it to her. At first she wasn't sure what she was looking at. It appeared to be a resort beside the sea. Then she realized it was a single dwelling: a fabulous house that cascaded down the side of a cliff through at least six levels. She could see gardens, a swimming pool, and a long dock with a ship that looked amazingly like Britt's moored at the end.

"What have you done?" she asked.

"I bought an island in the British Virgins. Last week, actually. Darrell's setting up his production studio nearby on Tortola. There's room for Marvin Stancell to stay with us for a month at a time. Your parents. Charlie and Sue." He looked into her eyes for the first time. Grief and regret. Hope and more hope, all in one glance. "The question is, will you and Bonnie be happy there? Or only happy-ish?" When she didn't answer, he continued. "I bought it for a vacation home. But now, well." There was a long pause. "I should be able to leave the country today under my Daniel Windsor passport. But I'll never be able to return without resurrecting Britt Jordan."

"Give me your hand," she said. When he turned and reached for her, she placed his right hand flat on her belly and gently stroked the delicate scrimshaw tattoo that covered his entire right arm like a sleeve. This was the tattoo that reminded her of Britt's detailed mind, the meticulous way he had of planning things just for her happiness. "It depends," she said.

"On what?" he asked.

"Well," she said slowly, "it depends on what your plan is for corralling this little rascal in a six-level house." And then she laughed, giving voice to the joyful vision of the future that rose within her.

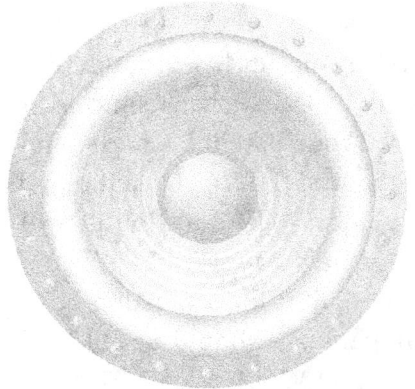

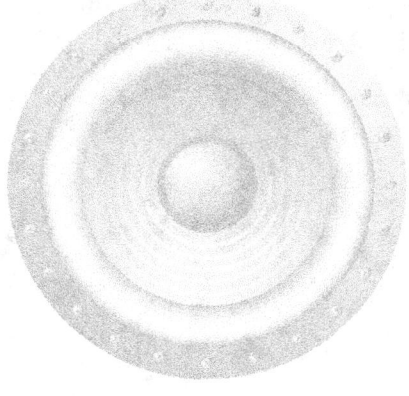

Epilogue

He stood at the window of his study, watching the setting sun melt into the waters of the Caribbean Sea. Those incredibly rich blues and greens and yellows and oranges took his breath every day. From behind him, on the other side of the closed door, he heard his wife's laughing voice, "Come back here, you stinker!" The sound of little bare feet running on tile floor and a giggling voice floated from the hallway. His child had entered the world wide open and hadn't slowed down or hushed since. Always in motion, already running at eleven months. The child had yelled for the first two months of life, and impish laughter had been the constant soundtrack of their lives ever since.

Smiling, he turned from the window and surveyed the mahogany-paneled study. He kept the décor austere; the sea was distraction enough. The cabinets along one wall were locked, but they contained no secrets or memorabilia of Britt Jordan. What they held were several albums worth of unreleased songs. So far, he had released one digital album of new music, to modest sales and some very satisfying reviews. He was not displeased with the results; he was simply in no hurry.

He did keep two mementos of his former life, not in frames, but beneath glass inside the top desk drawer. Opening the drawer, he glanced at the photo of his friend, Mark Blue, accepting the Grammy for Song of the Year posthumously on behalf of the songwriter, Britt Jordan. That season spent in North Carolina, as chaotic and disturbing as it had been, was still priceless with sweet memories, and the transitional music he'd produced was still special to him. He was glad his old friend was getting rich off the songs.

Again, the patter of bare feet and giggles came from the other side of the door. Again his wife's voice, "You scamp! What have you done with your clothes?" His child didn't quite get the concept of wearing clothes. He didn't know why Dena bothered dressing the kid. Fifteen minutes into his set tonight the child would be butt naked, and nobody would care.

He enjoyed sharing his new music with people over on Tortola in very small venues—sometimes only thirty people might show up. Yes, he had bigger plans for his voice and his music, but this was not the season for that. He would know when the time was right.

Meanwhile, he was known around the islands as Daniel Martin. Dena still called him Britt at home, and Bonnie called him Dad. And yes, he drew stares at times. Inevitably when he would forget and flash a dimpled grin, some tourist would approach him and say, "Has anyone ever told you that you look a little like Britt Jordan?" And he would reply in a distinct, crisp voice, "Yes, I get that all the time." He suspected that the locals knew exactly who he had been, but most of the ex-pats were trying to forget some former life or another. Nobody around here cared.

"Mama, your little stinker stole my lipstick again." This in Bonnie's voice. Earlier there had been a low-key skirmish between mother and daughter regarding Bonnie's plans for the night. Not yet fifteen, Bonnie had a boyfriend of sorts. As she had complained to her dad, "He might as well be my girlie play-mate, for all Mama gives me fifteen seconds alone with him." Dad was staying out of that particular skirmish. For now.

Dad and daughter had bigger plans than teenage crushes, anyway. Her art was maturing into stylized work, human subjects painted in muted colors, made truly memorable by her use of light and perspective. Acting as her agent, he had gotten a few pieces placed in prestigious galleries. Within a couple of years, he predicted a gallery opening for Bonnie Martin, maybe in Man-hattan. And this would require him to have a passport, if he were to travel with her. A lawyer was working on that for him.

Next to the photo of Mark Blue, also under glass in the desk drawer, was one other memento of his former life. As was his daily ritual, usually at this hour of the day, he glanced over the familiar words, torn from the last two pages of Ron Edwards's authorized biography of Britt Jordan, in the singer's own words:

I had no explanation for the good things that had come into my life, but I knew two things: I was hopeless before the night I woke up with a half-dead girl in my bed, only I was too arrogant to realize it. And I was hopeless after that night, only then I knew it. Still, I had no clue what to do about it.

So there it was, that word hope smacking my brain just two days before another young girl showed up, this one with a gun. Wrapped around the word, as thoughts often travel through my head, was the image of my wife's amazing smile.

Now picture me with a loaded pistol aimed at my heart. Like a stopwatch, a timer was set in my head, ticking down the final minutes of my life. No time to waste on anger or fear. No guarantee of anything other than this: I was going to use every ounce of my being to stay alive until my wife and child were safe. I had no hope of anything beyond that.

Into that scene, curling like a ribbon through my thoughts, came that word again. Hope. Again the image of my wife's smile, the sound of her laughter. Along with that, there was the certainty that I was not alone. There was no voice, yet there was a Presence whose thoughts at times melded with my own.

Another ribbon of a word swirled into the scene: gratitude. Oh, I had never been so arrogant that I didn't understand how it felt to be grateful to another person. But to express gratitude into thin air would imply the existence of something outside myself to accept my thanks, and such a thing seemed impossible. Yet the instant I poured a drop of gratitude out of the hopeless arena of my heart, acceptance grabbed hold with such swift intent, I felt a physical sting.

I was under no delusion that the Presence was there to rescue me from the girl with the gun. Nobody was going to keep her occupied for the next four minutes other than myself. And nothing was there to stand between me and a bullet besides every trick I had learned from twenty-two years in the spotlight. If I survived this particular shipwreck, or for that matter, if the girl survived, I was going to have to pull us both out.

Yet my friend, Charlie, had raised the question of whether there was somebody big enough to hang with you even when you're beaten. There was not a doubt in my mind: Somebody cared enough to hang with me that night. I had no guarantee of the outcome, and no clue how big this somebody was, but hope became my very heartbeat nonetheless.

If you're reading this book, then you probably also read the newspaper reports or saw the eyewitness accounts on national news: how I miraculously propelled my body five feet into the air to disarm the girl and take her down. Superman stopping a speeding bullet. This was no miracle or super-heroic effort. That was practice coupled with focus. It used to scare the heck out of my lead guitar guy on stage when I'd come at him from behind.

No, the only miracle that night came later.

I spent that night on the sofa facing the doorway where my life had narrowed down to one pinpoint of focus: Britt Jordan was done. Shot dead, quite possibly. But if I walked away still breathing, still able to put my arms around my family, even then he was done. I absolutely could not walk one step into the future dragging the weight of the man I had been.

While I sat there, my sleeping wife curled against my right side, my sleeping daughter stretched out on my left, I became aware that the Presence was back. Just breathing with me, thinking about things with me. Finally I asked, "Who are you exactly?"

"Somebody Big Enough."

"Wow!" I was utterly terrified. But I forced myself to keep breathing, keep thinking. It made no sense, after what I had come through that night, that I should be struck dead on the sofa with my family in my arms. After a few more breaths, I ventured, "So what do you want with me?" There was no answer, and it occurred to me what an arrogant question that was.

And so we hung out on the sofa, breathing and thinking. I thought about things my wife had said to me: "The real Britt Jordan is the one I hold in my arms every night." "Britt's real life began the night he met me." She had even gone so far as to call me a gentleman, which was a bit of a stretch. And yet the more I sat with those statements, the more I realized they were true. Quite true.

I thought about the totally self-serving life I had lived, the shameful arrogance that had nearly taken one girl's life, the image I had created which had drawn another girl into my home with a gun, and I felt strangled. Shipwrecked, in worse peril than the comic heroine tattooed on my arm. There was no hope for the real Britt Jordan to disentangle himself from the weight of the . . . dead one. And where that thought came from, I couldn't say.

My situation was impossible, and yet . . . there had been those words, floating like ribbon through my brain during the minutes my life ticked down, words that had seemed to meld with the thoughts of a Presence outside myself. Even with a gun to my head, those words: "This girl has no idea . . . she has no idea what I'm capable of . . . she has no idea how far I will go . . . I will go to the depths of hell if that's what it takes."

Surely not . . . surely those words had not been meant for me. And yet it seemed possible; in fact, logically, it had to be true. If Somebody were indeed Big Enough, then Big Enough would encompass any mess. Somebody Big Enough would and could go to the depths of hell to rescue a man like me. I had no idea what Somebody might be capable of.

Some of you who have stuck with my story up to this point probably know more about religion and such than I did that night. No doubt you understand on a different level what my thoughts meant. I might not have understood on a theological level, and yet I understood exactly. Forgiveness meant I had to let go and allow Somebody Big Enough to disentangle the real me from the stinking mess that was choking me. And Somebody besides me would have to deal with it, do whatever had to be done with such a mess. Maybe fling it out of the universe, sort of the way I flung that rock into the lake when I forgave my brother.

Now in case you haven't figured it out, I'm a visual person. I see algebra formulas in my head, for instance. I see the way a piece of music should be scored—every note, every instrument—and it's such a chore to convert it to paper. I see dawn in the back side of a sunset. It made perfect sense to me that a transaction had to be visual. And so I said, "Here's how this is going to go down. We're going to strip off my tattoo, which represents my former life, as Dena said. And you're going to deal with it, because I can't. And then I'll set about figuring out just what you are capable of. Are we cool?"

A word floated through my head: Gratitude. I thought a while longer about my life. About how, underlying all the addictions, obsessions, compulsions and exploits had been one constant: discipline. Again, it made perfect sense to me to say, "Done. An hour of gratitude every day. Now are we good?"

At once I felt so giddy that I threw something downright silly out there, like a gauntlet: "You know, a really nice visual for my gratitude hour would be if I had a son. Just saying." I thought I heard a laugh, but one of the women on the sofa with me snored right about then, so I can't be certain.

He shut the drawer, as he did every day at the end of his gratitude hour. Sometimes he took this time in the middle of the night, but he preferred to do it at this hour of day, with the sweet music of his family's voices floating around him. In the twenty months since that transaction had been made, he had learned enough about Somebody to realize he still didn't have a clue. He had learned that there are seasons to life, and this simply wasn't his season. At this moment, he was standing in the center of his priority.

Behind him, he could hear the doorknob rattling. He could picture his child on the other side of the door, standing on tiptoe, barely touching the knob. But the child was determined to keep trying. This time his wife's voice sang with melodious drama, "Here, let me help you with that." He turned to see the door open a few inches, Dena's capable hands giving their son a gentle shove into the room. The door was immediately pulled shut behind the child, and his wife's laughter receded down the hallway. He didn't have to see her face to imagine the mirth in those airship eyes.

"I guess you're mine now, huh?" He held out his arms, and his son ran toward him, hazel eyes bright, mouth wide open in a dimpled grin. Little tennis shoes pounding the floor, not a stitch of clothing otherwise. A scribble of pink lipstick on his belly. "Child after my own heart," he said, swinging his boy onto his shoulder. "What's your name, boy?"

"Da," yelled his son, smacking him on the head with his little hands.

"Not my name, your name. All anybody around here calls you is stinker. Do you know your name?"

The child smacked his head again, chortling with glee.

He swung his son off his shoulder and tucked him under his left arm like a wiggly football. "Come on, Rascal Martin, let's see about getting some pants on you. I've got a show to do in an hour." He reached inside the closet, pulled out his twelve-string guitar, and headed for the door.

About the Author

Sheri grew up in Mt. Airy, NC, and lives thereabouts with her husband. Together they run a couple of small businesses and plan their next vacation. A graduate of High Point University, her first job was writer at a marketing firm, and she's been scribbling ever since.

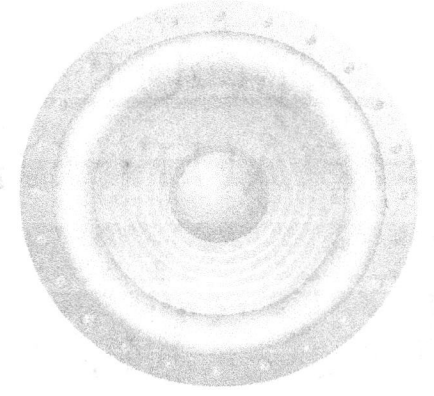

www.ingramcontent.com/pod-product-compliance
Lightning Source LLC
Chambersburg PA
CBHW070613260626
47161CB00007B/2417